Author of *The Rough Romance Trilogy*

SELENE CASTROVILLA

a novel

Luna Rising

Dear Reader,

As I've written in previous letters, I do believe in fate, and that I was fated to write this book. But unlike my earlier novels, this one took years to write. Why? Because love takes courage—and courage takes time.

LUNA RISING is a love letter to myself, and to every woman. One early reviewer wrote, "I think that Castrovilla exposes a deep dark secret that many women share. Sometimes we are so desperate for love that we hold on to any relationship that comes our way. Many women can relate to this book deeply, even though most probably would not admit it."

This is is not always an "easy" novel to read—or a "pretty" one, but it's honest. You know the saying, the truth hurts. Luckily, sometimes it's damn funny, too.

Please consider posting a review of LUNA RISING, as this is the primary way authors gain readers these days. Any shouts on social media are hugely appreciated!

I'd love to have your thoughts. Write to me on my website:

SeleneCastrovilla.com

I also have a Facebook fan page:

Selene Castrovilla (Facebook.com/SCastrovilla)

and I'm on Instagram:

Selene Castrovilla

and Twitter:

@SCastrovilla

May you rise, like Luna.

Love,

Selene

 Published by Last Syllable Books,

4251 New York Avenue, Island Park, NY 11558

All characters appearing in this work are fictitious. Any resemblance to real persons, living or dead, is purely coincidental.

Castrovilla, Selene

Luna Rising / Selene Castrovilla. – 1st ed.

p. cm

Summary: A middle-aged suburban wife and mom divorces her gay husband and sets out on a quest for love.

ISBN-10: 0-9916261-9-2 ISBN-13: 978-0-9916261-9-9

[1. Self-realization in women—Fiction. 2. Psychological fiction. 3. Mothers—Fiction. 4. Love—Fiction. 5. Man-woman relationships—Fiction. 6. Search for happiness—Fiction. 7. Women authors. 8. Domestic fiction.]

BOOKS BY SELENE CASTROVILLA

Melt (Book One in the Rough Romance Trilogy)

Signs of Life (Book Two in the Rough Romance Trilogy)

The Girl Next Door

Saved By the Music

Revolutionary Friends

Revolutionary Rogues

By the Sword

Upon Secrecy

Selene is pleased to have a piece included
in the charitable book anthology

Travel in the Sixties,

whose proceeds fund art/music therapy for Alzheimer's patients.

For Me

Acknowledgments

This book has been over a decade in the making. Thank you to everyone who has supported me—too many to name! (And some would wish to remain anonymous, I'm sure.)

Christmas on Long Island

LUNA PEERED THROUGH her peephole, watching Trip cut across her yard past the inflated Santa. He was an hour late—early for him.

Trip tramped raggedly through the pristine snow, leaving gopher-like piles in his wake. He stomped on Luna's welcome mat and swung the door open without knocking. Trip never knocked. Prepared for this, Luna had already moved to the side when Trip clomped into her foyer. She slammed the door closed behind him to keep the cold out. But the chill Trip carried was inescapable. It shanked her senses like a Slurpee brain freeze.

Trip looked good, snow boots aside. He'd literally cast them off to drip onto her hardwood floor. He now stood there in thick wool socks, wriggling his toes in a come-hither manner. Everything about Trip's body signaled "come" to Luna—overriding her distaste for his demeanor and his piecemeal wardrobe. But tonight's black leather coat was a sexy surprise—and a striking upgrade from the puffy Jets jacket he generally sported although he hated sports. That man wore anything he found at the Goodwill.

Trip planted a perfunctory kiss on Luna's lips and pressed a tan Kay Jewelers bag into her hands. She would've preferred a warmer greeting, but the bag held promise. What could it contain? Certainly not diamonds. Trip was too cheap for them. *Maybe a charm bracelet?*

The bag was rumpled. It had probably been crushed under a mountain of surveillance cameras and digital video recorders in Trip's car. Trip was a jack-of-all-trades, but providing electronic security to homes and businesses was his mainstay. Luna had always sought protection, but in a more primal, Tarzan/Jane way.

She reached in the bag, but there was no box. Instead, she touched yarn. *What the hell?* She extracted two pairs of men's gloves. One pair black, the other brown – and flimsy ones at that.

Were they a joke?

Did Trip have a *real* gift for her?

How could the man who'd been so tender also be this cruel?

Luna stared at Trip, who laughed. His brown eyes squinted even smaller than usual. It was rare to get a good glimpse of his pupils. Unveiled, they were filled with flecks of gold. So alluring—but they had a hunted look, like they belonged on a trembling fawn waiting for the crack of a gun. "Extras," he said. His voice was warm and soothing—a verbal fleece blanket. It had a mesmerizing effect. "Can you believe three people gave me gloves for Christmas? I kept these." He reached into his pockets and pulled out a pair that looked suede.

"But… this bag…," Luna spluttered. Trip's vocal hypnotism only carried so far, and the misleading tote was out of bounds.

He shrugged. "I found it in a dumpster. The gloves fit perfectly. Why waste wrapping paper, right?" He gave her a toothy smile, phony but still endearing.

Trip took his coat off. He perched it on her banister; obstructing the tin sign Luna had hung which read, *Joy*. It wasn't just a seasonal decoration—it was also her middle name.

Trip sauntered toward the living room. The leather wasn't his only wardrobe improvement. Donning a cable-knit sweater (much thicker than the re-gifted gloves) and slacks instead of his typical thermal shirt and worn-out jeans made Trip extra appealing. His face held the lone vestige of the rugged working man he was. He hadn't shaved. Luna loved Trip's scruff, especially when it rubbed against her while they kissed…

Stop thinking smutty thoughts! Don't ***you*** *deserve an upgrade?* a familiar presence chided inside her head—the voice which had been counseling Luna for over twenty years. She'd dubbed it Jiminy, after Pinocchio's conscientious cricket. But naming it didn't mean she heeded it. *Speaking of kisses, he didn't give you a decent one—heck; he didn't even say "Merry Christmas!" He just handed you a crumpled bag he dug from a pile of garbage. Rats probably slept in it!*

Jiminy always noted the ugly truth.

The uglier truth was that there was no other present in sight. The gloves were *seriously* her gift. Why would Trip do this? For Christ's sake (or, as her best friend, Sunny, would say, *Christ on a cracker!*), if you were visiting an acquaintance on Christmas night you brought them a nut platter or a ten-buck bottle of merlot. She'd been Trip's lover for four months.

Handing her nothing would've been better.

Way better.

She dropped the gloves on her counter and stepped into the living room. Maybe he'd say he'd been kidding, after all. *You're almost forty*, Jiminy said, as though she didn't know. *A little old for kidding, wouldn't you agree?* She ignored him.

Trip was flopped on the couch. He rested his feet on the holiday-adorned coffee table, shifting aside a ceramic snowman and framed pictures of her children from Christmases past.

Her kids thought Trip was ancient, but he was forty-nine. His balding head threw them. *He should shave it all off and be done with it*, she thought – not for the first time. But it was his head and hair, not hers.

Trip had a great physique, except for his skinny Kermit the Frog legs. It was his sturdy chest that attracted Luna the most. It made her feel protected, more than any of his security cameras ever could.

He opened his mouth to speak, but he didn't say what she'd hoped. "Got any eggnog?" He knew she did. He'd asked her to buy him some, and she always did what he requested. He clicked the TV remote. *The Santa Clause* was on. She started toward the kitchen, eager for a task that would distract her, however momentarily. "Babe, c'mere."

She turned back. This was it! He was going to reveal the joke! "Yes?"

"Come close."

Did he have a gift wedged in his pocket? Perhaps he was going to *tell* her about it? Trip liked to travel… maybe he'd whisk her off somewhere exotic! She hoped her ex, Nick, wouldn't be a dick about watching the kids for a week or so.

She squatted to just under eye level with Trip and looked up at him. His scent was so intoxicating that she almost fell on her ass. Trip touched her crown and ran his fingers gingerly through her hair. It was crazy, the way his weathered, calloused hand could be so gentle. "Aha! Got it!" he proclaimed. "Piece of lint." A minuscule fuzzy rested in his open palm. Trip pursed his lips, blew, and off the speck flew. Luna thought briefly of Whoville, and its beleaguered citizens, desperate to be heard. It was a story Dylan still enjoyed, while Ben had never liked it. He had nightmares about Whoville being boiled.

Trip gave Luna a pat on the head and turned back to the show. Luna teetered for a moment, then rose.

Inflatable Santa's suit shined red through Luna's kitchen window. She thought lawn blow-ups were ridiculous, but Trip had insisted on depositing it on her lawn a few days ago. (He had a shitload of Clauses in storage, thanks to garbage-picking behind K-Mart post holiday clearance one year.) "Your kids will love it," he'd told her. As if he knew what they'd love. The closest he'd come to meeting them was when they caught a glimpse of his male-pattern baldness as he slipped out the front door one morning just after they awoke. And so St. Nick had arrived and now waved incessantly at the Jewish neighbors across the street. They were the only audience on this dead-end.

The kids, who had in fact been unimpressed with Santa's presence, were sleeping at Nick's (her ex-husband, not the saint.) Luna had looked forward to her first holiday with Trip, ignoring the steady decline of their relationship like a child believing in Christmas miracles.

Maybe things were turning around. After all, they'd just shared an endearing moment. Picking the lint from her hair showed he cared, right?

Oh, please, Jiminy scoffed. Such a buzzkill. *Mister Critic detected a flaw, and then he petted you like a dog.*

"He was being sweet." Luna countered. Why couldn't Jiminy give her *that*? Why couldn't he leave it alone?

He's reduced you to canine behavior, Luna. Don't you see he's got you begging for scraps?

Luna didn't want to see. She just wanted to pour Trip his eggnog and get through whatever it took before she and Trip climbed under her covers. At least the orgasms he bestowed weren't re-gifted.

She'd coined the thing they did in her bed "making half-love." There was no other term that fit the situation.

To make love, both parties needed to keep their eyes open and focused. Luna was too well-acquainted with Trip's wrinkly eyelids. They looked like elephant skin, except they weren't grey.

Nor would she concede to tagging it "having sex." For Luna it was much more than that.

Technically they were "fornicating"—but that conjured thoughts of something gross involving horns, Formica and cats—while the word "intercourse" sounded like a seminar about cross-country highways.

"Making half-love" was the most satisfying label she could summon.

Luna imagined gliding her fingers across the hairs on Trip's back. They were double-arched, shaped like the wings of an angel. She thought sometimes Trip was a gruff herald, sent to teach her lessons she didn't want to learn.

He's just a jerk in need of manscaping, said Jiminy.

Doing her best to ignore Jimmy's comment, Luna turned to open a cabinet—but her gaze met those gloves on the counter. She felt her face redden, then sucked her emotions back. *One day your head's going to burst from all those feelings you're keeping inside,* said Jiminy. *Just like a bowl of spaghetti sauce cooked too long in the microwave. Pop! Splat!*

She considered this. It could happen…

Jiminy wasn't done. *Ask yourself: What would Sunny do?*

Sunny would've shoved Trip right back out the door. But then, Sunny wouldn't have invited him over. "I like to go to their place and then leave," Sunny once said about her dates. "Let them through the doorway and they want to lie around afterwards, all sprawled out. Nobody likes a lingerer."

No one, except for Luna. She wanted more than a lingerer—she wanted a partner who wouldn't leave. That certainly wasn't Trip, who would clomp back out the door soon after he woke in the morning.

She stared at the gloves. If love was for sale, Trip's knockoff would be in the dollar store. Was she willing to give up her dignity in exchange for a slipshod product?

The things from the dollar store never held up. You got what you paid for.

She sighed deeply, and then shivered. "You're right, Jiminy. I have to break up with him."

Hallelujah! Jiminy cheered. *Why don't you go do it right now?*

"It's not so easy," Luna replied. She reached into her cabinet and took out a glass. But instead of pouring Trip's eggnog, she poured herself some pinot grigio. Her hand shook as she gulped. *How* would she break up with Trip? She hated confrontation, almost as much as she abhorred sleeping solo.

*It **is** that easy!* Jiminy persisted. *Remember Dr. Gold's advice.*

Luna's chiropractor boiled life down to three rules, which dangled above his adjustment table. They read:

1. Breathe.
2. Drink water.
3. Everything always works out.

"Note," Dr. Gold told her during one visit, "it doesn't say, 'Everything always works out the way you want it to.'"

Boy, did Luna know that.

She took a deep breath and let it out, and then guzzled more *Pinot.* Water had to be an ingredient, right?

If you asked Luna about herself and how her life had worked out so far, here's what she'd say:

STATS ON LUNA

Name: Luna Joy Lampanelli (Her middle name was actually Gioia, pronounced 'Joya' and meaning 'Joy' in Italian, but she had gone to the English version because everyone mispronounced it 'Goya.' Luna was not a bean.)

Ethnic background: Italian (from the north, her mother would always remind her) and Russian.

Marital status: Divorced.

Children: Two sons: Ben, age 12, and Dylan, age 7.

Body: Slim with curves.

Hair: Brown, subtly highlighted with blonde.

Occupation: Writer of children's books.

Favorite physical activities: Sex and boxing (real, not kick).

Other likes: What a strange thing it was to classify 'likes'! Luna wanted to like everything, to appreciate whatever she was doing. This is what she wanted—she hadn't quite gotten there. It was difficult, training one's mind to heel, sit and stay in the moment. That said, the things she liked most were books, coffee and the color purple.

Dislikes: Being left in limbo, travel mugs (she hated that plastic taste), shitty/inconsiderate Christmas gifts.

Religion: A toughie. Both her mom and her aunt had experienced bad breaks with Catholicism and hammered their stories into her. Luna's only positive brush with organized religion came from random exposure to her aunt's subsequent zeal for Zen Buddhism, but it was more confusing than compelling, and saying "Mu" during a meditation didn't exactly make her popular with her schoolmates. As an adult she yearned for something to believe in, but what? And how? Immersed in their religions, Luna saw people as salmon—immobilized in a frosty lake of dogma. And even if they managed to thaw, how could they swim upstream? She toyed with starting her own ministry: The Church of the Frozen Salmon, but lacked the actual ambition to do it. Twelve Step meetings described a "higher power" less constraining than the gods in theological creeds, but she still struggled with the concept. Even addressing her higher power had been a problem: "God" was so almighty, "Goddess" too glib, and "HP" made her think of Hewlett Packard. Finally she acquiesced to "God," both for lack of a better idea and because a slight bow to tradition couldn't hurt. And anyway, as Jiminy reminded her, *What's in a name?*

Jiminy came from nowhere, in a dark moment when she was a teen.

Whoever—whatever—he was, he wasn't God. Jiminy was just too obnoxious.

Favorite writers: William Shakespeare, William Faulkner, J.D. Salinger.

Favorite dessert: Flan.

Favorite expression: Gandhi's "You must be the change you wish to see in the world."

Above all, Luna believed in love. Love could heal the human race—and her as well. Wasn't *that* what Christmas was all about?

Then again, love had turned her into this doormat.

Where had the independent woman who'd evicted her cheating ex and changed the lock cylinders all by herself gone?

Ms. Unstoppable had set out on a fast course for amore – hitting potholes, blowing tires and even overturning in a ditch or two. Then she'd crashed into Trip. Luna had seen stars the night their hearts collided. Now here she was with emotional whiplash, and backlash.

Without love, she'd been strong. In love—she was this wreck. It was time to start repairs, and that meant shelling out the high deductible of being alone.

Luna grabbed the gloves and started back into the living room. On her way, she removed Trip's coat from her banister and draped it on her arm.

Trip looked away from the screen. "Where's my eggnog?"

Luna wagged the gloves in his face. "Trip, I've had about enough…"

"Wait a minute. Don't tell me you thought those were your only gift?"

That halted her. She lowered the gloves. "They're not?"

"No, no, no, sweetie." Trip's voice was an analgesic, and he displayed an extra toothy grin. "I have something else for you."

Trip stood and took his coat from Luna's quivering arm. He planted a smooch on her lips, and slipped her a taste of his tongue. His whiskers brushed her cheek, like bristles sweeping away her doubt. He had something else for her!

Luna was reeling from their close encounter and heady with delight. Trip swung his coat on and said, "I'll go get it from the car."

ONE

13 months earlier

IT WAS BLACK Friday, but Luna was seeing red. The hell of a Wal-Mart stampede was preferable to discussing the purgatory of her farcical marriage—and yet here she was, in couples therapy.

Luna stood on a white vinyl mat that said "hers," staring at her husband Nick on "his" mat a few feet away. In the center of the floor, between them, "ours" awaited. This was Dr. Michelle Stepponi's version of relationship counseling. *Bullshit*, Luna thought. But she'd promised to try one session, after Nick pulled the kid card: "Do it for the sake of our sons!"

Sure, Ben and Dylan needed their dad around, but didn't she deserve happiness, too? Not to mention a faithful husband who didn't prefer men? *This is what you get for listening to drive-by psychics*, Jiminy scolded.

Jiminy was right. Though at the time, a lifetime ago when she was twenty-one and pumping gas to pay for NYU textbooks, it had seemed reasonable enough to listen to the blonde who'd rolled up in her pink Cadillac for a fill-up and claimed to know the future. "I see you with a Nick," she'd predicted as she paid. Then she drove away.

Luna took up with the first Nick she met, overlooking that he was a snarky, pot-smoking high school dropout. She'd put up with a lot over the years in exchange for his companionship and his willingness to do the laundry, but Luna drew the line at gay. *That* seemed pretty hopeless, given that she didn't possess a penis.

Dr. Stepponi was an eternally smiling psychologist with a sing-song voice and a saccharine view of life. In the pre-session phone call, she'd assured Luna that everything could be worked out—even the gay thing. Now she said, "You'll both have the opportunity to speak your minds, and then you'll come together in the center mat."

Luna didn't want to come together with Nick. She didn't want to be near the man who hadn't touched her in three years. He'd made her feel like there was something wrong with her: she was too busy writing, too consumed with the boys. She'd believed that their lack of sex was her fault. Until the day she went on their computer and "Gay.com–join now" popped up.

It was shopping season, but the gift she wanted couldn't be bought. Freedom was free, and yet it came with a cost—she'd have to put on her big girl panties and demand it. Yesterday's Thanksgiving fowl had been hard to choke down while mustering yet another performance of "we're happily married" in front of Nick's old-school Italian family. Nick would keep her as his beard until death did them part, if she let him.

"Luna, you'll go first," Dr. Stepponi sang. Her pink-walled office smelled as sickeningly sweet as her personality. Some kind of floral air freshener. So thick, it settled in the base of Luna's throat. The decor was too cutesy for such dire circumstance: baskets of silk flowers, a fuchsia couch with macramé throw pillows, a cheesy picture of a sunset—these seemed to deride the stakes at hand. But then, Dr. Stepponi's "therapeutic" mats were so absurd that they pretty much mocked themselves.

Are you really going along with this? It might be the most ridiculous thing I've ever seen, said Jiminy. *And I've seen centuries of absurdities.*

It might feel good to have someone hear what I have to say, Luna reasoned. *It might be vindicating.*

Why are you looking for vindication? Try peace of mind. It's awesome, Jiminy countered.

Luna wavered, teetering on "hers." Jiminy was right, of course. She stared at Nick, the man she'd thought she knew. As it turned out, you could only view so much of a person: whatever they *let* you see.

Here's what Luna knew about Nick:

STATS ON NICK

Name: Nicholas Paul Marone III

Ethnic background: Italian (unfortunately his ancestors were from Southern Italy, a line of lowlife scum according to Luna's mother, who had Venetian blood) and Czechoslovakian (his Slavicness had endeared him somewhat to Luna's Aunt Zelda, who was fiercely Russian.) Funny what made people like you.

Relationship status: Trying to stay married despite the exposure of his many hook-ups via the AOL chat room "Long Island Men for Men Now." All had been revealed once Luna installed computer spyware, which captured every word—and pictures, too.

Children: The two sons he'd given Luna were just about the only positive contribution he'd made toward humankind.

Body: He used to have a great physique, but lately Nick's belly had grown large and round. Luna thought of him as "Kung Fu Panda."

Hair: Dark and receding (as opposed to the Scott Baio locks he'd sported when they'd met.)

Occupation: Deli manager.

Other likes: Pot, cigarettes, mocha caramel lattes. And Lotto, which he poured money into like it was an investment plan.

Dislikes: Being challenged, tomato seeds.

Religion: Catholic. He was from one of those families that made sure their children had a proper religious education, even if all else failed. God forbid he hadn't been confirmed: he wouldn't be able to get married in a church (he hadn't anyway), or get into heaven (which remained to be seen.) Since confirmation, he hadn't been to mass. He still knew all his prayers, he just didn't say them anymore.

Favorite writers: Nick loved Fitzgerald's *The Great Gatsby*—the only book Luna had seen him read beside a nonfiction bestseller about ebola.

Favorite dessert: Most Hostess products¸ particularly Ding-Dongs, Twinkies & Ho-Ho's. Nick also loved Mounds Bars, but not Almond Joys. He never felt like a nut.

Favorite expression: "Never do today what you can put off until tomorrow."

Dr. Stepponi cleared her throat. "Luna, we're waiting for you to begin." Her voice delivered a jarring, remonstrative note. And once Dr. Stepponi stepped out of her nice-nice character, just for that moment, it was clear what a sham she and her whole exercise was.

Luna may not have had a penis, but she grew some balls. Looking Nick in the eye she said, "You're gay. You've been hooking up with strange men from chat rooms for years. I don't want AIDS, and I don't want you."

There was silence. Nick and Dr. Stepponi's mouths hung open.

Dr. Stepponi recovered. "Luna, this won't work if you're not open-minded."

"It's impossible to be open-minded enough for this charade to succeed," Luna said. Was she talking about the session or the marriage? Both, she decided.

"Luna, I told you… I'm not gay. I'm bisexual," Nick implored in his gravelly voice. The words didn't sound right in that baritone. It was as though Tony Soprano were confessing he went both ways. "I was in a period of transition. I'm finished now."

Yeah, funny how you finished just when you got caught, Luna thought.

What's funny about it? Jiminy asked.

Point taken, responded Luna.

"I love you, Luna," Nick said. "I'll make our marriage work."

Funny what passes for love these days, Jiminy said.

What's funny about it? Luna asked.

Jiminy said, *Point taken.*

Nor was it funny that Luna and Nick were paying $275 an hour for these shenanigans.

"Good, good, good!" Dr. Stepponi told Nick.

Everything's good, as long as her check clears, Luna thought. She wanted to settle up now, and go pick up the kids from Sunny's. She could've taken Ben and Dylan to the zoo today. Instead, she was stuck at this circus. She could still bring them somewhere when she got out of here. Maybe Nathan's. The food there was borderline fast food, but once in a while couldn't hurt and the boys liked the Nathan's game room.

Later, when they went to bed, she would write.

These were the things that made Luna happy—though it would be nice to have some sex too. God, she'd forgotten what it was like to kiss.

"Now you two meet on your mat in the middle, and hold hands!" Dr. Stepponi instructed.

Luna didn't want to hold Nick's hand. She felt like puking, really—between the air freshener and the falsely optimistic room.

Just say no, Jiminy said.

Nick was already on "ours," hand extended and face earnest. What a crock. It reminded her of that day so long ago, when she'd walked down the aisle all dressed in white. There he'd been, at the altar—waiting for her in his tux. It was supposed to be her happy ending, but the fairy tale was fractured. It was time to close the grim book and get on with life. "No," she said.

"Whhaaattt?" Dt. Stepponi and Nick exclaimed together.

"No," Luna repeated. "I'm done." She stepped off "hers" and headed for the pink door. Really, this place was more suited for selling Mary Kay, or fighting breast cancer.

"You're not acting fairly, Luna," Dr. Stepponi scolded. Like anything Nick had done could be called 'fair.' Luna kept walking. She grasped the handle and turned.

"Luna!" Nick's voice was pleading. "If you leave, how will I get home?"

Luna opened the door. Without turning around she said, "Frankly Nick, I don't give a damn."

Outside, Luna paused a moment to breathe in the fresh, chilled air. What a relief to be rid of that chemical smell. Luna's coat was in the car, but for once she didn't mind her exposure. The prickly bumps and raised hairs on her arms were proof that what had just happened was not a dream. She'd stood up for herself! *Yes!* She chirped open the Windstar and got in the driver's seat. She hated her minivan, but it was an unwritten law of suburbia that moms drove them.

Luna slammed her door shut. Her breath fogged the windshield, and her euphoria clouded. There she was, encased in a large metal box. Could there be any true escape from confinement?

Jeez, would you stop being so Dostoyevskyesque? Jiminy piped in.

Was the minivan even metal? She'd read somewhere that vehicles were made of plastic these days. Synthetics abounded...

Never mind manufacturing materials, Jiminy said. *You might want to get out of here before Nick comes out.*

"Right. "Luna started the engine and backed away from the Mercedes in front of her. It was a pale pink, and the license plate read: "CpleRX." The back seat was piled with shopping bags, probably bargains Dr. Stepponi had procured that morning. *I guess the good doctor gives herself retail therapy,* Jiminy said. *Let's hope she wasn't counting on your money for her credit card bill.*

"I'll mail her a check," Luna said. She couldn't bear not paying as promised.

You're too nice, Luna. Jiminy said. *That's why the world eats you alive.*

"That's not very spiritual, Jiminy."

Depends how you define it, Jiminy countered. *Spirituality is in the eyes of the beholder.*

At the corner light, she reached for the coffee she'd left in the holder. Half of the large Dunkin' Donuts cup remained. She took a swig. Cold, but marvelous nonetheless. Nothing beat caffeine therapy.

One hand on the cold wheel, Luna sipped and headed towards Sunny's. She tried to relax and think of fun things to do tonight with Ben and Dylan, but her troubles were storming in. Walking out of couples' therapy had been liberating, but *now* she had to stick to her guns and make Nick vamoose. He would not go quietly—Nick was no gentleman.

Oh God, how am I going to do any marketing with this going on? Luna thought. She had a book coming out in a few days.

Your book will be fine, Jiminy said. *You've concentrated on your career for long enough, Luna. It's time to focus on* ***you****.*

"But Jiminy, it's not just a job for me. It's my path."

Sometimes you have to clear your path before you can continue down it, Jiminy countered.

Before Luna could mull Jiminy's words, her cell phone rang. She looked down and saw the name: "Mom." Not exactly the person she felt like speaking with at the moment. She let it go to voicemail.

Now she felt *really* cold. Luna turned the heat on and drove a couple of miles. She wished her coffee was warm – she needed fortification before facing her mother's almost always caustic tone. But she had to make do with what she had.

Once the cup was drained, Luna pulled over and called her voicemail. "You have one new message," the robotic female voice said in its flat-lining way. Luna hit the pound key to listen.

"Luna." Loreena's seething voice made her daughter's name sound like an accusation. "Your father's at Southside Hospital. He's had a stroke."

TWO

LUNA CALLED SUNNY and told her the situation.

"Christ on a cracker!" Sunny exclaimed. "I hope your dad's okay."

"Can you keep the kids with you a while longer? I doubt Nick will be picking them up, 'cause I left him stranded three towns from home. It'll take him forever to walk home to get his car, and he'll never spring for a cab."

"Sure, no problem. Sounds like therapy was every bit as successful as I thought it would be," said Sunny.

"Oh yeah, mission accomplished."

"Well, you did him a favor. Fatsy can use the exercise."

The hospital had that sick smell Lysol couldn't camouflage. The halls were yellow, probably meant to brighten spirits, but it was a bit on the dark side and made Luna think of bile. Cardboard turkeys and cornucopias hung from the ceiling for the first stretch of the hall, but when Luna turned a corner the theme switched to Christmas and Hannukah: with green and red decorations outnumbering blue ones three to one. A grey-uniformed, dark-complexioned, thirty-ish maintenance man was on a ladder, swapping symbols of abundance and thanks for tributes to the most wonderful time of the year, with an obligatory nod to the festival of lights. "Hi, Mami," the man cooed as Luna walked past. Both pleased at being noticed and grossed out for the same reason, she continued to the elevator without responding or looking his way. God knew what he would say if encouraged.

Loreena was perched on the front part of a chair in an orange waiting room next to the elevator banks on the third floor. She might've been on the cushion's edge so her feet touched the ground—she was under five feet tall—but it probably also had something to do with the fact that she never relaxed. At home she ate standing at the kitchen counter. "They're doing some tests on your father," she told Luna. This in lieu of 'hello' or, god forbid, a hug. On the rare occasions when Luna received her mom's embrace, it was cold (Loreena literally felt reptilian in that there was no warmth to her skin) and smelly (she took so many vitamins that she secreted them.)

"How is he?"

Loreena sighed dramatically. A paper turkey in a pilgrim hat dangled a few feet above her head. The mami maintenance guy hadn't made it that far, and hopefully he wouldn't while Luna was there. She craved masculine attention, but with a tad more finesse. "It was bad. But they won't know *how* bad until his brain stops swelling."

Ugh. An image of her dad's engorged cerebrum popped into Luna's mind. She envisioned all his inflamed matter, largely unused and now wasted. How could someone with his genius IQ spend life so stupidly?

"When did he get home?" Luna asked, even though using the term "home" was questionable in relation to her dad, who was absent from the premises about 90 percent of the time.

"I pulled into the driveway last night and he was there, on the stoop. I said, 'You're too late for turkey, Lenny.' He was kind of slumped on the stoop. I asked him to get up so I could open the door and he said, "I don't feel so well, Babe."

Babe. What a ridiculous word for her father to use, Luna though. First of all, it was child-like. And second, it implied an intimacy that Lenny and Loreena did not share. How could two people who rarely saw each other be called intimate?

"What happened then?" Luna asked.

"He keeled over and started twitching, so I called 911."

That was a lot to absorb. Luna sank into the padded chair across from her mother, who took out her compact and blotted her skin. Loreena never went anywhere without her makeup.

Here are more facts about Luna's mom:

STATS ON LOREENA

Name: Loreena Risotto Lampanelli. Loreena's maiden name was a Northern Italian rice dish. Loreena had made overtures through the years that her ancestors created risotto. Loreena snubbed pasta, which she said was popular only "south of Rome, where no one has any sense of palate."

Ethnic background: Northern Italian, far above where people get mugged "at the bottom of the boot."

Marital Status: Married to a man who was barely around.

Children: One beleaguered daughter.

Body: Miniscule. But, for a shrimp, she had some incredible projection in her voice.

Hair: Dark brown, worn short with a flip at the bottom.

Occupation: Formerly an opera singer, but quit to have Luna. Through the years, she'd frequently reminded Luna of this sacrifice.

Favorite Activities: Yelling, stacking newspapers and hoarding things she bought in the thrift shop.

Other likes: Anything northern Italian, *The New York Times* (collecting issues, not actually reading them.)

Dislikes: Too many to list.

Religion: Agnostic.

Favorite writers: Anyone northern Italian.

Favorite dessert: Gelato.

Favorite expression: Anything spoken in Italian (not dialect) or written by a northern Italian writer.

The one constant about Loreena was that there was no constant. Mostly she ranted, but sometimes she took on a little girl voice, filled with questions. For Luna, the child voice had always been worse. Mothers were supposed to have answers.

Loreena snapped her compact shut, stowed it back in her purse and gave Luna the critical eye. "Your shirt is stained."

Luna looked down. There was a drop of coffee on her purple shirt. Practically microscopic. Leave it to Loreena to point it out.

Having been in this relationship for thirty-eight years, Luna knew what her mom was like. But disapproval never stopped stinging, just like memories didn't leave.

Luna looked past her mother, to one memory she'd never forget.

Thirty-three years earlier
Woodside, Queens

They lived in the center of a maze of dirty brick apartment buildings. Luna skipped along the winding asphalt path lined with chain-linked poles. She was in the circus, the chains were her trapeze! She stopped to swing. Mommy kept walking. Luna had to run to catch up. The air was sour with incineration. Still, Luna's mood was sweet.

At their building, Mommy said, "Stay outside. I'm going to take a nap." It was her angry voice, but Luna wouldn't have argued anyway. She wanted to stay in the light.

Luna dashed to the playground. Slide, swings, concrete slabs to climb. Playing out a story in her mind, she nested herself inside a cement cylinder. So busy, she didn't see the bodies blocking her exit on each side.

Laughing voices. "You're our prisoner," said one.

"You can never go home," said another.

They were older. Girls.

She hadn't been afraid curled up in that small space before. Now, trapped, she was.

She put her hand on her chest to calm her heart. It was beating so fast. She couldn't live like this forever!

She leaned back, shivered. The walls were so cold.

Not the slightest bit of light got in between those legs blocking her way.

She was all scrunched up. Her body ached, her head ached too. The hairs on her arms stood up.

She needed to get warm.

She had to get out.

HOW?

She crawled toward one end of the cylinder. Her hand slid along the strange surface, smooth paint but with grit underneath. She felt the coarseness so much more now, pricking her palms.

It seemed forever to go that short distance but finally she was there.

PUSH!

She gave a great big shove at the legs. They kicked. CONK! Her head met concrete. Pounding pain. The taste of salty tears and blood.

Shaken voices prattled at once: *She's hurt! We're in trouble!*

And then the legs ran off.

She was free!

Luna crawled out into the light. Her head ached, blood trickled. She headed down the asphalt path leading to her building, passing all those links she'd played with. They weren't trapezes at all. They were just heavy, thick chains. She wouldn't—she couldn't, ever—swing anymore.

She yanked on the red metal door to her building, stepping inside the dim hall.

She stopped by the elevator, stared at it.

No. She couldn't be closed in.

She climbed the stairs to her fifth floor apartment, gripping the green metal banister tight with each step.

Up, up, up she climbed. She was exhausted but at least she was moving, at least she was almost there.

She reached her door and knocked.

Dumbfounded and eyeing the blood, Mommy screamed. "What did you do to your new shirt!"

Luna didn't ask for a hug—Mommy still had her angry voice. It wouldn't help anyway. Mommy's skin was always like ice. Luna needed warmth.

She shuffled past the angry voice and into her room. She curled under the covers with Gus, her stuffed walrus. And she told him everything.

THREE

AFTER A WHILE, a nurse appeared and told Loreena she could go back inside. Luna followed her mom down another corridor with a bounty of harvest decorations on borrowed time, past rooms with doors open, curtains drawn around the beds.

Why did she peek inside? Morbid curiosity? Self-punishment? She couldn't deal with sick people. They made her feel so helpless. And she felt their emotional pain.

She always felt everyone's pain.

But there was no curtain drawn in Lenny Lampanelli's room. Her father was the only patient in the room.

Oh god, he looked awful. Like he was in the process of dying. His body writhed as though 1,000 volts of electricity were charging through him. He moaned in a voice that sounded like the ghost of him.

"It's okay, Lenny," Loreena said. Her tone was flat and unconvincing—at least to Luna. But Lenny didn't look like he heard her anyway. He was somewhere in his own orbit of pain.

"I haven't eaten all day," Loreena said. This was actually nothing new—she said it all the time.

"Go eat, Mom. I'll stay here."

"The food is probably atrocious. I doubt they have risotto."

"I doubt that, too."

Loreena sighed. "I'll just go get some tea."

"Whatever makes you happy," Luna said, knowing nothing would.

Loreena left, and Luna was alone with Lenny—or what remained of him.

She stared at her groaning father and tried to remember good things about him—anything to offset the present picture. The problem was that she didn't have all that much to work with.

STATS ON LENNY

Name: Leonard (Lenny) Lampanelli

Ethnic background: Italian (hopefully from the north, though it had never actually been mentioned) and Russian.

Marital status: Married but rarely there.

Children: One daughter, who'd missed him.

Body: Fairly tall and stocky.

Hair: Sandy brown (Luna had his coloring).

Occupation: Heroin dealer (and addict).

Favorite activities: Sleeping. On the rare occasions they ate together, he was snoring before he finished his meal.

Other likes: Leaving.

Dislikes: Conflict. Thought the years, whenever Loreena said something vicious he'd serenely respond, "Alright, Babe," no matter what she'd said. Soon after, he'd be gone.

Religion: Unknown.

Favorite writers: Unknown.

Favorite dessert: Unknown. (Never made it that far.)

Favorite expression: "What a fathead," which he said about other drivers in the infrequent times when Luna had been in the car with him. He didn't get upset. It was more of a calm observation.

The other thing Dad said a lot was "Goodbye."

Luna stood at her father's bed, touching the plastic handrail and trying to say something. But what? The room was devoid of decorations, with not one turkey or corn stalk in sight. Didn't stroke victims deserve festivity, too? She thought briefly of requesting a hanging paper candy cane or wreath, but nixed the plan because she didn't want to approach the mami man. She tried to click on the TV so at least there would be some background noise, but it only displayed an extension to call for rental. The inactivated TV made her feel so sad she had to hold back tears.

She finally gave up on conversation. What was the point in struggling? She doubted he could hear her. All her life she'd wanted to be with him and here he was—and not going anywhere, from the look of things.

Now that she had him, all she wanted to do was leave. Standing here only dredged up the past, and there was nothing good about that.

Thirty years earlier

They lived on Long Island now. No more concrete playground. No more chains. But still, Dad wasn't there.

Luna was eight, and she could call Dad at his friend's house and ask him to come and get her. He promised and promised he would but he didn't say when.

Finally, he said he would take her to the Halloween Parade in Greenwich Village.

New York City!

After trick or treating, she sat on her patchwork quilt and waited. She was a witch in pointed black hat with a bristly broom at her side.

She waited, waited, waited for her dad.

Raggedy Ann and Gus watched Luna from the end of the bed but she didn't want to play. She didn't want to read her books piled on the floor. She didn't want to watch TV, even though Batman was on. She didn't want any candy from her trick-or-treat bag. She just wanted to go.

Dad was late.

He was always late, but now he was really, really late.

Mom said it in her razor sharp voice over and over and over. "He's late, and he's probably not going to show."

Luna's lamp shined in the corner. Light coming from under, over, through the shade. Looking at the light usually felt good, made her feel warm and glowing inside, but tonight it was too bright. It hurt Luna's eyes.

Mom was getting louder, sharper; her voice could cut wood, could slice through Luna's broom. It felt like it was carving through Luna. Mom was angry, behind Luna, moving back and forth, her voice switching sides of the room, pinging against the walls. Luna held onto her broom, circled her hands around the smooth handle. Even though she didn't know any magic and it was just a piece of wood, still it felt good to hold on to something.

Mom didn't like that Luna liked Dad. "He's a bastard," Mom yelled. "You can't trust him; he's not coming. When will you get that you can't depend on him? He's no good!"

Luna sat on her patchwork bedspread, staring so much that the colors blurred. She wished Mom's voice would blur like that, mix the words together so they didn't make sense, so she wouldn't have to understand the truth.

It was cold.

This place was always so cold.

Her hat, her broom, her shoulders slumped. Her brown hair swept across her face and covered it like curtains but still there were colors through the spaces in her hair. Blue, red, yellow and green blend, blend, blended through strands; her mom yelled, yelled, yelled that Dad wasn't coming, and she got it.

She got it.

She was alone.

Her mom was ranting, ranting, ranting. Not talking to her, talking *at* her.

Loud, loud, *LOUD*.

Luna was alone.

Her dad wasn't coming.

She was alone.

Her broom dropped to the floor.

Something inside her fell too.

"I should go," Luna said when Loreena came back. It was cold in the hospital room. She had goosebumps. "I have to pick up the kids."

"Then go," Loreena said. She turned her back on Luna and clicked on the TV. She tsked at the screen displaying the extension, muttered something about thieves being everywhere, and dialed the number. After a short exchange in which she begrudgingly authorized the $4 daily charge, Loreena hung up and changed the channel. *Judge Judy* was on, and she was letting someone have it.

Luna was used to her mother not saying goodbye. She never got any closure from Loreena. She stood in the doorway, where she'd waited out the TV activation. "'Bye," she called. But Loreena just stared at the TV, immersed in Judy's admonishment. Luna was already forgotten.

Waiting for the elevator, Luna rubbed her arms and tried to shake off her chill.

Ding! It arrived. The doors slid open, and there was Aunt Zelda.

"Oh, child!" Zelda stepped out and wrapped Luna in her arms. And then Luna was warm.

FOUR

THE HUG HAD to end, of course. That was the bad thing about hugs. It was like when Luna was little, and Aunt Zelda came and held Luna's hand through the crib bars. Sooner or later she had to let go.

It was Aunt Zelda who had provided love and companionship in Luna's young world. And she'd helped Luna discover who she was—by bringing her crayons, a little box of bright colors. Luna held one and she knew. She gripped that crayon, she scribbled purple and she felt it: *This is right.* And though it would be years before she understood what it truly meant to write, she had peace and purpose in her heart. These things carried her through the dark.

Zelda tried to teach Luna *her* passion, propping a tiny violin under Luna's chin practically before the child could speak. As the years passed and Luna balked, Zelda bribed her to play, paying ten cents per music sheet line.

The violin was torture to Luna. She wanted to write.

Every moment she spent struggling over notes, she could be putting words to paper.

That's how much she knew what she was meant to do, and finally Zelda accepted it. When Luna was nine, her fiddle was retired and Zelda bought Luna a journal. "Far be it from me to fight your passion," she told Luna. "Write on, Love."

Here are some things about kooky, wonderful Aunt Zelda:

STATS ON ZELDA

Name: Zelda Lampanelli Belleford Lamar

Ethnic background: The same as her brother Lenny's, but the similarities pretty much ended there between her and her decade-younger sibling.

Marital status: Twice widowed.

Children: None. Before she was married, Zelda had been something of a free spirit with men. In trouble when abortions were illegal, she had a botched "backroom" procedure. But she couldn't love Luna any more if Luna were her daughter, rather than her niece.

Body: Tall, fit and slim—she had the build of a migrant worker.

Hair: Dark brown.

Occupation: Musician and visionary. Zelda had converted an old coffee barge into a floating concert hall in Brooklyn. She was pretty famous now, featured in the *New York Times* and on *Good Morning, America.*

Other likes: Gardening, the sea, whodunit novels.

Dislikes: Arrogance and cruelty.

Religion: Zelda had been raised by a devout Catholic mother whose life centered around her church. When her mother died, the priest refused to bless the grave because Zelda couldn't pay him. Zelda had renounced all religion until recently, when she'd become a Zen Buddhist. Her second husband's ashes were sprinkled outside the Zendo in upstate New York, though he didn't share her beliefs.

Favorite writers: She enjoyed anything she read, but particularly favored Agatha Christie, which she'd read with Luna during Luna's teen years.

Favorite dessert: Anything sweet, because during the Depression they barely had sugar. Nor did they have much butter, and now she never turned down a croissant.

Favorite expression: "Opposition breeds opposition." (Zelda offered many profound observations, but this was her favorite nugget.) And when they parted, Zelda never said, "Good-bye." Instead, she said, "Tootle-oo, old chum!"

Zelda had a strong, deep laugh. When Luna was a child and Zelda visited, Luna had laughed a lot too. The world had taken a different tone..

But there was nothing to laugh about now.

Zelda asked, "How is Lenny?"

"Not good..."

"Oh my..." Zelda's walnuty voice cracked. "Let's sit for a moment. I have to compose myself before I see him." This was a rarity. Zelda was the one who was always together. She held everything in place—she was the glue! *If she comes apart...* Luna shuddered. That wouldn't, couldn't, happen.

Zelda took one wobbly step towards the lounge area, then another. She lived on her floating barge, and because she came off it so infrequently, she didn't have "land legs." Luna took Zelda's hand to steady her, and Zelda squeezed heartily.

Attached, they inched across the white linoleum floor as though it were wet and they were in danger of slipping. Finally they made it to the chairs. They sat side by side, Zelda gripping Luna's hand still. Just like old times, except now Luna's hand was full-grown, and Aunt Zelda's was wrinkled and bony. Disturbing, how people lost the cushion between their flesh and bones as they aged. It was hard to feel comfortable holding Zelda's hand now. It made Luna think too much.

A shame it had to be like this. That it took Lenny's stroke for Zelda to leave her barge. Zelda's life revolved around that hunk of metal, and even though Luna was glad Zelda had realized her dream, she was jealous of it. Luna wanted her aunt to be the person who used to sit with her, read books with her. But once the barge was born, her aunt was consumed with concerts and fundraising. Now she was here, sitting beside her, holding her hand. Luna wanted desperately to discuss her problems and to ask, *How do I find the strength to deal with my life?* Zelda would know—she'd mustered so much courage in her years—but of course

Lenny dominated this moment. The man who'd never been there was suddenly *everywhere*, vapor in the air they breathed. And in a way, Luna hated him for that.

In a way, she hated her father, period.

Zelda was talking about the past again—the really long-ago past, when she had made the choice to leave her home and her ten-year-old brother behind. Their mother was dead, their father remarried. "I had a chance to go on the road with a symphony. I had to take it," she said—not for the first time.

"I know you did," Luna reassured her, as she had the other times.

"I didn't know my stepmother was so cruel, that she would treat Lenny that way."

"How could you?" Who could believe that wicked stepmothers really existed—that little Lenny would be sent to the garage to sleep like a dog. That his father would allow such a thing.

"By the time I realized something was wrong... it was too late." Zelda lamented.

"It's not your fault."

Left to his own devices, Lenny had looked for friends. The ones he found showed him a way to forget his troubles: Shooting up heroin.

"Do you think the drug use played a part in his stroke?" Zelda asked.

"I don't think it helped," Luna said.

They sat in silence for a while, holding hands. And Luna thought back to the day when she learned the awful truth about her dad.

Twenty-seven years earlier

They were on the barge's roof, painting it rustoleum red. It was kind of cool, giving the ugly metal a makeover. But Luna was too distracted to really give in and enjoy the process. She was tired of the big mystery surrounding her father's employment. Loreena just sighed and walked away every time Luna asked. Zelda tended to divert the question, or say "Ask your mother." But Luna wasn't giving up.

With every roll of her paint, she recited a different classmate's name, followed by their father's profession. "Jeremy Fitzhenry's dad is a defense attorney."

Roll.

"Stuart Weinstein's dad is an orthodontist."

Roll.

"Arlene Schumacher's dad works on Wall Street."

Eight rolls later, she got to her point. "What is *my* dad?"

Aunt Zelda dropped her roller and fisted her hands toward the sky. "He's a drug addict!" she proclaimed in her scratchy voice. At this high decibel, it sounded like a car screeching into a pole. Luna felt like she was the pole. "He's addicted to heroin and he supports his habit by selling it!"

Stunned by both the revelation and Zelda's tone, Luna fled the roof. Boom, boom! Steel thundered under her quick movement. She descended the steep metal ladder so fast that she lost her footing. She didn't fall—her tight grip on the cold rail saved her—but her stomach plummeted in a rush of panic, like on a roller coaster ride. She forced herself to slow down.

Finally at the bottom, Luna bolted inside the barge's dark chamber, flopped across the ratty couch Zelda slept on and tried to cry. She couldn't—she was too shocked. And anyway, it was a relief to know, even if the truth was horrible.

She lay there with her eyes closed. Soon the metal barge door creaked open again. Then footsteps. Then Aunt Zelda's cracky voice. "Child, I'm sorry… I never meant to tell you… but you kept asking…"

Zelda's warm hand pressed Luna's shoulder. "Forgive me, dear heart. The truth is, I've felt guilty for not being there when your father fell in with that bad crowd… But I had my music career, I was on the road…"

Luna pulled herself up and pushed into Zelda's arms. Wrapped in that hug, Luna absorbed Aunt Zelda's love—like a plant's roots soaking in nutrients from the soil. Maybe that was why Aunt Zelda loved gardening. She could see that her hands had the power to make what she loved bloom.

After a moment Aunt Zelda let go. She looked Luna in the eye.

"Come on, child," she said. Luna had a stray strand of hair hanging in her face. Aunt Zelda tucked it behind her ear. "Let's get back to work."

Aunt Zelda released Luna's hand and gave it a little pat. "Go home to your children, dear heart. I'll be all right, now that I've absorbed some of your strength."

Luna's strength? Now *that* was funny. "Are you sure?"

Zelda nodded, and stood. "I buried two husbands. At least my brother's still alive."

"Well, that's true." Luna said. She got up and headed to the elevator once more without bothering to mention a few things: How her father was the poster child for a life wasted. How his new physical condition was a metaphor for the metaphysical nothing he'd been for so long. How it was so devastating that he might very well wind up some kind of paralyzed vegetable with no hope of connecting and resolving his issues with Luna in one of those Oprah moments she'd always believed they'd have. No, these things she couldn't lay on her poor Aunt Zelda, who clearly had enough of her own shit to process.

And besides, Luna had to go and deal with her shit of a husband. She had to stop shitting up her own life. *And*, she had to make sure her kids didn't get hit with a bunch of shit.

The shit stops here, Luna thought. The elevator door opened. She waved goodbye to her aunt and stepped inside. Part of her waited for Aunt Zelda's usual "Tootle-loo, old chum!"—Luna would've given anything for some kind of normal—but the only sound was the slight rumbling of the door sliding closed.

FIVE

LUNA PULLED UP in front of Sunny's white, aluminum-sided house. A small one-story, it looked flat and incomplete. But Sunny didn't care about appearances. It had a roof and heat. Praise Baby Jesus! For a while, after Sunny's husband Sal decided to try crack at age 33 and subsequently wiped out all their savings chasing his high, Sunny hadn't been sure if she would be able to afford housing at all. Even now, years later, there were months when she barely pulled the rent together.

Luna grabbed her purple parka, got out of her Windstar and chirped the locks. She slipped the coat on as she walked, without breaking her stride. Luna wasn't a born multi-tasker, but motherhood had instilled efficiency.

Flower and Spunky, Sunny's two female "mixed breed" dogs, were in the process of doing their business on the lawn. Someone had once asked her what kind of dogs they were, and Sunny had answered, "The smelly kind."

Flower was brown, mid-sized and plump. Spunky was black and white, larger, with a tight, muscular physique. They were attached to the fence bordering the house on long chains that clanked when the dogs got riled up—which was whenever a man passed by. They would bark and strain to get at anyone of the male persuasion, but women didn't faze them.

"Hello, girls," Luna greeted them as she headed up the cement walkway. Flower and Spunky wagged their tails briefly, then went back to sniffing out spots to poop in.

Luna stepped onto the decaying brick stoop and read the newly hung wooden Christmas sign on Sunny's door: "Santa, I've been as good as I can be, what else do you want from me?" Yesterday in this spot, there'd been a turkey sporting a t-shirt that said, "Eat ham." Like at the hospital, Sunny wasted no time swapping out holidays. Luna knocked, and the door opened. "Oh, chickie," Sunny exclaimed. "How are you?"

"I'm okay, I guess."

Luna stepped inside and Sunny hugged her. This was a rare thing, because Sunny was not a touchy person. The situation had to be really dire.

But Sunny showed her love in other ways. The best was that she would always listen. Another, not as easy to swallow, was that she never failed to give her opinion on a situation—in a very snarky manner. She didn't mean any harm by it – that was just Sunny's "truth hurts" approach. Luna believed her best friend could make a bundle as a stand-up comic, but Sunny had permanent stage-fright.

Here are some other things (both funny and not-so-much) about Sunny:

STATS ON SUNNY

Name: Sandra Jacqueson (Miss Jacqueson if you're nasty.) Sunny hated her real first name because people always shortened it to "Sandy" no matter how many times she told them not to. This made her think of Olivia Newton John's sugary character in *Grease*, which subsequently made her want to hurl.

Age: 37

Ethnic background: Haitian. Black on USA census forms, but light-skinned enough to be routinely claimed by natives of any and all Hispanic nations as one of their own.

Marital status: Divorced from a crack-head.

Children: An eleven-year-old son (Layne, named after Alice in Chain's lead singer, whom she adored) and a ten-year-old daughter (Phoebe, a name Sunny just liked.)

Body: A few pounds over, but placed in strategically appealing areas. The term they used in on-line dating was "voluptuous." The term Sunny used was "fatty-fat."

Hair: Straight when she flat-ironed it. Most often she wore it pulled up in back, making her look really young.

Occupation: Cataloguing books for the county library system, working nights at a local library and doing laundry, house cleaning and child feeding when not occupied by the first two jobs. She was a single parent with the emphasis on single—her ex bounced in and out of town, jobs and jail, providing sporadic financial aid when he wasn't on a crack binge or serving time for funding it.

Favorite physical activities: None. Sunny didn't like to sweat.

Likes: Reading—she read voraciously. Movies, especially cheesy ones. She also loved *Star Wars*. Drinking—she enjoyed partaking in the spirits while doing that reading and movie watching. Snarking—she enjoyed ridiculing those who deserved it, and so many deserved it. Alternative music—as an alternative to talking to the people she'd later ridicule. Also, the TV shows *I Love Lucy* and *The Year Without A Santa Claus*.

Dislikes: Most people, clutter, chaos, mildew.

Religion: None to speak of. She'd had a brief bout with some sort of Protestantism, but it had passed. She was spiritual; she just disliked the group effort thing and preferred going solo.

Favorite writer: Stephen King.

Favorite dessert: Hostess cupcakes.

Favorite expression: She had a comment for every occasion, especially treasuring her many visual descriptions of Christ (i.e., "Christ in pajamas!") and her nifty all-purpose wrap-up phrase, "'Nuff said."

Luna had inadvertently nicknamed Sandra 'Sunny' the first time they'd met, fourteen years prior, at a summer barbecue. Sunny had been dressed in a black Alice in Chains t-shirt, black jeans, black open-toed platform shoes and black nail polish on her toes.

Looking her up and down, Luna had asked, "Why so sunny?"

Sunny appreciated the irony, and adopted the name on the spot.

Luna and Sunny's boyfriends, Nicky and Sal Marone—whom they'd later marry—were cousins. The barbecue was a Marone family get-together: big and boisterous. The two young women bonded immediately in that neither fit in with the drama du jour. The volatile Marone family didn't need the Grucci's to make fireworks—alcohol sufficed. After a few hours and more than a few Budweisers, the truth burst forth about who hated who, and exactly why. All this anger would be re-buried as soon as the sun peeked, but it was uncomfortable and unnerving to witness its exposure, however temporary.

As voices, tempers and blood alcohol levels rose, Luna and Sunny dragged their plastic lawn chairs across the gritty brick and cement patio, through air thick with smoke and malevolence, to the outskirts of the yard—planting themselves next to a bushy rhododendron. Strangers in a strange land, they learned that night that it was way easier to laugh at the craziness of the world when you had company.

They'd been providing each other company ever since.

Sunny smelled like cigarettes and cocoa butter. She released Luna and they went inside. "The kids are in the middle of a *Star Wars* movie marathon. They're up to the *Revenge of the Jedi.* Those ewoks are mad annoying, but apparently children enjoy them."

They stepped into Sunny's always-immaculate kitchen. Sunny couldn't afford much, but what she had, she kept tidy and clean. The white counters gleamed, the matching appliances shined, the paper towels and napkins were neatly stowed in coordinating seasonal dispensers, with Rudolph perched forlornly on each one (Sunny identified with outsiders.) Wooden chairs were tucked under a matching table, and when Luna put her coat on the back of one she took care to keep it aligned.

The refrigerator stood out, because it was covered with Sunny's extensive magnet collection. Magnets were the only things Sunny allowed to collect in her home, which was funny because Sunny was herself a magnet: for crazies. When she hit the street, the crazies approached. She was safe at her day job, because the county library system was closed to the public, but at night she worked in a public library that might have been a sanitarium. Crazies practically leapt across the counter to get at her. And it was worse when she wasn't working. Crazies found her everywhere. Gas station attendants, grocery clerks, oil delivery men: all were not only attracted to her, but felt no obligation to obey social boundaries. (This could've been because they were crazy.) Everywhere Sunny went, she was like that poor black-and-white cat accosted by Pepe Le Pew. It might not have been so bad if only she could summon men higher up the chain, but inevitably: if a guy was missing teeth, grooming skills and good sense, he'd be all over Sunny.

Luna had never thought about the correlation between Sunny's magnets and the fact that she *was* a magnet. She was about to mention this when five-year-old Dylan raced in from the living-room, where the sounds of a space battle were playing. Luna was glad to skip the *Star Wars* saga today—she had enough to battle through here on Earth.

"Mommy!" Dylan exclaimed with exuberance. It was nice to be exalted. She gathered him up in her arms and squeezed.

"Hey, Mom." Ten-year-old Ben said, joining them a moment later. She added him into the fold. The three embraced for several heartbeats before separating.

"Where's Daddy?" Dylan asked. He had blonde hair, a cherubic face and a vivacious spirit. Always, he smiled. With his looks and temperament, Luna had been tempted to take him for head shots and parade him among talent agents in Manhattan. Every mom wants to show her child off to the world! But she was afraid of becoming a stage mom and even more scared Dylan would become a child star. They rarely fared well as adults.

"Um… Daddy had some errands to take care of," Luna said. Dylan's left overalls strap was undone. Soon he'll be too old for overalls, she thought, as she refastened it. She wanted to freeze his boyhood, stick it in a bottle like time in that Jim Croce song. And yet she craved the independence that arrived when children became more self-sufficient, like Ben.

Dylan said, “I’m gonna go back to Star Wars. Phoebe and Layne are way ahead of me.”

“You do that,” Luna told him.

“May the force be with you, Mommy.”

“You too, baby. Tell Layne and Phoebe I said ‘hi.’”

“Okay, Mommy.”

Dylan zipped back to the living room. “My Mommy says hi,” he said to his cousins. For how long, Luna wondered, will he be so obedient?

“Hi Aunt Luna!” Layne and Phoebe shouted. She pictured the three kids together on the couch, the light of the screen playing over their faces.

Ben took a step toward the living room, paused and turned back. His complexion was darker than his brother’s, but nothing near his dad’s. People were always saying that Ben looked like Nick, but Luna didn’t see it. Nick’s hair was black, while Ben’s was brown—and Ben had none of those Italian spots on his face. She had to admit, the shapes of their faces were similar—but was that what made you resemble someone? There were only so many shapes a face could be. One thing was for certain, Ben had Luna’s hazel eyes and kind heart. “Is everything all right, Mom? You seem sad.”

Luna hesitated. So much had happened today! It seemed wrong to burden him with reality, but equally erroneous to spin a fantasy that everything was fine. “I’ve got a lot going on, honey. But don’t worry—no one died.” There was no point in telling Ben about his grandfather. He’d only met him a few times, anyway. It wasn’t like Ben was going to be asking for Lenny, so why deliver painful news? But *what* would she say about *Nick*?

“Is Dad really running errands?”

Ben’s eyes were so deep and expressive, Luna felt as if she could find the truths of the universe if she could only dive inside. But she had the same eyes as her son and she had no answers, only questions.

“Why do you ask?”

“Well… I was just wondering if maybe you were mad at him.”

"Mad?"

Ben furrowed his eyebrows, causing the worry-lines on his forehead (another thing he had in common with Luna) to look extra prominent. "Cause of… the stuff on the computer."

"What stuff?"

"The… pictures."

"What pictures, honey?"

"The wieners."

"What wieners?" Luna prayed he was talking about hot dogs, but knew that he wasn't.

Ben looked down at Sunny's black and white checkered linoleum. It was rare for him to break eye contact. "I was trying to go on the Disney Channel website on Dad's computer, and all these pictures of guys with their wieners showing popped up… they were pretty gross."

Luna wanted to say something reassuring, but all she could think of were vicious things about Nick. She took a deep breath and let it out. Then she did it again. Finally she said, "I didn't know about the wieners, sweetie. I'll make sure you never have to see them again. And as for Daddy…" She paused again. Oh, there was a lot she wanted to say about Nick. But she remembered how horrible it had been to listen to her mother rant about her dad, and she wasn't about to scar her son like that. She took yet another breath in and let it out. "Daddy's got a bunch of things to take care of right now, that's all." Like packing. There was no way Nick was spending one more night under the same roof as Luna. Period.

Ben still seemed unsure. "Is Daddy moving out?" He really *was* intuitive. He'd probably heard the fighting. Luna and Nick had been doing that a lot. She'd never done it in front of the boys, but kids always heard.

"Yes," she answered. She wouldn't lie to him. It wasn't fair. "Yes, he is."

"Well, that's okay. Maybe then you can be happy again, Mommy."

Luna stared at her son, and she was so grateful for him. "Maybe," she conceded. And in that moment she truly felt that she might be happy again. She grabbed Ben and gave him a squeeze. "Don't tell your brother yet, okay?"

"Okay, Mom." Ben's voice seemed mature all of a sudden—deeper. And she'd somehow gone from 'Mommy' to 'Mom.' Is that how childhood ended… in one sentence? In one revelation?

Ben went back to the movie. Luna pulled out a kitchen chair, scraping it over the linoleum, and sank into it. Sunny put a giant mug on a green plastic placemat in front of her. "I know you don't like my brand of coffee, dude, but I figured you needed a caffeine fix after that."

It was true. Sunny bought whatever canned brand was on sale at the supermarket, while Luna ordered whole bean from Zabar's—one of the few ways that Luna was a snob. But it was also true that right now, any coffee was fine. "Thanks." She took a sip. It was weak, but also heartening.

Sunny patted Luna's hand. "Everything will be alright."

"When?"

"Hell if I know."

They both laughed, and Luna felt better—if for no other reason than because she had this one friend in the world.

SIX

ONE FRIEND? JIMINY protested. *What am I, chopped liver?*

It was always unnerving when Jiminy piped in following hours of silence—even after all these years. She knew not to bother asking why he hadn't commented since she'd hauled ass from couples therapy. Questions like that he would never answer. Actually, he never answered *any* questions. He just raised them.

You're not my friend, Jiminy. You're my… Crap. What was he?

It doesn't matter what I am, Luna. It only matters that you know I'm here for you.

Yeah, when you want to be.

When you need me, he corrected. *But go have coffee with your one friend. We'll talk later.*

"Mind if we take this outside, chickie?" Sunny asked, oblivious to Luna's inner dialogue. "I'm dying for a cigarette."

"Sure."

They sat on Sunny's stoop with their cups of coffee. Luna tucked her coat carefully under her butt before she sat on the cold asphalt.

Sunny wore a sweatshirt, sweatpants and Happy Bunny slippers. She never put her coat on to go smoke. Apparently she had some strange immunity to freezing. Sunny sat downwind from Luna, so the smoke wouldn't blow in Luna's face. Luna shared the events of her day while

Sunny inhaled and listened. "Christ on a platter with parsley, dude. That's a lot of shit for one day."

"Yup."

"The only good thing I can say about Nick is that at least he's not a crack-head."

"Is that better than being some kind of pervert?"

"Hell, yeah! You've still got your jewelry and car, right? Sal took everything I had. Only consolation I have is that he's renting some room in a basement, living like the subterranean creature he is. And that's an improvement for him. Half the time he's homeless, or incarcerated."

"Wow," Luna said.

"Exactly," said Sunny. "And what about your dad? When will they know how he'll be?"

Luna shrugged. "It's up in the air. Like everything in my life." She stared at the bleak foliage in Sunny's yard. Bare trees paling in grey air. God, winter was getting old. She was impatient for spring, even though she had to turn another year older before it came. But, what the hell, spring was worth aging for. At least she had some progress to report at this year's end—though she had a lot more to do, starting with dealing with Mister Wiener. After that…

Luna's heart sped with anxiety at the thought of starting over, so she stopped thinking. She clutched her mug like a life preserver.

Sunny said, "Don't you wish we could be like those women on the coffee commercials who are all about celebrating the moments of their lives?"

"Yeah. Where's Jean-Luc when you need him?"

The dogs went wild, barking and rattling their chains. Sure enough, a guy had just turned the corner. He saw the dogs and crossed the street.

"There goes Jean Luc now. He got scared off," Luna said.

"Just as well," Sunny said. "If he's a man, he's a problem. 'Nuff said." She took a final puff on her cigarette and crushed it out on the asphalt at her feet. Black ash marked the spot. "So, what are you gonna do about your worse half?"

"Oh, the wieners have sealed Nicks's fate," Luna said. "I'm going to..." Luna's phone rang just then, interrupting her sentence. She checked the caller display. It said, "Liar."

"It's Nick," she told Sunny. She hit the answer button. "What?"

"*That's* all you have to say? *What?* After you left me with no money to pay Dr. Stepponi and no way to get home?'

"You're thirty-six years old, Nick. I figured you'd work things out." God, she was sick of having to hold the world up. She was dropping it, starting now.

"Well, I finally made it back. But I'm locked out. You have the key on the car ring."

"Oh, well..."

"Oh, well? You need to come home, Luna! The bank card's inside! I need to play Lotto."

In addition to thinking it was his due to win Lotto because he'd played for so many years, Nick was also sure that if he didn't play, his numbers would hit.

"It's *my* bank card, Nick. You don't have any money saved, remember?"

"Whaddaya mean? It's our money."

"No, it's mine. I write books, and the royalties get direct-deposited. You serve coffee and sandwiches off the books, and the money gets folded into your pocket. You don't contribute to the household, and when your hand comes out empty you hit 'our' bank account for more. But there is no more 'our.' 'We' are done, Nick. In case you didn't get that hint from when I walked out of that ridiculous therapy session, I'm divorcing you. You can't go in the house because it's not your house anymore."

Sunny clapped. "Yay! Go you!"

"Who is that? Sunny? Tell her to go fuck herself," Nick snarled. "And you can't keep me out of my own house."

"It's actually *my* house," Luna told him. "I guess you forgot that, too." Thank God she hadn't put his name on the deed. Aunt Zelda, who had given Luna the house after moving to Brooklyn, hadn't let her.

"You can't throw me out."

"Looks like you're already out. Saves me the trouble. I'll let you know when you can pick your stuff up."

"Don't fuck with me, Luna. I'm friends with half of the Nassau County cops, you know."

The number of cops Nick was "friends" with was always growing. The truth was that he served eggs to a few patrolmen every morning.

"Maybe your *friends* on the job would like to know about the pornography you've exposed our son to on your computer," Luna told him.

"What?"

"Ben saw a bunch of wieners when he was trying to go to the Disney Channel site. Are you proud of yourself?"

"I don't see how that's possible…"

"There's no need for you to speak anymore, Nick. The wieners have spoken for you. Face it: You have a problem, and I'm not going to let it affect our children. You're done. If you're outside the house when I get home, *I'll* call your cop buddies and let them see your collection of pics."

There was a heavy sigh. "Where will I go?"

"I think Sal's got a cellar room he's renting at the moment. Go crawl in with your cousin." Luna hit End. It was hard. She was afraid of what came next. Nick could get so mean! But she was more afraid of what would happen if she didn't end this charade right now.

Her kids were most important.

She was shaking. The phone rang again—"Liar" wasn't giving up. Luna put the phone on the pavement next to Sunny's cigarette ash.

"Good job!" Sunny said. She patted Luna's back. "I know that was hard for you. You're too nice to him to that user… though I could never understand why. It's about time you showed Fatsy the door."

"If only fatness was the problem. There's no dieting off deceit. Oh, by the way, he told you to go fuck yourself."

"Such wit. I am mortally wounded," Sunny said.

"I knew you would be."

The phone kept going to voicemail, then ringing again. Some texts came in as well. Sunny picked up the phone, deleted everything, and turned the power off. From around the corner the Roman Catholic church bells rang, marking either the beginning of an hour or the end of one, depending on how you looked at it. Sunny stood and said, "Let's order some Chinese food. The kids are gonna realize they're hungry as soon as the Jedis extract their revenge, which will be any moment."

*Sunny really **is** a good friend,* Jiminy amended. *And for the record, I'm proud of you, too.*

Thanks Jiminy, Luna answered as she went back inside to take the kids' orders. *I'm proud of me, too.*

After everyone had been fed and fortunes read aloud (Luna's was "You have a long journey ahead"—not the most thrilling news), the kids went back into the living room to catch some Disney Channel show. Sunny turned on Luna's phone, listening to and erasing all of Nick's venomous voicemails. "Your mom left a message, too," Sunny told Luna, handing her back the purple-encased phone. "She said your dad's not twitching as much."

"Thanks," Luna said, stowing her phone back into her purple purse. It had been her New Year's Resolution last year to surround herself with things that made her happy—and the color purple was one of those things. Nick was not. Why was getting rid of something—or someone—so hard? "You think he'll be outside when I get home?"

Sunny shook her head no. "His ranting was unintelligible for the most part, but I think he deduced that his cards are all played for the night."

"God, I hope so. But Nick doesn't generally know when to fold." She pulled her cell phone out again to check the time. "Holy crap! It's nine-thirty. The kids should be in bed!"

"Relax. They're young. One night past bedtime won't hurt."

Sunny was right. For the past few years Luna had been clinging to her schedule like a log on a river, trying to keep herself afloat. One missed bedtime was hardly cause for alarm or Child Protective Services.

Still, going home could no longer be avoided. She called for her kids, everyone said their goodbyes, and they were on their way. But to what?

SEVEN

LUNA PUT ON Disney Radio (God, Disney was everywhere!), and the kids happily listened to songs by their favorite child stars. She attempted to let the music distract her thoughts, but she kept imagining Nick waiting for them on the curb. He'd try and make her look like the bad guy. Ben wouldn't buy it—but Dylan might.

She couldn't bear for Dylan to think she wouldn't let Daddy in the house for no good reason. *Please don't be there, please don't be there...*

Her prayers were answered. Nick was nowhere in sight when she parked the van. Only Jingles was there—their errant cat, who came and went as he pleased. She'd originally named him Oliver—after Oliver Twist, because the orange cat was such a ragged stray—but the kids kept calling him Jingles because of the bell around his neck, which Luna bestowed after several bird massacres on her lawn. The new moniker stuck. Jingles followed them in, jingling all the way.

"Pajama time, guys," she said when they got in the door and she hit the lights. "It's late." She glanced at her kitchen table, with the extra leaf still in and so many chairs gathered around to accommodate Nick's super-sized family. They were all loud and nuts, but in a way she would miss them. Being an only child had given her an aversion to being alone, no matter how bad her company was.

But then Luna's eyes landed at the center of the table, on the ceramic turkeys Ben and Dylan had made in art school and proudly presented her with. She had her sons. She wasn't alone.

It was wonderful to have them, but of course not the same as adult companionship. With them her world was Disney, and sometimes she wanted Showtime. And of course her kids could not protect her. It was her job to protect them. How was she supposed to do *that* in this world where so much was beyond control, and where right was so often intermingled with wrong.

You think too much, Jiminy said.

It was true, but she didn't know how to stop.

Just be.

"Be" was too solitary for Luna. She always put something beside it: like "careful," or "worried." Or "afraid."

She followed the boys upstairs, where they had adjoining rooms. Dylan scampered into his and Jingles followed him, while Ben paused with his hand on his door knob. "Good night, Mom."

Luna felt a swell of loss. Yes, it was great that Ben was self-sufficient. But his independence also made her feel like she was shirking her duties—and in a way, his growing older made watching over him more of a challenge. Worst of all was this feeling of time marching, carrying her away from her boys' childhood. Luna missed the old pajama and story time, with Ben curled up on one side of her and Dylan on the other.

Tonight, she particularly mourned such moments. "Don't forget…" Luna started.

"To brush my teeth," Ben finished.

"And also…"

"To wash my face. I know, Mom. Everything's on my list."

Ben made a daily sticky-note list of everything he needed to accomplish and stuck it on his mirror. He even included "wake up" on top. When she'd questioned him about this given, he'd answered, "I like to be able to cross something off first thing."

Luna wavered in the hallway. More changes were happening—she felt movement in the air. "C'mon, Mommy," Dylan called from his room. Ben let go of his handle and gave her a hug. "It's okay, Mom," he assured her. "I'll be the man of the house now."

Ooooh, no. She wasn't going to burden her son like that. Luna took

Ben's hands in hers and looked him in the eyes. "Don't you worry about taking care of me, sweetheart. Relax. You don't have to be a grown-up yet."

He studied her for a few moments. Her hands remained tight over his. "Okay. But let me know if you need me to do anything. I'll put it on my list."

Dylan's room was a jungle. Across one wall was a rainforest mural. His bunk bed posts looked like trees, complete with leafy green tops. The upper bunk was encased in a hut with thatched roof. Dylan alternated between sleeping inside that house and below, where a menagerie of stuffed animals resided. The rest of his furniture matched the hut, in a Gilligan's Island way. Stepping into this space was like leaving civilization behind. Tonight, that suited Luna just fine.

Unfortunately, some things could not be forgotten. Luna had just buttoned Dylan into his macaw-patterned pajamas when he asked about Nick. "When's Daddy coming home?"

Luna bit her lip, so hard that she tasted blood. Through seeping saltiness she said, "Daddy's staying somewhere else, baby."

"Is he coming home tomorrow?"

Luna pressed her finger on her wound and thought. Should she wait to break the news? No. He'd resent her if she did. She just knew it. "No, baby. Mommy and Daddy aren't going to be together anymore."

His eyes widened. "You mean you're getting divorced?"

Such a big word for a five-year-old! "How do you know about divorce?"

Dylan rolled his eyes. "Everyone knows about it, Mommy. It happens all the time."

"I see." She checked her lip. The bleeding had stopped. If only everything could be fixed so simply.

"So, are you and Daddy getting a divorce or not?'

There was no beating around the bush with Dylan—not even here, in the wild. "Yes, we are." God, Nick was going to be livid that she told Dylan without him. *Oh, well.*

Dylan was uncharacteristically quiet for a moment. When he finally spoke, his voice was low. "Will I see him?"

"Yes."

"But we won't do our trips anymore?" Dylan loved family vacations.

"Not with Daddy. But you, me and Ben will go."

Dylan's head slumped. Luna sat on the floor and scooped him up in her arms. "We're still a family, Dylan. And Daddy's still your father."

He lay in her lap with his face pressed into her shoulder for several moments. Then he raised his head and asked, "Will you sleep with me tonight?"

"Okay, Baby."

"In the tree house?"

Luna sighed. It was so cramped in there, and she was claustrophobic. "Okay, Baby."

"I wanna lay on your arm."

"Okay, Baby."

Luna brushed Dylan's teeth and washed his face. Then, because it was already *so* late, she followed him up the bamboo ladder into his house without putting on her pajamas.

Jingles was sprawled on the comforter. Luna nudged him over, and then burrowed under the quilted monkey comforter with Dylan. Jingles jangled as he searched for a comfy space to settle in, electing to lie across Luna's feet. There was no storytime. Dylan was asleep the moment he curled against Luna, her arm cradling his neck. Unfortunately, real life had been tonight's tale. In silence, she wished for a happy ending for her kids—and herself. She managed to turn and kiss Dylan's forehead without disturbing him. Then she tried to sleep, despite the rising panic which resulted from lying scrunched inside close walls. Dylan wanted her there. She would endure.

EIGHT

LUNA WOKE UP before dawn with a jolt. It wasn't the cramped quarters, or the lack of circulation in her arm or her feet. It wasn't even the throbbing pain in her neck from sleeping in a bad position. It was something much worse: the realization that she'd forgotten to cancel Nick's American Express card. She needed to do it immediately, before he sent her permanently into the red. The combination of AmEx's lack of a spending limit and Nick's lack of conscience made that possibility all too real.

Gently, she extracted her arm from under Dylan's neck, and shifted away as carefully as possible so she wouldn't wake him. Unfortunately the same couldn't be done for Jingles, who let out a rebuking "Meow!" when Luna reclaimed her circulation-deprived feet. He jingled his way over to Dylan's stomach and tucked himself against it.

Luna climbed down the wooden ladder carefully, because her feet and her arm were numb and barely functional, and she was always wobbly pre-caffeination. She hobbled into the hallway, flipped on the switch and limped down the stairs, shaking her arms and kicking her feet like a Rockette to get the blood flowing. Now that she'd woken up a little more, she wanted to hurry. The kids didn't have to be up for another hour—they had art school today, where they'd made those ceramic turkeys. If she got done with Amex fast she could get some writing in.

Luna thought of early morning as "bonus hours"—-time she could devote to *NWaN—Novel Without a Name*. It was an ultra-personal endeavor she knew had the potential to be great, if she could just stop weeping as she wrote it. In addition to not having a title, she didn't have an end for it—which made her nuts. While many writers wrote blindly, she'd always maintained that if one doesn't have a destination, one will never arrive. Still, she felt compelled to press on through the pages, and the tears. She could never work on it during the "main" day, which was so quickly devoured by paying work, household chores and motherhood.

Her arms and feet were recovering now, tingling with warmth. She hopped across her kitchen tiles to shake out her flow even further. All circulations were go when she reached the phone. She hit speed-dial for Amex (which she normally used once a month, to pay her bill), and asked for a representative. She didn't want to use the automated system and risk canceling her own card, which she used for everything. While on hold, she jerked her neck from side to side to make it crack. Alas, the pain endured. Luckily she had an appointment with Dr. Gold later.

The representative was pleasant and handled the termination of Nick's charging abilities quickly and efficiently. If only the marriage could be ended that way. Luna learned that Nick had spent $171.89 at 7-11 the evening prior. Most likely the bulk of it had gone for cigarettes, with perhaps a nitrate-filled hotdog and a red-dye-loaded Gatorade thrown in. It could've been worse. Nick might've wasted a shitload of money on overpriced groceries, but for the fact that he never could think past polluting his lungs. And gambling, of course. She thanked God he couldn't charge Lotto tickets.

So Nick was cut off. Luna wanted to revel, but she had little capacity for joy until she had her coffee. She hit the button on her Krups and waited to hear the sounds of brewing coffee—and to smell that wonderful waft.

The Krups sputtered, but no coffee dripped down. After a few moments it started making loud sounds that sounded like the mechanical version of choking. Then smoke billowed out. *What the hell?* Luna hit the "off" button and checked the water chamber. Empty. She swung open the coffee basket. Full of yesterday's grounds. *Rats!* She'd forgotten to set up her coffee last night.

It was so hard measuring and grinding beans when she didn't have her clarity yet. It took her three tries to count the eight scoops, because she kept losing track. Clearly she wasn't going to get any work done on *NWaN* this morning. But instead of kicking herself for a missed opportunity, she elected to be positive. She had Nick out and it was glorious!

You're so right, said Jiminy. *You're doing great. Keep going!*

By the time the coffee was ready Luna had to wake up the kids. She managed to get through her morning routine of dressing Dylan and making breakfast without mishap. Another hour whisked by, the way those early moments do, and it was time to get the kids to art school. Luna looked both ways for Nick as she followed the boys and the jingling cat out the door. It was doubtful that he would be there, since he had to work—but she couldn't shake the foreboding that he would turn up anyway.

Thank goodness, she was wrong: Nick wasn't there. They waved goodbye to Jingles, who was pawing dirt next to a shrub to do his business. "Why does he poop on the front lawn, Mommy?" Dylan asked.

"He poops wherever he feels like it, Baby," Luna answered. "The world is his litter box."

"It's good for the plants," said Ben, who was definitely the resident optimist. "I learned in school that people mix manure into their dirt to make things grow better."

"What's manure?" Dylan asked.

"Poop," said Ben.

"Ewww," said Dylan. "Grownups are gross."

"They can be," Luna said. "Some more than others."

They arrived at The Creative Place, and Luna scoped the area. Nick wasn't there. *Phew!* He could've made a real scene if he'd wanted to be a prick. He was either thinking of the kids, or he couldn't get out of work (it was probably the latter.)

A dozen or so smocked students of varied ages were visible through the storefront windows, already at work on their projects. The boys were a little late, but it wouldn't matter. One great thing about this school was that everyone worked at their own pace. The teachers hopped from kid to kid, offering help as needed, but the kids followed their own visions.

Luna put the car in Park & hit Unlock. The kids unbuckled themselves and hopped out. "Have fun, guys! See you in a few hours! Love you!" Luna called to them. They waved and headed off. Until recently, Luna used to get out and hug them—until Ben had informed her that she was being embarrassing.

Luna watched her sons head into the studio, side by side. Ben walked with an assured and even gait—he was that sort of balanced kid. Half Ben's height, Dylan usually had pep in his step because he loved going to art school and seeing his friends. Today he kind of trudged, falling behind Ben—who stopped and put out his hand. Dylan accepted it, and the two scurried inside together, joining the other kids already seated at tables and working.

Luna stared at the door closing behind her sons. She was proud of how she was raising them, yet always afraid she'd teeter and fall right off that tightrope called motherhood. And today was a particularly shaky day. *You're a good mother, Luna,* said Jiminy. *Now you need to learn how to be good to yourself.*

Back home, it was time to sit down and revise her novel under contract. She only had an hour before her chiropractor appointment. Unusually she could focus, shut everything out except her task. But today her mind spun with real-life details, like calling her lawyer (an old high-school friend who years ago had offered to represent her any time she wanted) and changing the locks. Oh, and dealing with Nick's stuff. But it was Saturday—not the time to reach a lawyer. The locks could wait, since Nick didn't have a way in, anyway. And Nick's stuff would still be there after she got some work done.

Luna took a deep breath and exhaled. Dr. Gold had instilled deep breathing into her, promising it to be more effective than any drugs or therapy. She couldn't argue with its price, either. Allowing her mind to exhale proved to be the harder task. But there was no need to be on high-alert for Nick. He worked until four.

Her dad popped into her head. *Shit!* She had to call her mother and check on him. The phone rang five times before Loreena answered. "I was wondering when you were going to call," she said, in lieu of "hello."

"Sorry. I have a lot going on, Mom."

Loreena let out her signature *Hhhmmmppppffff.* "As usual, I'm left alone to deal with everything."

"That's..." Luna started to say it wasn't true, but she stopped herself. Her mother was baiting her, and she wasn't going to start down that twisting road which either had no end, or a dead end. Luna would say that she's there for her, but she *does* have a family to take care of. Loreena would say that she gave up her opera career to raise Luna, as though Luna had asked to be born. Then Luna's residual resentment and hurt would kick in, and she'd bring up the fact that Loreena had left her alone every night, scrounging for whatever supper she could find. Then Loreena would snap, "I had to work, didn't I?" And Luna would return loudly—because defensiveness and anger always manifested in her voice—"You got off work at five and didn't come home 'til ten or later!" And Loreena would say Luna was out of her mind and that wasn't true, and even though Luna knew it was true she couldn't prove it and that would make her madder—etc, etc. There was no point in going *there.* Besides, wasn't everyone alone? She remembered listening to a Buddhist cassette Aunt Zelda sometimes played while they were working. The deep male voice had said: "We are all of us alone."

"We are all of us alone," Luna told her mother.

"What kind of a thing is *that* to say to your *own mother*? After all I *sacrificed* for you through the years, you'd *think* you could show some *gratitude*."

Sacrifice and gratitude were the themes Loreena had been slapping Luna in the face with for years. In high school, when Luna had to read *King Lear*, Loreena had handed her a copy with the line "How sharper than a serpent's tooth it is. To have a thankless child!" highlighted, and, in case there was any doubt at whom this was directed, "Luna" was scrawled in the margin.

Luna took a breath in and exhaled. Again. And again. She would not engage today. In fact, Luna *was* grateful: that she was no longer a child, living under Loreena's roof and subject to her brand of life. If she could only stop being so angry with her. She sucked in another long breath and slowly exhaled.

"Hello?" Loreena's voice cut in. Sharper than a serpent's tooth was Loreena's tongue.

"So, how's dad?" Luna asked, hoping her mother would go with the shift.

Loreena sighed. "He's awake."

"Great! Is he talking?"

"He's spewing vulgarities."

That was a surprise. Luna had never heard Lenny go any further than "fathead."

"Why?"

"The doctor says curses are stored in another part of the brain—a part that was unaffected. Cursing may be Lenny's only way of expressing himself."

"Ever?"

Loreena sighed again. "We have to wait and see."

There was nothing more to say, and Luna really wanted to get off the phone. She told Loreena to call her if anything changed and hung up before the guilt parade took up its march again. Then she thought about calling Aunt Zelda, to counteract Loreena's effects. But Luna never bothered Zelda on the weekends, when there were concerts on the barge. Right now, Zelda was probably tackling the seating chart. She handwrote slips for all the ticket-holders and put them on their chairs.

Okay... to work...

Finally, Luna could enter the pages of her novel again. A bang at the front door jarred her from them.

NINE

SHE LOOKED UP and saw Nick's receding hairline through the window at the top of the door. *Crap!*

"Luna, let me in," Nick growled, a la the Big Bad Wolf. Only she doubted he had the lung capacity to blow her house down.

"Go away, I'm writing," she shouted back from her table.

"I'm not leaving without my toothbrush and clean underwear," he declared. "I mean, what the fuck is wrong with you?"

What's wrong with you is that you put up with him at all, said Jiminy.

Luna stared Nick's thinning hair. *He does have a right to his stuff. And I want it out of here.* Now that Nick was there, she felt better. Stronger. The dreading was gone. Soon Nick and his belongings would be gone, too. And the kids weren't home to see this. *Perfect!* She scraped her chair back and headed to the door to face him.

If looks could kill she'd be a goner, because Nick's eyes were shooting daggers at her. "You are *such* an asshole."

"Come in," she said, ignoring the comment. "Get your stuff and go. We'll sort out everything else later." She didn't know where all this nerve was coming from (maybe her many viewings of *The Wizard of Oz* through the years were paying off?) but she was sure embracing it.

Luna sat back down at the table. Nick wavered by the stairs, obviously wanting to say something, but not sure what. "I'm on a delivery, so I don't have long," he said.

"Then you'd better hurry," she said, eyes on her screen.

He sighed and headed up the stairs. The stink of tobacco hovered in his wake.

Of course there was no working while he was up there. She couldn't stop picturing him pawing through her drawers and purloining things. But what would he take, anyway? It wasn't like she had any money lying around, and what little jewelry she owned was stashed in the back of her underwear drawer. He didn't know it was there, and he sure didn't care about her panties. Still, he might tear the room apart, or something. She almost went up there, but she didn't want him to know how much he was distracting her. She sat there, fingers on the keyboard, waiting for his descent.

Ba-boom, ba-boom, ba-boom! His footsteps bounded down the stairs, accompanied by her favorite suitcase. She glanced up at him. "I want my luggage back when you're done."

"What the hell am I going to do with a purple suitcase, anyway?" he growled.

"I didn't realize you were so bound to gender clichés."

He glared for a moment. Then he said, "I'll be back later."

"Must you?"

"I want to see the kids."

"Fine. You can take them out to eat."

"How generous of you."

"Thanks. I think so too," she said. She was quaking inside, but she'd never let him know.

"By the way, you need to call American Express. My gym called a little while ago and said my monthly payment didn't go through."

This was the big moment. He was *not* going to like losing her credit. She stared at the last sentence she'd written, before his loud knock. Over and over she read it, a calming mantra, until she found the courage to tell him. "There's no problem."

"What do you mean?" Nick's voice rose. "I just said, the card didn't work."

Don't look at him, don't look at him... "I canceled it."

"Excuse me?" He bellowed now. "You canceled my credit card?"

Tap, tap, tap. She hit the keys without knowing what they were.

The only things that mattered were the act, and the sound. "You must've known this would happen. You charged all that stuff at 7-11."

"I only did that so I would feel like I had something, even if it was just cigarettes. You took everything else."

Oh, God. Now it was time for the pathetic pity party. Poor, victimized Nick. Tap, tap, tap. Braver with every keystroke, she spoke. "It's my credit card, even though your name's on it. I can't pay for you to run around playing anymore." She looked up from the screen and told him, "Grow up."

Nick paced and ranted. "How could you do this to me?"

Pretending to ignore him, Luna kept pseudo-writing. Her heart raced. She just wanted him gone.

From the far corner, there were sobs.

She kept typing.

Crash!

She sighed and looked. Nick had collapsed to the floor. Face-down in Jingles' bowl.

At least it was dry cat food.

Bite-sized morsels were scattered everywhere. Would Nick's cheeks have heart-shaped imprints? "Get up, Nick. You're taking too long on your delivery, and I have to go to my chiropractor."

"You and your chiropractor," Nick snarled, standing and brushing cat food off.

His face was as unmarked by the Purina as by shame.

"What about us?"

"Ever since you've been seeing him, you've changed."

It was true. Dr. Gold had helped her way more than any shrink. "So?"

"So, I think you're doing him."

"No, Nick. Dr. Gold has adjusted me, but sex has not been on the table. Only you equate everything with fucking—except our marriage, of course."

Nick made the unintelligible rumbly sound that was his standby when he had no comeback in an argument. He gripped the purple suitcase's handle and rolled towards the door. The wheels clicked each time they went over a cement line bordering tiles.

Finally he was in the doorway. She was so pleased that he was going that she forgot not to look him in the eye. Damn! It was sad how a person who'd pledged to love and cherish you forever could shoot metaphysical daggers through their pupils at you. With one foot out the door, Nick asked, "Who's going to do your Christmas decorations?"

This swelled her up with panic, because the holidays overwhelmed Luna—especially decorating. There was so much! She stared at Nick, paralyzed by his words. Then Jiminy piped in, *Never mind that—decking your inner halls is what counts.*

"Right," Luna said, accidentally speaking to Jiminy out loud.

"Right what?" Nick asked.

"Never mind," Luna told him. She forced herself to give him a steely look. She wasn't capable of conjuring a murderous one like his, but apparently it was ferocious enough to do the trick, because he looked away. Ha! "You're letting the cold air in, Nick. Buh-bye."

She looked back at her computer screen, and a moment later the door slammed. It was a relief, but also jolting—and she jumped a little in her chair.

"Why did I ever go out with him?"

Because a psychic told you to, said Jiminy.

"Oh, yeah." Funny the things you pushed to the back of your mind…

And not even a psychic you paid to go see. No, this was a psychic you just happened to pump gas for!

"Right." Now, it all came back. "God, I was so young and naïve!"

A lot has changed, said Jiminy. *Now, you're not as young.*

Seventeen years ago

Luna was twenty-one, an English major senior commuting to NYU from Long Island. To make some cash, she'd started pumping gas. It was a drab job which really sucked in the rain, and the inside of the station smelled of gas, even though it was nowhere near the pumps. But she brought in her literary anthologies—fortunately, her shift partner, Billy, enjoyed being read aloud to—and she could pay her car insurance, so the employment met her needs. Too bad there was no discount on fuel.

Ding, ding, ding! One cool fall evening a blue Subaru pulled in. Luna and Billy both came out. During slow periods they worked as a team. The customer was an attractive blonde woman. Billy washed her windows—kind of sloppily and streaky—while Luna pumped.

A big chatterer, Billy asked the woman, "What's the weather gonna be like?"

Luna said, "Billy, what do you think she is, psychic?"

The woman said, "Well, actually, I am."

"Cool!" Luna said. She totally believed in that stuff. "Can you tell me the person I'm destined to be with?" *Frank, Frank... Let it be Frank*, she thought. Frank was the older guy she'd recently lost her virginity and her heart to. Unfortunately, having gotten what he wanted, he wanted nothing more to do with her.

Give it up, said Jiminy.

I did, Luna responded. *And now he doesn't call me. I don't get it.*

"I see you with a Nick," said the woman.

Luna frowned. "Don't you mean Frank?"

The tank was full at $18.89. Luna squeezed eleven more cents in. Customers liked even dollar amounts. It made them happy.

The woman fished out three fives and five singles from her wallet, pushed it into Luna's palm and said, "The extra buck's for you. And sorry, but it's Nick."

She turned on her engine and drove away. It was a wonder she gave a tip, since her window was still pretty drippy from Billy's lousy squeegee handiwork. Luna passed him the buck—she was way more interested in what the woman had said than the dollar bill.

Billy accepted the money and tucked it into his overalls. He looked at Luna's thoughtful face and laughed. "You don't really buy all that psycho stuff, right?"

"I do," she admitted. And that was the end of their conversation, because she was busy sifting through her brain.

Nick, Nick… Where was there a Nick? Luna wondered.

Unfortunately, you thought of one—a high school dropout you met once at a party where everyone except you was stoned! Jiminy admonished her now. *I told you not to base your life on a passing remark.*

Luna stared at Jingles' scattered morsels. She needed to sweep them up. "I should've listened to you, Jiminy."

Can I quote you on that?

"On the other hand, then I wouldn't have had my kids."

I hate when people use their kids to feel better about their mistakes, said Jiminy.

"Maybe there are no mistakes," Luna mused. "Maybe there are only experiences to learn from."

You should write a self-empowerment book. People can't get enough of them, even though they all say pretty much the same thing.

"You think so?"

Sure… or else you could write fortunes for cookies. But first, let's get your life fixed up. I've been waiting for you to take action, Luna.

Luna checked her clock. "Time to go align my spine. We'll take it from there."

TEN

SITTING IN THE well-lighted, window-lined, earth-toned waiting room adorned with healing crystals and plants, Luna leafed through a holistic health magazine. New age meditative music played in the background. Strange how synthesized chords could comfort a soul. The sounds relaxed her, but they also reverberated inside—stirring reflection on her long, strange journey toward Dr. Gold. The road to chiropractic had been paved with decades of failed relationships with so-called healers of the mind.

Luna had tried them all: social workers to psychiatrists. But no matter how high the degree, they all had their own issues to contend with. She'd searched and searched for just one mental health practitioner who was less fucked-up than her, to no avail.

Her therapeutic journey had started out as a farce, based on a miscommunication and a lie. In high school, Luna had no friends until she met an older girl named Carrie. One of the first things Carrie told Luna was that she smoked pot and took mescaline. Luna said she didn't want to smoke pot, but she did enjoy mescaline –because she'd confused it with mesclun salad. Once she realized her mistake, Luna was afraid Carrie wouldn't want to be friends anymore if she admitted she was square. On a couple of occasions Luna had to fake taking a pill, and then sit there while Carrie tripped out. Carrie's parents smelled pot on her one day and sent her to a drug and alcohol treatment center. Carrie actually liked the therapy and told Luna about how she was able to talk about her problems with someone who didn't judge her. Luna wanted someone to talk to! Having no idea what it really felt like to be on mesc, she couldn't lie comfortably to the counselor about taking it. However, Luna *had* gotten drunk on occasion. She decided to embellish her experiences with alcohol. It worked! Paula, the counselor, embraced her as a client and complimented her for seeking help on her own. Luna looked forward to discussing her life, but that never happened. Paula spent most of each session recounting her own black-out drinking—and how she'd recovered and become a counselor. When Luna did manage to get an anecdote in, she always had to pretend that she'd been drunk when it happened—changing its tone and focus.

That didn't work—but what if she told the truth? When Luna entered college she tried the mental health facility at NYU. Her psychologist had big and bright Mad Hatter eyes. He kept talking about himself and calling her "my friend." She wasn't his friend, and she didn't want to know how he'd womanized until he met his current girlfriend. And he was, like, 50. Wasn't that a little old to have a 'girlfriend?'

She figured she just needed to keep trying, but years went by with no satisfying therapy. Sometimes she got fooled by a good beginning, when she poured everything out. But that high of being purged was short-lived when no solutions to her problems followed.

Her longest stint ran with a social worker named Charlene, who bore a Bride of Frankenstein grey streak through her hair and wore clumpy mascara and shocking blue eye shadow. She was bossy and steered the sessions the way she wanted, which usually involved some inner child process. Luna stayed with her for about a year, because of proximity (both to Luna's home, and more importantly, to a little coffee place where Luna always stopped off before her session.) The end came the day Luna recited one of her favorite quotes: "The best way out is always through."

Charlene said, "Or, you can go around."

Luna realized she'd been going around – and around and around – with Charlene for too long. Probably the coffee infusion had tranquilized her from seeing this sooner.

After breaking up with Charlene, Luna made one more attempt

to seek therapy, from a psychiatrist. He was the most expensive and, it turned out, the most crazy of all her analysts.

Dr. Zelderman was a stutterer. At $350 an hour, Luna felt she deserved a rebate. Also suffering from haphephobia—the fear of being touched—he'd made her sit clear across the room. She'd practically had to shout to communicate with him. This disturbing doctor rattled Luna to the point that she swore off shrinks, freeing up time to do the chores she'd avoided—like tackling her piled up mail. Flipping through her local Pennysaver, she paused at an ad for a holistic chiropractor.

Dr. Adam Gold's advertisement promised relief from chronic pains of all kinds—including stress. *Hmmm...* She'd heard that chiropractors worked wonders on people.

Why not give chiropractic a whirl? Luna thought. Especially when there was a coupon for 50% off her first visit.

A few days later, Luna headed to the chiropractor for her back and her neck.

She wound up working on her mind, as well.

Dr. Adam Gold was the perfect therapist.

The waiting room door swung open. "Thanks, Doc! See you next week!" a middle-aged man with a bouffant the color of black shoe polish said as he stepped out.

Dr. Gold followed, wearing his eternal smile and exuding his usual calm. "You're very welcome," he told his patient. Fiftyish, Dr. Gold wore wire-rimmed glasses and had a penchant for Hawaiian shirts. Today he wore a tan one with the requisite floral bursts.

"Well, hello Luna!" he greeted her. "Ready?"

"Ready." Luna followed him into his examining room, which was a perfect yellow—not too harsh or too faded. It had a fresh, natural scent—not overbearingly Febreezy or antiseptic. He'd decorated with gemstones and plants. Hanging above her, on a sign decorated with flowers and stars, were his three rules of the office, which she studied like the Torah every time. So simple, really. Why did she always insist on complicating her life?

"How are you?" he asked.

She took a deep breath in and let it out – as per rule number one – and thought. How was she?

"I see," he said. "Well, let's have a look at what's going on. Seating is now available at your table for one."

Luna took off her bulky sweatshirt and laid it on the windowsill with her purse. She climbed onto the brown, cushioned examining table, her body sliding on the smooth leather and her head against crinkly white paper. She gave Dr. Gold her right hand and rested her left one on her stomach area, on the over-sized black cotton t-shirt she'd bought as a souvenir of the London Underground. It said, *Mind the gap*.

Dr. Gold checked each part of her body before he began his adjusting. He'd touch an area with his finger, and know whether or not she needed help there. It was a little eerie the first few visits, and had required a leap of faith that she surprised herself by making. Now, she thought of it more like getting a diagnostic tune-up, like mechanics did on cars. She laid back, closed her eyes and did her best to relax in his hands. Even after many visits, this didn't come easy.

Here are some of the things Luna had learned about Dr. Gold over the months:

STATS ON DR. GOLD

Name: Dr. Adam Gold

Ethnic background: Hungarian.

Marital status: Married.

Body: Medium build, slim.

Hair: Peppered.

Favorite physical activity: Yoga.

Other likes: Meditation, serenity.

Dislikes: Prejudice.

Religion: Jewish.

Favorite writers: Authors who write about balance and all things holistic.

Favorite dessert: Fruit and yogurt.

Favorite expression: "Your body can heal itself given the right environment." (It was on a poster in his waiting room.)

On her first visit, Luna had asked if that included her heart.

Dr. Gold said, "Yes."

After a little while, Luna opened her eyes. The ceiling lights framed her chiropractor in soft fluorescence. She focused on his general head area, moving from hair to chin to cheek and finally making eye contact.

"I kicked Nick out," she told him.

"Good for you! That's an amazing step, Luna!" Dr. Gold's smile broadened. "So, how do you feel?"

"Ummm… . Glad, and relieved… but also scared."

"Fear is an illusion," Dr. Gold said. "You just have to believe that it's not real, and poof! It'll be gone."

"I'll try."

"You're doing a great job taking back your life."

"Thanks."

"You're welcome."

Dr. Gold was working on Luna's leg, which was propped up on his shoulder. She didn't like leaning on people—she felt like a burden. But he'd put her leg there, so she had to deal with it. "But something bad happened, too." She told him. "My dad had a stroke."

"I'm sorry. How is he?"

"They don't know yet. He's cursing a lot."

"Well, any form of expression is a plus." He kneaded deeply into her calf and looked at her. "The only thing we can do is deal gracefully with the circumstances life hands us and be in the present."

"Gracefully, huh?"

He gave her a wink. "It's either that, or descend into madness."

"Insanity?"

"You could say that, but I was referring to pure anger. However, getting mad *is* a form of insanity because it never solves anything. We attract more of what we concentrate on, so when we are angry we just invite more anger. Only acceptance and living in the moment bring us peace."

"You are a thin and Jewish Buddha," Luna told him.

Dr. Gold chuckled. Finished with the leg, he instructed Luna to sit up slightly and rest her head in his hands. *This* was difficult—to trust his hands with her head.

"Relax," he said.

Then he said, "A little more."

Then again, "A little more."

With her head in one hand, Dr. Gold pressed down on her shoulder with the other. It felt like he was shifting her physiological plane.

Again, her neck and shoulders tensed up.

Again, Dr. Gold told her, "Relax."

Why were the simplest things the hardest?

He worked on her in silence for awhile. She stared at rule number one, and said it to herself.

Breathe.

Dr. Gold asked her to turn over. He pressed on her back.

She said, "I just wish my life would be normal."

Dr. Gold laughed. "What's normal?" Crrraaack! He made a loud adjustment. "You're an extraordinary person, Luna. What others view as normal would never suit you. Just find your balance."

"How do I do that?"

Dr. Gold pointed to the rules. "These are more than a decoration."

Luna took a deep breath in and let it out. Again… and again.

Staring at number three she said, "I really *do* think my life will work out."

"Who says it hasn't worked out already? It's all how you look at things, Luna."

"That seems kind of quantum-leapy to me," she said.

"Not at all. It's just a question of choosing to be happy, instead of waiting for happiness to choose you."

Dr. Gold put his hands on Luna's neck and instructed her to relax again. Miraculously, she managed to do it this time. Craaack! He adjusted her neck. "That was amazing and horrifying at the same time," she said.

"Just like life. It's all how you see it," he told her. "No extra charge for the metaphors and similes." He gave her a wink. "Okay, stand up, and let's see if you're centered."

Luna rolled herself off the table. She felt right – and light. "It's amazing how you can shift so much stress out of me," she told Dr. Gold.

"You're the one doing the heavy lifting, Luna," Dr. Gold said, "I can only release what you allow me to."

She stood facing the window with her feet spread apart. "Where do you feel your weight?" he asked, even though he didn't have to. She knew the drill.

Still, it was hard to be sure where her weight truly lay. She swayed a few moments and did a toe to heel roll with both feet. "Weight's in the center of my feet," she finally determined.

"Good! You're all set!" He gave her another pat on her shoulder.

Now all she had to do was figure out how to *stay* centered once she left the room.

Luna rushed home to take advantage of the small amount of time she had before heading to pick up the kids. She was all set to work on marketing when she thought of *NWaN.* If she let a day go by without looking at it, she'd be allowing distance in. It was only a pipe dream—she had no idea how to get a women's novel published even if she did manage to finish it. But what good was life without a dream to chase? And so she opened the document where she'd left off—at a kiss. Her character Serena's first kiss since her divorce. Only a few paragraphs, but the scene had been a killer to write.

Reading it over, Luna was struck by the simple and genuine happiness in the moment. She was pleased that her writing had such an effect on her, but also bummed by how empty her life felt. She hadn't kissed in so long that it felt like she'd *never* been kissed. How had she even written about a kiss, and so convincingly?

Suddenly, urgently, she needed to rediscover the sensation of a kiss.

She felt awakened after a hibernation. How strange, to be roused by her own words.

Ding-ding-ding! Luna's cell phone alarm went off. Time to go, and she'd written nothing new. But that was okay, as long as she'd immersed herself in Serena's world. Boy, had she.

It was time to start living life again, like Serena. Could she find someone to kiss? *Where? How?* The task seemed momentous! Maybe Sunny would know. If not, at least she'd have something humorous to say.

ELEVEN

THE KIDS SPRANG inside the house clutching new paintings for Luna's walls. Both boys complained that they were hungry, so Luna settled them on the couch with a SpongeBob episode and called Nick. It went to voicemail. "The kids want dinner soon," Luna told him. "Call me back." She gave the kids a bowl of fruit to split, and decided that if Nick didn't call back within the hour she'd feed them.

In the meantime, she called Sunny and shared her kissing melancholy.

Sunny said, "So come out with Phil and me tonight. We're going to a bar. You can get drunk and make out with someone. Easy peasy."

"I didn't realize you were still seeing Phil. You never mention him."

"Yeah, well, you know Phil. There's not much to mention."

It was true. Sunny was dating a twenty-five-year-old who worked with her at the library. Luna called him "The Coconut." Not only due to his haircut, which somehow brought coconuts to mind, but also because he had the personality to match.

The Coconut was a stunning mediocrity, pretty much incapable of social interaction. It was exhausting holding up both ends of a conversation, so Luna avoided speaking with him.

Here are some of the things Sunny had told Luna about The Coconut:

STATS ON THE COCONUT:

Name: Phil Findley

Ethnic Background: English.

Marital Status: Single

Children: None

Body: As skinny as his predecessor, Sal.

Hair: Brown, close-cropped with blunt bangs.

Occupation: Library clerk.

Favorite Physical Activities: Lifting an alcoholic beverage to his lips, sprinting to the bathroom to avoid puking on the floor.

Other likes: Reading (though all he had to say about any book he'd read was "it was good"), Sunny.

Dislikes: None. He just went with the flow. Even after puking from excessive drinking, he'd just gargle and drink some more.

Religion: He was okay with all of them.

Favorite Writers: He expressed no preference.

Favorite dessert: Vanilla wafers.

Favorite expression: If he had one, he didn't say.

Dating the Coconut was an accident, induced by a particularly hard night of drinking combined with a long sexual dry spell. When it came to intercourse, Sunny was like a camel in the desert. But even camels had to drink eventually. One evening, parched, she was at a co-worker's retirement dinner. Many drinks in, someone commented that The Coconut and Sunny should hook up. Even though she worked most nights behind the desk near The Coconut, she'd never talked with him, or even given him a thought. He blended with the furniture. She'd sized him up at the party, shrugged and said, "Okay. Better than nothing." What she didn't know was that The Coconut's idea of hooking up translated to Sunny's idea of getting snagged on a fishhook.

As far as he was concerned, once they'd fornicated, they were a couple.

"I can't believe you're still going along with this couple thing," Luna said.

"He has his pluses," Sunny explained. "He buys me drinks, and he goes away on command. Except he keeps pushing to stay over – and you know how I feel about that. But the kids like him, and he takes them to their soccer games. He does anything I want him to, like the laundry and grocery shopping. He's a good egg."

"Sounds romantic."

"Oh, yeah… the romance never ends with Phil. But you're the one who nick-named him. So, tell me, how much passion can you get from a coconut?"

"You've got me there," Luna conceded.

"He also buys me really good gifts, and he likes to make out at bars." It was strange, because Sunny usually hated public displays of affection, but when she was drinking she loved to suck face. Luna had watched her do it countless times with Sal.

What could it feel like, kissing a coconut?

Luna asked Sunny if the kissing was good.

"Well, he's not a natural at it, that's for sure," Sunny said. "I kind of have to coax him along. But he's willing to do it anytime I want, which is convenient."

Sounded like Sunny was settling, but who was Luna to judge? She'd be willing to kiss a coconut too.

Right now, she'd kiss pretty much anybody.

They agreed to let their four kids have a sleepover at Luna's, under the supervision of Luna's trusted teenage neighbor Betty, whom Ben and Dylan adored. Luna tried to call Nick again, to find out when he was coming and to let him know he'd be dropping the kids with Betty.

Again, the call went to voicemail.

"Mommy, we're hungry!" Dylan called from upstairs.

"Okay, sweetie!" Where the hell was Nick?

Just then he called back. "I can't take the kids out. You cancelled my card, and my boss won't give me an advance."

The old Luna would've felt bad and given him money. But the new Luna just said: "Okay then."

Click! She hung up and boiled some water for pasta. *Good thing I didn't tell the boys their father was coming.*

Jingles jangled into the kitchen and sat at her feet while she cooked.

The Achy Breaky Bar pushed Long Island's redneck boundaries. It was the kind of place you'd expect to find sawdust on the floor. Through the dim lighting, Luna spied walls covered with Nascar photos. There was lots of pool-ball clinking and cursing. The air was moist with Budweiser. It was smoky, because rednecks didn't think much of anti-smoking laws. Someone dropped change in the jukebox and "I Walk the Line" came on.

Every redneck bar needs at least one guy with a mullet to be complete, and lucky Luna sat next to him. He had that weatherbeaten, Willie Nelson look. She decided to talk to him anyway.

But what would she say? It had been years since Luna stepped in a bar, and small talk escaped her then.

How about introducing yourself? asked Jiminy. *You get all worked up over nothing.*

You're right, she answered. To mullet man she said, "Hi, I'm Luna."

He said something back, but she couldn't make it out.

"What's that?' She leaned in closer.

Again, she couldn't understand him. "Sorry?"

He said it a third time, and finally she got it. His name was Bobby.

Why was his speech so garbled? Had he had a stroke?

Bobby pointed to the bartender. He was offering to buy her a drink, she presumed. She accepted.

Sipping her vodka collins (she had been going to order a beer, then decided some hard liquor was in order), Luna told him a little about herself.

Then she had to let him talk.

She tried to understand what he said, but it was so hard. All she wanted to do was make out. Yes, he was yucky, but that meant he wouldn't judge her harshly. She needed someone who would be complimentary, not impatient with her rustiness.

Would she be able to kiss him? What if she'd forgotten how?

He kept saying the same thing over and over, obviously trying to communicate something important.

But *what?*

He pointed to his neck.

The bartender came over. "Bobby's trying to tell you about his throat cancer," he told Luna.

"Oh! Are you okay?" she asked Bobby.

Bobby nodded, and took a sip of his Bud.

The bartender said, "He can't talk so good ever since they took out his tongue."

Luna's jaw hung open in disbelief.

Inside her head there was laughter from Jiminy.

You knew about this? she fumed at him.

No. I told you I don't see the future. I'm just along for the ride. But, wow, that was pretty funny.

Luna didn't find it amusing. She turned to Sunny, wanting to vent, but Sunny was using *her* tongue with The Coconut.

Meanwhile, Bobby was still talking – about who knew what.

Luna didn't want to be rude, so she nodded politely.

Kenny Rogers' "The Gambler" played on the jukebox.

Looks like you crapped out tonight, said Jiminy.

Yeah, she agreed. *What were the odds?*

When Sunny finally came up for air, Luna practically dragged her to the ladies room. Safely out of earshot, she told her about Bobby.

"Eeew," Sunny said.

"That's not nice."

"Never said I was."

This was true. "Oh my god, I just wanted to kiss someone," Luna moaned. The stall door said, "Kim and Colton 4eva" in black magic marker. Luna wasn't looking for anything like "4eva." She was just looking for a French kiss "2nite."

"Clearly the universe doesn't feel you're ready," Sunny said.

"You think?"

"Could there be a more obvious sign than a redneck with no tongue?"

"Good point."

The ladies room door squealed open, and two bimbo-types with big hair, three-inch thick eyeliner, skin-tight minidresses and stilettos wobbled in. Laughing, they bolted themselves into adjoining stalls and chatted loudly while peeing.

Luna envied them. She had nothing to even smile about.

"Cheer up," said Sunny.

"How can I cheer up? You have The Coconut, Nick has his parade of inappropriate men, Kim has Colton… and I have tongueless mullet man. Oh, and let's not forget: The universe is conspiring against me."

"I didn't say that! I said the universe thinks you're not ready."

"Yeah, well, screw the universe." Luna looked in the mirror. She wasn't bad-looking. And yet she felt ugly.

Sunny patted Luna's back. "Let's go get you some whiskey shots."

"Yuck!"

"Just get them down, and everything will be better."

Sunny was right again. The whiskey scalded going down, but after that nothing mattered.

She wished she could duplicate that carefree feeling without the vomiting that followed the next day.

TWELVE

AFTER LUNA PICKED herself up from the bathroom tiles and flushed her barf, she remembered to check on her dad. Loreena answered the phone by saying, "I just came home so I could feed the cats. I've been sleeping in a chair in your father's room. What are the odds he'd do that for me?"

Million to one, Luna thought.

"Not that you'd do it for me, either."

Luna let that jab pass. "How's dad doing?"

"He talks a little, other than cursing."

"That's good."

"It takes him forever to get a word out."

"Still, that's progress. Right?"

"I suppose. But speaking of right, he's paralyzed on his right side."

"Permanently?"

"No one knows these things, Luna." Loreena's voice was sharp, but then it morphed into a sigh. "They wanted to send him home to me in a few weeks and then send an ambulette to take him to rehab every other day, but I told them I couldn't handle him. Plus I don't have a ramp for the wheelchair.

"What's going to happen?"

"There's a rehabilitation facility in Long Acre that will take him while I find an aide to help me and have someone make the house handicap-accessible."

"Oh… well, that's close." Long Acre was the town between Island Harbor, where Luna lived now, and Little Beach, where Luna had grown up. Luna shuddered, thinking about her old house, where Loreena still lived. It was not a warm and fuzzy atmosphere.

"I'll have trouble getting there when it snows," Loreena said. Leave it to her to focus on the worst-case scenario. Luna started to say something reassuring, but why bother? Loreena looked for misery in any situation.

After a few seconds of silence, Loreena asked, "Are you planning on visiting your father again?"

Luna wasn't planning on anything, really. She was trying to stay in the moment, like Dr. Gold had advised. Unfortunately, it proved easier to avoid stress over what was coming up than to block out the past. She was prone to flashback, maybe because she was a writer, or maybe that was one of the things that had made her a writer. Everywhere there were connections to things that had happened before. And triggers, shooting her back in time.

So here she was, ricocheting again…Back in her father's car.

Twenty-five years earlier

She saw her father about once a month. He'd pick her up from the barge in Brooklyn – she served Oreos and coffee at the concerts – and give her a ride home. She imagined this alleviated his guilt for being a beyond-sucky dad. Getting the ride didn't change her feelings toward him. She just preferred the car to taking the Long Island Rail Road at night. Plus, he always gave her money.

Lenny waited outside for Luna, even though Zelda was his sister.

She got into her father's blue Buick and yanked the door closed. Something was the matter with that door. You had to pull it hard to get it closed, and bump your body against it to get it open. Inside was a cigarette odor, unsuccessfully masked by the air freshener hanging from the rear view mirror. That smoggy, choky feeling lingered no matter how many little cardboard trees he strung. At her feet lay empty coffee containers with the lid tabs bent back.

"Hey, Kiddo," her father said. He always said that. His chestnut brown hair – same color as hers – was slicked back, with a few strands hanging loose. His face resembled James Earl Jones', except it was white.

"Hi," she said. She couldn't even bring herself to call him 'Dad' anymore. He was just this once-a-month driver.

The car was running and the heat was on, even though it was summer. She wanted to unroll the window, but it was broken.

"What's up?"

"Nothing."

"How's Zelda?"

Why don't you go in and ask her yourself? "Fine."

He backed up and turned around, heading up the street.

"Can you stop somewhere for tea?" she asked. Once in a while she drank tea, when she felt a little achy. People said it was soothing. It hadn't worked for her yet, but in an attempt to do something proactive, she kept trying.

"Sure."

He pulled up to a deli and handed Luna two bucks. She bumped the door open, went inside and returned a few minutes later with a Styrofoam cup in hand.

Her father frowned. "Is there lemon in there?"

"Yeah…"

"Please don't drink that, Luna. I heard that the acid from the lemon juice eats into walls of the cup, and you actually ingest it."

"You're kidding." *The man abandons me and worries about a lemon.*

"No, it's true."

She stared at him.

"Please pour it out."

Rolling her eyes, she bumped the door and leaned over the street. The tea's plastic cover squeaked as she opened it, like it was complaining about how stupid this was. She dumped it at the curb. Steam rose from the gutter. The offending rind lay in a puddle, tangled with the bag.

Luna slammed the door closed. "Okay, let's go."

No sense starting a Revolution over tea again.

She didn't even like it. It tasted like nothing. Watery nothing. You had to add lemon to get any flavor at all.

She should've gotten coffee. But she wasn't going to ask for it now.

If she were to say anything to this man next to her, it would be something like, "Why didn't you save me from my mother? You knew she was nuts." But she didn't want to get into that. She was afraid of the answer.

Lenny headed onto the Brooklyn-Queens Expressway.

Luna stared at the lamps illuminating the road. Easier than looking at him. The tires grooved on the pavement, except when they hit potholes. Passing cars swooshed by. Lenny was a right-lane driver.

He was breathing pretty heavy. It sounded like he was gulping down air.

Is he on heroin now?

Wouldn't he have to be, in order to function?

He'd be all sweaty and crazy if he needed a fix.

God, she wished she didn't know this about him...

Especially that he was a dealer.

Are there drugs in the car?

Near Kennedy Airport, the quiet was broken.

Sirens blared.

Red and blue strobe lights flashed behind them.

Had the police read her mind?

Oh my god, they're going to arrest him in front of me! Luna's pulse pounded. *What will they do with me? How will I get home?*

Lenny seemed unaffected. He kept driving.

"Pull over!" a voice on speaker from the police car thundered.

She was having a heart attack.

No, worse.

Her heart was extracting itself from her chest, just yanking its way out.

"Alright, alright. Keep your shirt on," Lenny said. He inched over to the side.

Luna wanted to ask him, "What now, Dad? What will we do? What will *I* do?"

She wanted to tell him she was terrified.

But before she could get the words out, the police car zoomed by.

It had only wanted to pass them.

"What a fathead," said Lenny.

When they reached her house about a half hour later, Luna was still quivering. Lenny was clueless about Luna's state.

He pulled money from his pocket. A twenty and a ten, folded together. Thirty bucks. What he always gave her at the end of the ride.

But before he could hand it over, Loreena appeared at the side of Luna's door. She was wearing a hair net, a rainbow tie-dyed sweatshirt she'd bought at a thrift shop, and her angry face.

She wrenched Luna's door open. "You get her drunk again, Lenny?"

"Babe, that was years ago. Can't you let it go?"

When Luna was about four, Lenny had given her a sip of his beer. She'd loved it – so much that she chanted for it whenever she saw him. "Beer, beer, beer!"

They were in a convenience store once, and she'd spotted the Budweiser logo. "Beer! Beer! Beer!"

"Pipe it down, Kiddo," he told her in a hushed voice. "You're gonna get me in trouble."

"Beer! Beer! Beer!' she'd proclaimed, tugging on Lenny's leg.

"Shhhh! I'll get you the beer, but you gotta be quiet," he said.

And he did buy her a beer, which she'd chugged. "Easy, easy!" Lenny exclaimed, tilting the bottle before she drained it. "You've gotta learn how to sip, Kiddo. Hope you don't throw up all over your mom's newspapers when we get home."

She hadn't puked. But she *had* burped loudly in Loreena's face – a big, smelly, hops-filled belch.

"She's drunk!" Loreena screeched.

Lenny shrugged. "Sorry, Babe."

He'd limped down the driveway at a pretty fast pace and gotten in his car. Loreena leaned against the open screen door, shouting obscenities at her retreating husband. She couldn't go out after him. Her favorite show,

All in the Family, was starting. The opening music drifted from the little black-and-white kitchen TV.

Luna slipped past her mother and stumbled down the driveway. "Why are you leaving, Daddy?" she asked in a slurred voice.

"See you, Kiddo," he'd said. "Gotta go."

Now he said, "Jeez, she's not drunk, Loreena. Smell her breath."

"Yeah, he wouldn't even let me have tea with lemon," Luna interjected. She wished she didn't have to inhale Loreena's heated, hating breath. It was laced with sardines – a dinner favorite of hers.

Loreena ranted on. When she was in this mood, no one was right but her. Ever.

"Sorry, Babe," Lenny said with a shrug. He extended the money toward Luna. "See you, Kiddo. Gotta go."

"Yeah, see you." *Thanks for leaving me with a raving lunatic.* To Loreena she said, "Can I get out, please?" Loreena stepped up to the curb, into the patch of green spiky-leafed things growing in front of the sidewalk. She called them plants, but they looked like weeds. Loreena favored them because they didn't have to be mowed.

"Oh, perfect, now I've stepped into my garden…" Loreena screamed.

Luna got out of the car and slammed the door closed. Lenny raised his windows.

Loreena's tirade continued, even though Lenny couldn't hear her. He was in motion now. Loreena pounded on his hood, but he didn't stop. Thirty bucks was really not worth this scene. A neighbor across the street was peering from behind his white curtains, and several dogs in the area were howling in response to Loreena's bark. *Great.*

Luna watched her father back away from the madness. Chug, chug, chug, chug. His carburetor breathed as heavy as him. His wheels crunched leaves littering the driveway. Then he shifted into drive and was gone, leaving a cloud of exhaust in his wake.

All these years later, Luna still smelled it.

THIRTEEN

"HELLLLO!" LOREENA PROJECTED into the phone. "Are you still there?"

"I'm here."

"I've been waiting for an answer for a *solid* five minutes, Luna."

"What was the question?"

Another dramatic sigh came through the receiver. "Are you planning on visiting your father again?"

"I'll pass… until he's in the rehab." Luna braced herself for an angry tirade on how selfish and uncaring she was. Instead, Loreena said, "That's probably for the best. Frankly, I'm not even sure he's cognizant of his surroundings. He answers yes to every question I ask, like 'Are you feeling better?' but who knows if he understands what he's saying. He was always yessing me before. Maybe he's just on auto-pilot now."

A pounding struck up in Luna's forehead, like someone was chiseling in there. She wanted to deal with the situation gracefully, but it felt like her head was going to burst off her shoulders. She needed to get off the phone, but the only excuse she could come up with was, "I have to go pee."

Not very graceful, but it did the trick. Loreena said, "So go pee."

Luna said "goodbye" as usual, and also as usual, Loreena hung up without another word.

Luna swallowed two extra-strength Tylenols and rummaged through her closet for a cardboard box. Damned if she was going to languish in her pain. The weather was unseasonably warm and she was going to let her sons take advantage of it. "C'mon, boys, let's go to the playground!" she called up the stairs.

"Yay!' Dylan yelled, and both boys bounded down the steps. Luna bundled Dylan into his coat, and Ben buttoned himself. Luna threw on a poncho and hat, and down the block they headed, to the schoolyard. Luna didn't love playgrounds, but she wasn't going to stop her kids from enjoying one – and this playground had no cylinders, anyway. What it did have was a humungous, winding slide that the boys loved.

Luna broke off two pieces of box and gave one to each boy. She sat on the slightly chilled bench and watched Dylan and Ben climb up steps and head down the big slide – their speed accelerated by the cardboard they tucked under their tushes. Again and again they did it, laughing and giggling while Luna snapped their pictures with her cell phone and forgot to feel shitty. "C'mon, Mommy, you do it too!' Dylan implored.

Oh, why not? she thought. Her headache was gone – she was up for it! She tore off another piece of the box and headed up the stairs.

Whoosh! The world blurred as she plunged. Dylan, cheered, "Go, Mommy!" She panicked at the bottom but managed to pop up on her feet, albeit unsteadily.

"How was that?" Ben asked.

"A little too fast for my taste. I think I'll leave the cardboard to you guys," she answered.

"Yeah, you looked a little scared, Mom. Your face got all red."

"Do it again, Mommy!' Dylan implored. "Let's all do it again!"

Luna put the cardboard to the side and climbed back on the slide with the kids. Without the box, the ride was actually pleasurable. They did it a bunch of times, and then played tag on the spongy foam that padded the playground. Luna was "it," pretty much assuring that both boys would remain "safe." And they did.

They walked home in twilight, past all the houses sparkling bright with Christmas lights. "When are we gonna have our lights on, Mommy?" Dylan asked.

Oy. "Ummm…"

"I can put them up, Mom," Ben volunteered. "I helped dad last year."

"Thanks, Sweetie, but I can't let you go on the ladder—or on the roof."

"Oh, fine."

Luna didn't know how she would get the lights up without asking Nick. Then Jiminy piped in, *You can hire people to do things, Luna. What about that guy who mows your lawn?*

Great idea! "I'll ask Henry to put up the lights tomorrow," Luna told Dylan.

"Yay!" Dylan cheered.

They turned the corner to their street. An unfamiliar red Datsun was parked in front of their darkened house. *What now?*

When they got close the driver door opened. It was Nick. "Daddy!" Dylan whooped. Both boys hugged their dad.

"I'm taking you guys to the Chinese buffet," Nick told them.

"Yes!" Ben exclaimed. He loved the snow crab legs.

Luna felt the urge to call Amex and make sure Nick's card was still cancelled. She gave Nick a questioning look. "I borrowed money from a friend—and his car," Nick told her.

Who was this friend, and what kind of "friend" was he? Luna glanced inside the car. Were the seats sticky?

Stop! She commanded her brain. The kids missed their dad. She had to let them go. It would be cruel not to—and she'd look like the meanest person in the world to send him away.

So she kissed her kids and let them go off with Nick, bundled herself up and got into her minivan. Might as well go buy a Christmas tree while she had an unexpected free moment. She could surprise the kids with it when they got home.

She drove to the parking lot on the main drag in town, where they were selling trees. When she got out of the car a chill ran through her. The temperature had dropped in the few minutes she'd been driving, to the point that her breath was fogging. She gave her hat a tug to settle it firmer onto her head, and pulled up her scarf – but her nose had to remain exposed, so she wouldn't feel like she was suffocating.

She stood at the entrance, staring at the rows of trees. A sappy smell permeated the air—the scent of trees bleeding out.

After all, they were dying: hacked and hauled from their home in the forest to spend their final moments in some suburban household, as a decoration under which to stick flat-screen TVs, Xboxs and more toys than any child could need. Luna was guilty of excess just like everyone else, but it suddenly seemed so sad that a tree brimming with such robust scent would be dragged to the curb as soon as January hit, a trail of prickly needles its only legacy.

Wasn't it ironic that this holiday celebrated a birth?

What was the lesson of Jesus Christ's life, anyway? Where had his compassion landed him?

Up on a cross, nails through his palms and feet.

Betrayed and forsaken.

Such morbid thoughts! She'd never dealt with buying a tree before. Nick had always gone to pick one out. Facing all these trees at once made her think of her childhood, and the fate of all of the trees in her youth. Each year, the brown and brittle evergreen would remain next to the TV until Easter, at least. Her mom couldn't bear to throw anything away. Sitting there watching her shows, Luna heard the patter of shedding—like the tree was gently weeping. She tried to concentrate on the Fonz, *Laverne & Shirley* and *Three's Company*, but the branches' growing bareness could not be ignored.

"You need some help?" a hillbilly-accented guy in lumberjack clothing asked her. He must've been one of the tree hackers. She avoided his gaze, focusing instead on the sign nailed into some poor pine: "All trees $35!"

She wished she could pay $35 to buy back the roots for one of these trees. But at least she didn't have to participate in this grisly ritual. "No thanks."

"No one beats our deal," he told her. His words billowed out in a cloud. "Guy a couple of miles down is charging $45 a tree."

"It's not the price," she said.

"Then what is it?" he asked.

What would be the point in telling the truth to a guy who had sawed these trees down for profit? "I can't make this decision myself. I'll come back with my husband."

He broke into a smile, displaying spaces where several teeth should've been. "Yeah. Tree shopping's a guy thing, I guess."

"I guess," Luna said, although she couldn't see why that would be the case. Tree chopping, yes—but wasn't shopping supposed to be a woman's game? Well, not *this* woman.

She got back in her car and headed to Ace Hardware, where she bought a fake tree and, at Jiminy's suggestion, new locks for the doors. She wasn't sure she could handle changing the cylinders, but he insisted she could. So she took it on faith that he was right. After all, 'twas the season to believe.

Luna got the tree out of the box and in its stand before the boys returned. The packaging had promised easy assembly, which proved true: the tree was in three pieces marked "1," "2," and "3." Any child could have put them together; this was way simpler than Legos.

But the finished tree was gaunt, to say the least—what she might call malnourished, if it could have been nourished. Sparse was too kind a word for the branches. WTF? The photo on the box depicted a full, fluffy specimen. Was it even the same tree? If so, what kind of angle did they shoot it at?

The kids are gonna hate it!

It just needs some primping. Bend the branches into the spaces, Jiminy advised.

But when she twisted a branch into one spot, another patch opened.

"Christ! This is as impossible as filling the gaps of my life. Can't anything be what is seems?"

Maybe your perception's off, Jiminy said. *And I wish you wouldn't use the Lord's name in vain.*

"Are you serious?"

No. I was just trying to throw some levity into the situation. God knows, you need to lighten up, Luna.

"Do you mean, God literally knows? Or are you just using an expression?" She still wasn't sure what Jiminy was – or who had sent him.

Up to you to interpret, my dear. It's all good.

"Is it, Jiminy?" It sure didn't feel that way. But whatever Jiminy would've asnswered – if he had answered – was lost because the front door swung open. Her boys were home.

"Mommmmy!' Dylan cheered, rushing into her arms.

"Hey, baby." She hugged him hard.

"Guess what? I made the ice cream come out of the machine all by myself!"

"Wow!"

Ben strolled over for his hug. "I had a pile of snow crab legs. I sucked the meat right out of them."

"Yum!" Luna mustered up a smile, even though she felt kind of bad for the crabs. She wasn't a vegetarian, but she felt like she should be.

Nick sauntered in. Luna felt a pang of panic. What if he *doesn't* leave?

He'll leave, Luna. He's just a big pussy in wolf's clothing, Jiminy reassured her. *And it's not even wolf's clothing. It's Banana Republic. Hardly bad-ass. No self-respecting wolf would wear that.*

Luna laughed.

"What's so funny?" Nick asked.

"Nothing. Just glad to see the kids."

"Imagine how I feel," he snarled.

"Okay, Nick. The boys need to go bed. Say goodbye."

Nick stared at her. After a few beats he said, "Alright, I'm going."

See how good assertion feels? Jiminy asked.

It *did* feel good.

And it's like a muscle. The more you use it, the more it develops, he added.

We'll see.

Nick hugged the kids, then focused on the tree. He smirked. "Nice. Pick that out all by yourself?"

Ignore him, Jiminy said.

But now everyone was staring at the so-called tree. "Mommy, why are there so many holes?" Dylan exclaimed.

"It's a fake tree," she told him. "I'm trying to save real trees' lives. I'll figure out how to make this tree look better – just give me some time to work on it."

"If you say so," he said dubiously.

"I'm glad you saved the trees, Mom," Ben said.

"Your mother didn't save any trees, Ben," Nick said. His goodfellas voice gave his words an extra condemning tone. "The trees were already chopped down."

"Yes, but if everyone stopped buying the trees, no one would cut down any more," Luna said.

"Do you really think that's going to happen?" Nick snickered.

"I'm just being the change I wish to see in the world," Luna told him, meeting his insolent glare. He turned away, mumbling something about her needing robes and beads to be Gandhi junior. She was surprised he knew who to credit her reference to. Maybe it was just a lucky guess.

"Say goodnight to Daddy," Luna told the boys.

Nick hugged them both, and then he left – just like Jiminy had said he would.

Things are only obstacles if you see them as such," Jiminy said, as Luna clicked the lock behind Nick.

Maybe so, Jiminy. I'm just not sure how to stop seeing them as such.

FOURTEEN

LUNA STEPPED BACK into the living room. God, the tree belonged with Charlie Brown. "This tree has potential," she said, mustering some enthusiasm in an effort to convince herself as much as the boys. We'll decorate after school tomorrow. But for now: to bed!"

The boys looked mopey. "Oh, come on," she said. "You can't be that disappointed in the tree, or the fact that it's bedtime. What's wrong?"

"I wish Daddy could stay with us," Dylan lamented.

"Stupid wieners," Ben mumbled, staring at the floor.

Luna studied her dejected boys, wondering if she was destroying their childhoods. Was it wrong to throw out their father, even if he was a gay sex addict? It was hard being in charge. What if she'd made a wrong move? Should she have continued with the sham? The sound of bells came from outside, and then a thump. It was Jingles jumping onto the deck, of course. But she wished it was Santa, coming early to grant her wishes. That gay husbands could be set straight, or at least show some remorse. That someone could actually be honest and keep the promises they'd made.

"I'm sorry, guys. I don't know what else to say," said Luna.

Then Dylan brightened. "It's okay, Mommy. I just remembered, Daddy said we could get a dog when he gets his house," Dylan said.

Leave it to Nick to one-up her in theory, mentioning a home he was incapable of acquiring anytime soon—unless Lotto finally paid off.

"Alrighty, then," Luna said. "Better not tell Jingles. He'll get jealous."

As if on cue, the cat meowed loudly at the deck door. Luna unlocked it and let him in, He rubbed against her leg in appreciation.

No doubt fueled by the sugar in his ice cream, Dylan rocketed up the stairs. Luna held Ben behind. "It's not just because of the wieners, sweetie," she told him.

Ben looked down again. She wasn't used to him turning away. She said, "Daddy and I had lots of problems. The wieners were just an example of them. He wouldn't be here even if you hadn't seen them, or you hadn't told me."

He looked at her. "Really?"

"Really."

He hugged her, and she returned it tightly, squeezing her arms against this boy she'd carried, too big to carry now. She nuzzled her nose into his crown and smelled Johnson's No More Tears – she still bought it, he had such sensitive skin. Now he washed his hair himself, but he was far from grown up emotionally. She had to make sure he knew he could count on her. She said, "You can tell me anything, baby."

Luna dreamed she was kissing a man in the dark. She felt the moistness of his lips on hers, she tasted his tongue, and even though she didn't know him or even what he looked like, it didn't matter because they were sharing this moment. They had this connection. But the morning came and there was no man, there never had been a man, there hadn't been a man kissing her for three years – and even before that it wasn't like Nick had been the make-out king. Luna felt like she would explode if she didn't find someone to kiss – to touch. It was still dark out, and she had a half hour before she needed to wake up the kids. She reached deep under her bed, straining until her fingers touched the photo storage box she housed her rabbit vibrator in. It couldn't kiss her, but at least it would touch *something*. Made of cold rubber and sans cotton-tail, the only thing this object had in common with bunnies was the prong on its side with ears that twitched the clit while the massive faux-penis pulsed inside the vag. She tried not too use it often – not only because it couldn't be healthy to insert chemical compounds inside her (did the government regulate the cancer risks of plastic sex toys?) but more because it was a lonely endeavor. Nevertheless, her rabbit was always there, ready to jackknife into her cunt when the going got *that* tough – which was way more than she could have ever said for Nick. She closed her palm around the mini-missile and shoved it in before she could give it a good look. The bunny ears actually had a little face underneath, which she'd found quite creepy the one time she'd made the mistake of looking at it. Who wants an animal gnawing away at their mound?

The rabbit was inserted, and she hit the two switches, pushing them to their maxes. One to make it swirl, the other for intense, vibrating action. Sometimes she started with a slow twirl, but today she just wanted this done. She closed her eyes while her rabbit whirled and whirred, and she imagined it was a man doing this to her –or at least, doing something humanly possible along these lines. She imagined him caring about her at least enough to want to please her, to massage her clit and rhythmically pound inside to make her come. This had never really happened to her, but she'd read about it. She *had* come with Nick a few times, completely by accident, usually when she'd been so angry with him that it sparked a passionate rage that propelled her up that mountain to glory. Once she'd let out a cry in unexpected joy. He'd frozen, and told her sharply that she was too loud. After that she never let herself get carried very far, because half an orgasm was purgatory with no way up or down.

The rabbit was burrowing furiously, and she couldn't help but climb. And for a few glorious seconds she peaked – and then she burst into tears. Her rabbit slipped out and onto the bed, and there it was – a writhing, rubbery mechanism with pointed ears. This x-rated Easter bunny meant nothing, cared nothing. It just obeyed. Where was the joy in that?

Oh God. Was she doomed to battery-operated orgasms for the rest of her life?

No time for wallowing. She had to safely stow the rabbit under the bed. She tucked it back in its box and shoved it *way* deep – in case Dylan decided look under there for some reason. She didn't want him asking what *this* toy was for.

She swiped at her eyes a few times for good measure, woke up the kids and fed them breakfast. When they left the house to head to school, she grabbed up her laptop so she could work on her social media book-promoting in public. She needed to be around people so she wouldn't fall down the rabbit-hole again – literally. It wouldn't do to alternately vibrate and cry all day. Work needed to be done.

There were two nearby diners. One had great coffee, but the other had wi-fi. She sacrificed the better java for the connectivity.

The gum-cracking waitress, who was a ringer for Linda Lavin's character Alice, took Luna's order for pancakes and coffee, and Luna turned on her computer to get down to business. But the screen said "unable to connect" when she tried to get online. Alice came back and Luna asked if there was a problem with the internet. Alice replied, "You might say that. A busboy got fired for going on the computer and looking at porn. On his way out he took all the wi-fi equipment and tossed it into the soup of the day. Modem minestrone, coming right up!" Alice grinned and gave her gum a good crack. "Gotta admit, it was kind of a funny thing to do."

"Rats," said Luna. "Now my goose is cooked."

"That's not as good as my modem joke, and it doesn't really work because it's not a soup reference," Alice said.

"I wasn't going for humor. I'm dismayed. I have work to do!"

"Oh, relax," Alice chided. "Drink your coffee and read the paper."

"I don't have a paper," Luna pointed out. She would've added that she didn't want a paper – that she couldn't stand reading about the world's troubles, that *truly* no news was good news, and furthermore, she could still *write* something on her computer because she didn't needed internet for Word – but Alice had already snatched up the one from the table next to Luna's booth, where a man was just standing to leave. "You're done with this, right?" she asked him. Before he could respond she'd plopped *Newsday* in front of Luna. "Problem solved. Cha-ching!"

Luna looked past her at the balding, paunchy, previous possessor of the paper, who shrugged and walked away.

"Um, thanks," Luna told Alice. She didn't have the heart to not read it now.

"No problem, babe," Alice said. "I'll be right back with your food."

Pondering how freely the term "babe" was bandied about, Luna flipped past the front pages of devastation and woe to Part II. The inner section of *Newsday* was a benign sanctum.

Or so she thought. But today's cover featured a pile of bodies. Luna gasped, and nearly dropped her coffee. Was is a mass killing in some militant country? A cult suicide? She shoved the paper to the corner of the table, but her grim thoughts about humanity wouldn't be pushed aside.

Oh, calm down, Jiminy piped in. *You're going to give yourself a nervous breakdown. Take another look. Those people aren't dead.*

Luna pulled the paper back over. It was true. The story was about something called snuggle parties. These people were lying together, cuddling in something called a puppy pile. They seemed so content – so peaceful.

Oh, wow.

There were people who felt like she did. Other people wanted to be touched.

She wasn't alone after all.

Before she even read the whole article, she knew she *had* to go…

Soon.

Luna's steaming pancakes arrived, and she dug into them while she read the article. When she'd finished, she thanked Alice profusely for the paper and tipped her extra well. Then she went home and went on the internet. She still had that social media work to do for her book, but first she Googled the snuggle parties and got the information. They were in Manhattan.

So close!

She made a reservation for the Saturday night party.

Luna was so caught up thinking about snuggling that when her phone rang and she saw it was Nick, she didn't even mind.

"I'm gonna be sharing Sal's basement for now," Nick growled—or maybe it wasn't actually meant to be a growl. His gravelly voice put all his words in the worst light possible. "I took the day off tomorrow to get my stuff. Make sure you're there to let me in."

"Okay," she said, still distracted by her thoughts.

The phone made a beep, signaling that the call had ended. It was only then that Luna realized that Nick was going to be wreaking havoc on the day of her book launch. Talking about raining on a parade.

Any parade that leads Nick permanently out of your house is cause for celebration, Luna. Your launch will be fine. Try worrying about you, Jiminy counseled.

Luna looked back at the pile of serene people. She wanted serenity, too. And serenity started with a completely Nick-free home. "Okay," she agreed.

Luna's head churned with so many contrary thoughts, and she still hadn't done any social media work. She needed to spill all her news out so she could focus on tweeting. Sunny was at work, but if she left her a message Sunny would call back when she could. Sunny was that kind of friend.

"Dude," Sunny said. "I'm on a break. What's up?" She made a sucking noise, clearly inhaling from a cigarette.

"Oh, a lot!" Luna first told her about Nick coming for his stuff.

"That's rocking good news!" Sunny said. "You'll be rid of his shit—and him, for good!"

"I know, but still… ."

"I get it. I'm out of sick days, but if you want I'll skip work and come be your bodyguard."

That was tempting, but Sunny couldn't afford to lose anything from her paycheck. "No, that's okay. I'll manage. But could you pick the kids up from school and take them to your house? In case he's still here." Sunny worked from seven to three, and she picked up Layne and Phoebe from school anyway.

"No problem. Ka-chow!"

"I have good news, too," Luna told her.

"Thank the Baby Jesus! So, spill."

Luna blurted out the story of how she'd discovered the snuggle parties. There was a long pause at the other end, punctuated by another sucking sound.

"Christ in a yarmulke!" Sunny exclaimed. "You want to touch a bunch of sketchy *strangers?*"

"Yes."

"Dude, you need to talk to a therapist."

"I'm done with therapy. Remember the across-the-room stutterer?"

"Then talk to your chiropractor."

"I just had an adjustment. I'm not going back before the party. And anyway, my mind is made up. This feels *right.*"

"Okay," Sunny said dubiously. "But really. Cuddling people you just met? I don't even like hugging my friends—no offense."

It was true, which made her slobber fests with The Coconut even more dumbfounding. But Sunny was a woman of contrasts. There was no point trying to figure her out.

"I know it's the place for me," Luna said. "I don't know about cuddling all of them—but I'd like to snuggle with at least one of them."

"Well then... enjoy that." Sunny's voice softened. "I hope you find what you're looking for there."

"Thanks." Luna stared out her window at the water's current, moving so rapidly.

Sunny asked, "Do you want me to take your kids for a sleepover on Saturday night?"

"Oh, that'd be awesome!" Luna said. "And... there's one more thing... ."

"What's that?"

"Would you go shopping for pajamas with me?"

FIFTEEN

NICK SPEWED ALL kinds of verbal abuse while he and Sal carried furniture to a U-Haul parked on the street. Luna was letting Nick take whatever he wanted—like half of the pieces to the entertainment center, which made what was left look incomplete and asymmetrical—but still he couldn't make it easy on her.

Nick blamed Luna for his infidelity.

She hadn't been a good cook, housekeeper, lover, you name it.

On and on, he vented, while she said nothing. Sal's insane-sounding Woody Woodpecker laugh followed each of Nick's cutting comments. What was funny about this scene?

"You showed no interest in decorating this house," Nick spat out as the ottoman went bye-bye. "What kind of woman doesn't care about where she lives?"

Sal laughed.

"What kind of man picks out swatches for curtains?" Luna countered, finally lured into the fight.

Sal laughed.

Just let it go, said Jiminy. *Don't get sucked down to his level.*

Ignoring Jiminy, Luna followed Nick and Sal out to the lawn. "You deliberated every last detail. It was the hardest you ever worked in your life, which isn't saying much, because you hired people to do all the actual labor. You wouldn't even pick up a paint brush."

Sal laughed again. Nick was red with anger. They hoisted the ottoman into the rear of the U-Haul.

Luna got in Nick's face. "And I paid the bills."

Sal started to laugh, but Nick shot him a murderous look and Sal sucked it back. They headed into the house for more things.

What Nick didn't want, he dumped. The bedroom floor was littered with his old clothes that no longer fit. The living room had a pile of partially-burnt candles and keepsakes accumulated through the years—all surrounding the Christmas tree, which actually looked great now that it was decorated. Maybe that was another thing that set Nick off – the fact that there was going to be a family Christmas in this house without and despite him. It turned out that what made a tree special was not its height or it girth – it was the spirit put into trimming it. Luna had let the boys put the ornaments wherever they wanted, and they'd strung garlands all around it as well. Perched on top was a cowboy hat they'd elected to use in lieu of a star or angel. Yee-ha! Luna thought of her boys' beaming faces as they'd admired their work. She had to keep them in her mind. These were the things that counted.

But it was hard to retain happy thoughts when she headed into the office and faced that floor, the worst victim of Hurricane Nick: a sea of magazines and books and assorted paraphernalia had been tossed from the desktop and bookcases to the floor so Nick could take the furniture away. The rubble was knee-high—and it had been Nick who had accumulated all this clutter to begin with! His message of contempt and hate was so palpable that she felt it clogging her throat. God, she'd been married to this man. She'd borne his children… .

Happy release day to me.

But it *was* a happy moment, a double release—Luna kept telling herself that, even as she quivered—from Nick's abrasive tone, from her fear of what came next in her life. Nick may have been jerky, but at least he had been *there*. There was something terrible about being free.

How will I go it alone?

Don't ask questions; just go, said Jiminy.

But… where am I going?

Up to you. But the great thing is, you don't have to decide now. You just have to keep moving, shake everything off. Your soul needs exercise just like your body does.

Nick and Sal were heading through the kitchen with boxes. Sal went out the door first. Nick paused, and motioned toward the purple tiffany lamp hanging above the table. "You had to have that lamp. You're a control freak."

Luna could've pointed out the incongruity between that statement and Nick's earlier claim that she'd been uninterested. Instead she said, "Okay, I insisted on a lamp, and you had sex with men. Touché."

"You're such an asshole," Nick said.

"Hey, you're the bottom, not me," she said. Another lovely tidbit of information she'd gotten from the computer. He was taking that, too. Not that she wanted the sticky-keyed, gay-porn-infested machine. She probably needed to sterilize that whole room.

Nick shut up. Luna doubted he wanted his cousin hearing anything about his secret life. It had to stink, living a lie. But it was no longer Luna's problem.

Hallelujah, said Jiminy.

Nick and Sal finally finished and drove off. Luna sat in the quiet. *Her* quiet. She stared out the living room window and spotted the egret she often watched while she was musing for the perfect word. As usual, he plodded along the shoreline on his search for nourishment.

What a slow process, she thought – not for the first time. She wondered how he could bear such painstakingly slow movements.

She forced herself away from the scene, to face her interior. After all, Sunny and the kids would be there in a couple of hours.

I should clean.

But where should she start?

She spotted her wedding album in the living room rubble and picked it up.

It was grey faux-leather with bulky gold-rimmed pages.

It smelled stale, and its surface felt craggy—covered with intersecting lines like someone's palm.

Luna stared at the cover, embossed with the words: "Our Wedding. Luna and Nick." She opened it.

The first pictures were of Luna getting ready. Or rather, pretending to prepare. She'd already been finished, of course. Who would pose for wedding pictures without being made up? Not even Luna.

Then came Nick. In his tux.

Tears sprang to Luna's eyes. *Oh, stop,* she scolded herself. But it was the tux that made her cry, not Nick.

That tuxedo was a sham—a promise that wouldn't be kept.

She turned a few pages.

There they were. The happy couple. Bending under their wedding party's human arch. Frozen forever in that entrance to marital bliss.

Pictures really *were* all you had left from a wedding.

And they were a problem when you wanted to forget about it.

She couldn't throw the album away, or burn it. For one thing, she looked too good in the pictures. And for another, she wanted her kids to have proof that their parents had once been happy.

Had they been happy?

She was going to go with 'yes' on that one. The path of least resistance.

Luna flipped to the last page. The one of her and Nick waving good night.

She remembered how faint she'd felt at the end of the evening – all that money spent, and they hadn't had a moment to eat until later in the hotel room where they finally dug into their foil-covered take-out swan. The ninety-five-dollar serving of chicken divan, scalloped potatoes and mixed vegetables lost its allure all mushed up in Reynolds Wrap, and it didn't taste so great cold.

Her wedding and her marriage had two things in common: She hadn't been able to really enjoy either one, and both had left her dizzy.

Luna slapped the book shut and removed it from her lap.

It was a relief to put it aside.

Those gilded pages were ridiculously heavy.

Here's to lightness, said Jiminy.

"Yoo-hoo! We hear it's someone's book launch day!" Sunny's voice came from the doorway.

"Mom, you didn't lock the door," Ben scolded, coming in behind Sunny. Ben was vigilant about safety and security—even more so since Nick had gone. He'd started checking the house doors and windows every night before bed.

"Sorry, sweetie," Luna called from the top of the stairs. She'd just stowed the wedding album in Ben's closet.

"Oh, and congratulations on your book, too," Ben added sheepishly.

"Thanks."

Dylan, Layne and Phoebe walked in, too. "Mommy, did Daddy come get his stuff?" Dylan asked. Luna had told them last night, so they wouldn't be surprised to see all of Nick's things gone.

"Yes, baby. But it's okay. You'll still see him. He only moved across town."

Dylan looked sad.

"We're gonna have ice cream cake after dinner," Sunny told Dylan.

"Yay!" Dylan said. He bounded upstairs to play.

Everyone else stood around the pile Nick had left. There wasn't enough room to sit, because Nick had taken the couch and left only the love seat. "Dad took our furniture?" Ben asked.

"Yeah."

"Why'd you let him?"

"I just thought it would be easier, to let him take what he wanted. We'll get new stuff," Luna said. "It'll be nice. A fresh start."

"But what will we do now?" Ben asked.

Luna slumped. She had no answer; she was out of ideas. She didn't want to be in charge anymore; she was tired of thinking. She really felt that her head just might explode.

"It's okay," said Sunny. Her voice was extra-soothing, like a nurse on a mental ward. "We'll use garden chairs." She sent Layne and Phoebe to the shed.

"I didn't mean to upset you, Mom," Ben said.

"You didn't, sweetie. It's just… today was a bit much."

"I got you this card," Ben said, handing her a purple envelope. He'd written "Mom" inside a lop-sided heart, and drawn stars all around.

It was one of those sentiment-filled "Special Mother" happy birthday Hallmark cards Luna had always cringed at when shopping for Loreena. She couldn't imagine giving such a warm thing to her cold mother.

But *her* son had picked one out, crossing out "birth" and scrawling "book" above it. Thank goodness she'd managed to be the kind of mother who deserved a gushy Hallmark card. "I mean it, Mom," Ben told her. "I love you."

"I love you, too, baby," Luna said. They hugged.

Layne and Phoebe returned with the chairs. Then they went upstairs with Ben.

Sunny said, "I know you're gonna feel sad and overwhelmed, because I did when Sal left, and you're a big mush. But remember, having to use garden chairs is better than having a big ole user/loser taking up space in the house. Less is more." She opened her large pocketbook and revealed a bottle of champagne. "Let's celebrate."

"Okay."

"I saw you have new locks on the kitchen table. I think you should get a move on them, in case Fatsy finds his key and decides he wants to come back for more goodies."

Luna sighed. She hadn't been able to deal with the locks—even opening the package seemed daunting because of what came next. Hardware was scary. "I need a locksmith."

"No you don't! Order the Chinese, and then I'll show you how to change them."

"Are you sure?"

"Absolutely! For one thing, doing it yourself is empowering. But more importantly, it's way cheaper."

"Okay. I'm pretty sure there's a screwdriver around here somewhere." And she found one in the rubble.

It must've been super busy in the Chinese place, because by the time dinner arrived Luna had changed the two lock cylinders under Sunny's guidance, plus they'd managed to bag up the garbage in the living room and dragged it to the curb. The living room was clean, though nearly empty. A love seat and half of an entertainment center didn't do much to fill in the room.

The tree was by itself in the far corner, by the window. "It looks nice set apart like that," Sunny told her. "Like a shrine, or something."

It actually did look good, especially with the lights on. The room glowed with the colors.

"See, everything works out," Sunny told her.

As per rule number three, Luna thought. Unfortunately, she couldn't wholeheartedly believe this even though she wanted to. There was so much chaos in her life. How could it *ever* work out?

Everyone ate at the kitchen table (Nick had left it, along with that lamp he abhorred.)

Just as they were finishing, there was an ominous *beeep!* outside. Luna and her kids knew whose car locked with that high-pitched honk.

"It's Nona," said Dylan.

Shit, Luna thought.

Loreena rapped on the door moments later. Phoebe was closest to the door, so she answered.

"Oh, hi!" Loreena greeted Phoebe. She was always nice to Sunny and her kids.

"Hi," said Phoebe. She moved aside and let Loreena in.

"I was on my way home from the hospital, and I needed to use a bathroom." Loreena took a look around and focused a glare at Luna. "Are you having a party without me?"

"No, Mom," said Luna. "We're just having dinner."

"Oh? I haven't had a thing to eat all day." Loreena said this every time she arrived on Luna's doorstep. "You might have invited me over."

"I had a lot on my mind today," Luna said. "Go to the bathroom, and we'll work something out with the food."

Loreena made her *Hhhmmmppppffff* throat noise and walked off. Luna got a dish, and everyone contributed what was left of their food onto it. The kids hadn't eaten all that much and the plate was impressively full.

Everyone had grown quiet, like the joy had been sucked right out of the room. Then Ben asked, "Why was Nona at the hospital, Mom? Is she okay?"

"Ummm… she's fine, sweetie. Unfortunately, your grandpa is staying there. He had something called a stroke." This was a sucky way to break the news, but she figured she'd better tell the kids the whole truth now.

"What does that mean?"

"It's kind of like an earthquake went through his body, and now he's recovering from the aftershocks."

"Is he going to get better?"

Luna was not one of those unduly optimistic parents. She didn't want to create false hope. "We have to wait and see."

"Should we go visit him and cheer him up?"

"Not yet, baby. One day we will."

"We can bring him a Build-A-Bear," Dylan piped up. "I like to make them."

"Sure we can," Luna told him.

Returning, Loreena scraped her chair across the tiled floor and sat in front of her brimming plate. She picked up her fork and speared a sugar snap pea. She plopped it into her mouth and chewed thoroughly as everyone watched, finally swallowing. Then she turned to Luna and asked, "Do you have any tea?"

She did this every time she came over. The answer, same as ever, was no. "Don't you have a teabag in your purse?" Luna asked. "You always do."

Loreena foraged through papers and tissues, finally locating some white tea. "Do you want me to make it?" she asked.

Luna didn't feel like explaining how to use the microwave to her mother yet again. Loreena never remembered which buttons to press, and there was always a complicated debate over how many minutes to heat the water. "That's okay, Mom."

Loreena scraped her chair back and stood, wandering toward the living room with her plate in hand. She couldn't just sit and enjoy. "What happened to your furniture?" she asked.

Luna sighed. She really didn't feel like getting into it right now.

"Daddy moved out," Dylan told her.

"Really?" Loreena brightened at the news.

Luna shot a worried look at Sunny. Would Loreena say something about Nick that would upset the kids?

The microwave dinged.

"Saved by the bell," said Sunny.

"Can we have cake, Mommy?" Dylan asked.

"So you *are* having a party," said Loreena. "And I wasn't invited."

"It's cake. Just cake," Luna said. "And you're here now." To Dylan she said, "Yes, sweetie."

The kids stuck six candles into the ice cream cake that said "Happy Launch Day"—one candle for each book she'd published. "Do you have a new book?" Loreena asked.

"Yes, Mom," Luna answered, not surprised that her mother had forgotten the news she'd shared several times over the past few months.

Everyone sang "Happy Release Day to You" – even Loreena, once she caught on to the words. Loreena never missed an opportunity to sing. Her operatic voice was filled with vibrato. It was about three octaves above everyone else's.

Luna made a wish: for her book to be loved by its readers. She wanted more than sales. She wanted her words to linger.

Dylan helped her blow the candles out.

Everyone cheered. Except Loreena, who sipped her tea.

After everyone left, Luna gathered her sons in her arms. "Thanks for making my release day special," she said, squeezing them both tight.

Then she let them go and faced them. "Are you sad about Dad?"

They both nodded.

"I'm sorry you have to go through this. I tried to make the marriage work, but we weren't happy together."

"We know," said Ben.

"Can I call Daddy?" Dylan asked.

"Sure, baby." Luna got the phone, dialed Nick's number and handed the receiver to Dylan.

While Dylan was talking to Nick, Luna apologized to Ben for not telling him about Lenny. "I didn't want to upset you more, with all this going on about your dad," she told him. "I was going to tell you when he got a little better. I figured it didn't really matter—it's not like you see him that often, anyway."

"You don't have to hide things from me, Mom," Ben said. "I can handle them. I'm big now."

"You sure are," Luna agreed. She felt like crying. She hugged him instead.

SIXTEEN

THE SNUGGLE PARTY was located on the top floor of a five-story Upper East Side walk-up.

Between anticipation and climbing, Luna was a bit breathless when she walked in. She smelled fresh-baked brownies.

Right away she recognized the creator of the snuggle parties from his picture in *Newsday*. He sat at a folding table in his small kitchen, collecting money.

"Hi, I'm Finn," he said when it was her turn.

"I'm Luna."

Finn was blond and classically Nordic. Dressed in a Superman t-shirt and Scooby-Doo pajama bottoms, Finn had flair.

The whole scene was so odd. Luna struggled for something to say. "Are you of Finnish descent?"

"Swedish," he answered. He gave her a smile, revealing very large, sparkling teeth. "You can get changed in the back room, behind the curtain."

Luna put on her new purple plaid pj's and joined the eleven others waiting to begin.

Before the snuggling, there would be a welcome circle with rules.

Finn's living room was narrow, which actually made it cozy. There was a futon against one wall, and pillows strewn all over the tan, shag-carpeted floor. Glistening white lights were strung around the wooden ceiling beams. Luna leaned on a pillow propped up against the brick wall next to the fireplace. Her legs were pointed forward, crossed at the ankles.

She was going for that casual, relaxed look.

It was a Bohemian atmosphere, with everything and everyone at floor level. The snugglers eyed each other, probably trying to figure out whom they'd like to cuddle with and if that person would possibly agree.

Luna was too overwhelmed to size people up. Breathing took up all her energy. It felt new, like each breath was the first one she'd ever taken.

Finn took a spot in the circle. "Welcome, everyone," he said in an oh-so-soothing voice. He was really good-looking. The kind of guy she'd get a crush on if she weren't careful. She decided never to snuggle with Finn. "I've been, among other things, a bartender for ten years. During that time I've witnessed a great amount of misunderstanding and miscommunication among people." He paused and gave another one of his big-teeth grins. "That's why the rules must be laid out so we can all be clear and enjoy ourselves."

Everyone nodded.

"Rule number one is no sex."

No problem, thought Luna.

They proceeded through the list of rules and things to consider. "You are encouraged to say no if you don't want to snuggle, and to think of no as a complete sentence," said Finn.

Luna doubted she'd be voicing that sentence.

Finn said, "Don't make a request unless you are comfortable with getting a no. When you leave room for a no, people will feel freer to say yes."

The rules were getting a bit long. But they had given Luna a chance to warm up to the room, and even look at the other people.

She spotted a guy she'd like to kiss.

He resembled Barry Manilow in his younger years – skinny and kind of geeky, but friendly.

He was checking her out.

Maybe he'd like to kiss her too.

The snuggling began.

What now?

Should she approach the guy?

What if he said no?

Next thing she knew, he was sitting next to her.

But he didn't say anything… .

Somehow, she managed the words. "Would you like to snuggle?"

"Yes."

They lay down together, pressed into each other.

God, I'm touching a man, Luna thought.

A man's touching me…

Moon River" came on. The song was grainy and raw.

They held each other hard and listened. It felt like ghosts were floating around Luna, or maybe they were angels. She thought she might cry, but then she didn't.

It was so bittersweet in the arms of this man she didn't know.

Luna's head was against his chest, cradled in his arm. Through the cotton of his t-shirt she heard his heart. It sprinted, like hers.

"I like your cologne," she told him. It was musky and deep—protective.

He said, "I'm not wearing any. It must be my deodorant. It's Right Guard."

She said, "Maybe it's you."

This was possibly the corniest thing she'd ever said.

He must've liked it, because he asked her, "Can I kiss you?"

"Yes."

Their lips touched. His were so cushiony. She melted right into them.

He slipped her his tongue then, and she latched on with hers. They locked in place. *Kissing's like riding a bike*, she realized. (She actually didn't know how to ride a bike, but everyone said that once you learned, you never forgot.) Not only did she remember how to kiss, but it seemed easier now.

She rolled onto him for better leverage, and they were solidly smooching.

After about ten minutes Finn asked, "Are you two all right?"

"Um-hum," they both managed, without releasing their grip.

"Are you gonna come up for air anytime soon?"

"Uh-uh," they said.

They kissed until the party was over.

When Luna rose, he tried to follow, but couldn't. "I need a minute to lie here," he said. "You're some powerhouse."

She told him, "That's the first time I kissed someone in three years."

He said, "I'm glad you didn't tell me beforehand. That would've been a lot of pressure."

Luna left the party lighter. For blocks and blocks she took in the nippy Manhattan air like it was the freshest air ever, and maybe it was. She didn't feel cold. All she felt was alive.

She danced in the moonbeams bouncing onto the asphalt.

And when a powdery snow began to fall, she twirled in the dusty flakes.

The city belonged to her.

The world belonged to her.

The next morning, Luna woke up feeling like she was dying.

No, that wasn't it.

She wasn't dying. She wanted to die.

As high as she'd climbed last night, that's how far she'd plunged.

A splat on the sidewalk.

"What's wrong with me?" she cried out.

Just rest. We'll talk later, said Jiminy.

"Great."

When she woke up again her head was pounding in desperate need of coffee. Thank goodness she'd set it up before she'd left for Manhattan last night. She trudged downstairs, hit the button on her coffeemaker and leaned against the counter with her head bent low, waiting for her fix.

When the gurgling stopped and the coffeemaker beeped, Luna filled her cup and brought it to her computer. She wanted to work on her novel, at least to type a few lines. Maybe if she got something written she'd feel better.

Maybe her words would convince her that she was worth something.

She stared at the blinking cursor, waiting impatiently for her to carry on from the previous paragraph. It should've been so simple to just carry on. Just keep typing. But it hurt so much. It was killing her to write this book. It was like she'd slit her wrist open and was dripping crimson onto her keys. Splat. Splat. Splat.

Splats were today's theme.

The pain felt intolerable. What the hell was she bothering with this for, anyway? Who would ever want to read such misery? Who would ever care about her story?

Why not delete it?

Why not erase the whole fucking thing and play "let's pretend everything's perfect" like the rest of the valium-popping, liquor-swilling, vow-breaking population of Long Island? What was the point of being a martyr when no one would even notice?

She highlighted the whole thing and dangled her finger above the 'delete' key.

Sorry, babe. You can't hit delete, Jiminy told her.

"Says who?" She was tired of his interspersed irony coming out of nowhere.

Says you.

"What the hell does that mean?"

You want to be the change you wish to see in the world. And guess what? This book ***is*** *your change.*

"I don't see how my story can be a lesson for anyone."

It's not for you to see, and it's not going to be a lesson. It's a change.

"What's the difference?"

Nobody wants to learn a lesson. But they can't help experiencing a change.

"You're too deep, Jiminy. You're giving me a migraine."

I'm just the deepest part of you, Luna.

"Oh, God."

Right.

"I gotta get some more sleep. I'll write when I get up."

Good thought.

And when she woke again, that's what she did.

She wrote until evening, and then she went to Sunny's to have dinner and pick up her boys.

Sunny was sitting on her stoop, smoking. "I hope you don't mind, but Mary Fabarino packed all the kids in her minivan to go see some Disney flick." Mary was a neighbor of Sunny's with two kids. She was one of those "as seen on TV" super-moms who super-sized her kids' schedules due to her fear of one dull moment leading to their ultimate ruin. In a way Luna envied Mary's energy and devotion, but she also found it disturbing. Sunny continued, "I didn't see the point of calling and waking you up to ask. I mean, why would you say no?"

"I wouldn't," Luna said. "I'm glad they're having fun."

Flower and Spunky were attached to the fence again. Barklessly, they watched Luna as she walked slowly, trying to avoid icy patches. The temperature had sunk, and the town was frozen.

Sunny wore a black wool jacket. She gripped her pink Happy Bunny mug with the caption: *Let's focus on me.* "I'm waiting for the girls to do their business," she told Luna. "I don't want to leave them outside."

Flower and Spunky didn't seem interested in peeing or pooping. They were now in a frenzy, yapping at a teenaged boy rounding the corner. Sunny sipped her coffee and said, "I've decided I will bark for nobody."

"Problems with The Coconut?" Luna asked, bending to sit. Her puffy purple jacket made a swishing sound as she pulled it over her butt.

Sunny sighed. "The honeymoon is over."

"And you weren't even married." Luna's legs were shivering. She was still in pajama pants, which were pretty thin.

Sunny shuddered. "Thank god! I can't imagine doing all that divorce paperwork again!"

Luna wrapped her arms around her legs and squeezed. "I thought you were having fun with him."

"I was having fun because of him. He took the kids out and gave me some alone time. I got to sit and read books without anyone harassing me for a ride. That was awesome."

"So, what's the problem?"

"The problem is, he's needy! Once he wanted me to wait to eat a sandwich because he needed to go buy mayonnaise for his!"

"And?"

"And I was hungry! Plus, he wants to touch me all the time…"

"I thought you liked that. The way you guys were at the bar…"

"That's what you do at a bar. You make out. But when we're watching TV, he needs to keep the hell on his side of the couch! Criminy!"

There was a silence then—a winter's kind of crisp quiet—except for the dogs rattling their chains like Ghosts of Christmas past.

"He's got an alcohol problem, too."

"You like to drink."

"I don't drink beer in bed!"

"He does?"

"He did. I asked him to stop, because I didn't want the kids to find empty cans under the bed, and also because it was tacky. Then he brought over gin and poured it in a cup."

"Huh."

The church bells rang in their eerie way. They played "Silent Night" every hour during the holiday season. "Christ in a miniskirt, can't you make them switch up songs?" Sunny begged the sky.

"How's the sex?" Luna asked.

"Ha! Like you can even call it that. You know how a conversation with him goes, the way you have to hold up both ends yourself? That's what sex with him is like."

This seemed normal to Luna. Nick had been pretty passive in the sack. But Sunny had a high standard. Sal may have been a loser and a crack-head, but everyone had a talent—and his was in the bedroom.

"So, bottom line: you're done with The Coconut?"

Sunny nodded. "I've just got to tell him. He *is* a good egg. It's just… I'm cracking from the strain of all his mundane."

Luna wanted to laugh, but she couldn't bring herself to do it.

"Chickie, what's wrong with you? Didn't you have fun at that party?"

Luna told Sunny she'd kissed a guy. She told her how she'd danced in the streets afterwards. "But this morning I felt so empty. Worthless."

"Sounds like you crashed after a high," said Sunny.

"Kissing made me high?"

Sunny shrugged. "Everyone's got their drug."

Precisely, said Jiminy. *She nailed it.*

"So what do I do now?"

Sunny gave Luna a hard look. "You've always been a relationship person. Look how long you stuck with Mr. Gay Dot Com. Face it: You don't want to touch strangers."

Right again, said Jiminy. *This girl is pretty insightful for a mere mortal.*

"Yeah." Luna traced her foot on a patch of ice just to the side of the walkway. "I don't think I should go to any more snuggle parties. Finn is the kind of guy that could convince everyone to drink the Kool-Aid."

"And he's got those big teeth." Sunny had seen a picture of Finn on the web. "You can't trust a guy whose chompers take up his whole face."

He's got a mouth like Gary Busey, said Jiminy. *'Nuff said.*

"I'm gonna try meeting someone online," said Luna. "Maybe speed-dating, too."

"That sounds okay. But…"

The dogs piped up again.

Sunny continued, "I'm just not sure that your happiness equates with finding a man."

I second that emotion, said Jiminy.

"Tell that to Disney," Luna said. She opened her mouth to say something else, but the moment was interrupted by clattering steel. From the ends of their taut shackles, Flower and Spunky stood on their hind legs and howled at a guy starting up his blue Mazda.

Sunny addressed the dogs: "Would you girls please concentrate, so we can go inside? My ass is freezing!"

Flower and Spunky squatted.

SEVENTEEN

LUNA DIDN'T LOVE the internet, especially after all Nick had done on it, but it *did* seem to be her best option for dating. Everyone was doing it. So that night, when the kids were asleep, she turned on her computer for something other than a writing-related task.

Which site should she try? The other day, she'd heard a woman in Dunkin' Donuts telling her friend she'd met someone on CraigsList.

Luna had thought CraigsList was for finding apartments and swapping tables. But she went on-line to check and there it was: a personals section.

Hey, it was free. Worth a shot..

She wasn't sure what to write in her ad, but wound up with this:

A Lot of Love to Give

Loving, attractive, late-thirties female seeks mate to hold hands and cuddle with.

She almost added, "Must have tongue," but she figured mullet man had been a fluke. And anyway, she could weed out any speech impediments on the phone.

But would you hang up? Jiminy asked.

"Yes, I would," she answered.

Yeah, right, he said. *You waste a lot of your life being too nice.*

Within the first few minutes of posting, Luna's e-mailbox had been inundated with answers and photos from men.

She was flush with the thrill of attention.

She wrote back to a few that seemed particularly sincere. And before she left the computer to go bake holiday Shrinky-Dinks with the kids, she'd secured the phone number of a guy named Glen.

When the kids were in bed, she called him.

He sounded good!

Here's what he told her:

STATS ON GLEN

Name: Glen Rolf.

Ethnic background: German and Middle Eastern.

Marital status: Separated.

Children: Two daughters in their twenties.

Body: Tall and beyond buff.

Hair: Curly brown.

Occupation: Owner of a Gold's Gym franchise.

Favorite physical activities: All.

Other likes: Protein shakes.

Dislikes: Losing control of a situation.

Religion: Christianity.

Favorite writers: Whoever wrote the articles in sports and health magazines.

Favorite dessert: Apple pie.

Favorite expression: "Winning isn't everything; it's the only thing."

They decided to meet. Glen lived further out on Long Island, about an hour away. They agreed on a diner, midway between them.

Two days later, Luna headed to the Shorefront Diner. Shrinky-Dink ornaments made by Ben and Dylan swung from the rearview mirror—a wreath and a Christmas tree. She pulled into the lot of the typically grandiose Long Island diner, decked out in sparkling silver façade and lights that rivaled Times Square. She parked facing the bright ruby sign. Neon glowed through the minivan, illuminating the wreath and tree, which swayed slightly. She watched until they stilled.

Leaving her bulky, unattractive coat in the passenger seat, Luna got out of her van and ran toward the entrance. She wanted to look sexy in her first impression, even if that meant a few seconds of cold.

A Muzak version of Jingle Bells played inside. The counter sported shiny garlands and a mechanical Santa who waved. *Ho-ho-hope,* she thought. She'd passed under a mistletoe hanging in the doorway. Would she get a kiss on the way out?

She spotted Glen at the counter, waiting. Actually, she figured it was him due to a process of elimination. He was the only one sitting there.

"Hi! Are you Glen?

He nodded.

"I'm Luna."

"Hello," he said, without a smile.

Hmmm…

True to his word, Glen was a tall, burly guy. A bit intimidating. He'd described himself as "built like a linebacker" on the phone. Luna didn't know exactly how linebackers were built as opposed to any other backers, but he seemed to fit the general football bill. He barely fit on the counter stool.

The big-haired waitress tried sitting them at a booth near the front of the diner. Glen pointed to the back dining room, "We'd like to sit in there."

"That's closed, Sir," she told him.

"Perfect. We have some private business to discuss," he said.

Business? Luna wondered. *A strange way to describe a date.*

The waitress wavered, seesawing between toe and heel on her thick, non-skid rubber soles as she thought. Then she said, "Follow me."

Luna and Glen slid across from each other in their private booth. He ordered coffee for both of them.

"Something else?" The waitress asked.

Luna would've liked something else. Some kind of snack at least. But before she could voice her request Glen said, "We'll let you know." He pushed both menus toward the edge of the table, away from Luna.

The waitress returned with their coffees, banging them down. In the far corner of the room, a dessert case beamed like a beacon toward Luna. Glen swirled a whirlpool of sugar into his black coffee, scraping his spoon along the cup's bottom like nails across a blackboard.

He stared at Luna. His eyes were steely gray.

She tried to start a conversation. "So, you mentioned football on the phone. Did you play in high school, or college?"

Glen leaned over the red Formica tabletop, so close his face was inches from Luna's. "My father never let me play football. He said I wasn't good enough – that I'd never be good enough." His breath was hot, his voice distressed.

"Sorry to hear that."

"Ancient history," he said. His voice was magically calm now. "But we are here to talk about today, yes?"

"Yes."

"Here's what I have in mind." His voice had morphed into a cool whisper. "I want to humiliate you."

"*What?*"

"It's called erotic humiliation," he said. "I always had these urges to do… things… so I did some research on Google and found the name. It covers everything I have in mind."

Luna just stared. Words failed her.

As nonchalantly as if he were listing ingredients in a recipe, Glen proceeded to name the degrading acts. "I want you to do what I want exactly when I want it. Like get on your knees and deep throat my cock so much you choke, while I call you my filthy little whore. And then open your mouth wide so I can piss in it. Stuff like that."

Stuff like that???

"And when I'm ready I wanna doggy-fuck you from behind like the bitch that you are. I wanna hear you bark while I ram you, and I don't wanna stop till your pussy's so sore you're howling for mercy. Oh yeah, and you gotta request permission to come. Three barks in a row. That's how you ask."

Luna was sure she felt her eyes bulging out of her head.

"Don't worry, I'll treat you like a lady in public," he assured her.

Glen splattered the paper placemat advertising local businesses with brown drips from his spoon. Coffee pooled and soaked into ads for sewage treatment, a tanning salon and a bridal shop.

Luna didn't touch her coffee.

She found her voice, finally. "I don't think I…"

He interrupted her. "But we won't be in public often. Can't take the chance of my wife finding out about us."

"You said you were separated!" Like that mattered, anyway. His being married was the most miniscule of the problems.

Apparently he'd hidden a lot of things on the phone.

Like the fact that he was bonkers.

"I meant mentally," he said. "My wife doesn't understand me."

It would take a panel of top shrinks at a Vienna symposium to figure this guy out.

Glen then revealed that he wanted to give her catch phrases which would be her cue to "perform" at any given time. For example, when he said "ocean," she was supposed to lick her lips provocatively.

Luna doubted she could flick her tongue across her mouth erotically for any stakes—even a million dollar book deal. It seemed like such a silly thing to do. How could she not laugh?

Plus, it could lead to chapped lips.

But Glen was not laughing. He wanted her to try it now.

"Give me some time to practice," she said, figuring it was better to humor him than to refuse. *Just play along until you get the hell away*, she told herself.

She worried about what would happen when they left. She didn't want to be alone with him in the parking lot. He could force her in his car!

On the other hand, she was kind of alone with him now. In a second, he could reach a little further across the table and snap her neck with those bear-like hands of his.

She decided to make a run for it.

"I have to go to the ladies room," she told him. Clutching her purse, she headed toward the front of the diner. Safely out of Mr. Crazy's view, she pushed through the kitchen's swinging doors.

"Is there a back exit?" she asked the surprised cooks.

One of them pointed, and she headed toward it. The scent of the diner's fresh-baked goods filled the air, and she teetered for a moment in a sugared-brain fog. Was there time to get a large sprinkled cookie? Diner cookies were the best…

Just go! Jiminy said, and the sharpness of his tone slapped reality into her. She could get a cookie at some other diner… as long as she wasn't locked in Glen's trunk.

Luna sprinted into the cold night, toward her Windstar in the lot.

She thought of Glen's catch phrase—"ocean."

An ocean was what she wanted between her and Glen.

She couldn't cross it fast enough.

EIGHTEEN

LUNA WAS GRATEFUL for the caller ID on her cell phone, so she was able to decline calls from "Crazy." Glen also emailed her several times. She deleted them unopened.

The meeting had not been a promising start to her dating life.

But Luna was determined to proceed. What else could she do?

She decided to try speed-dating.

It was in a Greenwich Village bar/lounge called Madame X, modeled after a 1920s French bordello. The walls and couches were scarlet velvet. The lampshades were beaded. The dim red lighting gave skin a crimson hue. Madame X didn't look like the kind of place one where would find their soul mate.

If you can see that, why are you going through with this? asked Jiminy.

Well, I'm here already, so what the hell. A girl can hope.

Yeah, hoping always works out, Jiminy said. *Just like at the diner.*

She stepped up to the bar for a drink. The bartender had curly black hair and striking green eyes. And dimples. "Sex in the bathroom?" he asked.

"Excuse me?"

"It's our most popular martini," he said. "Chocolate vodka, Frangelico hazelnut liqueur, creme de cacao, three olives and a vanilla sugar rim. Yummy and it relieves tension." He gave her a wink.

"I don't think so," she told him. She couldn't handle sex in the bathroom, real or in a glass.

Elbows propped against the bar, he leaned closer. "Your place or mine?"

She studied him for a moment. "Is that another drink?'

"It is."

"You might want to clarify these things," she told him. She ordered a white wine.

The place was packed with speed-daters raring to go. It smelled of alcohol and perfume. The women were looking va-va-voomish, which was intimidating, because Luna was not the va-va-voom type. She disliked makeup except for the basic foundation, which she wore because she looked red-nosed without it. But lipstick... well, she didn't see the point of something you had to continually check and make sure was still there. The worst was when it partially came off, because then the wearer just looked deranged. There were enough things to do over and over in life. Why add applying lipstick to the equation?

But tonight she'd worn it as well as eye shadow, mascara, blush, the works.

She knew what she was up against and when in Rome...

Ever stop to think that maybe you don't belong in Rome? asked Jiminy. *This is not your scene, Luna.*

Shhh, she told him. *I can handle this. After all, I've got glitter.* She'd spotted "iridescent body shimmer" in CVS. It reminded her of pixie dust. Wearing a few dabs made Luna feel brave.

She wore a body-hugging silky blouse trimmed with lace, the kind of top that looked like border-line lingerie. She looked good, but still, her jeans were not quite as alluring as the short skirts some of these women wore. She did have a cute pair of burgundy Nine West shoes, though. Comfortable, unlike the spiky slivers most of the other women precariously balanced in. Luna's footwear slipped on like a clog, but had a thick, raised heel. Its tapestry stitching really dressed up an outfit *and* raised her height.

A whistle blew. Time for the women to sit at the tables.

It blew again. The first man arrived.

He wasn't bad looking, as far as she could tell in the red light.

"Hi, I'm Steve."

"Luna," she said.

"So, what do you do?"

She told him, and then asked what he did. He was a sales manager somewhere.

"Interesting," she lied. "So what's your favorite dessert?"

"Why do you want to know that?"

"Thought I'd mix it up a little."

"I fail to see how my favorite dessert could be the judge of anything."

"I'm not trying to judge you… I just thought it was a fun question," she said.

The whistle blew.

Steve got up. "Baked Alaska," he said, shaking his head.

The next guy was Randy. He worked in banking.

"Interesting," she lied.

She asked him about his favorite dessert. "I don't like sweets," he replied.

The whistle blew.

The evening wore on. Faces blended. It was annoying telling the same story of what she did for a living over and over, and no one liked her dessert question. She told one guy she was shy. He said, "Shy girls don't wear glitter."

The last guy was Ari. Tall and lean, he looked old for 45. Not bad, just… older than 45. He was Israeli.

Ari told Luna that when he was twenty he'd lived in Africa, working for a human rights organization. He'd adopted an orphaned chimpanzee.

How cute was that?

Luna liked Ari at least, way better than the drips who'd preceded him.

The whistle blew, but Ari stayed. They sat and talked for a while. Then, they kissed.

Woohoo! Another kiss under her belt!

They were supposed to go on-line and make their dating selections. If people picked each other, they'd receive their contact information.

"Come home with me," Ari said. His thick accent made it sound like a command.

"I don't think so..." she told him.

"I will be a gentleman."

"I have to get going... ."

"Just for a little while. It's a short walk from here."

She thought for a moment. He seemed sincere enough... and she *was* enjoying herself. "Um... Okay."

Here are some of the things Luna learned about Ari:

STATS ON ARI

Name: Ari Luz

Ethnic Background: Israeli, but raised in Vienna.

Martial Status: Single.

Children: None.

Body: Tall and thin, but worn-looking and stooped.

Hair: Graying.

Occupation: International investment banker.

Favorite physical activity: Bicycling.

Other likes: The Wall Street Journal, Forbes.

Dislikes: Changes in plans, disappointment.

Religion: Jewish.

Favorite writers: Anyone who writes books on economics.

Favorite dessert: Weichselstrudel.

Favorite expression: "Do not live in a town where there are no doctors."

By the time they got to his place, Ari was talking like they were already a couple. Partnering had been on his to-do list for awhile, and he'd checked it off now. He spoke about relationships like they were a business merger and theirs was complete.

Luna wasn't ready to merge quite yet, but she did like the attention. And she did want somebody to take care of her… to love.

But it was a little early to know if it would be him.

The apartment felt sterile and smelled like Pledge. "This is not my real residence," he told her. "My mother is on an extended visit to New York, so I let her live there. I'm renting this place by the month, furnished."

Convenient, though the furniture was depressingly neutral.

He sat on the beige couch. "Join me." He patted a cushion.

She sat next to him. They kissed some more.

He was getting a little adventurous near her pants. "I'm not ready for that yet," she told him. After her three-year hiatus she needed to take things slow, but she didn't want to share that. So she said, "I don't want you to think I'm some kind of first-date slut."

He moved his hand higher, inside her blouse. That, she allowed. She liked it.

"Our bodies were made for each other," he said. "You will see."

That was how it worked in general, but she didn't point that out. "I've gotta go," she told him.

He tugged at her arm, but she pulled herself up.

"When will I see you again?" he asked.

"Next weekend," she promised.

The weekend came.

Since Sunny hadn't broken up with The Coconut yet, Luna decided it would be fun for the two couples to go out together. Nick and Sal had all the kids for the night, and were doubtlessly plying them with saturated fats and sugars but what the hell, they were their fathers and one night of crap couldn't hurt *too* much. She picked Ari up from the train station and brought him to Sunny's. "Where is the rest of it?" he asked, staring at the small, boxy house. "Was it lost in a hurricane?"

"No, this is all of it."

"Why do they not put a top floor on it? Is it a trailer? I saw one in a movie." Luna was guessing there weren't many trailer parks in Vienna.

"Nope. It's a regular house."

They got out of the van and headed up Sunny's walkway. Ari didn't pick up his feet when he walked, it was more like a shuffle. Why hadn't she noticed the other night?

Sunny and The Coconut were waiting inside. Slouched on the couch watching music videos on his computer, The Coconut wore a red-striped flannel shirt, like a lumberjack. Ari scanned him critically. "Are we not going to dinner?"

"We are," Luna told him.

Ari looked stiff in his charcoal dress shirt with a dark gray tie and jacket. Luna wore a similar blouse to the one she'd met him in. She had it in several styles. When she found something she thought she looked good in, she bought it in every variation so she could just be done shopping. Sunny wore a black cotton blouse and black jeans: standard Sunny attire.

Soon after introductions, Sunny tugged Luna into the kitchen. "Excuse us," Sunny called to the men. "I wanna show Luna a new recipe."

On the other side of the swinging door, Sunny said, "Oh, no."

"No?" Luna asked.

"No," Sunny repeated. She was emphatic.

"Why no?" Luna asked. She knew Sunny was talking about Ari.

"Did you see those shoes?"

Luna recalled that they were slip-ons. "European style?" she asked.

Sunny snorted. "European, my ass. They're like the ones my dad wears. Orthopedic trying to be stylish. You got yourself an old man. Get out, fast."

They went back to the living room, where Ari questioned The Coconut about the music video playing on-screen.

"What is its purpose?" Ari asked.

"Music," The Coconut responded.

"But music is to listen to. Why do you watch it?"

The Coconut shrugged.

"Ready, guys?" Luna asked.

The men stood. The Coconut nestled up to Sunny and touched her arm. She swatted his hand. "We talked about that," she said.

The Coconut hung his head.

The dogs barked from the bedroom. "I couldn't let them out with a strange man here," Sunny explained. "They can barely deal with Layne and Phil."

"I had a monkey once," Ari told Sunny. "When I lived in Africa. It was quite an exciting life. I lived in a large tree house."

"You don't say." She glanced down at his shoes. "I'm thinking that was a long time ago."

"It was, actually."

On the way out, Sunny whispered in Luna's ear, "Yeah, before he went geriatric."

NINETEEN

THEY DROVE TO Mother Murphy's.

"I do not like Irish cuisine," Ari said on the way over. "It is so peasant-like, and it revolves around alcohol."

"You don't drink?" asked Sunny.

"Of course I drink," Ari answered, disdain in his voice. "But I do not drink the things the Irish drink." He shuddered.

"Not to worry," said Luna. "This is an Italian restaurant. The wife is Italian, and she makes the meals. The husband, despite his peasant, Irish ways, learned how to make pizza and he does that up front."

"Pizza. Cool," said the Coconut.

"Really?" asked Sunny.

"I do not like much Italian food either," said Ari.

"This place has a large menu, with a lot of healthy choices," said Luna. *It's just dinner. Deal with it.*

When they got out of the car, Sunny pulled Luna to the side. "We would've had a better time if we'd gone out without these tools."

Luna glanced at Ari, who trudged toward the entrance in his old man shoes. *Why doesn't he pick his feet up?*

Then there was The Coconut, who walked blandly and blankly alongside Ari. *Is there a thought in his head?*

"You're right," she told Sunny.

Inside, Ari glared at the multitude of Christmas decorations dangling in every conceivable area. It was like Santa's sleigh had exploded in

Mother Murphy's. Garlands, candy canes, ornaments… . There was even a tree with presents underneath it, as well has stockings hanging, each with the name of a Mother Murphy's employee scrawled in glittery red script.

"Look," Luna said, pointing at the tiny plastic menorah perched on a table next to the large tree.

Ari scowled. "This is an insult."

It *was* a pretty cheesy token.

"They bring matzoh to the table on request," said Sunny. "I was with some ladies from the library a couple of years ago, and one of them was Jewish, so she asked for it."

"Matzoh is for Passover," Ari snarled.

"Oops," said Sunny. "My bad."

They sat at a table for four. "*Not* very stylish," said Ari, brandishing the paper napkin from his setting.

"Similar to your shoes," Sunny said under her breath.

"What's that?"

"I said I like your shoes," said Sunny.

"Thank you." He glanced down to admire his footwear. "You cannot find these here. I bought them in Vienna."

"You don't say. Too bad, I would've bought Phil a pair," Sunny said.

This might've alarmed a young man who was many years away from geriatrics, but fortunately The Coconut went with pretty much anything without comment.

Sunny took another good look at the shoes. "They sure don't scream 'Fifth Avenue,'" she told Ari.

Ari read the menu thoroughly, tsking all the way.

"They have cous-cous," offered Luna.

He glared at her. "In an establishment such as this, I would doubt its authenticity."

"What's wrong with this place?"

"The furniture is plastic and metal, not wood or tiled."

"So the décor isn't upscale," Luna said. "Can't they have tacky tables and still have real cous-cous?"

"Unlikely," said Ari.

"Nothing worse than imitation cous-cous," muttered Sunny.

"What?"

"I said it's a shame about the cous-cous. There's just no couth in the world anymore."

Ari made a long sigh of sacrifice. "I will make do," he said. "That is the Israeli way."

"I could picture you schlepping through the desert," whispered Sunny.

"What?"

"I said, 'Your people have been through so much.'"

He bowed his head. "It is true."

This is going to be a long dinner, thought Luna. Thank God Ari's hearing wasn't super sharp.

They sat in a silence punctuated by conversation from other tables and rhythmic crunching. The Coconut gnawed on a sesame-coated breadstick.

After the third or fourth child whined loud enough for them to hear, Ari asked why there were children in the restaurant.

"They must've slipped out of their restraints at home and followed their parents here," Sunny said. "Just be glad the shackles on *my* kids held."

"May I take your order?" the waitress mercifully asked at that moment, before Sunny could carry the absurdity any further, because she certainly would've.

"Could I get a glass of pinot grigio right away?" Luna asked. Alcohol was the only way to get through this meal.

"I'll take a Bud, no glass," said Sunny.

"That is crass," said Ari.

"Exactly," said Sunny.

After the waitress returned with the wine and Budweiser, Luna ordered the filet of sole. Sunny ordered eggplant parmesan. The Coconut ordered two slices and a Guiness. Ari requested Gumppoldskirchen to drink, but the waitress thought he'd sneezed and blessed him. Then he tried to order Viennese lager, but they only had German. He made a sour face and ordered a glass of merlot. Having settled on his drink, he went on to quiz the waitress about the ingredients in various dishes before finally acquiescing to the balsamic chicken when she assured him it contained no peppers, carrots or corn, all of which gave him indigestion. Having secured the order at last, the waitress made a run for the kitchen.

"And no paprika," Ari called to her fleeing back.

"Why no paprika?" Luna asked.

"It inflames arthritis."

"You have arthritis?"

"I do not think so, but why take the chance?"

"Old man," Sunny coughed into her napkin.

"What?" asked Ari.

"I said, 'Here's to friends!'" Sunny raised her Bud. "Cheers!"

She winked at Luna, who couldn't help laughing.

The rest of the meal proceeded better, at least for Luna, who was enjoying her wine.

Sunny and Luna laughed about things the way they always did, while Ari stared like he was from a foreign country, which he was. (Actually, he was from two of them.)

Apparently Luna and Sunny's offbeat humor failed to cross borders.

The Coconut didn't have much to say either. It was almost like he wasn't there.

Sunny wouldn't have missed him, until it came time to pay their half of the check.

The group ordered dessert. Easy for The Coconut, who chose vanilla ice cream. Easy for Luna, who ordered crème brulee, which was like flan with a crust. Easy for Sunny, who opted for another Bud so she wouldn't kill her buzz. Not so easy for Ari, who asked for Weichselstrudel.

"We don't even have apple strudel," said the waitress.

"Then I will have Sachertorte."

"Not here, you won't," said the waitress, who was getting a bit snappish.

"Can't you have a normal dessert?" asked Sunny. She took a swig of beer.

"I am trying, but they do not have any," Ari said.

Fortunately, they did have espresso, which appeased him. Thank God it came with a lemon rind.

After they dropped off Sunny and The Coconut, Ari asked if he could come back to Luna's house.

"Ah, no." she told him. There was no way she was letting this critic take a gander at her housekeeping. Nor did she feel like explaining the lack of furniture.

"Then you will accompany me to Manhattan?"

"No, Ari… I have to pick my kids up in the morning. I'll see you next weekend."

She dropped him off at the train. He trudged onboard.

And why do you want to see him again? Jiminy asked. *As your friend Sunny pointed out, he's a tool.*

Luna sighed. "I guess it's because the beginning was good."

Newsflash: Beginnings are always good. It takes a while to find out what a person's really like.

"The beginning with Glen wasn't good."

He was an extreme. Leave it to you to find the one person who couldn't contain his craziness through the first date, said Jiminy. *Man, I have my work cut out with you.*

"No one's asking you to stick around."

You're asking, he said. *You just don't know it.*

Luna kept her word and met Ari at his not-real apartment the following Saturday night. She was a bit tense, because she figured he'd want to have sex. She wanted to have it too, of course… but it'd been such a long time. What if she'd forgotten how?

Last night on the phone she'd told Sunny, "I feel like a virgin again."

Sunny said, "Imagine the possibilities!" She was still against Ari, his dinner demeanor had done nothing to sway her. But she told Luna he would be good practice. "Get on top and go for it!" she told her.

Luna said, "I have my period. It came early." Or maybe not. She never kept track of it, and was always surprised when it arrived.

Sunny had said, "Hey, virgins bleed."

Ari and Luna started kissing and moved their way into the bedroom. He got her pants off, then started for the underwear.

"You might want to get a towel," she told him.

"Why?"

"It's that time of the month."

He pushed her away like she was rabid. "Why would you do this?"

"I didn't 'do' it. My period came, that's all."

"Did you not know?"

"It's irregular." At least, she thought it was.

He let out a sound that was close to a growl. "It is disgusting."

"It's nature," she said. Back at NYU, she'd studied human sexuality. Her professor had emphasized that a woman's period was the most dynamic phase in her cycle, when she was filled with kinetic energy. The ancient Romans were in tune with this. Warriors were allowed to return to their wives during menstruation. Obviously, they kept better track of dates than Luna.

She didn't share any of this with Ari. He didn't seem open to a history lesson, or anything else. He sat on the bed with an erect posture, his back facing her. But apparently only his posture was erect.

She asked, "So… Can we at least cuddle?"

Really? asked Jiminy.

I just wanted to be touched again… to be held, she told him.

Get a grip, said Jiminy. *This guy can't give you what you're looking for.*

"No," Ari said. His voice was cold, his accent sharp. "I have to work in the morning. I need my rest."

"Tomorrow is Sunday," she said.

"I work every day. That is part of my service to my clients." He clicked off the lamp and climbed into bed, pulling up the covers. Luna stood in the dark, but she felt illuminated.

Jiminy was right.

Ari didn't deserve her "virginity"—or her at all.

And as for cuddling with him… .

It would've been fruitless anyway, like snuggling up to a sword.

Luna was surprisingly calm. She felt around the floor for her clothes, put them on, and left.

TWENTY

IT WAS CHRISTMAS Eve. As a present to herself, Luna decided to join Match.com. They charged a fee. That had to attract a better class of people than Glen, right?

Did you get what you paid for?

She had plenty of time to fill out her profile. The kids were with Nick at Uncle Alfonso's house. Nick's family always had a big Christmas Eve celebration, with all kinds of fried seafood. "A WOP tradition," Loreena had said on the phone earlier. As if Luna didn't know. Loreena reminded her every year.

"Northern Italians don't eat deep-fried foods," Loreena said. "You just don't care what your kids ingest, do you?"

Luna was not taking the bait. However, she didn't have it in her to hang up on her mother, who after all did have a sick husband to deal with, so she sat there with the receiver perched on her shoulder, saying nothing until Loreena finally switched gears. "Do you want to go out for Christmas dinner tomorrow with the kids? Since you no longer have any obligations… ."

"We're going to Antoinette's," Luna told her mother. Antoinette was Nick's younger sister. She had a wild Puerto Rican husband, three children and two grandchildren. Nick's mom lived with them, and she was cooking her usual ziti and ham Christmas dinner.

"Why would you subject yourself to pasta when you're getting divorced?" At least she didn't get started about the civilized people of the north eating rice.

"For the kids' sake. They like being with family, especially their cousins. I won't take that away, and I'm going because I want to be with them."

The night the boys had slept over at Nick's, they'd asked him if their family was still going to have Christmas dinner together. He'd answered, "Of course!"

He'd probably had no intention of including Luna. Someone who took furniture from her house and dumped what he didn't want on the floor would seem to have little sentiment in his heart for her. Nevertheless, she was now included.

"Well, I would be glad to get away from those people and have some peace and quiet if I were you," Loreena said.

"By the way, you're still invited," Luna told her.

"Oh, okay. I'll bring pignoli cookies."

"No kidding." Loreena always brought pignoli cookies. They were her favorite.

"By the way, they're going to move your father to the new place the day after tomorrow."

"That's his birthday."

"Oh, you remembered."

That remark could've been taken in so many ways, most of them bad. But Luna simply said, "Yes, I did." The day after Christmas was an apropos birthday for Lenny, who had always arrived late—if ever.

"Will you come help me settle him in?"

Luna bit her lip. It was not an easy thing to consider. But she had to help her mom out on this one. "Sure. I think I'll bring the kids, too."

"That would be nice." Another ambiguous comment. Loreena's tone sounded sarcastic, but there was always the chance she didn't mean it to be.

"Gotta go, mom. See you tomorrow. Merry Christmas."

Luna had hung up and finished her wrapping. She thought about calling Aunt Zelda, but nixed the idea because there was a concert on the barge and Zelda wouldn't be able to talk. Besides, she'd become a Zen Buddhist at age fifty, so the birth of Christ meant even less to her than it did to Luna.

Luna's wrapping was done. The gifts were in the closet. The gingerbread houses the kids had made earlier rested on the kitchen table. The tree waited patiently in the living room for the gifts she'd put under it later, after the kids had returned home and gone to bed.

The stockings were hung by the chimney, just like in the poem. Red with fuzzy white tops and their names in green glitter: "Mom", "Ben" and "Dylan." The kids had already put gifts in her stocking, purchased at their school holiday fair. But they were keeping their "main" gifts for her in their rooms.

She filled out her Match.com profile and sipped wine, looking forward to the promise of Christmas morning like she was a little kid again. She had every reason to believe she'd wake up to matches in her inbox.

After all, she'd been good.

The kids woke up practically at the crack of dawn. Dylan still fervently believed in Santa. Luna was pretty sure Ben was onto the truth, but he went along with the charade.

Luna headed down the steps with her video camera. The boys knew the routine: they waited until she was recording to rush down the steps. "Ooo, Santa ate his cookies," Dylan exclaimed, pointing at the plate of crumbs on the coffee table.

"Of course he did, honey," Luna said. "And his reindeer ate their carrots."

There were bits of carrots scattered around the table, since reindeer did not possess the etiquette of eating over a plate.

In all the years she'd been doing this, the boys had never questioned how the reindeer got in the house. She'd had an answer prepared: Santa came down the chimney and let them in the front door.

This was the magic of Christmas, taking that leap of faith.

The boys ripped into their presents while Luna recorded footage. When they'd finished, Luna made her traditional holiday breakfast of French toast, with some help. The boys each cracked two eggs into a bowl. After they fished out the few stray bits of shell, Ben poured the milk and Dylan sprinkled in the cinnamon. Then all three chefs beat the ingredients together, and the boys took turns dunking the bread.

By this time, Luna was sorely in need of coffee.

Then it was time for Luna to open her gifts, which the boys proudly brought from upstairs. "We picked them out ourselves, Mommy!" Dylan said. He'd gotten her two bouquets of colored, wooden tulips. "One was not enough," he told her. She loved them, because they were from Dylan and because they would never die.

Ben had selected jewelry: purple beads on a silver necklace and bracelet. She loved them, because they from Ben and because they were purple.

Her stocking contained purple pens and pencils and mini notebooks. And at the bottom was a set of three rocks with the moon hand-painted on them. "That's because of your name, mom," Ben explained.

It was one of those happy moments in a life you wish you could just hold on to forever, or at least store it in a jar somewhere so you could take it out and relive it at will.

They all hugged. Then the kids went to play their new video games and wait for Nick to come. He'd been working the morning shift at the deli for triple-time.

Luna decided to check her in-box.

There was one match.

She was excited until she saw the guy was twenty-seven.

Twenty-seven?

What would they have in common?

Some match. *How could a twenty-seven-year-old be interested in me?*

If this was how it was gonna be, she might have to ask for her money back.

He was cute, that was for sure. She read his profile. He liked music. *Who doesn't like music?* He liked taking walks and holding hands. *Yeah, right. That's what they all say.*

In his personal statement he said he was "looking for someone understanding who believes in change and second chances." *Terrific. Probably a bank robber or bomb maker or something.*

Disgusted, Luna left the site.

Christmas dinner at Antoinette's was relatively uneventful. Luna was surprised by everyone's good behavior. Not one argument erupted at the table, and more importantly, no one confronted her for tossing Nick.

Did they *know* she'd tossed Nick? Sal was on Nick's father's side, long estranged from Nick's mom since the time he got caught kissing another woman in the meat freezer of the deli the family once owned. Nick's mom had been bringing him a surprise dinner, but she's the one who got a shocker. Nick's dad and his girlfriend were forced to chill when Nick's mom slammed the door and bolted them in, not bothering to call her brother-in-law to let them out for a couple of hours. Even after getting the deep freeze, Nick's old-school dad wanted to stay married. But Nick's mom didn't.

No extended Marones were present tonight. These days, it took a death in the family to get the two sides together, glaring at each other from opposite sides of the viewing room.

And what did it matter if they knew? This bunch was famous for playing "pretend nothing's wrong." Their family pastime was burying their heads in the sand. The last acknowledged unpleasantness had been Nick's parents' divorce and that was thirty years ago. Only alcohol brought truths to the surface but tonight nobody was drinking. A Christmas miracle.

Loreena showed up with her box of pignoli cookies while everyone was chomping their way through a giant cannoli and a variety of other pastries. "Oh, am I late?" she asked.

"About two hours," said Luna.

"Do you have any food left?"

Luna made her mother a plate of ham scraps and the ziti left in the corners of the pan. Loreena claimed to despise pasta, yet she ate every year at these dinners. This was the one place where she never asked for risotto.

To take her mind off of her mother's incongruities (a thought process which, if unchecked, inevitably spiraled into reflections about her childhood which were better left unlooked at) Luna went into the bathroom, took out her phone and checked her Match.com account again, hoping for another match.

There were a couple more guys, but they looked like complete rogues.

There was also a message from the twenty-seven year old!

He said he'd read her profile, and she sounded so wonderful.

He hoped he would be so lucky that she would give him a shot.

He confessed the reason why he needed a second chance: he was an ex-crack addict, and he lived in a halfway house.

Luna knew she should've hit 'delete' and been done with him, but his note was sweet.

And he was interested in her!

Oy vey, said Jiminy.

"Can't you be an optimist?"

Only when there's a possibility of something working out well, he answered.

"Oh, zip it. You said yourself, you can't see the future."

A blind mute could see how this will end.

Luna decided to talk to Sunny.

She gave her a call. "I have a Match dot com dilemma."

"Come on over! We need to exchange presents anyway."

"Cool."

Pretty much everyone who didn't live at the house had left, though Nick was still hanging with a couple of cousins who had stopped in for dessert, and Loreena lurked in the background picking at cannoli crumbs and pignoli nuts. Nick's mom would sit and have tea with her later, once she was done putting the food away. Luna knew this from past years. She never understood why Loreena would want to be in the company of the mother of the man she'd focused much of her considerable rage and hatred on for considerable years, or for that matter, why Loreena would want to come to his family's house at all. But it was one of many questions that could never be answered.

Luna wished her mother and everyone else a Merry Christmas

and then said goodbye to the boys in one of their cousin's rooms for a sleepover. She kissed them and told them she'd see them in the morning.

Sunny opened the door beaming. "I gave myself the best gift ever!"

"What's that?"

Sunny poured Luna some eggnog, but Luna shook her head when Sunny offered to spike it. She had to drive home. "I broke up with Phil!"

"That's not nice, doing that on Christmas."

"How many times do I have to repeat myself? I'm not nice!" Sunny took a big slug of her eggnog. "I didn't plan it, but he did something so ridiculously stupid I just couldn't look at him anymore."

"What was it?"

"I sent him out to pick up Cool Whip for my pudding pie, and he came back with Miracle Whip."

"That *is* ridiculously stupid. Did he have an explanation?"

"He said they didn't have any Cool Whip, and he didn't want to come back empty-handed." She gave Luna a deep look. "Can you imagine using Miracle Whip on a pie?"

Luna shuddered.

"It's a miracle I didn't whip *him*," said Sunny.

"I understand your frustration," Luna said. "But I'm still surprised. You're missing out on his presents!" Sunny loved gifts and Phil gave thoughtful ones. He'd given Sunny a bunch of stuff last year, including Alice in Chains CDs to replace the ones she'd worn out and Sponge Bob pajamas.

Sunny said, "There's no greater present than his absence. Now I can watch my *Fellowship of the Ring* DVD in peace. It'll be a silent night tonight. Bless the Baby Jesus, amen."

Luna didn't know how Sunny could be so callous. Part of her was appalled, and part of her was envious. Could she ever treat someone with such indifference?

"Speaking of Baby Jesus, did you hear they stole him from the manger again?" Sunny asked.

Every year, a nativity scene was displayed outside town hall. The little bed remained empty until Christmas Eve, when Baby Jesus was placed inside at some late hour. And every year for as far back as Luna could remember Baby Jesus vanished sometime after twilight on Christmas Day. If you didn't get a look at him in the sunlight, you'd missed your chance.

"I thought they put in a security camera at the top of the manger."

"They did, but someone came from behind and cut the cord," Sunny told her.

"Do you think it's the same person every year?"

"Probably it's their Christmas tradition. Some people sing carols, some bake cookies, and some snatch Baby Jesus."

"What could they possibly do with all those Baby Jesuses?"

"Damned if I know. They must have a closet full by now."

Luna said, "I always wondered, didn't Joseph get upset that his wife got pregnant by someone else?"

"Good point," said Sunny. "And why didn't he have sex with his own wife? He must've had some set of blue balls."

Sunny and Luna exchanged gifts. Sunny unwrapped her first gift, which was a clear plastic egg filled with pearly-white goo. The packaging said, *Angel Snot: The gift of precious fluids from Heaven's Messengers.* "I love it! I'm going to keep it on my desk at work," she told Luna.

She unwrapped her second gift: *What Would Jesus Wear? Jesus dress-up magnets.*

"Just when I thought the snot could not be topped," said Sunny.

"Now Christ can really be in pajamas," said Luna.

Sunny got Luna a Shakespeare action figure with removable quill. "Cool! I'll prop him up when I'm writing," she said.

"I figured you would," said Sunny.

Sunny's second gift was a metal *It's Happy Bunny* sign. It read: *Sucky losers not allowed.*

"To hang outside your front door," said Sunny.

"I hope this works," said Luna.

"It will if you enforce it," said Sunny. "Anyway, tell me about your dating dilemma. What's wrong with the dude? Erectile dysfunction? Ditch him! Anything else, we can work with."

"He's kind of young. Twenty-seven."

"Young can be good. They've got stamina."

"You said The Coconut wasn't good," Luna reminded her.

"That had nothing to do with his age. It was his type: 'B' for boring. Youth doesn't trump dull."

"Do you think addicts can change?"

"Uh-oh. Why do you ask that?"

"He said he used to be addicted to crack."

"How long ago is 'used to be?'"

"I'm not sure, but he lives in a halfway house right now. He's got a ten PM curfew."

"Well… I have a few friends that got off drugs. They were serious about it. But it's tough. Look at Sal. He's cracked back out a few times, and his mother's wallet has paid the price. Then again, Sal's an idiot. Is this guy an idiot?"

"Doesn't seem so." Luna was confused. "So… Should I give him the benefit of the doubt?"

"I think you have a bigger problem."

"What's that?"

"If he has a ten PM lock-down, how are you ever gonna have sex?"

Luna shrugged. "We'll deal with that later, if necessary. Right now, I just have to be sure this is a good thing for me."

"He told you all this drug stuff in his email?"

Luna nodded.

Sunny whistled. "Well, everything's out in the open. It can't get worse than crack. Unless, of course, he's a mass murderer or something. But what are the odds on his being a junkie *and* a serial killer?"

"So what should I do?"

"Is he cute?"

"He is."

"Then meet him. At least you'll have some eye candy. But watch your purse."

TWENTY-ONE

WHEN SHE WOKE up, Luna called Alex. He had a beautiful voice filled with good humor. The kind of tone you could feel wrapping itself around you and keeping you warm.

Luna decided to go for it.

But before she could meet the ex-addict who could be her potential boyfriend, she had to again face the ex-addict who was her father.

What are you hoping to get out of seeing your father again? Jiminy asked.

"Nothing."

Good. Then you won't be disappointed.

Luna picked up the kids and took them to Build-A-Bear at the mall to make the grandpa they barely knew a birthday/get well teddy bear. They chose a tan one, and Dylan insisted on dressing him in an old-time train engineer's outfit: blue pin-striped overalls, a matching cap and a bandana.

"Grandpa doesn't work on a railroad," Ben told Dylan. "You don't even know if he likes trains."

"I don't care," Dylan responded. And Ben didn't care enough to argue.

Just as well, because the store didn't have any heroin-addict accessories for the bears. Not a syringe or a tourniquet in sight.

Lenny was parked by the window in his new room at Blue Skies Extended Care Facility when they walked in. Well, a wheelchair was an improvement over a bed, Luna thought.

The room was not an improvement over the hospital. It looked like a hospital room, with two beds and curtains to separate them. The other bed was unoccupied, just as it had been in the hospital. Was it better to be alone in this sterile room, or to have the company of a person one didn't know or choose? Would it make a difference to her father, anyway?

"H-hi!" Lenny exclaimed when he saw Luna and her boys.

Ben said, "Happy birthday, Grandpa!"

Dylan added, "We made you a bear!"

"Th-thanks!"

Luna wondered if her dad knew what they were talking about and if he even knew who the boys were. They'd grown so much… and he'd never really *known* them.

Dylan propped the bear on Lenny's lap. Lenny touched it with his left hand, rubbing his finger on its soft paw. Inadvertently, he triggered the squeezable mechanism that Dylan had also insisted on including: a high-pitched voice that squealed, "I love you!"

"H-holy s-shit!" Lenny exlaimed. Oh God. Were more curses to follow?

"You shouldn't swear, grandpa," Ben said.

"O-okay," Lenny agreed. His hand rested on the paw, but mercifully the voice didn't go off again. He was wearing blue button-down pajamas that looked new. The right side of his face drooped, and his glasses were askew, but hey, they were on. Could he read anything and comprehend it? His hair was greasy-looking, but at least it was combed back. Someone attended to him.

"How do you feel, Dad?" Luna asked him.

"O-okay."

"Do you want some cookies?" She'd brought a plate.

"O-okay." But when she extended the tray he just stared at it blankly and continued touching the paw.

"I don't think he understands you, Mom," Ben said.

"I'll give him a test," Luna said. "Dad, do you want to go to Mars?"

"O-okay," Lenny said.

The boys laughed, but Luna didn't find it funny at all. There seemed to be no point in this conversation with her father, which kind of mimicked their entire relationship.

There was a little jade Buddha on the windowsill. Clearly Aunt Zelda had been there. Too bad she'd missed her, but she'd see her on New Year's Eve. Luna and the boys always rang in the New Year on the East River.

"Where's Mom?" Luna asked Lenny.

Lenny shrugged. "F-fuck…"

The boys looked uncomfortable. Why had Lenny cursed? Was he trying to say, "Fuck if I know?" Or was it just some random utterance?

She didn't want the boys to hear any more cursing, and she didn't think this visit was doing them any good in general. "Grandpa's been through a lot," Luna told them. "We should let him rest."

"But we didn't bring him a birthday cake," Dylan said. "Everyone needs a birthday cake."

"Nonna will bring him one," Luna said. There was about a one-in-fifty chance of that, but whatever. Luna couldn't take anymore right now. She couldn't be in charge of making sure Lenny got his cake. It was all she could do to take care of her sons.

Lenny had left her in Loreena's hands while she was little, and she had managed to get by. Now it was his turn.

It wasn't a case of revenge, or turning the tables with a vengeance. It was just how things had turned out.

Who are you trying to convince? Jiminy asked.

"Tell Grandpa goodbye, boys," Luna said, trying to tune Jiminy out.

"Bye-bye, Grandpa!" The boys both exclaimed, and they waved. Probably they were intimidated by the wheelchair, and didn't want to go closer, especially to kiss a man they barely knew. Luna wouldn't push them. She didn't kiss him either.

Lenny was staring at them through those slanted glasses, and touching that teddy bear. He didn't say anything.

"Happy birthday, Dad," she told him.

"H-happy b-birthday," he parroted back, as they left the antiseptic-smelling room.

Luna took the kids to a pizza place down the block from Blue Skies. It was just the thing to shift their collective mood. And even though it was December, they had Italian ices for dessert.

Luna dropped the boys at Sunny's for yet another sleep-over. "Thanks again," Luna told her.

"They're no trouble at all. As a matter of fact, my kids are less trouble when your kids are here, because they all entertain each other. Ka-chow!"

"I'll call you after the date and check in."

"Have fun, Chicky. You deserve it."

"Thanks." She almost believed that.

Luna and Alex met at Dojo in Greenwich Village, a restaurant both cheap *and* good. The smell of spices and beer filled the air and some kind of funky instrumental music was playing. They were seated at the very last table in the rear, facing the beige wall.

Luna joked, "Nobody puts Baby in the corner."

He laughed, but Luna wondered if he'd ever heard of *Dirty Dancing*. He was so damn young.

She didn't ask.

Alex was *very* cute. He looked like a younger Johnny Depp.

Luna felt all tingly.

Simmer down, said Jiminy. *Remember, this guy lives in a halfway house. Can the metaphor be any more obvious?*

Well, I can meet him halfway.

Cute. I can see you're determined to learn the hard way on this one.

I definitely want it hard.

That's gross.

Thank goodness Alex was oblivious to Luna's inner dialogue. He reached across the table and put his hand on her arm. "You're very beautiful," he said.

Wow.

"Thank you," she said, for lack of a better line. Who could think of witty banter with all these vibes rushing between them? Luna felt like an electrical circuit, all charged up. Fortunately, Alex moved his hand off her arm to take a sip of water. Now she could (hopefully) concentrate on their conversation without jumping his bones.

Here are some of the things Luna learned about Alex:

STATS ON ALEX

Name: Alexander Polaner (no relation to the jelly-makers.)

Ethnic Background: Czechoslovakian

Marital Status: Divorced (Yes, in his young life he'd already managed to take the plunge, even in his drug haze. A girl from Uganda had convinced him she loved him, but somehow stopped once she'd obtained her green card.)

Children: None.

Hair: Sandy brown.

Eyes: Intense green.

Occupation: Attending a computer school in the Empire State Building, and working an office temp job.

Favorite Physical Activities: Basketball, hockey (not that he'd played either in a while.)

Other likes: Trying to find himself (See also: Religion). Staying clean. Pickles. *Star Wars* (though what Luna thought of as the "original" *Star Wars* movie, he thought of as *Episode Four: A New Hope*).

Dislikes: He said he didn't have any. He was a pretty mellow fellow.

Body: Nothing to complain about! He had the body of a healthy twenty-seven-year-old. You would never know he'd been all cracked out.

Religion: Raised Protestant, he was studying different religions now, trying to decide which one he liked.

Favorite Writers: Melody Beattie & Louise Hay.

Favorite Dessert: Cheesecake.

Favorite Expression: "One day at a time." (Luna knew this as a TV show. She'd grown up watching its reruns.)

They finished dinner. Luna excused herself and headed to the ladies' room. Part of her worried, *What if he leaves?* She peed at breakneck speed and returned to the table.

He was still there.

She said, "Oh good, you didn't run away."

He looked at her intently, with those amazing eyes. "No, never," he said.

After dinner, they walked down St. Mark's Place. It was chilly, but not as bad as late December could be. There was the bright mix of lights from buildings, street vendors and passing cars, the soft orange glow of cigarettes in passing hands, the brash sounds of honking horns and music competing from stores and vehicles, the murmuring chit-chat from sidewalk traffic they dodged.

And there was them.

He slipped her his hand.

She accepted it, sliding her fingers around his.

It felt like they were alone now… like everything else in this big, noisy city had vanished.

They got in her van and he kissed her.

Kissing Alex was even better than the snuggle party kissing because it wasn't random. Alex wanted *her*, not just any stranger.

You ***are*** *strangers*, said Jiminy. *Don't you get it? Just because you had dinner together doesn't make you a couple. Slow down, Luna.*

But that tingling was back, and it was all that mattered. Luna was falling hard.

Good grief, said Jiminy.

All good make-out sessions must come to an end, and this evening had a curfew. They realized they were cutting it close when they defogged the windows and the clock, which said "9:46."

Less than fifteen minutes to make it to his halfway house in Spanish Harlem.

"What happens if you're late?" she asked him as she sped uptown, dodging lights and taxis. This was like Cinderella's mad dash home, except now Prince Charming was in jeopardy.

"They lock me out and report me to my probation officer."

"Do you have somewhere to go in case?"

"Ummm... no."

Poor Prince Charming...

Some prince, said Jiminy. *Honestly, Luna. Wake up! This isn't a fairy tale.*

Luna was too busy pressing her pedal and honking to pay Jiminy any attention. They had to make it to the halfway house on time... She couldn't leave Alex on the street. Nor could she bring him home.

She got stuck at a red light and cursed.

"Don't worry. We'll get there," Alex told her. He rubbed her leg. She was acutely aware of the scent of him.

"You're a gem," he said. "You know that?"

As a matter of fact, she didn't.

But it was certainly nice to hear, even in that panicked moment.

They made it with a minute to spare, literally.

She pulled up to the curb. "Go, go!" she urged him.

He said, "I have to get my kiss goodnight."

And he did.

Luna coasted on that kiss until she hit the RFK Bridge. Then, she wanted conversation. "Did you have something to say, Jiminy?"

No reply. That was Jiminy all right.

"Petulant little bastard," she said, hoping to draw him out.

But the silence remained, so she turned the radio on.

TWENTY-TWO

A COUPLE OF nights later, Luna and Alex went to see the holiday lights on the houses in Dyker Heights, Brooklyn. Two weeks before Christmas she and her boys had gone with Sunny, Sunny's kids and the Coconut. Little did The Coconut know it was to be his last outing with Sunny, who hadn't even invited him. For weeks she'd stealthily avoided mentioning the upcoming excursion in The Coconut's presence, but Phoebe slipped and told him the day before they were going to go, and so there he was. He'd worn an absurd woolen hat with pointed top.

"You look like an elf," Sunny informed him.

He'd shrugged and tried to link his arm around hers, but she'd elbowed him away.

Despite Sunny and The Coconut's less than romantic foray, Luna had longed for a man to share the glistening lights with.

And now, she had one!

Luna and Alex held hands and walked close because it was cold, and because they wanted to.

The streets glowed from the light the houses cast on them. It was as if Luna and Alex had been transported to a magical land. But Luna could not relax completely into the twinkling setting, even though she was getting something she desperately wanted—just like in a fairy tale. She felt an uneasiness tugging at her, pulling her back into her real world of worry.

Alex had such an air of peace, despite all he'd been through. She asked how this was possible.

Alex smiled. "It's easy," Alex said. "You just gotta surrender."

What did that mean? "Could you explain that? What am I supposed to surrender to?"

The shining lights seemed like beacons. They framed Alex's face. "To God… or whatever you want to call your higher power. Call it Fred if it makes you happy."

Luna wasn't sure she was comfortable with *any* higher power, even one named Fred. "And what does it mean to surrender?"

"It's like this leap of faith. You put yourself in his hands. That's the best way I can describe it. All religions have it. When people are raised with something, they don't question it. If you come to it later in life, it's harder."

She looked at him dubiously. Her religious training had consisted of a couple of trips to the Zendo with Aunt Zelda, which were confusing. Most of the time no one spoke, and when they chanted, it was in Japanese. "How do you know so much about this?"

"It's the main thing they teach you in addiction recovery."

"And surrendering helped you?"

"Helped me?" He laughed. "Luna, it saved my life."

Alex was safely stowed in Spanish Harlem, and Luna was on her dock in the dark. Sitting on one of the built-in benches, Luna thought about surrender.

She was terrified.

She'd learned early that she was no one's priority. Even Aunt Zelda had something more important.

People had always let her down.

What if God rejected her?

Moonlight reflected in the rippling water. It was calm out here at midnight. The wildlife slept somewhere in the marsh, probably the fish were resting, too. Why couldn't she quell the uneasiness she felt? Why couldn't she just 'be?'

There was an order in the universe, she knew it.

It was obvious in nature.

And something had led her this far.

She'd gone down the path kicking and screaming. Look how long it took her to ditch Nick!

What would it be like to let go of her guard and her fears and her doubts and just live?

She decided to take the leap.

She watched the water for a while, trying to relax. Prepare. What was the protocol on surrendering, anyway?

How do I start? What's the opening line?

She'd never prayed before.

No, that wasn't true. It came back to her now. Once, years ago, she had:

Zelda had blurted the truth about Lenny's addiction, and Luna had wished fervently that her father wouldn't come home. She became obsessed with the fear of seeing him shoot up. She'd heard about this – apparently rock stars did heroin a lot. If she saw her father do it she might literally lose her mind.

That's when she thought of God. But it wasn't easy to pray, given what little she knew about him.

STATS ON GOD:

Name: God

Ethnic Background: Unknown.

Marital status: Unknown.

Children: Depends on whom you ask.

Body: Unknown. In paintings he was wearing a long, flowing robe. Even if the artists did know what God looked like, his physique was impossible to pinpoint.

Hair: Silver and flowing.

Occupation: Watching over the world. He lived in the clouds and apparently could see everyone at once. This might seem far-fetched, but after all, Luna had believed in Santa Claus until Miriam, a girl in her second-grade class, felt the need to enlighten her. Under questioning, Loreena had admitted she'd lied. Still, it might be possible to see everyone at once. Annoying, but possible. This guy God must've had lots of patience and concentration skills.

Other likes: Goodness, honesty.

Dislikes: Sinning.

Religion: Depends on whom you ask.

Favorite writers: Unknown.

Favorite dessert: Unknown.

Favorite expression: Depends on whom you ask.

All these blanks made it hard for Luna to muster up faith.

The other kids in school went to churches and temples. They accepted everything they were taught, believed the biblical tales they read. But how could all the religions be right when they contradicted each other? As for the Bible, Luna didn't like those stories. Some of them were downright upsetting. Like Noah's Ark. She couldn't stop thinking about all the innocent animals and children who drowned.

If there was a guy up there watching, why was he leaving her all alone down here with a mom who got off work at five but wasn't home until ten (on an early night), even though it was a fifteen-minute ride? And why had God given her a dad who sucked? Her aunt was no help with the Zen stuff, which was too confusing. Zelda didn't want to discuss God at all, so Luna was left to sort this out herself.

She figured: Why *not* talk to God?

There was nobody else.

"Please, God, don't let me see the needle," she begged once, leaning into her patchwork quilt with her eyes closed. "Please..."

That would be too much.

On the rare days when her father was there, she'd prayed.

Creaking up the right side of the stairs toward the bedrooms—the left side was piled with papers, boxes and shoes—she'd chanted it. Turning the corner midway, facing the banister fully loaded with Mom's wardrobe draped over, she'd pleaded: "Please don't let me see my father shooting up. Amen."

And maybe God had listened, or maybe it was luck, but she never had.

She stared at the water now, reflecting on that day all those years ago when she'd prayed not to see her father's needle. It was the one thing she'd ever asked of God.

He hadn't let her down.

She'd never reconciled whether it was God or dumb luck that protected her from that sight. Part of her felt it easier not to believe in God—because he was such an uncertainty, and who needed more of that?

But part of her—the deepest part—did believe. If not in the God everyone else subscribed to, at least in the force that had spared her when she'd begged.

She called on that part now, and she let it speak.

"Thank you," she said.

The words felt right.

She got on her knees on the dock's wood surface and she pushed her palms into grain. "Thank you," she said again.

She wanted to say "Thank you, God," but somehow the "God" part wouldn't come out.

Really? asked Jiminy. *Is it that much of a struggle? You did it when you were a child. Why not now?*

"I guess… because so much has happened. It's just harder to say the word now."

You're a writer, Luna. You should know: What's in a name?

"You're right." She was tired of fighting the current, of bucking the system. It was a lot of resistance for no payoff. "I'll bow to tradition this once."

Atta girl!

"Thank you, God." Luna closed her eyes and took a deep breath. When she opened them, the egret she often watched was plodding along the shoreline. An odd sight—she'd never seen any birds at night, other than the occasional duck.

She said, "Thank you for my kids, and my books, and my friends."

She stared at the unhurried, deliberate bird. In the daylight she'd observed that he walked slower than she typed. "But I'm also in pain. I don't know why or what to do. Will you help me?"

Did the bird just glance at her?

She took another breath and exhaled. She hadn't breathed like that since Lamaze. She said, "I surrender."

The bird was so serene. Almost mystical—a beaked maharishi.

She said, "Just let me know what you want me to do. I'm listening."

The egret took off. *Whoa!* All these years, and she'd never known he could fly. *Why didn't he ever do it before?* She watched him stretching his white wings through the air. Grace.

She wanted to soar.

She said, "Amen."

TWENTY-THREE

LUNA AND ALEX were in a midtown hotel. Not a cheap place—and she'd paid for it.

It was either that, or never have sex.

He couldn't afford the hotel. He could barely pay for dinner. If she'd waited for him to save up, it would've been months.

He'd lied to the halfway house people about where he was staying. He was allowed to sleep out on weekends, as long as it was with family or a close friend. Apparently sex in a hotel room—or anywhere—was frowned upon. His friend Juan was covering for him.

Luna's emotions spanned a broad spectrum. Nervous – she was going to have sex! Thrilled – she was going to have sex! Curious – was she going to have good sex?

She sat behind Alex on the bed, raising his Marilyn Manson T-shirt over his head and off of him. He had a great body—so muscular, so young.

Then she noticed a tattoo over his left shoulder blade that said "N.A."

He sighed and said, "We need to talk."

"Do you want to tell me who 'N.A.' is?" she asked.

"What?"

"Right here, on your back." She traced the letters with her finger.

"Oh—no. That's not a person." He laughed.

"What is it?"

"It stands for Narcotics Anonymous."

Now she laughed. "Wow. I didn't see that one coming." *Talk about devotion.* Luna didn't understand the compulsion to indelibly inscribe things into one's skin. She rubbed his shoulders and asked, "So what do you want to talk about?"

He sighed again and said, "I'm not ready to be monogamous."

He slumped his head, looking down at his Conversed feet and the burgundy carpet.

He said, "I haven't really had a chance to date since I've been clean. I want to explore my options."

They sat quiet for a moment, him staring at leather and fibers, her staring at blue ink and skin.

Maybe "N.A." really stood for "not available."

Jiminy was right.

As always, said Jiminy. *Things would go a lot better if you'd just accept that.*

"Is that okay?" Alex asked.

What could she say? The room was nonrefundable.

It would've been nice to know this beforehand.

You can still walk away, Luna, Jiminy said. *You could wait for someone whole.*

I can't, Jiminy. I'm in too deep. And besides, what whole person would want me?

If you feel that way, make yourself whole.

Yeah, right.

"I guess it'll have to be okay," she told Alex.

The foreplay was incredible. Alex touched and kissed her all over, trying so hard to please. He brought her up to the edge so many times... Then he entered her.

I'm having sex!

It felt so amazing... She'd never known it could be like this.

She was sooo close to climaxing...

But then an image jumped into her head: She pictured Alex inside another woman.

"Oh, God," she cried out—but not in a good way.

She burst into tears.

He pulled out of her. "What is it? Did I hurt you?" He grabbed her up in his arms.

"No..." It was all she could say at the moment.

She breathed in and out, trying to calm down, focusing on his safe, strong scent.

And then she fell asleep.

The next morning they were lying in bed. Alex had found The Game Show Network and put on an old episode of *The Price Is Right*, which was filling in all the silence Luna and Alex couldn't. Contestant number one was spinning the wheel in the showcase showdown. *Beep, beep, beep, beep.* The wheel went round and round, finally halting at five cents. "I take it you'll spin again," said Bob Barker.

"Yes, I will, Bob," contestant number one squeaked out excitedly.

"So how many people are you sleeping with, anyway?" Luna asked Alex.

He said, "Uh... one."

He laughed. He did that a lot.

"You," he said, in case clarification was needed. Or perhaps to clarify that what they'd done the night before counted as sex, even though neither of them had climaxed.

That's something, she thought.

What, she didn't know.

She said, "That's good."

The woman on TV spun again. *Beep, beep, beep, beep*. She got one dollar. What were the odds? The audience moaned, the music even groaned, she covered her eyes in dismay... she was over. "I'm sorry," Bob said in his sad voice. He hugged her. "Buh-Bye."

It did make Luna feel better, being Alex's only lover.

Luna started to touch him, then lumped up a handful of the lime green comforter in her palm instead. She wanted to have sex with him—good, complete sex—but first she had her own clarifying to do. "Listen, I gotta tell you..."

The room smelled of some cheesy air freshener, on top of PineSol, and it was a bit nauseating. Then again, she was overdue for coffee. Everything seemed sickening when she needed caffeine.

He was waiting. She forced herself to continue. "If you start sleeping with other women besides me, eventually I'm not going to be able to take it. I'll probably hang in for a little while, but then… no."

Beep, beep, beep, beep. Lots of wild cheers! Someone else hit one dollar and won a cash bonus!

"What about just one other woman?" he asked.

"Still no."

The curtains were brown and thick, double-layered to block out the sun. As if the sun's beams could manage to find their way through all the tall buildings and billboards. There were so many signs outside! They were near the entrance to the Midtown Tunnel, where advertisers had a captive audience every rush hour.

It was a pretty dismal scene inside and out of this $300-a-night hotel, and the room was small too.

That was Manhattan for you.

Next time they'd try Queens.

He asked, "What about if we found someone to join us, like a permanent *ménage à trois?*"

"This isn't a movie, Alex. It's hard enough for two people to get along." She didn't know if she could share him, even in those circumstances.

The bed was pretty ugly. Some kind of Formica. With the requisite ugly lamps perched on matching Formica nightstands on either side. *God, hotels suck.*

The no-flavor pseudo-coffee packets they put in the rooms in those pre-measured filters sucked the most. No way could she drink that brownish water.

She had to go seek her fix soon.

"We could try," he said. He touched her cheek. It felt good, despite her withdrawal symptoms.

"You'd stay then, right?" he asked.

She said, "I guess." But she wasn't sure at all.

He kissed her neck.

On the TV, Bob congratulated the woman who had won the showcase showdown spot. Upbeat music played. He said, "Now stay tuned for the next half of our show, where lots more prizes are up for grabs… *if* the price is right!"

Alex kissed lower… and lower.

I'm his only lover… I'm his only lover… Luna recited to herself.

Her mantra was working, blocking those sad thoughts.

Alex straddled her. "Do you want to take up where we…"

"Yes!"

It didn't take long to reach the edge again.

"Come on, baby," said Alex. "I know you're close."

"Oh, God!" she screamed—this time, in the good way.

She was there.

"I feel like a stud," Alex said afterwards.

"You *are* a stud," Luna said. "That was incredible." There was so much more Luna could've said, but one thing far outweighed the rest. "I need coffee so bad."

Alex went out and got her a large Styrofoam cup from a diner on the corner.

After she'd drunk it, they made love again in a heated hurry because check-out time had come.

New Year's Eve arrived. Luna, Ben and Dylan were onboard the barge.

Aunt Zelda had long ago accepted that Ben and Dylan were too fidgety to sit in the audience, so she assigned them to refreshment duties. Ben cut chunks of havarti for intermission, while Dylan laid out neat rows of crackers and artfully layered Oreos into a basket. It always startled Luna to see Dylan do something neatly, when his half of the bedroom looked like an homage to Oscar Madison. The first time she'd asked him: How was it that he could be so ordered here, while at home he dropped everything he owned, wore and finished eating straight onto the floor?

His face got very serious. "This is my *job*, Mommy," he told her.

And so it was, because Aunt Zelda paid each boy twenty dollars—a small fortune!

Luna also pitched in (though she worked gratis), filling up glasses of champagne. She wouldn't let Aunt Zelda help, because Zelda deserved to sit and enjoy the fruits of her labor. Not only the task of building the barge, but the painstaking effort she made at every concert including this one, greeting each of her guests with a resounding, "Welcome home!" as they checked in for their seats.

Luna and the kids worked all through the first half of the program, trying to make sure they were prepared for the intermission rush. The sold-out crowd was especially demanding on nights like this, when the higher admission cost included refreshments.

The champagne was the most challenging. It took so long for the bubbles to subside! If Luna tried to rush the process, the cups invariably ran over. So she had to make sure plenty were already poured. This required tiptoeing to the deck with her bottles to pop their corks, so the bursts wouldn't disturb the concert.

Luna thought about Alex. But the work kept her so busy that she couldn't obsess too much about him.

Intermission came, and the clamoring crowd was served. Many of the patrons found Ben and Dylan cute enough to tip, which made her children even happier. When the music started up for the second half, they cleaned up as much as they could without making noise. Then they sat in the galley, scarfing Oreos and playing tic-tac-toe on the back of a program.

Luna sat next to Aunt Zelda in the rear of the room, which was only twenty rows from the stage. She tried to concentrate. Again her mind roamed to Alex. Was he safely stowed at the halfway house like he'd told her? Or was he seeing someone else?

She pushed these destructive thoughts from her mind and let the music in. Bach's Brandenburg concertos. Favorites of hers. Twelve musicians vigorously performed their parts—an unusually large group for the stage, which sagged a bit under the extra weight. There was a harpsichord—a rare treat. Luna loved that special, unmistakable tinny pitch. It was welcoming, like an instrumental version of Aunt Zelda.

At the end of the concert the musicians played *Auld Lang Syne*. The song sounded so sad, especially when the whole audience chimed in. For a moment Luna felt like crying, even though she had no idea what "auld lang syne" even meant. Then Aunt Zelda sashayed up the aisle, jumped on the stage, raised her glass and toasted her audience. "Thanks for another great year of sharing in the music with us!" she proclaimed. "I built this barge for you, and I'm so very pleased you like it!" She blew the audience kisses and they cheered. Aunt Zelda sure could work a crowd.

Afterwards, everyone climbed the metal stairs to the roof.

The countdown began. Everyone chanted: "Five, four, three, two, one… Happy New Year!!!"

Luna hugged her children fiercely and kissed them as fireworks lit up the Manhattan skyline.

"Oh, dearhearts, it makes my heart sing that you are all here!" Aunt Zelda told them.

The kids were looking ragged. It was late, and they were coming down from their Oreo high.

Luna's cell rang. Was it Alex?

No.

It was Nick.

The call was for the boys, she knew, and she passed her phone to Ben.

Why hadn't she heard from Alex?

He could easily have lied to the people at the halfway house and spent the night with someone else.

She'd told him she didn't want to know, and she didn't.

But just the possibility hurt.

The kids finished wishing their dad a happy new year, and Dylan handed Luna the phone. The fireworks were over and the sky was dark except for a few random stars, but Manhattan still shone bright. The building lights never went out.

"Can we go home, Mommy?" Dylan asked.

"Sure, Baby," she answered. "Just give me a minute."

She dialed Alex.

"All circuits are busy. Please try your call again later," a computerized voice said. *Yeesh. So much for technology.*

Then her phone rang. It was Alex!

"Hey," he said. "I know you're with your kids, and I'm supposed to be in bed already, but I wanted to wish you a happy new year."

"Same here," she told him. The kids were eyeing her, and she couldn't say more. Inside, she bubbled. Her wish had come true! Her prince had called!

"I can't wait to see you this weekend," he said. She heard a grin in his voice.

"Same here," she said again. Maybe he could sense her grin, too.

She drove home with her foot light on the gas, because inside she was floating.

TWENTY-FOUR

JANUARY WAS TRADITIONALLY bleak.

No more lights, no more mistletoe, certainly no more presents. The first month of the year was one long hangover.

It was almost unanimously agreed: All January offered was cold weather and gray. On line at the post office, pushing carts through Stop and Shop, on the ellipticals at the gym: Everywhere, voices complained.

Luna was perhaps the one person who didn't succumb to January's dreariness. While others trudged, scowled and moped, she glowed.

Her life was coming together.

True, Alex lived in a half-way house, was practically broke and recovering from crack addiction, and wanted to find a third party to join them in bed. But he'd move out of Spanish Harlem eventually and find his own place, and then she could stop shelling out for hotels. He'd graduate from his computer school and earn better money, and then he'd be able to pay for more than cheap dinners at Dojo. He'd stay clean; his one year anniversary at N.A. had just passed. And as for that third party joining them, he hadn't mentioned it since that first night together.

Maybe he'd forgotten or changed his mind.

Maybe she was enough for him.

She drove into Manhattan to pick Alex up at the Empire State Building. She was bearing gifts: two Star Wars toy figures from Burger King and a jar of Ba-Tampte Half Sour Pickles, which he'd mentioned he loved.

Traffic slowed as soon as Luna hit the light at the end of the Midtown Tunnel. Horns blared around her, but Luna didn't care about a little vehicular congestion. She had an afternoon tryst with Alex ahead of her.

Her mini-van crawled to Thirty-Fourth and Fifth. She spotted Alex in his brown trench coat standing by the curb. He climbed in, sticking his briefcase against the bag with the figurines and the pickles. The paper made a crumpling sound. He slammed the door a little too hard. "Hey," he said. No smile, no kiss hello.

She leaned over to kiss him, but he pulled back.

"What's wrong?" she asked.

He said, "We need to talk."

"Did I do something?"

"No, no, not at all. Can you just find some place to park?"

She couldn't.

They were sandwiched in a honking, practically standing-still jam.

They had to stay on Thirty-Fourth for several blocks because no turns were allowed.

This might be hell on earth, thought Luna. The bus in front of them farted blasts of black exhaust at her windshield. The cabdriver behind blasted his horn long and hatefully, as though she'd chosen to plant herself in front of him. *Beeeeeep!*

Staring at the bus, she asked, "Do you not want to sleep with me anymore?"

There was a beaming, extraordinarily busty woman pictured in the ad for Georgi vodka on the back of the bus. She wouldn't be so happy if she had to breathe all this bus soot seeping through the crevices in her van. Or if her boyfriend was about to break up with her.

Alex wouldn't let Luna kiss him. Could it be any clearer? "Do you not want to sleep with me anymore?" she questioned him.

"I wouldn't say that," he replied.

She asked, "Then what would you say?"

He would say nothing. He pursed his lips and shifted his feet uncomfortably on the floor. They inched their way to Eighth Avenue, panic and sadness swelling in her because she knew it was over.

Finally she turned on Eighth and pulled over in front of a Dunkin' Donuts.

This hadn't been worth the trip.

Couldn't Alex have just called her to end it?

She killed the engine and waited for the kill. He was having a hard time making eye contact with her. "Of course I want to keep sleeping with you… But… ."

She hated buts.

Buts sucked ass.

Behind him, Dunkin' Donuts beckoned. But she didn't want coffee. She felt so queasy, she might throw up from one sip.

"But what?" she asked.

He stared out the windshield, straight ahead. He couldn't glance at her, not even peripherally. "But I promised someone else that I wouldn't."

There it was.

Just like that, he was dumping her.

Just like that, she couldn't even touch him anymore.

"You met someone else?" *Duh.*

He nodded.

"Have you slept with her?"

"No."

Next time you should hold out! Jiminy yelled. Easy for him say. He wasn't the one deprived for three years.

Who needed this scolding little voice anyway?

"Fuck you," she whispered to Jiminy.

"What?" asked Alex.

"Not you," she told him, though it applied to him as well.

I'll be going now, said Jiminy. *Maybe this will teach you something.*

I don't think I can take any more lessons, Luna thought. "So I guess the *ménage à trois* plan's a bust?" she asked Alex. Her voice cracked. She was going to cry, dammit. *I'm trapped in my car with a man I can't touch and I'm about to bawl.*

"She's not interested in something like that."

Like I am. "How old is she?"

"Twenty-five."

Ouch. "Do you prefer her because I'm so much older than you?" she asked.

"No."

"Is she prettier?"

"No."

Her stomach was doing flip-flops. Wouldn't vomiting be attractive right now. "Then... What is it?"

He looked at her, finally. But now she didn't want him to. It was the thing that finally made the tears come.

He said, "All I can tell you is I see gold in this girl."

You said I was a gem. But Luna didn't have the guts to say it.

She turned away from him, looking at the traffic passing by. Mostly yellow and black taxis. Blurred by tears, they looked like swarming yellowjackets. *I was so stupid to think this could ever work out,* she thought. "Get out, just get out of my car and leave me alone," she told him, still facing away. The dumb tears wouldn't stop... . *Can I have some dignity, at least?*

Her cold skin prickling with goose bumps. Each breath from her stuffed nose made a nasally, snorty sound as it struggled through snot. She was such a mess and wanted him gone. *Why* wouldn't he go?

"I want to stay with you until you calm down," he said.

She could barely catch her breath from all the heaving sobs. What the fuck good was this asshole who wouldn't touch her?

She pressed up against her plastic van door, curled up as far from him as she could get. The pop-up door lock jabbed her arm fat. She'd been overweight for awhile after childbirth. Working out had slimmed her down, but that dangling skin never went away. *He doesn't want me because my arms jiggle like the thing that hangs from a turkey's neck.*

She moved off the lock and took hold of the steering wheel, running her fingers over the indentations. Somehow, she managed to verbalize the question: "What did this girl do to get you to be monogamous?"

He said, "She asked."

Luna calmed herself finally, counting passing cars like sheep.

She really wanted to go to sleep. Crying was exhausting. She was sticky and hot and mucousy, and she could feel the blotchy patches on her face.

The van was silent, until Alex unclicked his seatbelt and stretched. He knocked into his briefcase, which rustled the paper bag. *Oh yeah, the gifts*, she remembered. He sure didn't deserve them. But she'd brought them, and it'd be worse if she held onto them. "That bag's for you," she told him.

"For me?"

"Yeah."

He reached down and crinkled paper, taking out Luke Skywalker and Yoda.

"I saw them on a Burger King commercial and picked them up for you," Luna said.

"Gee, thanks."

Then he pulled out the jar of half sours. "Wow. . . . I haven't had these in so long. . . ."

"I know." They'd discussed how there were no kosher pickles in Spanish Harlem.

He stared into the glass. What was so captivating about crammed kirbys? Maybe they'd triggered an epiphany! *Does he realize how wonderful I am? That this twenty-five- year-old would never match up in thoughtfulness – never bring him brined cucumbers?*

He said, "I want to tell you a secret."

So much for awakenings. She wiped at the snot dripping down her nose and waited for whatever came next. What more could he possibly reveal?

He said, "I don't just go to N.A. I'm also a sex addict."

What did that mean? And why was he less willing to share that information than the fact that he had been addicted to crack? And most of all, why did the pickles prompt this admission? Was it their phallic, swollen thickness?

But who cared anyway? None of this would matter once he stepped out of her van and her life. "Okay. Whatever."

"That's another reason why I think it's good to be with this other girl. Because she'll keep me in line."

Ridiculous reasoning. Twenty-seven-year-old ex-crackhead logic.

"And I'm a love addict, too," he added.

Now that was just silly. "Like in that Robert Palmer song?"

"Who?"

"Never mind."

"The meetings are for both sex and love addicts," he said.

"That's crazy," she said. But then, so was this conversation.

"Why?"

"The sex addicts will eat the love addicts alive," Luna said.

Alex laughed. *Glad I provided you with amusement while you broke up with me,* Luna thought.

Paper crinkled again as Alex put his gifts away. Was he finally hitting the pavement?

"Hope everything works out for you," she said, trying to speed up the goodbyes. This needed to be done. Her prince was abandoning her, and she just wanted to get out of there before her van turned into a pumpkin.

"Don't say that," he said.

I can say whatever I want, she thought. *You did.* "What's the problem with wishing you well?"

"Those words are so final. But this isn't goodbye! We'll still be friends," he said. "They teach us that in SLAA—Sex and Love Addicts Anonymous. Men and women can be platonic."

It was a little late for platonic.

And anyway, he'd just broken her heart.

What kind of a friend did that?

But Luna was too exhausted to talk any further, so she just waved her hand vaguely. He could relate to noncommittal. After all, that's what he'd been.

Thank the Lord Jesus he finally opened the door and stepped out on the sidewalk with his briefcase, toys and pickles. And then, in a final contradiction, he said, "Goodbye, Luna."

"Buh-bye."

Her flippant, Bob Barkeresque farewell was lost on Alex. He closed the door and waved. Her tires squealed as she peeled away—not the easiest feat in a minivan.

Luna drove up and down streets for a long time, trying to find her path home through the garment district. Lost in an urban maze, even though she'd been through the area a million times.

Caught in January's frigid snare, after all.

"Why? *Why?*" she called out. To God, and to Jiminy.

Neither answered.

After zigzagging aimlessly for a while, she pulled over next to a long row of garbage bags, stacked like sand sacks on the front lines. The sidewalks were deserted, the buildings were secured. This part of Manhattan shut down at five p.m.

Staring at the mounds of waste, Luna swallowed a last lump of mucus and called Sunny.

"Done with your boy-toy for the night already?" Sunny asked.

"He dumped me," Luna said. The garbage smelled rancid. *No, wait...* the smell was too strong to be outside. There was half a cup of coffee in her holder. She poked her nose through the plastic lid and sniffed. *Ewwww.*

"Oh, shit. I'm sorry," said Sunny. "What happened?"

"He met someone else."

"Well, those crackheads are flighty," said Sunny. "At least he got you off."

"Ex-crackheads," said Luna. She was going to hurl the coffee out of her door when a rat poked its head around one of the garbage bags. *Ick!* She felt like she should park somewhere else, but lacked the energy to move. It wasn't like he could get inside the van anyway, right? "I loved him."

"Really?"

"I guess." Keeping her eye on the rat, who'd gnawed into a bag and was chomping away at something, Luna thought about it. "I don't even know what love is. When I'm with a guy, I see the best in him. I probably would've given Glen a chance if he wasn't so scary. And Ari—if he'd slept with me, I would've stayed with him. I'm a wreck."

"You just don't know what you want yet. You should take a breather."

"I know I don't want to be alone." The rat turned toward her. For a moment they locked eyes. His nose twitched. "I've spent so much time by myself already."

She started the engine and jerked the van away, phone perched in her ear. She was on that rat's radar now, and she didn't like it.

Sunny couldn't relate. "I *love* to be alone. I can't stand people! But I do like what the male species has to offer, at times—like a certain organ. . . ."

"Could we not talk about that?" Luna missed Alex's organ already. She'd never see it again.

She parked half a block up, past the piles. "It's not fair. I'm doing the God thing. It's just hard to read the signs."

"N.A. was a pretty clear sign," said Sunny. "And so was tongueless mullet man."

Luna started crying again. Sunny said, "Alex was right about one thing."

"Yeah? What?"

"You *are* a gem. I just wish you could see that."

Luna stared out at the desolate charcoal buildings lining the street. "I wish I could, too."

TWENTY-FIVE

LUNA WAS STARING at the blinking cursor on her blank Microsoft Word document when Sunny called. "What's up?" Sunny asked.

"Nothing."

"That's what you've said every day for the past week. You have to snap out of this. Have you written anything?"

"Nope." The last thing she'd typed was "sex addicts" and "love addicts" and "meetings" into Google's search engine. "Sex and Love Addicts Anonymous" had popped up. Go figure. It sounded ludicrous, but there it was.

"What's going through your mind?"

"I'm thinking of getting a dog."

"Do my smelly girls attract you that much?"

"I just want unconditional love."

"Yeah, well, you'll also get poop to scoop, chewed shoes and probably fleas."

"You should do an ad for the ASPCA."

"I'm just saying… . You're not a dog person."

"How do you know?"

"Because if you were, you would've already had a dog sometime in your life."

"I had a puppy when I was in second grade."

"And?"

"My mom brought it back to the pound because I couldn't house train it. I'd walk it, then it would pee on the rug."

"See?"

"I was in second grade! I didn't know how to teach a dog anything."

"And you do now?"

"Well… no."

"'Nuff said."

"I'm going back to my cursor. Only a couple of more hours before the kids get home." Luna had been pulling it together to help Ben and Dylan with their homework. Serving dinner was out of the question. The Chinese place was doing big business with her.

"Hold on, I called you for a reason. Why don't you come out with me and Lois tomorrow night? She invited me to a bar."

"Lois the butch lesbian who skydives?"

"Yes, but this won't involve lesbianism or skydiving. Lois is a good time!"

"She barely speaks."

"Well, she's a quiet good time. We have fun."

Luna looked down and scanned her clothing. It hadn't changed in three days. "Can I wear my pajamas?"

"You probably could. But I thought maybe you'd want to look good in case there's some cute guys there."

"Cute guys?" That perked Luna a bit. "What kind of a thing is this?"

"It's hard to describe. They call it Burning Man Happy Hour."

"Sounds insane, dangerous and drunken."

"It's basically a weekly reunion for people who go to Burning Man every year."

"And Burning Man is… ?"

"Insane, dangerous and drunken. Well, I guess there isn't that much danger, except for sunburn or winding up on a government watch list for being a complete wacko. Basically, about 40,000 people go live in the desert for a week."

"Oh my God. Why?"

"They build a community and create tribes based on the things they like. Lois skydives. Some people do sculpture, some paint, some have sex all day. Whatever. One tribe just gets drunk and stays that way—that would totally be my group. Not that I'd go to the desert, for fuck's sake. Anyway, there's practically no rules. It's scorched anarchy."

"Sounds awful!"

"Obviously these people are freaks. Which will make them very entertaining." Sunny loved observing foolishness.

"And you think I should date one of these burning men?"

"No. I just thought that suggestion might get you out of the house and your pj's."

"Oh, fine."

The next night, Luna met Sunny and Lois by the Long Island Rail Road information booth in Penn Station. Sunny and Lois worked together, so they'd come in on a different line.

"You look good, Chicky!" Sunny told Luna.

"Thanks." It was a funny thing, but showering, getting dressed and putting on some nice jeans and a blouse did make Luna feel better—or at least, less of a blown-off loser.

"Hey," she said to Lois, who looked extra butch in a wife-beater, exposed under her green half-buttoned men's dress shirt, collar up. The bottom half of her outfit consisted of faded jeans and Nike black-and green-suede skateboarding sneakers. She dressed like Ben, except she'd topped off the outfit with a green plaid Balboa hat. Ben didn't do hats.

Lois nodded.

Sunny was wearing her usual black-from-head-to-toe ensemble: black blouse, black dress pants, black platform shoes.

"Who's ready to party?" Sunny asked.

Neither Luna nor Lois responded. "Woo-hoo! Good times!" said Sunny. "Take me to the vodka, please," she told Lois.

Lois was tall, with a Herman Munster gait. She barreled through the rush-hour crowd, leading Luna and Sunny through the subway's turnstiles against the spilling stream of commuters. It was lucky Luna had a

Metrocard already, because Lois didn't pause to ask. Luna paid for Sunny, too.

"Criminy, this girl would be a good foot soldier," Sunny huffed from the rear. Lois was already at the top of the stairs, on the platform. The train roared in. Luna and Sunny hustled. Lois was holding the sliding doors open with her butt. They got in and circled around a pole to hang on.

The train roared downtown. To shift her mind away from herself, Luna tried to make conversation with Lois. "So what's the story with Burning Man? Why do so many people go?"

"It's fun."

"And the groups have themes?"

"Yup."

"Lois told me some of the tribes are really funny. Like, one of them huddles under a sheet and just wanders around stumbling into things," said Sunny.

"You don't say." Luna wondered how Sunny had gotten that much information out of Lois.

Lois nodded.

"So what's the basic premise of the whole thing?"

"Freedom," said Lois.

"Aha," Luna said, for lack of anything else. Trekking into the desert sounded way more cumbersome than liberating.

The train rumbled on. Sunny was no longer paying attention to the conversation. She'd become too distracted with people-watching. Luna never looked at fellow subway passengers. You never knew who would take offense.

After a few moments Lois added, "And no judgments."

"Huh." Luna didn't feel particularly judged anywhere, except for the criticism she heaped on herself.

The lights in the car flickered.

"And, no worries," said Lois.

"Sounds like Never-Never Land," Luna said.

Lois shrugged.

The train pulled into their station.

The bar was on Delancey Street, near the Williamsburg Bridge. Heading in, Luna felt a ping of panic. She didn't do well in social situations under normal circumstances, not really getting the art of mingling. *What do you say to people?* Tonight she was feeling especially awkward.

"Don't worry, Chicky," Sunny said. "You don't have to talk to anyone but us. Unless you want to." It was like she was psychic! "But maybe you'll feel braver after a drink or two."

A possibility, albeit slim.

Luna and Sunny followed Lois up to the second floor. It was a dim faux paradise of leafy trees and winding vines with wooden benches lining the walls and a retractable roof overhead.

As it was winter, the roof remained closed. The scent of chicken and ribs floated through the room from an indoor grill by the rear window. Koi swam around a pond in the center of the room. People who must have been the Burners huddled in clusters, laughing easily as alcohol slid down their throats.

The place was packed. Good thing music wasn't playing—the noise level was already high. They leaned against the wall's shellacked wood paneling, sipping and chatting. Well, Luna and Sunny were talking. Lois mostly nodded. Sunny was scanning the eclectic crowd, looking for odd behavior. So far there was nothing outlandish, though one girl with cotton candy colored hair was hula-hooping with a tropical drink in her hand.

Then a guy in fatigues and combat boots walked by with a ferret in his hands.

Sunny gave Luna the thumbs up. She was having fun now.

Luna wasn't exactly having fun, but she was in her first decent mood since Alex had left. It was good to be among other adults, even if they were odd. And the wine was helping.

A dark-haired, dark-skinned guy in leather pants sidled up to the end of the bar. He caught Luna's eye and she felt the zap of mutual attraction. *Wow! I never thought I'd feel that again!* He headed right for her. "My name is Memphis," he said in a Barry White deep voice. He drank an amber, antiseptic-smelling alcohol, clinking ice as he brought the glass to his lips. His race wasn't clear—he could've been Hispanic, black or a blend of a couple of things. His eyes had an exotic Asian shape to them. They protruded slightly.

Luna introduced herself, Sunny and Lois. "Pleased to meet you," he said, presumably to all of them, but focusing on Luna. She was grateful for her pinot grigio. She'd never be able to handle talking to a guy without it. Being dumped gave her zero confidence, but the wine was counter-balancing.

Memphis talked about Columbia University (his alma mater), his experiences at Burning Man and his addiction to nicotine. All this he directed at Luna, with an occasional nod at Sunny and Lois. It was obvious even to Luna: he was flirting with her. It took her a while and the rest of her wine to feel comfortable with his attention. Her second wine helped even more, and she found herself excited and flattered. But this was a guy who schlepped out to the desert to escape society's rules, and then met with people weekly to relive the experience.

Was he really relationship material?

Memphis headed downstairs for a cigarette, promising to be right back.

"So what do you think of him?" Luna asked Sunny.

"He has bulging eyeballs," Sunny said.

Lois laughed. Who knew she was capable of laughter?

"Jeez, can you ever say something nice?" Luna asked Sunny.

"Occasionally," said Sunny, draining her martini. "But there's nothing nice to say about those popping peepers."

"So you think I should blow him off?"

"I didn't say that, I just said what I noticed. Other than his freak-show eyes, he seems like a nice enough guy."

Lois nodded.

Memphis came back reeking of tobacco, for which he apologized. "I know… disgusting habit." He hung his head in mock shame.

"No big deal, my ex-husband smoked," said Luna.

"Glad you said 'ex'," Memphis said with a sly smile.

Lois noticed some of her skydiving friends across the room. She took Sunny over to meet them.

"I thought they'd never leave," Memphis said in his gritty voice. "Not that I don't like your friends, but I like you more." He smiled largely now.

"I like you, too," Luna said.

Memphis bought Luna another drink and they chatted. He loved literature, so that was a good starting point. Here are some other things he told her:

STATS ON MEMPHIS

Name: Memphis Fang.

Ethnic Background: African American and Chinese.

Marital Status: Single

Children: None.

Body: Thin and wiry.

Hair: Black, slicked back with gel.

Occupation: Corporate recruiter.

Favorite Physical Activities: Running, swimming, racquetball.

Other Likes: Reading, experimental cooking, celebrating the full moon (he belonged to a group that howled at the moon in unison, which he felt cleared his kinetic energy), heading to the desert once a year to express himself.

Dislikes: Whining, pushiness, self-centeredness.

Religion: Raised a Buddhist, but didn't follow it these days.

Favorite Writers: Hemingway, Faulkner, Joyce.

Favorite Dessert: Torte.

Favorite Expression: An Einstein quote – "A man should look for what is, and not for what he thinks should be."

After four pinots, Luna was feeling lightheaded. Memphis took her out for some air. He had a Marlboro perched on his lips, but then their eyes locked like they did earlier. He dropped the cigarette to the pavement, grabbed her up and kissed her. He tasted like that antiseptic alcohol he'd been drinking (apparently so potent it washed out the tobacco), but she didn't even mind. His kiss was sweeping and strong, like the twirling mops at a car wash. *Whew! What a rush.*

They stood there for awhile with their tongues locked, until a chill ran down Luna's body and Memphis led her back inside.

"So, what tribe do you belong to at Burning Man?" she asked him when they were back on a bench upstairs.

"BDSM," he said.

"Um, hate to sound ignorant but—What does that mean?

"It's a complex acronym."

"Oh." Like that explained it.

"It's derived from the terms bondage and discipline, dominance and submission, sadism and masochism."

Holy cannoli! She suddenly felt a long way from suburbia, where stuff like this was never, ever mentioned.

"Does that bother you?" he asked.

"I… I don't know." She stared at him, trying to reconcile his words with her mind. "It scares me."

"Don't be afraid." His smile looked large and freaky. She was buzzing, *and* bugging. He continued, "We don't have to do that. Either way, it's fine."

"Are you the… sadist?"

"I play the dominant role, yes."

"Oh, wow." She'd seen pictures of women hanging from ceilings, bound in so many ropes they looked like cocooned grasshoppers about to be consumed. *God, are there any normal men out there?* "Does sex even happen during all this bondage stuff?" How could anyone penetrate those restraints?

"Oh, it happens," he answered. "But like I said, no pressure. We don't have to do that."

He kissed her again. Damn, they really had chemistry. Too bad he wanted to torture her.

TWENTY-SIX

LUNA AND SUNNY took the train to Freeport to get Sunny's car. Lois had gone home with one of her skydiving friends—a lipstick lesbian named Francesca.

"So?" Sunny asked, when the train was out of the tunnel and they could hear each other without straining.

"So what?"

"So I saw you making out with Mr. Eyeballs."

"And?"

"What did he have to say for himself?"

Luna thought briefly about not telling Sunny. This was embarrassing. No, wrong word. This was mortifying. But Sunny was her best friend, and that was that. "He said he's into BDSM."

"Which is..."

"Basically, it's bondage."

"He wants to *torture* you?" Sunny's voice was a little loud for the Long Island Rail Road. Luckily, the car was nearly empty.

"I don't think 'torture' is quite the word—" though it was the word she'd thought of, too.

"My ass it isn't. Have you seen those women in hoods? They look pretty tortured to me."

"You can't see their faces."

"Exactly! Is this what you're looking for in a relationship: pain and dehumanization?"

"I wouldn't wear a hood. I'm claustrophobic."

"Christ on a sesame seed bun with a pickle! Why would you want to have anything to do with this man's insanity at all?"

Luna stared out the window, at the darkness blurring by. The train's hum seemed disturbingly loud tonight. "Is it so different, to be a physical submissive instead of an emotional one?"

"You are fucked up. You *really* need a shrink."

"I told you, I'm done with shrinks."

"Then talk to your chiropractor."

"I know what he'd say. He says the same thing anytime I ask advice."

"Which is?"

"He says nothing is right or wrong. The question is whether it makes me happy."

"And does it?"

"I don't know."

"That's why you're fucked up!"

"Can't I just play it by ear?"

"With a man like that? No."

"He said we don't have to do that stuff."

"Yeah, right. You don't have to do it yet. Next thing you know, you'll be in a ratchet gag."

"Ratchet gag?"

"I saw one on-line once. You can get the picture from the name. *Not* an attractive look."

Bing! The train announcement system sounded. "This station is Jamaica," said a computerized voice

They were halfway there.

The lights flashed on and off, the way they always did at Jamaica.

Sunny sighed. "When you go out with him, make sure you keep your cell phone on."

Three nights later, Luna was buzzed in and clomping her way up to Memphis's fourth-floor walk-up. *You should listen to Sunny*, Jiminy chimed in. *She cares about you.*

Jiminy picked the darndest times to chat. "Sometimes I think *you* don't care about me."

Why's that?

"You come, you go. Anytime you want."

Hey, it's not like I'm getting paid for this. Do you have a specific complaint?

"I called out to you that night Alex dumped me. You didn't answer."

After the way you spoke to me earlier? You're lucky I didn't ditch you for good. Trust me, Luna. I care.

She stopped climbing and sighed. "So, you think it's wrong for me to get involved with Memphis?"

It's wrong for you.

She thought for a moment about this. Then she started to climb again.

Suit yourself, said Jiminy. *But then, you always do.*

Just to be clear, Luna told Memphis she wouldn't wear a hood. "On this, I'm firm."

"I've never used a hood," he said. They were standing in his entranceway, just past his front door. She didn't want to come in any further without this clarification. "And I told you, we don't have to do that at all."

But like a vampire who just couldn't stop himself, he reached for her neck all the same.

Sunny was right. Could the ratchet gag be far away?

She blocked his hand. "Not tonight, not this first time."

He said, "That's fine." He put his hand on her waist.

She asked, "Can you please be tender?"

"I can." But his voice was so not tender.

He smelled of alcohol and tobacco, like last time. Yet his skin had another scent—a nice, fruity one. His soap, no doubt. She was surprised Memphis didn't use Axe.

He pulled her blouse over her head and unhooked her bra. There was something so sexy about him making this bold move right there in his foyer. never used a hood," he said.

He squeezed her nipples. Not that hard, but still… it was a squeeze.

It felt good. *That's worrisome*, she thought. But then she stopped thinking because the feeling of his fingers was soooo amazing.

She came on the spot, just standing there. She almost fell over from the intensity, but he held her up.

"I need to fuck you now," he said.

He took her hand, led her into the bedroom. She was still quivering from her orgasm, and shaking for more. He stopped at the bathroom for a condom but never let go of her hand.

The sex wasn't tender, but Luna didn't care.

He pounded her so hard and she came and came. *"Ohhhh Godddd!"*

It was surreal, like she was swimming in an impressionist's ocean. Her consciousness drifted in and out, up and down… the only constant was pleasure.

She felt his hand on her neck, not pressing, but there.

Letting her know he was in control.

For a few drifting moments it didn't matter if he wanted to dominate her. If that was the admission price to this heaven, so be it. She just kept releasing, releasing, releasing….

Then she was back. Fully aware. Memphis was staring, studying her with those widened, stark eyes.

His right hand still gripped her neck, his other worked her nipple.

She didn't want to think about his fingers around her throat. She was a sparrow in his palm. He could crush her just like that.

She didn't want to look at him scoping her.

She could come again if she closed her eyes. So she did.

She screamed out again in exquisite pleasure, lifting off onto a cloud.

Then she fell asleep.

She woke up sometime in the night. Memphis was unconscious, his hand still on her throat. She released herself, taking hold of his wrist and moving his arm beside him. He sighed and rolled over, squishing himself against his pillow.

He looked so innocent and peaceful like that…

She thought back to their encounter.

This time he hadn't hurt her.

But what would he do if he could have his way?

And then there was the more disturbing question: to get more of those crazy-good, ever-lasting orgasms, would she let him have his way?

Memphis's books were the first things she saw in the morning. He had a shelf next to the bed, filled with classics. The sun was shining on them through the window: Shakespeare, Hemingway, Faulkner, Fitzgerald, Joyce, Melville… But no female writers.

Next to the bookcase was a dim open closet. The sunlight couldn't reach that far.

There was a black leather studded bodysuit hanging on a door hook, mask included. Luna shuddered. Even unoccupied, it looked cruel.

She *did not* want to see Memphis inside it.

He was curled up with his pillow.

Again, she noted how chaste he looked, lying there…

Stop! No affectionate thoughts! She chided herself. *Serial killers probably look sweet when they're sleeping.*

This wasn't love. Memphis was like a conduit, guiding the orgasms that were stored up inside of her.

That's all he was.

A conductor.

She couldn't allow herself to love him, ever.

Memphis was no innocent.

That leather get-up in the closet, that hand around her neck—that was Memphis awake.

Luna pushed the black covers off of her and slid out of Memphis's bed

She put her clothes back on and left, without waking him to say goodbye.

A few nights later Luna and the kids had dinner at Sunny's. Afterwards, the kids watched a movie in the living room, while Luna and Sunny sat in the kitchen. "I'm not going to see Memphis again, so you can take yourself off high-alert," Luna told Sunny.

"What happened?"

"I realized that there actually is a difference between being a physical submissive and an emotional one."

"Amen to the baby Jesus!" Sunny extended her beer towards Luna's glass of seltzer. "Cheers! Here's to enlightenment."

And here's to keeping it coming, added Jiminy.

TWENTY-SEVEN

LUNA MANAGED TO get by without thinking about a man until the beginning of February, when the stupid Valentine's Day ads ran so rampantly that they were impossible to ignore. She'd just finished listening to one for a rose company and felt ready to throw herself into a thorny bush when she got a call from a 561 area code on her cell. "Hello?"

"Cuz!" It was her cousin Dom. "What's going on?"

This was an unexpected question.

The last time she'd spoken to Dom was just before she'd learned that Nick was a paying member of Gay.com. When her husband wouldn't touch her, but she didn't know why.

She'd thought she could turn to Dom. Growing up, they'd been distant – due to the fact that their family sucked at getting together – but he'd been an usher at her wedding. That night, as they shared a dance, he'd said he'd always be there for her. Soon after, Dom got married and moved to Florida with his wife, Jill. They'd opened up a beachfront steakhouse. But even though he was far and they didn't speak, Luna carried his words from her wedding in her heart. She'd always wanted a brother, and Dom was the closest thing she had. So she'd called him.

"My marriage has fallen apart," she confided, pouring her heart into her cell phone. "Nick doesn't want me anymore. I haven't had sex in three years."

"Don't you have a vibrator?" he asked. His voice was staticky and distant.

"Yeah…"

"Then what's the problem? You're covered," he said.

"The problem is that I'm lonely… I want to be held…"

There was an uncomfortable silence on the line. Then he said, "Let me have Jill call you back."

But that call never came. Not that Luna wanted to talk to Jill anyway. They'd barely ever spoken before, other than bs niceties.

After a week she'd deleted Dom from her contacts.

What had she expected to get from that conversation with him, anyway?

Empathy.

She thought he'd at least listen.

Now he was calling. A little late to reach out again.

Now he wanted to know what was going on. Well, she'd tell him.

"I'm divorced," she said.

"That's cool."

Cool?

"I got a surprise for you… Jill and I sold the steakhouse, and as of tomorrow we are back on L.I.! We're having a 'coming home' party on Saturday night. Can't wait to catch up!"

"Oh… I…" Luna wasn't sure if she wanted to go. She hated parties.

Before she could decide, he said, "I'll text ya our new address. Ciao!"

That was Dom, making assumptions and not listening. He had the attention span of a three-year-old.

Here are some other things about Dom:

STATS ON DOM:

Name: Dominick Rissoto

Ethnic background: ¾ Italian and ¼ Ukrainian

Marital Status: Married

Children: None.

Body: Moderately tall, excessively muscular.

Hair: Shaved bald, because he was going bald. (By now, he might actually have gone bald.)

Occupation: Former steakhouse owner.

Favorite physical activities: Weightlifting, cardio.

Other likes: Partying, living in the moment, most sports (bowling didn't thrill him, and he called tennis gay), Muscle Milk laced with vodka.

Dislikes: The bottom of the bottle, maturity.

Religion: Like Luna, he was raised without one.

Favorite writers: Whoever wrote for Muscle and Mad Magazines.

Favorite dessert: Anything with rum.

Favorite expression: "What, me worry?"

Luna hemmed and hawed about going to the party, but in the end she went.

She still wanted a relationship with her cousin, even though he'd been a douche. Maybe he'd grown up a little. Maybe he'd missed her. Maybe later was better than never.

Luna didn't know any of the other guests at Dom and Jill's party, and Dom clearly had no intention of catching up with her as promised. *This sucks.*

Dom had rushed over, given her a big a squeeze, and left her in the doorway – returning to his card game at the dining room table. His buddies were loud –and sauced. She smelled the group tequila breath from across the room.

Jill was in the living room gabbing with a bunch of her clones – frosted blondes, perfect make-up and manis, and most probably matching pedis too. Young, slim builds, which would be Botoxed and tummy-tucked as needed in future years. They were all over-smiling to show off their whitened teeth and nibbling the olives from their martini glasses.

Luna eyed the door. She'd passed a Dunkin' Donuts on her way there, and her laptop was in the car. No way was she going to vegetate here when she could be writing. *Do I need to tell Dom I'm leaving?*

Then she saw a guy sitting alone on a loveseat, apart from the yentas, watching TV. He waved.

She went over to him. "Do I know you?"

"Don't think so." He smiled. His face was rugged in a Tom Selleck way, and his hair was auburn. "Just trying to be friendly."

"Oh." She stood there, not knowing what to say. She really was shy, and she didn't have any glitter on to make her braver.

He was watching the movie *Top Gun*. Luna had never seen it, but she recognized Tom Cruise and Kelly McGillis.

"Name's Ray, but everyone calls me Red." He extended his hand. She shook it.

"I'm Luna," she said. "Dom's cousin."

"Dom used to work for me, back when he was in high school." Red said. "I'm a butcher. But don't worry, I left my cleaver back at the shop."

She laughed.

"You don't wanna hang with the girls?" he asked, nodding toward the laughing platinum crowd.

She shook her head no.

"Wanna sit?" he asked, patting the seat next to him "It's okay. I really don't have my cleaver."

So she sat, even though she had no desire to see *Top Gun*. Not her type of movie, and she could live without Tom Cruise. It was a close fit on that small couch – almost impossible not to touch Red in some way. Loveseats were meant for… lovers, she supposed. She pressed against the side fabric.

"Do I alarm you?" he asked.

"No! I just… didn't want to be forward."

"Then I will." He rested his hand on her leg. It was shocking, but she liked it.

"Hey, you didn't slap me," he said. "There's hope for this relationship."

Relationship?

He smiled again. "Kidding."

"How come you're not drinking with the guys?" she asked.

"I'm in recovery. I've got nine years."

Oh, joy. Another addict. "N.A.?"

"Nope. A.A. The original, and still the best."

Well, A.A. was probably better than N.A. It was harder to beat crack than alcohol. And nine years was *definitely* better than the few months Alex had. *And,* Red was older than young Alex… he was clearly a few years older than Luna.

Whoa! Now she was getting ahead of the moment.

They were just talking, right?

Even if his hand was pressing on her leg.

And even if that hand felt so good.

Onscreen, Tom Cruise was flying a plane. "You think we could watch something else?"

"I love this movie!" Red said. "But, maybe my attention could be diverted elsewhere…"

He leaned in and kissed her.

And she kissed him back.

They were kissing and kissing, and then there was a throat-clearing noise next to them. "Yoo-hoo! Are your jaws permanently attached, or what?" Dom asked.

They unlocked lips and turned toward him. "Apparently not," said Red. "What's up, Dom? How can we help you?"

"I couldn't help notice that you've been making out with my cuz for awhile…" His words slurred.

"Your keen awareness of details was the biggest reason I hired you, Dom."

"Really?"

"No. You were good at hacking up meat."

Dom beamed. "Everyone said I served the best looking steaks in Boca – and I got my practice working for you."

"Thanks."

Dom blinked a few times, as his dulled thought process caught up with him. "Anyway, since Luna has no bros, I feel I should defend her honor."

No bros? Wow, that was cheesy, Luna thought. Once again Dom was late. Where was this chivalrous knight act when she'd needed it?

He really was more like a fire-breathing dragon. If someone lit a match near his Jose Cuervo breath, there'd be a blaze for sure.

"That's very noble, Dom," said Red. "I aim to treat your cousin real nice. I'm taking her out for Valentine's Day."

"You are?" News to Luna.

Is it good news? asked Jiminy, popping in from nowhere as usual.

"Yes, But it would be nice to be asked." *Oops!* She'd answered Jiminy out loud again. It was confusing, when he jumped into the middle of conversations.

"I was gonna ask you... but I was too busy kissing you." He gave her a big smile. "So, would you like to have dinner with me on Valentine's Day?"

"I would."

"It's settled then," Dom said, slapping Red on his back. "Carry on... but not too far on my loveseat!" Sauntering back to his pals, Dom stumbled on the ottoman.

Luna and Red laughed – it was impossible not to. "You're close?" Red asked.

Luna shook her head. "Our family doesn't do close."

"Join the club."

They talked for awhile. Luna told Red about herself and vice versa. Here are some of the things Luna learned about Red:

STATS ON RED:

Name: Ray O'Rourke

Ethnic Background: Irish

Marital Status: Single

Body: Tall and solid

Hair: Thick auburn, cut below the ears.

Occupation: Butcher shop owner

Favorite physical activities: He used to love motorcycle riding, until he crashed his bike years ago.

Other likes: History, philosophy, psychology.

Dislikes: Doubt, indecision, waiting.

Religion: Raised Catholic, now a twelve-stepper, but a non-spiritual one. He didn't work the steps. He went to the meetings for the coffee and donuts.

Favorite writers: Hegel, Rousseau and Freud.

Favorite dessert: Anything without rum.

Favorite expression: "There are no jokes."

Their conversation was interrupted by the sound of a chair scraping. One of Dom's friends raced from the kitchen, down the hall, into what was presumably the bathroom. "Huhhhhbluhhhhh!"

After heaving for several seconds, the guy flushed, made a gargling sound and came back.

"You okay, dude?" Dom asked.

"Yup." And then the guy continued with the card game.

"Butch is a trooper," said Red. "Hasn't taken a sick day yet."

"That guy works for you?"

Red nodded.

"Butch the butcher?"

"Butch the meat cutter," Red amended. "I don't even call myself a butcher when I'm in the shop. People find it grisly." He made a mock-ferocious, teeth-baring face. "Dom brought in Butch to be my apprentice when he moved to Florida. He's bulky – strength is a prerequisite – and he's got good eye-to-hand coordination." Red laughed. "Poor Butch. Puking's one of the things I don't miss about drinking."

"You threw up often?"

"I did."

The smell of alcohol-permeated barf floated in the air. "Eww," said Jill. She got up from the couch, resting her tropical-looking drink on the coffee table, and headed into the kitchen. She came back with a can of Febreeze and sprayed it liberally. "Sssssssssssssss…"

Now the air smelled like fresh, sweet vomit.

"You wanna go outside?" Luna asked. She felt like *she* might heave from the combined scent.

"Sure," said Red. "But I gotta tell you something first."

"What?"

"Remember I told you about that motorcycle accident I had?"

"Yeah…"

"Well… My right arm is paralyzed, and I walk with a limp."

Luna stared at him. *How did I make out with this man and not realize he was only using one arm?*

"Is that going to be a problem?" he asked.

"No… But I can't help wondering… How do you cut meat?"

He stood and offered her his left hand to help her up. "Carefully."

They walked outside. He took her hand with his left one, and they strolled. "I can take care of myself pretty well," he told her.

"I'm sure you can."

They were heading past a parked white Jeep. Red let go of Luna's hand, then shoved her against the truck. "Whoa," said Luna. *Even Memphis wouldn't do this without asking.*

Red gripped her hair and conked her head against the Jeep's side window.

"Hey! That hurt!" Luna said.

Red didn't say anything. He kissed her.

And she let him.

Here we go again, said Jiminy.

But Luna wasn't listening.

TWENTY-EIGHT

TWO DAYS LATER, Luna and Sunny were sitting in Sunny's kitchen, drinking coffee and eating the Entenmann's chocolate donuts Luna brought. Luna thought that sending Sunny on a sugar high might make her more mellow when she told her about Red. Judging by the way Sunny gagged on her donut when Luna got to the part about the Jeep, the plan was a bust.

"Are you shitting me?" Sunny asked. She spit crumbs out with her words.

"No," said Luna.

"The guy knocks your head against glass and you're gonna go on a date with him?"

"He sent me flowers. He apologized if I thought he was aggressive…"

"*Thought*?" Sunny broke in. "There's no room for debate. That mofo assaulted you."

Luna waved off Sunny's words. "And he's called me—a lot."

"So you're saying he's a stalker."

"No… I like it."

"You like the attention. But do you like him?"

Good question, said Jiminy.

"Oh shut up, both of you!"

"Both of us?" Sunny asked. "Is that Jiminy dude here, in my kitchen?"

For all those years Jiminy had spoken to Luna, she'd kept him to herself. But after she'd prayed on the dock, something had made Luna tell Sunny about him.

Sunny was kind of jealous. "How come I don't get a talking cricket?" she'd complained.

"He's not a cricket… He reminds me of Jiminy Cricket, that's all. I guess he's my conscience, or something."

"My conscience doesn't talk to me," Sunny said.

"Maybe your conscience gave up on you," said Luna.

Sunny glared. Then she laughed. "Probably."

Now Luna said, "He's not in your kitchen. You know he doesn't appear anywhere. He just talks in my head."

Tell her I said 'hi,' said Jiminy.

"He said 'hi,'" Luna told Sunny.

"Hey, pipsqueak," Sunny said.

"That's not nice!" Luna said.

Sunny gave her a 'duh' look.

Hey, fatty-fat, Jiminy said.

"I'm not repeating that!" said Luna.

"What did he say?"

"If you must know, he called you fat."

Sunny shrugged. "Fair enough. So Jiminy, why is it that I don't get a little voice inside?"

Tell her she can have one anytime she cares to embrace it.

"I didn't embrace you, did I?" asked Luna.

Yes, you did, because you heard me. You're a tough case, but your friend is Mission: Impassible.

"Hey! What's he saying?" Sunny asked.

"He says you can have a voice when you're ready to hear it."

"Hmmpf. Typical Godspeak."

"He's not God."

"Whatever."

I haven't got all day. Jiminy interjected. *Can we get back to the question?*

"Anyway, answer the question," said Sunny. It was eerie, the way she and Jiminy were on the same page.

"I *do* like Red," Luna said. And she did. "He's intelligent. He knows about everything."

"Uh huh. Like head-banging," said Sunny.

What she said, said Jiminy.

"Listen, I'm going out in public with him. What could happen?"

"Yeah, like you're not gonna let him lure you back to his place, you horny thing."

What she said, said Jiminy.

"Drop it! I'm an adult, and I'm going," said Luna.

"I think you're more of an adolescent – and a reckless, mindless one at that," said Sunny.

Jiminy said, *She's said it all.*

One thing Red could *not* do was drive, so Luna picked him up. He gave her a kiss and a heart-shaped box of chocolates. "You look gorgeous," he told her.

She beamed.

They headed to the Outback. "The steaks are not bad there, for a chain," Red said. "And I love the blooming onions."

The crowded restaurant was decked out in red and white balloons, and the chalkboard sign declared, "Be ours, Mates!"

The wait was long, but nice. They sat on a bench and held hands until their table was ready.

At the table, Red still held her hand across the table – except when he needed to eat. Luna didn't need any wine. Red's attention was inebriating.

He ate steak like a caveman, but it wasn't like he could use the silverware properly. He admitted that Butch and his other employees did most of the slicing, while he handled customer schmoozing and the business aspects of the shop. "There's a lot of marketing strategy involved in selling meat," he said.

"Like what?"

"Well, say the people are buying a lot of top rounds. I gotta figure out a way to move the sirloins, too. It's all about turnaround. I gotta sell it fast, while it's fresh."

"So what's your secret?"

"That's where the schmoozing comes in."

Dessert was a special Chocolate Thunder from Down Under drizzled with red and white sprinkles. "So, wanna go back to my place?" Red asked, as they ate their last forkfuls.

"Uh... excuse me. I have to use the ladies room," Luna said. She slid out of the booth and headed to the bathroom, almost colliding with a busboy because she was so distracted.

She wanted to go to Red's... but she was a little scared.

What if the head conking was a prelude to something else?

Jiminy was silent. Apparently he'd already said his piece and was leaving it up to her. Free will, and all that jazz.

But she wanted to talk to someone.

Not Sunny—she would just say not to go.

She decided to call Dom.

"Cuz! What's up? We're a little busy getting busy here, if you know what I mean. It's Valentine's Day."

"I know it's Valentine's Day. I'm out with Red."

"Really? When did you meet Red?"

"Oh my God – at your party. I was making out with him!"

"You were? You little minx! I don't remember much about the party, except my bud Butch puked."

"Right."

"So what's the problem?"

"The problem is, Red banged my head on a Jeep window outside your house..."

"Did the window break?"

"No..."

"Then there's no problem."

"Look, I'm afraid that could be a sign of something..."

" The guy's a cripple, for Christ sake. How could he hurt you?"

"I guess..."

"Besides, Red's a pussycat. I never saw someone hack a side of veal as tenderly as he did, back before the accident." There was a female voice in the background. "Coming, Pookie!" Dom called.

Pookie?

"Gotta run, cuz. The bathtub water's getting cold. Have fun, you divorcee you!"

I guess it's safe at Red's, Luna thought.

Red was paying the bill when she returned. "I thought I was going to have to hoof it home," he said with a wink.

"No need to worry," said Luna. She took his hand. "I'm ready to go to your place."

It didn't take long to get naked.

But before she took her clothes off and got in Red's bed (a Tempur-Pedic he was quite proud of) she told him, "I don't want to go all the way. Are you cool with that? Even with my clothes off, no means no, okay?"

"Of course," he said. "Anything you want."

He certainly was enthusiastic, and complimentary. "You're hot," he told her.

They made out, and she let his hand roam her body. But then he rolled on top of her, like he was preparing to penetrate. "Hey, don't go any further, Red."

He was brushing against her...

"Stop it, okay?"

He said nothing. It was like he didn't hear her.

She tried to move, but he was just too heavy. She was pinned down, even her arms. "Red, I don't want to do this anymore. Let me up."

Nothing again. He was zoned off somewhere. His face was up against hers, but he wasn't even looking at her. His eyes were dead. He was spreading her legs apart.

"NO!"

No response, not even a flicker of recognition. He was in a trance.

She tried to close her legs but he forced them open with his knee. Damn, he was strong.

He pressed himself inside her. He was a machine, pushing and pushing with no emotion. All she could think was, *I'm being raped by a cripple.*

She attempted to move in some – any! – way, but she was sunken into the lush mattress. Trapped, cocooned like a fly. The spider was on top of her…

Do something! She commanded herself.

She reached her head up to bite him, but then something happened. He didn't finish – at least she didn't think so. No, he just went limp inside her.

Thank God, she thought.

Thank God he didn't finish.

And then she thought, *What a thing to be grateful for.*

He smiled at her. Just like that, he was back – and acting normal. "Aren't you glad we didn't wait?"

Jesus…

He was crazy.

Red stared at her, wanting an answer. Still on her.

"Yeah," she said. "I'm glad, too."

As soon as Red moved off of her, Luna got out of the bed. She grabbed up her clothes and locked herself in the bathroom to get dressed.

From the other side he called in, "Why so modest? We just made love!"

She zipped up her dress – the tight dress she'd gone out and bought just for this date; now she felt pinned inside it – and she rammed on her heels.

She was relieved that he'd moved away from the bathroom when she reemerged. She had a clear path toward the door. " 'Night, baby," he called after her. "Sweet dreams. I'll give you a buzz in the morning."

Luna got in her car and clicked the car lock shut. The seat was freezing and her breath was blasting out clouds but she didn't start the engine. She picked up the heart Red had given her. It was cold, too. She opened the door, flung the heart into the street. She was so skiddish that the sound of her door slamming spooked her, even though she'd made it.

She tried to cry.

She tried to scream.

She could do neither.

It's okay, said Jiminy.

"The hell it is."

This too shall pass… if you let it.

"Spare me the Bible rhetoric. I just got raped."

Luna, why do you think I came to you?

She leaned against the door and hugged at herself. She was so cold. "I don't know."

Of course you do. I came to restore your faith.

"In God?"

Among other things. As we've discussed, God is just a word. It's what you do with that word that counts.

This was too much to think about at the moment. Luna stared out at all the garbage cans by the curb, waiting for morning pick-up. She felt like crawling into one of them. "I guess I hit rock bottom," she said.

Jiminy said, *Almost.*

TWENTY-NINE

DRIVING HOME, LUNA decided she wouldn't tell Sunny what had happened. She could hear Sunny's response already: "I wanna go kick some crippled ass!" – and she just wasn't up for Sunny's outrage and possibly her I-told-you-so's, warranted as they were.

She crept into the house, not wanting to wake anyone up. Beth, her babysitter, was her next-door neighbor, a college freshman who commuted to her nearby school. The kids had known her for years, and adored her. She was fast asleep on the bottom bunk of Dylan's tree-house, while Dylan cherubically slept above.

Inside his room, Ben slept with equal peace.

At least everything was calm and right at home. Why couldn't she have just stayed there?

Inside her bathroom she ripped off her dress and took a shower in the hottest water she could stand. She slipped on her cozy flannel pajamas. Then she tiptoed back outside and stuffed the dress in the trashcan waiting for pick up on the curb.

The next day, Luna set about the task of making the kids breakfast. Beth had declined to stay, saying she was on a special smoothie diet. It was just as well, because Beth might've asked about Luna's date, and Luna might've burst into tears. The kids were only concerned with how long the food was going to take.

She wanted to be a flapjack-flipping, PTA mom like on TV, or something realistically close. She wanted to close her mind to what had happened to her, and do things that mattered – like parenting.

The thing she'd never had.

"Yay! Pancakes!" Dylan exclaimed, digging into his stack. He was so easily pleased.

"Thanks, Mom," Ben said.

"You're welcome," Luna said. "Love you guys."

The phone rang soon after the kids left for school. It was Sunny. For a moment, Luna thought she'd tell her what had happened at Red's. But Sunny's tone was agitated.

"What's wrong?" Luna asked.

"I was accosted by a wacko with drawn-in eyebrows and three teeth looking for a hand-out when I was heading to my car this morning," said Sunny. "There's no protection against the crazies." She made a sucking-in sound, which meant that she was lighting a cigarette. "Do all crackheads run out of money at seven a.m.? 'Cause this happened two days ago with some creep in a filthy fedora. Him, I heard coming – calling out to me! I got in the car and kept the window rolled up."

"I don't know about crackheads and their funds, but that makes sense," said Luna.

"Yeah, I guess I'd have to ask Sal."

"So what did you do about this eyebrow character?"

"I didn't have to do anything. She took a look at my car and said, 'Oh, I see you're having hard times, too.' Then she walked away."

"Lucky."

"Yeah, but tonight I have to sit amongst the crazies!"

Sunny's day job was at the library system that ordered books for all of the county's libraries. Her evening job was at one of those libraries. Good, because Sunny loved books. Bad, because crazies migrated to libraries like immigrants had come to Ellis Island. "It's gonna blow!" Sunny exclaimed. "There's a new nutcase who's been coming in and hugging me every night."

"You let him touch you?"

"Hell, no! But the counter is short, and his arms are long. He keeps lunging when I'm not looking."

She made another sucking sound. Her final, long drag. "I gotta go back inside. Shit, I miss the days you could smoke at your desk."

"Have a good day."

"I'm gonna try… Hey, how'd that date go?"

No way she could get into it now. "Great. It was great."

"Guess I was wrong about Red. I'm glad." She hung up.

You never lied to Sunny before, Jiminy said.

"Yeah, feels weird," said Luna.

But she had other things to think about. One thing, specifically.

Red.

He called. She didn't pick up. He left this message: "Last night was so incredible. Call me, baby."

He called again, after a half hour: "Why aren't you calling me back, baby?"

Fifteen minutes more: "What's wrong, baby? Call me!"

Ten minutes later: "Did I do something? Talk to me, please!"

The next time the phone rang, five minutes later, Luna answered. "Don't call me anymore, Red."

"What? Why?"

"Because you…" she couldn't get the word "raped" out. It was just too ugly. "You forced yourself on me."

There was a silence. Then he said, "Luna, I'm sorry. I must've misinterpreted what you said."

"I said, 'Stop.' I said, 'No.' How could you misunderstand?"

"I was just so excited to be with you. You're so beautiful, I was distracted. I wasn't listening… I didn't mean to hurt you."

She wanted to believe that, because it was better to accept that then to think he'd just wanted to take advantage of her. But, still…

"Whatever. Doesn't matter. Goodbye, Red."

"Luna, wait. Can't we at least still talk sometimes? Chat on the phone? And then maybe, somewhere down the line, if you feel comfortable… we could go on a date again in public?"

Wow. He was really working for it. No one had ever done that before. They'd just taken what they wanted and left.

Maybe this could work. Maybe she could be a PTA mom, and talk to Red, too. Build up a rapport. Then date casually. People did that, she'd heard.

Normal people.

"Hello? You still there, Luna?"

"I'm here," she said. "Okay. You can call me tomorrow."

"Yes! I'm so happy. You're one special girl, Luna. I couldn't bear to let you slip away."

The next day, even though it was February and the year was half over, Luna went to the school and paid her PTA dues. There was a notice that they had no volunteers to run the approaching Parents as Reading Partners program, so she signed up to do it. What the heck – she didn't have to look far for an author to do a visit. It would actually be pretty cool to talk to the kids about writing.

She went home and waited for the call from the man who date-raped her. She could barely write, typing the same sentence over and over like Jack Nicholson in *The Shining*. (But at least she deleted it each time.) Sunny called, and told her about a new guy she met on Facebook.

"He likes Metallica, and all the other bands I listen to!" she said.

The cornerstone of a solid relationship. "So when are you gonna meet him in person?"

"I don't know. We're messaging right now."

"How 'bout a phone call?"

"Eventually."

Luna wished she could have Sunny's cavalier attitude. But Red never called, and she was upset.

It seemed illogical to be distressed about a rapist not calling, but there it was. He'd said she was too good to let get away. What happened?

Why didn't he want her?

Again Luna thought about telling Sunny everything, but she just couldn't do it. *Maybe this is what shame feels like.*

After a week of waiting, Luna erupted. It was like all the rejection and poor treatment in the past had amassed inside, filling her until she burst.

She scrawled a note to Red on a yellow legal pad: "Red, I hate you and I hope you die. You suck and deserve to be alone. Die, die, die. – Luna." Rip! She severed the page from its gum binding.

She grabbed a roll of duct tape and drove to Red's house. Rip! Rip! Rip! Rip! She tore four pieces of tape and attached the message securely to Red's front door.

Luna felt elated after that. It felt so good, letting her feelings flow. She headed to TCBY for a celebratory frozen yogurt.

Dom called while she was crunching her carob chip topping and reading the current book she carried in her shoulder bag: *Fear of Flying*. "Hey, whatever happened with you and Red?"

"It didn't work out. Why?" The sounds of the yogurt machine whirring and cash register ringing came from behind the counter. Even though it was February, the place was bustling, with a line of customers and most of the tables occupied.

"I just heard from Butch that Red collapsed in his shop this morning. The hospital doctors found an infection that started in his leg and spread, and something about a blood clot. He's in surgery right now."

Whoa. In her shock she sucked down a chip whole. For a second she felt like she was choking, but then she coughed it out onto her tray.

"You there?"

"Yeah." She stared at the chip she'd hacked back up. "Sorry to hear that."

"Well, he's in Huntington Hospital. Thought you'd wanna know."

"Thanks."

She ended the call and stared at the page she'd been reading. She scanned the same paragraph three times without grasping what it said. Finally, she flipped the book closed. Suddenly TCBY felt incredibly loud.

Luna had a lump in her throat that would not go down, even though she'd downed all of her yogurt. All she could think about was the timing of her note. She must've taped it to Red's door when he was already in surgery – Right?

Oh, what difference did it make? It's not like she had the power to induce injury to someone via her wishes – Right?

With our thoughts we make the world, said Jiminy.

No way, thought Luna.

According to Buddha: Yes way, said Jiminy.

Oh, fuck, thought Luna.

She thought about going back and removing the note, but decided to leave it. The damage was already done.

And the lump was psychosomatic. It would go away – eventually.

Her phone rang again. It was Sunny. "It's off with the Facebook guy," she said.

"Already?"

"He told me he puts in different light bulbs when he has company, so he can save money with lower wattage ones when he's alone."

"Well, that's odd. But so what?"

"I'm not dating someone who's so cheap he screws around with light bulbs! Criminy!"

"If that's how you feel," said Luna. She didn't have the strength to argue Mr. Cheap Watt's cause. She needed to share the truth about everything. "Got a few minutes?"

"Sure, I'm on my lunch break. What's up?"

Luna took a deep breath and let it out. Fiddling with her spoon, she told Sunny about the date rape.

"*What?* Why didn't you tell me when this happened?"

"I'm not sure. I guess I wasn't up to talking about it." She flexed plastic and considered the people around her again. People with normal lives, like the one she wanted.

"I can understand that."

Snap! She broke the spoon's handle as she told Sunny about speaking with Red again.

"*What?* Are you insane?"

"Possibly. But there's more." Luna told Sunny about how angry she got when Red didn't call back. *Snap!* She broke the spoon again, and again.

"Are you for real?"

"That's not the worst part." Using a jagged piece of spoon to stab at the chip she'd hacked up, Luna owned up to the note.

There was a silence on the line. Then Sunny said, "Dude, that's a bit much."

"He got me angry." The chip was reduced to a tiny mound of brown specks. She moved on to her yogurt cup. Jab! Jab! She made a jagged rip across the cardboard.

"Clearly. And he deserved it. I'm the first one to say, 'Let's go kick some crippled ass!' But you don't usually have this kind of rage."

Luna stared at her mutilated cup. "I know. I think I was burying it inside… I just wanted all the guys to like me… so I never told them how bad they made me feel. Even Nick. It's so important that men like me."

"Oh god, Chicky. I just don't know what to say." There was a cigarette-lighting pause. Sunny's finger triggered the flame. "Except, of course, to say that all those guys sucked. Especially Nick. Fuck him!"

Luna wanted to decimate something else. She shredded a napkin, but that did nothing for her. "I know that, but something in me is crying out for approval."

"This is awful. I can't even think of something witty to interject."

You don't even know the worst part, thought Luna. Luna didn't want to voice what had happened next, but she knew she needed to come clean completely. She forced the words out. "There's more. Red collapsed from a blood clot, or something. He's in surgery!"

"Well, that's the first good thing I've heard. Karma is a biatch."

Interesting reaction. Was Sunny right? Had Red brought this on himself? Or…

Luna stared at the tray of destruction she'd served up and asked the horrible question: "You don't think I could've caused the problem, do you?"

"How? By wishing him dead? You think you have the power to

wound with your thoughts? 'Cause if you can perform medical magic, cure my cramps!"

"Yeah, I didn't think it was me. But Jiminy implied it."

"He just wants you to think lofty thoughts in general. He's a pocket Dalai Lama."

At the next table, a couple started to argue. Apparently their relationship wasn't perfect. But Luna doubted the guy had date-raped the girl, and obviously they'd been in communication. "Why do I have to uphold some higher standard?"

"That's just you, babe. You always did – until now. Don't let this dirt bag drag you down to his level."

The couple was still arguing. "Yeah. I know. I'm gonna give up the man hunt and seek some help."

"A new shrink?"

"No." The guy got up and left.

"Dr. Gold?"

"Nope." The girl pressed her head into arms, which were folded on the table.

"Then what?"

The girl raised her head. She scraped back her chair, got up and walked out. "I'm gonna join Sex and Love Addicts Anonymous," said Luna.

"Dude, that's a bit much."

THIRTY

AT HOME, LUNA searched "Sex And Love Addicts Anonymous" on Google and found their website. The SLAA founders had reworded Alcoholic's Anonymous' Twelve Steps to fight sex and love addiction. It was, they said, a progressive disease. Incurable, but also arrestable.

Do I have a disease, like cancer? Luna wondered. Whatever it was, it definitely progressed. That much, she knew. She read on.

SLAA members shared a common denominator, repeating obsessive/compulsive patterns, and they were united in dealing with them.

Wow. Wouldn't that be great, to meet other people who felt the same as she did?

The kids were coming home soon, so Luna skipped the rest of the reading material and searched for a meeting. She needed to go, to break free from whatever it was that made her accept Red's behavior.

Otherwise, what would she progress to next?

Most alarming was that relentless tug in her heart, urging her to find a man.

Any man.

To protect her.

She felt like she had the shakes, but her hands were steady.

That's your soul trembling, said Jiminy.

"Can't I ever just sit in peace?" she asked.

You can, said Jiminy.

"When?"

Eventually.

God, she hated that word.

There was a 7:30 pm meeting in Long Acre.

While most of the meetings were in churches, with addresses provided, the Long Acre listing offered only the name "Stan" and a phone number. She called.

Stan sounded like a nice-enough guy. "The meeting's in my house," he told Luna. "That's why they don't list the address on the site."

"Okay," said Luna, though she wasn't thrilled with walking into a stranger's house. Right now, she was going to do whatever needed to be done.

"We don't have many women at the meetings," he said. "But it's always nice to get a female perspective."

This was also not exciting news. She was fine not being around women, but sitting around with a bunch of male sex and love addicts didn't sound like the safest thing to do.

"Don't worry," Stan said. "We're all on the same path to recovery."

"Sure," said Luna.

Then Stan gave Luna his address. "You can just walk in. But make sure to use the side door," he said. "My wife wants nothing to do with the meetings."

Luna was early. She sat in her minivan on Stan's block, sipping Dunkin' Donuts coffee and eating a corn muffin. She tried to be neat, but crumbs were everywhere: on her jacket, on her jeans, on the floor. It was amazing how much area those crumbs could cover.

"So, Jiminy. What do you think? Am I headed in the right direction?"

*Do **you** think you're headed in the right direction?*

"Holy crap. Can't you just give me your opinion?"

It's your opinion that counts, he said. *But I **will** say that any forward movement is good, as long as you learn from your previous experiences.*

Luna checked the time on her cell phone. 7:25. She scooped up the remains of the muffin from inside the waxy bag and dropped them in her mouth. Coffee in hand, she got out of the minivan, slamming the door shut and chirping the lock.

Her purple Converses mushed through slush – the remains of a recent ice storm – and she wished she'd worn boots. She never thought of obvious things like that. By the time she sloshed down the sidewalk and then up the un-shoveled driveway to Stan's side door, her sneakers, socks and feet were soaked.

Luna turned the knob and pushed the door open. The door creaked like it was complaining about something. She wiped her feet on the worn mat (the word "welcome" was faded, but she could still make it out) and stepped inside, creaking the door closed again.

There was a flight of steps going down.

Okay, this is off-putting, she thought. *I'm gonna sit in a basement with a bunch of male sex and love addicts.*

Too late to turn back now, said Jiminy.

As if to cement that point, the door creaked open again and a guy walked in. Tall, built and bald, he looked like Mr. Clean. She backed up to give him room.

"Oh, hey," he said when he saw her. "Sorry, I didn't mean to scare ya."

Her face must've shown how freaked she was getting. "You didn't. Not really," she stammered out. "It's this whole situation. I've never been here before…"

"Yeah, I get it," he said. "I'm new, too." He extended his hand. It looked like it'd been through a few rounds at a fight club. "Name's Joe," he said.

His grip was strong. Joe could do some damage with that hand. "I'm Luna."

The stairs were noisy like the door. They led into a small foyer, which was attached to a full kitchen. There was a large picnic table on the right, covered with a heap of papers and books. They literally looked like they'd been dumped there.

A plaque hung on the wall. It said:

1. Out of clutter, find simplicity.

2. From discord, find harmony.

3. In the middle of difficulty lies opportunity.

—Albert Einstein, Three Rules of Work

Through an adjacent doorway came voices. Luna and Joe headed into the meeting.

"Welcome!" said a middle-aged man with a gut. He was one of five guys seated in a circle of nine folding chairs in an otherwise bare, paneled room. "I'm Stan. You're just in time. We're about to open with the Serenity Prayer."

Luna didn't know the Serenity Prayer (or any other prayer, for that matter.) She listened while everyone else – including Joe – recited:

"God, grant me the serenity to accept the things I cannot change,
Courage to change the things I can,
And wisdom to know the difference."

Stan recited the twelve steps. Wow. They sounded pretty formidable. And, she'd need a sponsor to do them.

Luna scanned the room for possibilities.

Two empty chairs away from her sat a young guy who was sweating heavily and staring down at the brown-tiled floor.

No.

Next to him sat a hot Latino guy who secreted sex.

Hell, no.

There was Stan, with his gut. He was Mr. America compared to the guy next to him, whose swollen belly looked about to burst with child, or at least with donuts.

No, to both.

Not because of their stomachs per se, but due to the fact that they were creepy middle-aged guys. Luna wasn't sure she'd feel this way about Stan if she'd met him anywhere else. But the other guy would've repelled her anytime, anyplace. He exuded eau de pedophile.

The guy next to them looked so ordinary; he was probably a serial killer.

No.

That left Joe. He was intimidating, but seemed like a nice guy. Too bad this was his first meeting.

The men took turns doing five-minute shares. The sweating, floor-staring guy was addicted to phone and internet sex – to the point that he couldn't pay any bills and had to move back with his parents. That piled extra shame on him, because he had to make sure his parents didn't hear him talking to the girls. He'd forced himself to stop last week, and now he was going through physical withdrawal.

Holy moly. Luna never thought anyone could react like that when drugs and alcohol weren't involved.

"Thanks for sharing," said the group.

The Latino guy was all choked up about the random sex he had with women he picked up in bars.

"Thanks for sharing," said the group.

Stan talked about flirting with himself, which Luna uncomfortably felt was code for masturbation, or at least pre-masturbation.

"Thanks for sharing," said the group. Luna thought she heard Joe snicker.

The ordinary-looking guy echoed Stan about fighting off flirting with himself.

"Thanks for sharing," said the group.

The disturbing ten-month-pregnant guy actually *was* a would-be pedophile, caught online talking to an undercover cop who'd pretended to be a teenage girl. Mr. Grotesque said he knew it wasn't a girl – that he was just role-playing – which would've been pretty sick anyway even if it were true. But Luna didn't believe him. He was on probation, and court-ordered to attend these meetings.

Mr. Grotesque said nothing substantial. He packed his minutes with platitudes like, "Life is a journey, and you have to go through some pretty dark places to get to heaven."

Luna had heard something similar in the children's movie *Firehouse Dog*, which she'd watched on Netflix with Dylan: "To get to paradise you have to take a road so dark there are no stars." It sounded better in the movie, but it was some pretty vague bullshit either way.

Mr. Grotesque was wrapping it up. "I know I'll get to heaven someday." How, he never mentioned.

"Thanks for sharing," said the group.

Then Joe spoke: "I'm here because I can't let go of my ex-wife. I mean, I don't think about her sexually, but I wanna take care of her. I got a new wife now, and two kids, but I still hang out with Drew. I don't even think it's wrong, but people say I gotta disconnect with the past to make way for the future." He cleared his throat. "I don't know if they're right. I just know that I made a promise to look after her, and something in me won't let me stop, and maybe I don't wanna stop."

"Thanks for sharing," said the group.

It was Luna's turn. What would she say? *The truth.* "I had a boyfriend who told me about Sex and Love Addict's Anonymous. I kind of thought it was a joke. But since then, I've seen myself sliding into some disturbing behavior. It's like there's two of me: the little girl who doesn't understand boundaries and the adult who can only watch that girl beg for love." God, it was hard getting the words out. Was she in the right place? Was this meeting a haven along the dark, starless road toward paradise?

All those eyes were upon Luna. She wanted to turn away – eye contact was so scary – but she needed to connect with at least one person. Her first impulse was to pick the Latino guy, but that would only lead to more trouble.

She looked at Joe.

"I'm scared," she said. "I don't know what if feels like to be happy with myself. I keep going from guy to guy, and the results are more and more disastrous. I want to stop being so desperate. I'm willing to do whatever it takes."

Joe nodded.

"Thank you for sharing," the group said.

The meeting ended as it started, with the Serenity Prayer, which Luna still didn't know. She held hands in the circle with Joe and the sweating, eye-averting guy, and she tried to take the words in.

When they left, Stan gave out flyers for an SLAA retreat coming up in Pennsylvania. "It's co-ed," he told Luna.

"Thanks," she said.

Everyone thumped up the basement steps, out the creaking door and into the slush.

"How did you know that prayer?" Luna asked Joe as they tramped down the driveway. The water was again seeping into her sneakers.

"A twelve-step staple," he said. "I been in AA for sixteen years. At the beginning and the end of every meeting, it's all about the search for serenity."

"Does anyone find it?" asked Luna.

"In patches," he said. "That's why they keep coming back." They walked a few feet more. "So, wadja think?"

"I don't know. That was a lot to handle."

"Those guys were a bunch of sissies. What the hell does flirting with yourself even mean? Do they wink and say 'Hey, how ya doing' to their reflections in the mirror?" Luna couldn't help laughing. "And what's wrong with masturbation? I say, if ya wanna jerk off, then jerk off! Yeesh."

"So you're not coming back," said Luna,

"No. And *you* shouldn't be around all these wackadoos either."

"I might go to the retreat."

"Pennsylvania? Pretty long way to go." They were at the street. He said, "I think you should work with me."

"In what capacity?"

"I could sponsor you."

"But I'm not in AA."

"The steps are the steps, no matter what brought ya to them."

There was something about Joe that felt right. Like they were meant to know each other. But not in a sexual way. Which was weird, for Luna.

"Okay."

"Got a minute? We could go for coffee now and I'll go over surrendering."

"I already surrendered," she told him, launching into a description of that night on the dock, with the egret.

Joe held up his hand to stop her. "Very nice, but ya gotta do it again."

"Again?"

"And again."

"How many times?"

"I been doing it every morning for sixteen years." He gave her a deep look. "Get used to it."

THIRTY-ONE

THEY WENT TO a diner a few blocks away and slid into the two sides of a red vinyl booth. It was a dive—the menus were sticky and the waitress cracked gum while she took their order.

Over greasy French fries and oily coffee, Joe told Luna an abridged version of his life. His childhood had been violent; his drinking had begun early. "I started sampling the bottles my dad left laying around at night, after he beat up my mom and blacked out. A sip here, a slug there. It was all about feelin' good. Even for just a little while."

"I'm sorry…"

"Why? You had nothin' to do with it," he said. "Don't matter, anyway. Just part of my story – what brought me here."

Here's some other things Luna learned about Joe:

STATS ON JOE:

Name: Joseph Sullivan

Ethnic Background: Irish

Children: Two sons

Body: Muscular but misaligned from all the abuse it had endured.

Hair: None

Occupation: A former professional boxer; now a boxing instructor and personal trainer.

Favorite Physical Activities: Hitting bags; hitting jaws.

Dislikes: Moronic behavior; liars.

Religion: None. He dealt with his higher power his way.

Favorite Writers: Bill W. & the other founding members of AA

Favorite Dessert: Irish chocolate cake (made with mashed potatoes), but without the icing (made with Irish Cream liqueur.)

Favorite expression: "I feel like a million bucks, all crumpled up."

Joe's fiery temper and fast hook had given him a promising boxing career, until his drinking brought that to a halt.

At eighteen he'd decided to crawl out of an El Camino passenger window and "surf" on the hood while in moderate nighttime traffic on the Brooklyn Queens Expressway. He'd been so hammered on Bacardi 151 that he registered no pain during or after the forty mile per hour fall onto the metal grooves lining the Kosciuszko Bridge. He picked himself up, got back in the car, and he and his friends proceeded to a massage parlor in Manhattan.

The masseuse tried to work around Joe's blood and bruises. She told him, "You hurt very bad. You need hospital."

Joe said, "Nah, I'm fine, just gimme a hand job."

The next day Joe woke up in agony and discovered he wasn't fine. That fall had fractured his back and many other bones. His boxing career was through.

"Even after all that I still drank," Joe told Luna. "Drinking was all I had. Then one day I was walking home from the liquor store and I saw this big puddle by the curb. I stopped short just as I was about to step into it, and I was all proud cause I kept my feet dry. But then I looked in the water and I saw my sorry-ass reflection. Something in me snapped. I gave up. I surrendered."

"What do you mean?"

"I mean I fell into that puddle on my knees and I turned my life over to God. I gave up control. I told him: 'You win.'" He dropped another fry in his mouth. A dribble of ketchup missed and plopped onto the plate. "You asked about finding serenity. Well, that was the first taste of serenity I felt, ever."

Luna took a sip of coffee. This was a lot to take in, and not a story she'd expect to come from a tough-looking guy like Joe. "Sounds good," she said. "But I don't want to drop into any puddles."

Joe's blue eyes were piercing. "The puddle's in your mind."

I like this guy, said Jiminy.

They chewed and drank in silence for a few moments. Then Joe asked, "So what's your story? Were ya always so pathetic?" This would've sounded rude from someone else, but Joe said it with a smile.

"Kind of," Luna said. She told Joe about Nick. Then about her search for men since her divorce, and how things had gone wrong and wronger.

She told him about Red.

When she finished, Joe said, "That's a bit much."

"I know."

"You said that jerk-off was in recovery? I'll bet he never worked one step."

"He didn't. He said he went to the meetings for the coffee."

"Oh, bullshit. The coffee at meetings tastes like sewer sludge. He probably went to pick up damaged chicks."

"Great." Luna hung her head. She was a damaged chick, too.

"Ya want me to bust his skull? I got no problem with that. Just say the word." He crunched on a particularly well-done fry. "I been looking for someone's face to bash in."

"I'll keep that in mind, but Red already got what was coming to him… and then some."

"Let me know if you change your mind," Joe said. He flicked a greasy crumb across his plate. "Don't worry. We'll work it all out. If I could get my life together – for the most part anyway – so can you."

"What are you gonna do about your ex-wife?"

"Absolutely nothing," said Joe. "Sometimes, that's all there is to do." He stood and slid his jacket on. "And judging by that crew we just met, my problem seems pretty minor."

"What about the serenity?" she asked.

"What about it?"

"You said the first time you felt it you were in the puddle."

"Right."

"But earlier you said serenity comes in patches."

"Right."

"What makes it leave?"

Joe thought for a moment. "It goes away when I try to take back control of my life. Pretty often, because I'm so thick."

The check came. "I've got it," Luna said, figuring that treating Joe to coffee and french fries was the least she could do.

Joe snatched the paper from her hands. "Thanks, but I don't take no handouts."

"Have it your way." Luna shrugged. "Why are you helping me, anyway? Don't you have enough on your plate?"

"It's one of the Twelve Step traditions, to sponsor others in need. Ya gotta give back, ya know?"

That sounded fair. Which was more than she could say about most things.

Joe paid the check. On the way out, Luna said, "I'd like to try boxing with you, too. I've always been interested in it."

"Oh, yeah? Waddaya like about it?"

"I like the sounds of the gloves making contact." She thought about how to describe it. "It's kind of… glorious."

Joe beamed. "It is."

On her way home she called Sunny and told her about the meeting, and about Joe.

"Dude! That is all so very odd."

That about summed it up.

Curled up next to Dylan in his bed that night, Luna tried to envision the puddle. She kept seeing a lake, which would be no good to drop into because she couldn't swim. She finally drifted to sleep.

THIRTY-TWO

LUNA WAS AT Iron Island gym, training with Joe for the third time this week. She'd taken to boxing like a bird to flight.

While she hit the various bags (speed, upper-cut, heavy, banana, double-end and angle) Joe talked to her about the steps. Physical training and spiritual sponsoring all in one sweaty hour: who could ask for anything more?

The first three steps had been a breeze: admitting she was powerless over love addiction and that her life had become unmanageable (it was pretty impossible to ignore how out of hand it had gotten), coming to believe that a power greater than herself could restore her to sanity (she'd done that already, but discussed it more with Joe), and made a decision to turn her will and her life over to the care of God as she understood God (aka: surrender, which she'd done repeatedly every night that week. She hoped that God wouldn't get sick of her voice.)

Then she hit step four.

Whoa.

This step consisted of making a "searching and fearless moral inventory" of herself.

What an undertaking!

She'd stayed up late working on it, detailing all the things she'd done with men, and brought it with her this morning. Joe was reading it while she did her rounds.

Luna bashed into the thick black punching bag, relishing the slamming sounds her gloves made: the satisfying thuds of leather connecting with leather. She grunted, hit harder, harder. Perspiration seeped into her headband, her waistband, her sports bra.

She hit, hit, hit, until the bell rang.

"Good," said Joe, glancing up. "Take a drink."

Luna gripped her water bottle with her bulky red and black gloves. She took a long slug, put the bottle down and wiped her mouth with her sleeve.

The sound of weights clinking reverberated throughout the cinder-block-walled, equipment-packed gym. A man groaned loudly. *Boom!* He dropped the barbell he was holding above his head.

A huge sign on the right-hand wall said: "ellar of pain."

"What happened to the c?" Luna had asked Joe on the first day.

"That fell off years ago," said Joe. "Back when this gym was hard-core."

"It's not hard-core now?"

Joe shook his head. "They had pails next to the equipment. You could puke in them and keep going."

Still, Iron Island was no Curves.

The pop music that blared through Iron Island was out of place. An ellar of pain needed heavy metal, or some kind of rock 'n roll at least. But the gym's owner favored Top 40, past and present. Today a pre-pubescent Michael Jackson wailed soprano: *One bad apple don't spoil the whole bunch, Girl.*

Also incongruous was the scent of warm chocolate chip cookies floating in the air. There was a bakery next door. The smell wrenched Luna's stomach, particularly combined with the odor of clinging sweat. "You'll get used to it," Joe had told her.

The bell rang again. "On the upper-cut bag. Go!"

Luna pounded away. Joe continued reading.

Bam! Bam! She slammed upper-cuts until the bell rang again.

"What do you think?" she asked Joe.

"This is all very well-written," he told her.

"Thanks."

"But it ain't a pretty little story for *Woman's Day*." He folded the paper up and shoved it in Luna's gym bag. "Ya gotta dig deeper."

"Deeper?"

"Forget about sentence structure and get down to the bones." He grinned maniacally, like The Joker.

"I don't know what you mean. I wrote about… everyone. What more do you want?"

"It's not what I want, it's what *you* want. Ya wanna examine your motives for doing these things, and eliminate the behavior that triggered your actions so ya don't repeat them."

Oh, God. He sounds like Jiminy, Luna thought.

I told you I liked this guy, said Jiminy.

The bell rang, but Luna stayed motionless. "This is too much…"

"No, it ain't. For fuck's sake, I did it. So why not you?"

Why not her? "But I don't know what else to put down."

"Well, for one thing, I don't see nothin' 'bout resentments."

"I don't resent anyone."

"The hell ya don't. Think about what your parents did and tell me ya don't resent them. Not to mention your adoring ex. Feeling all warm and fuzzy about him?"

"Shit."

"That shit's poison in your system. Ya gotta get it out."

She understood.

She felt the truth of Joe's words reverberating inside her, in places she'd padlocked and forsaken long ago.

She didn't want to revisit them.

Joe put his hand on her shoulder. "Ya wanna get through this?"

"Yes."

"Then get it all down," he said.

"Okay."

Ding! The bell went off, ending the round. She'd missed the whole thing. "You're not getting off that easy," Joe said. "Next round, you hit twice as hard."

Luna nodded.

Joe reset the timer and the bell rang. "On the heavy bag," he said. "Go!"

Through everything, Luna managed to write. Her next children's book, which she was reasonably sure would be published since her latest book was doing really well and getting great reviews (the best was when kids Tweeted her and told her they loved it!) and her women's novel – which was all in blind faith.

But at least she had faith now – even if she had no ending.

She wrote a little bit each day, and included in her daily chats with God a request for divine plot intervention.

The next Monday, she wrote for an hour after the kids went to school. Then she headed to Brooklyn. She was due for a visit with Aunt Zelda.

Zelda's teeth were out again. Luna spotted the sag in her aunt's cheeks the moment she walked in the barge's door. Finding her new set of chompers uncomfortable, Zelda preferred to go au naturel when she was alone. "Dearheart!" Zelda gummily exclaimed. "I didn't know you were coming."

Besides dentures, Aunt Zelda possessed a little memory problem these days. "I told you I was coming on Monday," Luna reminded her, averting her eyes from the grinning prosthetics resting on a floral imprinted napkin. She tried to pretend they were castanets.

"Oh, is it Monday?"

"It is," Luna said. "I'm gonna use the ladies room. It was a long trip." She hoped that Aunt Zelda would pop her clickers back in while she was gone. It felt discomfiting to see her aunt so slumpy. Bad enough, Zelda plodded with a cane these days, when she used to parade. She was the Energizer bunny, finally winding down.

Luna walked toward the lavatory on the floor her aunt had created, using hundreds of interlocking mahogany strips to mask the stark steel beneath. So much work had gone into making Zelda's vision come true. Even the wood had been ugly until Zelda worked her magic.

Luna thought back to when she was ten. Zelda had sat Luna down on the ratty tan couch in the center of the dark, cavernous room. They were surrounded by second-hand lumber Aunt Zelda had been gifted. It was a repulsive green, like the color hospitals used in their halls. The sofa's cushions were ripped, and a spring sprung at Luna's butt. "You really think you can fix this place?" Luna had asked.

Taking Luna's hand and squeezing, Zelda had looked Luna in the eyes. "Dear Heart, there's beauty in everything," she'd proclaimed in her theatrical voice. "You just have to trust that it's there."

At ten, that had been easier to accept. Especially when Aunt Zelda had demonstrated, grabbing a paintbrush and dunking it in a can, then spreading clear, thick glop over one of the vile green pieces of wood. Then she'd traded the brush for a flat-bladed tool, scraping away the paint until it was a sticky clump on the floor. The grain beneath the paint was exposed: a warm mix of brown and cream.

"Behold… Beauty!" Aunt Zelda said.

And, slowly, the barge *had* become beautiful.

As an adult, Luna didn't see much beauty in the world. Could she somehow find it? Was it really everywhere, in everything? Had Aunt Zelda been exaggerating or overstating… or was it possible that she was just nuts?

Luna didn't know the answers. She just knew that she had to pee.

When Luna returned, Aunt Zelda's face was magically lifted. "Sit down, baby. How was the drive?"

Luna scraped a folding chair across the brick floor, sat and rolled her eyes. "The usual." Driving through Brooklyn on Atlantic Avenue was like enduring a living version of the Mario Brothers video game – each section with hurdles. Under the el, over a bridge, or just navigating stretches riddled with potholes and errant drivers. All that was missing was the electronic music and the bleeping sounds. At the end of the road was Aunt Zelda, an improbable princess in her towering barge.

But Atlantic Avenue beat sitting in standstill highway traffic.

Luna liked to move, even if the ride was treacherous.

Aunt Zelda took a swig of red wine. She was boozing it up quite a bit these days, which allowed for some interesting comments to the patrons of the barge. One day someone said to her, "You're very famous!"

She'd responded, "Oh, my. I hope I don't turn into a statue."

"And how are *you*?" Aunt Zelda asked Luna now.

Luna told Aunt Zelda she'd entered a program, and had determined to forgo male companionship until she'd worked on herself.

Aunt Zelda raised her eyebrows. "Why?"

"Because I keep attracting jerks."

Zelda took another gulp of wine. "That's too bad." She gave Luna a look of pity. "Darling, you're a goddess and your standards are high... You're going to be lonely."

"Perhaps," said Luna.

"You know my motto: get in, and get out. Like they say in the music world..."

"I love you, darling, but the season is over," Luna recited to Aunt Zelda. She'd heard it often enough.

Aunt Zelda reached out her bony arm and slapped Luna on the leg. "That's it!"

"I'm not cut out that way," said Luna. "I care too much."

Aunt Zelda shrugged. "Hey, guess what I found the other day when I was digging through an old box of things?" She reached down to the storage shelf built into the table and pulled out a small pair of Keds canvas sneakers. "Remember these?"

They were Luna's. White, until they'd been stained red by the Rustoleum Luna had dripped all over them, helping Aunt Zelda paint the roof.

"Dearheart. I couldn't have built this place without you," said Aunt Zelda.

"Of course you could've," Luna said. "I wasn't much help. I was just a kid."

"It was your heart and soul I relied on," said Aunt Zelda. "No one's ever loved me like you."

"Ditto," Luna said. She often thought she'd be locked up on a mental ward if not for her aunt. "By the way, have you been to see Dad since his birthday?"

"Oh, poor Lenny." Aunt Zelda let out a heavy sigh. "Yes, I went over there last week and brought him some pizza. Wow, did he eat it with gusto."

"Do you think he knows it's you, and what you're talking about?"

"Certainly I do."

"I asked him if he wanted to go to Mars, and he said yes."

"So? Maybe he wants to go to Mars. Lenny always *was* a fan of the space program."

"I don't know. I can't deal with him right now. Does it make me a bad person to not visit?"

"Not at all, dearheart. You are human, and must do what you can to shelter your heart." Zelda gave Luna a slap on her thigh. "All right! Let's go out on the town." For Zelda, that meant taking a ride into nearby Red Hook and getting some coffee. She didn't get off the barge very much these days, so when Luna came they took an excursion but didn't go far because Zelda always had so much business to attend to.

Luna held her aunt's hand as they climbed across the barge's creaky ramp onto the pier, crossed the road and headed into the barge's parking lot. With her black wool scarf wrapped around her head, Aunt Zelda looked like she'd just escaped from the Cossacks.

Slowly, Aunt Zelda hoisted herself up into Luna's van and they were off across potholes and cobblestones.

"Lumpy Brooklyn," said Aunt Zelda.

Luna parked in front of a diner that sold decent coffee and a custard pudding they both loved. Zelda sat in the car while Luna got their order to go. Then Luna drove to a spot facing the river and turned off the engine again. They ate, not saying much, because nothing much needed to be said.

Back in front of the barge, Luna bid Aunt Zelda goodbye. "I can make it back in myself," Aunt Zelda said, as always. "You just go. Beat rush hour."

"I love you," Luna said.

"I love you too, dearheart," Aunt Zelda said, giving Luna's arm a good squeeze. She added, "Remember, it's all there if you can find it… and somehow, you'll muddle through."

"Right," Luna said.

Aunt Zelda creaked open the door and slowly got out.

Then she winked. "Toot-a-loo, Chum!"

THIRTY-THREE

DR. GOLD WAS holding Luna's head in his hands. It was Tuesday, spine time.

"Relax," Dr. Gold said, as usual.

As usual, she attempted to comply.

"A little more."

She was doing her best…

"A little more."

He tried adjusting her neck, but nothing happened. She was just too stiff. "A little more," he said again, with a laugh.

Staring at the fluorescent lights beaming down on her, Luna sighed.

"What's the matter?" Dr. Gold asked.

"I'm tense about my future."

"Why?"

"I don't know what's gonna happen."

"No one does."

"True."

Crack! Success! As usual, Luna wondered how he didn't actually snap her neck, because it sure sounded like he did. Dr. Gold said, "If you can take the load of eternity off your shoulders, it'll be a big release for you."

"Sounds good…"

"Just ask yourself, 'Is this something that's okay for now?'"

"Hmmm…" said Luna.

Dr. Gold settled her head back on the crinkly paper over the cushion. He said, "If you stay in the moment you can't lose."

"I try to stay in the moment, but then all these things come popping out at me…"

"That's your anger. You need to let it go."

"*How?*"

"By staying in the moment."

"Good lord, this is like an Abbot & Costello routine. Who's on first?"

Dr. Gold laughed again. He picked up her left wrist and pressed into it. He said, "You can't be angry if you're living in the moment. Anger runs contrary, it's a distraction. Does it serve any purpose?"

"No."

"Okay. So the first step to staying in the moment is to accept yourself for who you are right now."

Luna considered this. It sounded reasonable. "All right."

"Then, instead of focusing on specific issues, focus on the process. You're thinking that if you've worked on a problem for x amount of time, it should be solved. But guess what? Life is not linear."

"Tell that to the math teachers," said Luna. But she knew there was no straight path to happiness. You had to veer into some pretty dark places, just as Mr. Grotesque at the SLAA meeting and the movie *Firehouse Dog* had said.

"It's like coming here," Dr. Gold continued. "It doesn't matter what I worked on last time. What matters is what you need me to concentrate on now."

This made sense, yet she wanted to cry.

She wanted to be done.

"Let's review rule number three," said Dr. Gold. Luna looked up at the sign, even though she already knew rule number three was "Everything always works out."

"Yeah, I've got that," she said.

"Good. Turn onto your side," he said.

He pressed several spots along her thigh and butt.

"Okay, so if you know everything will work out, you can let go of your issues and live in the moment." He pressed into a spot mid-thigh. "And when you're in the present moment, specific issues cease to matter – it's your state of being that counts." He sat and perched her right leg over his shoulder. "And you have to have faith that you're in the right place – that this is where you're meant to be at this moment."

"How do I do that?"

"If you're in the moment, you're aligned with your higher power."

Funny how you keep getting the same homilies from different sources, said Jiminy. *Another funny thing is how you keep repeating lessons until you learn them.*

Luna wasn't listening to Jiminy. She was distracted by Dr. Gold, who was doing the part she hated most—pushing his finger into the center of her chest. It hurt in such an uncomfortable, squirming way that she felt like there was no coming back from it. "This makes me want to run screaming from the table," she told him.

"Try not to."

"It feels like you're piercing my heart." He laughed yet again. She really amused him. "*Are* you piercing my heart?"

"No."

"Every time you do this it hurts more."

"That means you need it more."

He had an answer for everything, dammit.

This was taking forever. She really wanted to bolt. Oh God, the pressure—it felt like her chest would cave in!

She blurted, "What *is* it? What does this spot mean?"

He looked at her for a moment. Then he said, "It's an emotional center."

Then he stopped pressing. *Finally.*

"I just don't feel like I'm worthy," she said.

"Of?"

She thought for a moment. "Happiness."

Dr. Gold worked on her left forearm. "Are you alive?

"Yes."

"Do you have a soul?"

"Yes?"

"Do you do your best to be a good person?"

"Yes."

"Then why wouldn't you deserve happiness?"

She told Dr. Gold, "Because of what my parents did."

He asked, "Are your parents God?"

She was silent for a moment. Then she said, "No. They're not."

"It's okay to feel this way right now," said Dr. Gold. "The key is to accept and embrace the process and work on what your heart says you're ready for, not what your head thinks logically should be next."

But it's my heart that always gets me in trouble.

Releasing Luna's arm, Dr. Gold said, "Alrighty, roll over on your side, sit up, then stand with your feet together."

This was the end, once again.

Luna paused, considering her gravity. She pressed her black Nikes into the brown carpet, put her hands on her hips and swayed in a semi-hula, to stir her molecules up a little and see how they settled.

"Yup," she finally said. "Feels right in the middle."

Behind her, from the other side of the table, Dr. Gold said, "Good. You're centered."

"Thanks." Luna turned and looked at him, right in his green irises.

He smiled.

Luna's step work was progressing. After two more tries she produced what Joe called an "okay" inventory of herself for step four.

She breezed through five, six and seven.

Step eight was kind of like step four, except it was an inventory of her relationships. After she finished that, she had to make amends to people.

As if on cue, Cousin Dom called.

"Cuz… What went on between you and Red?"

She did *not* want to get into that. "Why?"

"He called me."

"And?"

"He came home from the hospital and found a note from you."

Damn. She'd forgotten about the letter. *I should've gone back and taken it down.*

"Did he tell you what it said?"

"He did."

"Dom... All I can say is that it wasn't unfounded."

"He wanted me to tell you something."

"What?"

"He said he's gonna outlive you and piss on your grave."

Red wants to piss on my grave.

Luna couldn't get the thought out of her head.

She had no urge to spew vicious words back.

But she *did* have to do *something*.

Even though Red had deserved her outrage, Luna needed to make amends to him.

She wrote him a new note: "Red, When I wrote that you should die, my intentions were metaphorical. I meant that you should die spiritually and be reborn. I would never wish actual death on you or anyone. It's just that you hurt me and for some reason, this time I reacted to the pain. – Luna"

She drove to Red's house and taped the new note to his door.

It felt like she had made amends to herself.

That's the best kind of amends to make, said Jiminy.

THIRTY-FOUR

THE RESURGENCE OF her experience with Red had shaken Luna. She told Joe, "I need to go to that SLAA retreat." It was coming up the next weekend.

"Why? You're doing good," he said. "You'll be fine. You don't have to drive to Pennsylvania."

"I feel like I should."

"Do what you need to do," he said. "But be careful. They say it's gonna snow."

Luna dropped the kids off at Nick's apartment (he'd finally moved out of Sal's basement, and had a place with actual bedrooms for the kids) and packed her van. The flakes tumbling outside were getting heavier, blanketing everything. The ducks in the water took off, quacking and flapping their wings frantically like their feathered butts were frozen. But Luna couldn't imagine the snow lasting, despite the warnings on every news channel. Spring was in five days.

You just can't accept expert advice—or even the evidence you're witnessing, said Jiminy. *Have fun on your journey.*

By the time she drove across the Verrazano-Narrows Bridge into Staten Island, she realized that the snow *would* keep falling. It was even faster and thicker now. Apparently Mother Nature hadn't consulted a calendar. But Luna wasn't worried. The snow was pretty, and she preferred it to pouring rain.

She got to New Jersey. Thankfully, the Garden State's highway department kept the turnpike clear. The road was nice and smooth, even if she had to keep her speed down to forty. *This isn't so bad.* She stopped at rest area for a cup of coffee and sang along with the radio.

It was nearly dark when she hit Pennsylvania. She was sixty miles from her destination, which would've been less than an hour away on any other day. But the sky was dumping snow by the bushel, and for some inexplicable reason the turnpike was unplowed. Luna reduced her speed to twenty, tripling her remaining traveling time. The temperature had dropped, and the road was all ice under the snow. The radio was a distraction instead of a comfort. She hit the "off" button and drove to the sounds of her tires and wipers hard at work. A few times she skidded, and terror shot through her heart.

If someone had been driving beside her…

She didn't want to think about it.

Luna crept through the darkness for three hours, and finally her exit was next. She was paying what she thought was close attention, but there were no lights on the highway, the snow made visibility suck even more, and the regular exit signs had been removed while the road was under construction.

Honk! A humungous tracker trailer was passing her. She moved to the left to make room. Too late, she saw the tiny exit sign pointing to a ramp on the right. *Shit!* No way could she chance going over all the snow between her and the exit. She could fishtail into the truck!

The next exit was twelve miles away.

That meant twenty-four more miles of edging down this treacherous road. Now she was doing fifteen miles an hour and still felt like she might crash at any moment.

Luna did the math and felt sick. She knew what a metaphor it was, to have missed the exit and been forced to inch further in the night, out of her way and then back. But frankly, it was a metaphor she could've done without.

She almost called out to Jiminy, but even if he answered, what would he say? *I told you so.* She felt around the passenger seat for her cell phone.

Sunny picked up on the third ring. "What's up, Chicky? Having fun with the addicts?"

"I haven't gotten there yet," Luna said. She shared her predicament. "I'm scared, and the worst part is, I'm all alone."

"Stay on the phone, I'll talk you through it," Sunny said.

"I can't. I need to use both hands in this snow. I can feel the car losing its grip..."

The car wasn't the only thing losing it's grip.

"So put me on speaker."

"I can't—the speaker sucks on this phone. People soundalike they're lost in the netherworld." Kind of like she was.

"What are you gonna do?"

"I guess I'll pray."

"Call me when you get there," said Sunny. "Godspeed."

"Thanks," said Luna. The call ended.

Praying was awkward. She still didn't understand her higher power—which made it hard to address. It was like writing a 'to whom it may concern' letter.

She opened with the serenity prayer—it was always a good ice breaker, and also ironically appropriate.

"God," she said, staring at the dark ahead, "Grant me the serenity to accept the things I cannot change, the courage to change the things I can, and the wisdom to know the difference."

This was definitely an 'accept the things I cannot change' moment.

She said, "Please lead me through this, and help me get safely to where I need to be."

She couldn't think of anything else to add that wouldn't be redundant. So she just said, "Thanks."

She drove in silence for a while, then decided to try the radio again. "Bad Day" came on.

Tell me about it, she thought.

She turned off the radio again and started chanting, "I'm going to be okay. I'm going to be okay."

After a while she modified it.

"I'm okay," she said.

Over and over.

"I'm okay."

And then she finally was.

Free from the horrific highway, Luna had a few more miles to go. It seemed like she'd ventured into some uncharted forest. Poking her way through several inches of unplowed snow she wondered, *What God-forsaken place am I headed to?*

The road ended at a driveway. She saw the sign for her destination: "Gaston Abbey." She snaked down the path, inching around the parking lot to the front door. Studying the harsh gray facade and the looming granite statue of Mother Mary in front, it hit her.

This place wasn't God-forsaken at all!

This place had forsaken everything else *for God.*

She called Sunny. "I made it! You won't believe it though – this place is an abbey, as in Westminster Abbey – it's all religious!"

"Didn't they tell you that when you signed up?" asked Sunny.

"It said 'abbey' on the paper, but I thought it was a fancy word for 'inn.'" She paused, then added, "Actually, the word 'abbey' made me think of the 'Abbey Road' album cover – you know, with the Beatles crossing the street."

"See any Beatles?"

"Nope, no Beatles," Luna said quietly, still taking in the fact that she'd driven hundreds of miles to get to *this.* "There's nothing here except the snow-covered cars of a few dozen sex addicts… and the hand of God."

"Christ on rye with a pickle," said Sunny.

Luna stared at Mary – the poor woman who, rumor had it, got pregnant without even getting to enjoy her husband.

She sucked in a breath, let it out. This was an interesting choice to house a bunch of sex and love addicts; that was for sure.

"I'll tell you one thing. After what I went through, this is it. *Something's* gonna change in me here."

"What's that?"

"I don't know yet… but you'll see."

"Have fun with that," said Sunny. "I'm gonna go have some Bailey's over ice."

THIRTY-FIVE

LUNA PARKED AND trudged with her bags through the snow to the door. It was locked, and there was no bell. "Come on now!" she implored, staring up to the sky. When she looked back at the door a woman was heading toward her.

"You're lucky," she said. "There's no one at the desk this time of night. I just came down to get something."

The woman showed Luna to her room, which was small and Spartan – basically a monk's cell.

"There aren't any locks on the doors," the woman told her.

"Do you think that's a good idea with this crowd?" Luna asked.

"We joked about that," the woman said. "Anyway, there's a lounge down the hall. You might want a snack."

Luna might very well want a snack. She hadn't had dinner.

The woman said goodnight and Luna unpacked a few things – toiletries and her notebook, which she put by the bed. She wanted to be sure and get all this down later.

Then she headed to the lounge.

There were a few people in there, men, mostly—and some very good-looking ones, as luck would have it—and a couple of women. Luna introduced herself and snagged a pear, slurping into it unceremoniously. It was too late in the evening to be lady-like.

"Is that your pear, or ours?" one of the men asked.

She stopped mid-crunch. *Oh God.* Was she eating their prayer pear or something?

Juice oozed down her chin.

"I saw it in the basket... Is that okay?"

"Oh yeah... the food's for everyone. I just thought we were out of them. You're lucky you found it."

That was the second person who'd described her as lucky since she'd gotten there.

Too bad she didn't see herself that way.

Not one bit.

The tricky thing about love addiction was love itself: a worthy and noble thing, unlike alcohol, drugs or even sex. It was hard to believe that anything bad could spring from something so pure.

This was the discussion at breakfast, while a cast iron sculpture of Jesus wearing Teflon pantaloons stood sentry in the center of the table. Luna sat near him, crunching corn flakes and of course, self-administering a massive dose of coffee – possibly the only thing that could get her through this.

There was no escaping Jesus in this place. He was in paintings lining the halls, and perched on crosses just about everywhere else.

And he was getting to her.

What's your beef with poor Jesus? asked Jiminy.

I don't like the idea that God had a son and allowed him to suffer so much, Luna said. *I can't stand the thought of someone being sacrificed, especially by his own father.*

That ***is*** *a bit much*, said Jiminy.

The conversation continued around Luna.

The worst thing about love addiction, according to the general consensus, was that there was no balance. It was a constant free-fall from one extreme to the other.

Luna decided to chime in. "It's kind of like puberty," she said. "Maybe love addiction is really arrested development."

No one said anything. *Way to stop a conversation*, she thought. *Good job, Luna.*

To the others she said, "Or maybe not." She took a sip of coffee. "Hey, what's in a name, anyway?"

Luna felt a label was as helpful as a Band-Aid. Useful for a little while, but eventually whatever was underneath needed to be exposed if it was ever going to heal.

She might've said this to the others, but breakfast was over.

She had a lot to say, she realized. She'd lived this life of abuse and shame and finally she was learning how to accept herself – and here was a safe space to get it all out.

Unfortunately, there was no time. The day was booked solid with workshops, and a meeting in the evening. There was already a speaker for the meeting, and that person would have forty minutes to share. Other comments would be limited to five minutes max. That's the way it went.

Damn.

But then, as if on cue, the retreat leader made an unbelievable announcement: the evening's speaker wouldn't be able to make it! He asked, "Would anyone else like to share their story?"

Luna's hand went up almost on its own.

Everyone looked at her. She was so overwhelmed by this sudden opportunity that she had trouble speaking.

"Yes?" the leader asked.

Luna found her voice. "I would."

The thirty-five retreaters were seated in the abbey's oval, foliage-filled, glass-topped atrium.

Luna sat by the fireplace at the front of the room, in an antiquish dark wood chair with intricate carvings. There was yet another statue of Jesus next to her. A woman came over and covered him with a sweater. "He's too distracting," she said.

The room buzzed with conversation until 7:30 struck and the meeting was called to order. Instantly a focused energy sparked inside the space, so palpable that she felt it embracing her. She even smelled it. It was as pungent as if everyone in that room had been wearing the same strong perfume.

They said the serenity prayer, and then Luna was introduced.

All eyes were on her, and she was ready. She looked right back at them.

And she told her story.

From Halloween when she was eight to Nick and the disastrous relationships since her marriage ended.

She told them about Red.

"Some of these things weren't my fault. But some were – or at least, I could've been more cautious." Her glance fell on a super-sized Jesus on the back wall, and she fidgeted in her chair. "The mistake was in the rush. I had to get somewhere, to be something. I don't even know where or what. I just couldn't be comfortable being with myself. I chose the first wedding dress I tried on, and why not? After all, I chose the first man who was willing to stick around. And after the divorce, I was in another rush – to make up for lost time."

"I don't regret anything," she said. "It's all been part of the journey. The thing that's been the hardest is to stop looking for approval in others."

Luna got the five-minute warning. "I'm nearly out of time, so I'll close with a phrase that's been running through my head as I tell my story. 'Looking for love in all the wrong places.' " She looked mega-Jesus in the eye. "I want my life to be more than a cheesy country-western song."

Luna thanked everyone for listening.

"Thank you for sharing," they all said.

Walking back to her room, Luna felt both elated and exhausted.

Wow.

She was dizzy with all the words she'd said, and the thoughts still swirling through her.

I need to lie down.

She headed back to her room and sprawled across her cot. Still the thoughts wouldn't go, but they were different now.

They were new.

Revealing.

Suddenly she was filled with knowledge, like it'd been poured straight into her.

She understood her higher power.

It was a part of her, inside all along.

Awesome.

I am God, she marveled. *I just have to surrender to myself.*

Amen, said Jiminy.

She could see the puddle now.

Lying on the thin tiny mattress that night, she watched Joe's puddle glimmering, caught in between dreams and consciousness.

What was she afraid of, if God was inside her?

Why was she still trembling, afraid to take the plunge?

"Jiminy, talk to me," she called out.

He didn't answer.

When she woke up, she knew why she felt so scared.

She didn't want to be God—to be responsible for herself.

She wanted someone to protect her. Still, and after everything she'd been through.

She wanted the Hollywood happy ending.

But she was willing to wait for it.

At least I'm not throwing myself at the first man I see, she thought.

That's a really good thing around here, said Jiminy.

"So how was it?" Joe asked when Luna arrived at the gym for her next session.

"It was a lot to handle," said Luna. "I need a break."

"From?"

"From the twelve steps… from thinking about everything. I'm all thought out. I just wanna box for awhile."

"Suit yourself," he said. "But I'm gonna push you extra hard on the bags now."

That suited Luna just fine.

THIRTY-SIX

AUGUST ALREADY! THE spring and half the summer had flown by, along with Luna's 39th birthday. She was determined to find her way to happiness, but taking care of the house was a psychological strain. Every detail was daunting, and it was one thing after the next.

First, it was the air conditioners. She'd carted them from the shed and heaved them upstairs. One for her room, one for the boys. She could've hired a handyman – or even asked Joe to come help – but she'd wanted to do it herself. How hard could it be, to put in air conditioners? She took boxing lessons, for Christ's sake (or, as Sunny would say, Christ in long johns with fuzzy slippers!). She could do it! She could install the air conditioners and show her sons the meaning of independence! But the problem was not carrying the units. It was the moment of installation, when she had to let go for one breathless second and trust that the teetering mechanisms would stay in place and not crash to the ground. The problem was that no matter how much boxing she took, how much self-help work she did, how solid she felt when she was with Sunny—still, there were moments like this when there *was* no control, and things could easily waver and fall two stories, and there was nothing she could do. She managed to hold in her hysteria in front of Ben and Dylan, but as soon as she got their unit balanced (as well as she could ascertain, because the hanging in a window part seemed precarious now) and humming, she headed down the creaking stairs and outside, slamming the screen door with the big rip in it behind her, and let it all loose. She wanted to feel the victory in having installed the air conditioners without dropping them, but all she could do was quiver with anxiety for whatever unforeseen task was coming, because there was never an end to them.

The bees came next.

There were bees nesting in a Hefty bag amongst clothes Nick had left behind.

She'd dumped the bag onto the second floor deck while cleaning her bedroom in March and forgotten about it – until the day in late June when she glanced up from her lawn to see Nick's tube socks and tighty-whiteys spilling out over the deck's edge, out of the overturned bag. Sensing that the neighbors might not like this, she went to retrieve the apparel and dispose of the bag. That's when she discovered the bees, which, understandably, didn't like being stirred, and swarmed out in protest. Ben, who'd been watching from the window, was afraid of them. He yelled out, "Bees!" and slammed the window closed, leaving Luna outside with them. She'd yanked the window back open and lunged inside, bringing several uninvited guests with her. It took an hour to coax them out again. A couple of days later, she and Sunny did a sneak attack, hoisting the bag over the railing before the bees knew what was happening. Luna and Sunny high-fived each other and stared down at the burst of clothing, only to have to hightail it away when a bee flew back up at them.

Then the washing machine rinse hose had the audacity to burst, after she'd so carefully connected it. She'd burst too, sinking onto the toilet and crying. Eyeing the water pooling on the floor, Dylan had asked, "Mommy, are those all your tears?"

Luckily Sears repairmen came quickly.

The worst thing was the office – untouched since Nick had dumped everything and left. She could never deal with it, nor could she pay someone else to – not only out of embarrassment, but also because there just might be something she wanted to keep buried in that rubble. Whenever she worked up the courage to try and face the mess, her hand trembled when she touched the doorknob and she walked away without so much as twisting it. She convinced herself it didn't matter – she didn't need an office. She wrote at the kitchen table, or on the deck in the summer.

She told herself she'd take care of it when she was ready – and she hoped one day she would be.

Luna also worried that she had scarred the boys with the divorce.

They seemed to be taking it okay. Nick was doing the single dad thing remarkably well. When they were with him, he cooked dinner every night and watched movies with them.

Still, they were a fractured family.

In the fall there would be a full schedule again: classes, tests and clubs for the kids, PTA and soccer mom duties for Luna.

She decided to take the kids away, before the return of their obligations.

She picked Boston. Not too far to drive to, and she knew the general layout of the place.

Within two days of her impulse, they were on their way.

They were playing a license plate game on the highway when the Fung Wah drove up, two lanes across from them. It was a bus with daily rides between Chinatown in Manhattan and Boston.

"We could've taken the Fung Wah!" Luna exclaimed.

Ah, well, this way we get to go at our own pace, she reflected.

And apparently their pace was a lot quicker than the Fung Wah's. They exited for gas. They stopped at a rest stop for a bathroom break and ice cream. Then they got off again when Luna spotted a Dunkin Donuts sign and couldn't resist her Pavlovian craving for coffee. When they resumed their ride, the Fung Wah bus was behind them.

"I can't believe it! How slow *is* that thing? We stopped like a billion times!" Ben exclaimed.

"Let's race the bus," said Dylan.

"I don't know, guys," said Luna.

But the kids were adamant. They expected total victory in this unexpected contest with the Fung Wah to Boston.

"Hurry, Mommy," Dylan implored.

"Go, go, go," urged Ben.

"I'm doing my best!" Luna announced to her two backseat drivers.

The Fung Wah bus was on their heels. It changed lanes and picked up speed.

It was next to them now, engines revving.

"C'mon, Mom!" the boys cheered in unison.

Flooring it, Luna put a good, final space between them and the bus.

"Ha! That's right, Ma. Shift into nitro!" Ben was triumphant. "What now, Fung Wah? What now?"

That was the last they saw of the Fung Wah.

In the wake of their triumph, the kids were both quiet, curled up in their seats and reading books. The only sounds came from outside – tires against highway pavement, wind against windows. Dylan had Gus, Luna's old stuffed walrus, tucked next to him with his fins crossed. Luna had found Gus in the closet recently – the poor creature had a piece of his left tusk missing, but otherwise he'd survived the years unscathed – and she'd introduced him to Dylan. Now, they were inseparable.

Ben was reading his daily ten-page installment of *My Brother Sam Is Dead*. He paced himself so he'd never have to rush. He was almost done, and ready to write the report he had to hand in the first day of school.

Luna glanced in her rearview mirror at her two boys.

She was so lucky.

That's what she needed to remember always.

Now you've got the right idea, said Jiminy.

Luna pulled the van up to the old-fashioned inn she'd booked a family suite in. There was a kitchen, which Luna loved because she could cook some meals and save money, and even more because she could have her morning coffee the moment she woke up.

None of this impressed the boys, who were appalled that there was no pool. The way Ben and Dylan reacted, it was as though they'd been told they had to sleep hanging from nails in the closet.

Luna laughed, and apologized that she'd caused them dismay.

Next time, she promised them, they'd hit a chain hotel.

Over the next three days Luna and the kids explored Boston. Then they branched out, visiting the battleground in Lexington. From there it was a few minutes into Concord, where Ralph Waldo Emerson and Henry David Thoreau had lived.

Emerson and Thoreau were philosophy's rat pack.

Luna loved Emerson's great dictate: "What lies before us and what lies behind us are small matters compared to that which lies within us."

Emerson had been a Unitarian Universalist minister and his words tended to have that 'almighty' feel.

Thoreau had written a passage which had helped Luna get through her awkward, lonely teen years: "If a man does not keep pace with his companions, perhaps it is because he hears a different drummer. Let him step to the music he hears, however measured or far away."

Thoreau was the renegade of the pair.

First, Luna and the boys toured Emerson's house. Then they headed up to Walden Pond, where Thoreau had lived in a cabin.

It was hard to say why she loved Walden Pond at first sight. She'd seen light glisten on water before – she saw it every day, actually, at home – and maybe the familiarity had something to do with it. Still, she'd been around water and nature in other places which had done little for her. There was something utterly perfect here, something conducive to spirit and soul which instantly struck a chord of harmony in her heart.

Maybe it was Thoreau's ghost tickling at her, whispering, "Our life is frittered away by detail. Simplify, simplify."

Luna smiled at that thought. After all, she *was* simplifying her life. She'd been releasing the clutter she'd been carting around – the sorrow, the desperation, the loneliness. These were the details weighing her down, taking up precious time where she could be a mom, a writer, a happy person.

Simplicity was the key.

What would it take for her to toss every piece of garbage from her mind in one fell swoop and be free?

People were swimming, splashing around in the pond. She wondered if they were happy in any consistent way.

Did details drag them down, too?

Dylan wanted to swim. Even though they had no bathing suits or towels, she waded in with him. He was in shorts, she was in sweatpants – but it didn't matter. They danced in the water, played a dunking game, and collected rocks to bring home.

Ben, ever the pragmatist, didn't want to get all wet without the proper equipment. Luna told him they had clothes in the van to change into, but without a towel he was a 'no.' He sat on the stone bench in front of the pond and started his book report.

Stepping back onto the sand, Dylan reached down and scooped up what turned out to be a rubber band. He held it over Luna's head, a halo. "You're an angel, Mommy," he said.

Luna squeezed her arms around him. "You too, baby."

Maybe this was heaven on earth if only they'd let it be. Maybe all they had to do was see it, embrace it, accept it and let go of the rest.

Maybe it was that simple.

Just say no to hell.

Afterwards, Luna and Dylan made their dripping way back to the van and changed, and Ben basked in his dryness. In the past Luna wouldn't have wanted to get all wet either – generally she thought of swimming as a giant nuisance – but something had made her take that plunge with Dylan. She was so glad she had.

On the highway home, Luna and the kids passed the Fung Wah bus parked at a rest stop.

They waved.

THIRTY-SEVEN

BACK FROM VACATION, Luna made a decision.

"I'm gonna try dating again," she told Joe. They were doing pad work—jabbing, hooking, ducking, slipping and talking about love.

"Don't do it. You ain't ready," he said. "Uppercuts!"

"Gee, thanks." She drove her fists up into the pads until the bell rang.

"Rest. Hey, you want me to lie, or what?"

"Possibly."

"What makes you all gung-ho to do this? You horny?"

"No… well, I guess maybe yes… But that's not it. I just feel good. I've been living alone for nine months. I've been okay."

Not exactly true… she'd nearly fallen apart every time something in the house broke down. But she wanted to concentrate on the positive. She'd survived. *That* was positive.

"What's your game plan?"

"I thought I'd try CraigsList again."

"*CraigsList*? Are you *shitting* me? That's where you buy a table, not get a date."

"Yesterday, I heard a guy on Howard Stern say he met someone on CraigsList. It was love at first sight."

"That's ridiculous. That ain't love." The bell rang again. He held up his right pad. "Double hook. Twist on your heel!"

Luna complied, or at least she thought she did.

"TWIST!" he hollered. "Holy shit, for months I been telling you to twist. What the fuck does it take?"

She tried again. She responded to being yelled at. "Better," he said. "Twenty. Go!"

Luna twisted and thudded, twisted and thudded. In the background Cher crooned "If I Could Turn Back Time."

Joe said, "It took me six or seven years to fall in love with my wife."

Luna almost fell over mid-twist. "Really?"

"Yeah. In the beginning I would've told you it could never happen. But people can grow on you."

Twist, thud, twist, thud.

Over and over, catching Joe's steady blue eyes in-between each move.

Then he said, "Love is a consequence."

Twist, thud, twist, thud. "That's an unusual concept," she said.

"It's true," he said. Then he said, "Jab, jab, double left uppercut."

She struck the pads silently for a few moments. Consequence seemed almost a dirty word, although she didn't know why. Maybe it was too grown up.

Luna liked the immediate.

She asked, "What about the Zen saying, 'leap and the net will appear?'"

Joe said, "You're mixing metaphors. Jab, jab, right, right uppercut."

Thud, thud. "Am I?" Thud, Thud.

He laughed. "What the fuck do I know about metaphors? Sounded good, though."

The bell rang. Joe yanked off Luna's gloves, tossed them to the corner under the mirror, ripped the Velcro seal on her wraps and unraveled her. The wraps landed in a heap at her feet. "Let's go," he said.

He put a thirty-pound weight on what Luna called "the butt machine" and motioned her on. She stepped onto the platform, bent under the shoulder lift, spread her feet so they were centered, pulled the safety bar out and pushed up, lifting the weight on her shoulders.

Lift, squat. Lift, squat. The first couple were never bad. She said, "Don't you at least believe in unconditional love?"

"The only unconditional love we have is for our kids."

Up, down. Up, down.

By the fourth she was feeling the strain in her thighs and her rear. She felt it in her chest too, which stopped her from responding.

Up, down. Up, down.

Up, down. Up, down.

Her legs were trembling. "Jesus, Joe…" she managed.

He said, "Jesus wasn't really sacrificing anything to die for our sins. He knew he was going to heaven. I don't have that kind of faith."

Up, down. Up, down.

Up, down. Up, down.

Was he even keeping count here? "I have to stop," she told him.

"Two more."

Up. "Uhhhh!" Down. "Uhhhh!"

Up. "Uhhhh!" Down. "Uhhhh!"

"And rest," Joe said.

Luna slid the locking bar forward and moved out from under the shoulder rest. She wobbled down.

That's why she paid him – she'd never push herself this far.

She leaned against the machine for support. In between recuperating huffs she said, "So you're saying even Jesus didn't offer unconditional love?"

"I'm saying he had nothing to lose. It was a no-brainer for him."

Sunny didn't like the idea of Luna dating again, either. They were having lunch at the Chinese buffet near Sunny's job.

"Remember Mr. Ocean?" she licked at her chopstick provocatively.

"You did that pretty well."

"Remember the old man?" Sunny stuck her left foot out of the booth and pointed her chopstick at her shoe.

"How could I forget Gumppoldskirchen?"

"Remember crackhead Alex?" She stuck a chopstick in her mouth and sucked it like a pipe.

"Ex-crackhead Alex," Luna amended.

Sunny waved that detail away. "Remember the sadist?" She poked her chopsticks at her throat.

"Hey, I broke that off."

Sunny jabbed a chopstick towards Luna's private area. "Remember Date Rape Red?"

Luna hung her head. "Yes." She stared at her bowl of hot and sour soup.

"Chicky." Sunny's voice softened. "I'm sorry. That wasn't funny."

"None of this is very amusing."

"I hate bringing all this up, but I'm trying to talk some sense into you. You don't have the greatest track record."

Luna looked up now. "What should I do? Just give up completely? I'm not you, Sunny. I crave companionship."

"I understand the concept of companionship. That's why I have my smelly dogs." Sunny sucked in a wad of vegetable chow mein and chewed.

"Don't you ever want to date?"

"I dated Phil for a long time."

"Please. You had sex with him when you were drunk. Then he kept hanging around like a lost puppy even though you swatted him away."

Sunny was still chewing. She swallowed and asked, "What's your point?"

"And the same thing happened with Sal. You were drunk in a bar and went home with him. The only difference is that there was an actual attraction." Luna wasn't eating. Thinking about those guys she'd dated had quelled her appetite, and she didn't love the Chinese buffet anyway. The food always looked like it had been sitting too long, and the sauces were all extra gunky.

Sunny still had plenty of appetite, and she was fine with the food because there were vegetarian options. She was chewing again because she only had an hour lunch break to chow down, but she managed a "So?"

"So, have you ever gone on a legitimate first date?"

"I guess not," Sunny answered after a sip of Coke to wash down her vegetable egg roll.

"Exactly."

Sunny shuddered. "Dating sounds horrific to me." She crunched into another egg roll.

"Well, it can be… but sometimes it's nice. I had a great time with Alex until he dumped me."

Sunny brushed crumbs from her chest. "And then you were a mess."

"Does that mean the whole thing was a waste… because it ended badly?"

"You tell me."

"Look, I was in a low spot in my life, and I shouldn't have been out there. Things were bound to go wrong. But I've done a lot of work on myself. I want to give dating a shot."

Sunny shrugged. "I guess you're the best judge of yourself." She gave a salute with her chopstick. "Mazel Tov."

Luna felt better with Sunny's blessing. She drank her soup and downed one piece of skewered chicken, even though it was a tad dry.

They opened their fortune cookies. Sunny's said: *You make the world a brighter place.*

"Must be confused by my name," said Sunny.

"You make *my* world a brighter place," said Luna.

"Aw, gee. Ditto for me. Too bad we don't have lesbian tendencies, or we'd be all set."

Luna's said: *Luck is falling hard on you.*

"Talk about a good news/bad news scenario," said Sunny. "You'd better wear a helmet."

THIRTY-EIGHT

LUNA WENT HOME and wrote an ad for CraigsList.

She was looking for honesty, and that's what she led with: "As Billy Joel sang, honesty is such a lonely word. But I know it's out there somewhere."

She went on to describe herself, and the kind of relationship she wanted.

"I've got a lot of love to give," she wrote at the end.

Luna was about to post her ad when Jiminy spoke up. *Are you sure you want to do this?*

"Why? You don't think I should, either?"

My opinion doesn't matter, replied Jiminy. *The question is: Do* ***you*** *really think you're ready?*

"I do."

Then go for it.

She hit the "post" button.

The responses rolled in quick. Most were atrocious: "i just happened to read your post on craigslist and liked what you wrote. that sounds kind of generic, but i really did and was thinking we may share a similar outlook on things and be looking for someone similar. i'd love to find out more."

Kind of generic? But that was nothing compared to the other problems with this note. Luna cringed from poor writing skills and grammatical errors. When did capitalization fall by the wayside?

Some of the men were downright creepy: "I am an NRA shooting instructor looking for a good female friend for LTR and yes SEX also so I am glad to hear you have a VIGINA!!"

Luna actually hadn't mentioned she had a vagina. Wasn't that a given?

There were also a fair amount of husbands who claimed to be on the verge of divorce: "My marital status is married, but it's about to change in the following month. Divorce is on the way since this is a no turn back situation."

Sure.

Luna wound up answering no one. She didn't feel sad about it.

Proud that she hadn't reached out to anyone who seemed "off" (which was everyone), she deleted all the e-mails and figured she'd try again in a couple of weeks.

But then she got another response in her in-box.

And somehow, before she even opened it, she knew this one was a keeper.

She was going to have a relationship with this man.

The subject of his email was: "A bottle of red, a bottle of white, what shall we toast tonight?"

Inside he wrote: "I'm not Mr. Universe, and far from Bill Gates in wealth, but I have a deep heart, an open mind and lots of room to listen." He kept his note short, putting in just enough details to reveal that he was actually writing a response for her specific ad.

He closed with, "Maybe I'll have enough luck that you will reply. If not, enjoy life and best wishes in your search. He's out there, trust your heart and a few friends :)"

His name was Trip.

She wrote him back.

When Trip learned that Luna's screen name was Lady Macbeth, he sent an email quoting Shakespeare. That *really* got her. He'd played a witch in *Macbeth*, in college. She loved that.

One of the excerpts was this, which he'd dubbed his "Shakespeare mix" – a collage of Bard quotes:

Does thou hint of an inner being that pulls at the

skin of your mortal costume? I sense you protest too much, yet desires are truer then you speak! Unleash if you must, but beware of the moonlight, since it has the power to fold us within.

With the name 'Luna', she was well aware of the moon's pull, and perfectly willing to surrender to *that* higher power.

He also wrote, "You do know, in order to be a Lady Macbeth, there needs to be a Macbeth." How intoxicating! Problems aside, Macbeth and his wife had a tremendous passion for each other.

But they also had a pretty bad ending.

All in all, *Macbeth* was one of the darkest tragedies in literature.

Luna wrote back suggesting she and Trip try a romantic comedy, like *All's Well That Ends Well.*

As their electronic conversations progressed, Trip talked about his roots in the "wilds" of Jamaica, Queens, before moving to Long Island. His early years were spent in a three-story apartment building near the El, a large cemetery and a rock quarry. They had a small back yard, in which they housed a pet chicken named Fred.

He wrote about the theatrical productions he'd worked in during college, both on-stage and back, doing scenery and technical work. Besides *Macbeth*, he'd had roles in *Blood Wedding, Billy Budd, Bye, Bye Birdie,* and *Seven Nuns in Las Vegas.*

Here are some other things Luna learned about Trip:

Stats on Trip

Name: Lucas Tripodi

Age: 49

Ethnic background: Italian and Spanish.

Marital Status: Never married.

Children: None.

Body: Looked pretty good from the pictures.

Hair: Nearly none.

Occupation: Installing cameras and digital video recorders for security systems (where he secured the bulk of his income), fixing computers, light contracting, pyrotechnics, and anything else his clients asked him to do (if he didn't know how to do it, he figured it out.)

Favorite physical activities: Scuba diving, dumpster diving.

Other likes: TV crime dramas, Halloween, selling things on EBay.

Dislikes: He seemed to have a problem relaxing.

Religion: Another lapsed Catholic. He didn't follow the tenets, but he still believed in a traditional God.

Favorite writers: N/A – Books put him to sleep, literally.

Favorite Dessert: Pistachio ice cream.

Favorite saying: "Better late than never."

Typically, Trip composed his emails when he *finally* got home. One night at 2 a.m. he wrote, "I know, WOW, I work too much."

They IM'd frequently, something Luna usually found aggravating because it was hard to type correctly and keep up with the conversation. Somehow, with Trip, it was fun. They were sending questions back and forth, and he wrote, "Tats?"

Unfamiliar with computer lingo, Luna didn't understand that the question was short for "Do you have any tattoos?" She thought of Tweety, and typed, "Putty tat?"

He wrote, "Where?"

She wrote, "What?"

Finally, Luna realized he'd meant 'tattoos', but their banter reminded her of a character on the '70s TV show *Welcome Back Kotter,* famous for such muddled conversations.

She wrote, "Now we are Vinny Barbarino."

Luna's communications with Trip turned sensual pretty fast. She couldn't help it. If she felt it, she expressed it. It was part of that honesty thing. What some called boundaries, she called lies. It started with a simple reference from Trip at the end of an email in which he was sharing a chunk of his history. He wrote, "In the next chapter, I'll give you some food, fun and sex, but now I have to go to work."

She wrote him back, "Gosh, you had to go and mention sex. I was doing so well and now my mind is ablaze..."

He responded, "Mind ablaze, hmmmmmmmm, DO TELL!"

Luna told.

Oh God, said Jiminy. *Just when I thought we were making progress.*

But Luna was too caught up in sexy talk to hear Jiminy.

Modems sizzling, Luna and Trip agreed to meet in that Mecca of on-line first-date spots: Starbucks. Well-traversed and providing caffeinated stimulation, the cozy, earthy coffeehouse was perfect. She didn't love their coffee, but it wasn't great coffee she was after. And anyway, who could really taste anything but anticipation when they were about to meet someone?

She'd arrived early, ordering a vente soy misto (steamed soy milk tamed the harsh coffee to the point where she could endure it), and parked herself at a table near a power outlet for her laptop. The plan was to write. Edit, actually. She was too excited to type anything new.

But the editing wasn't going well either. For some reason the persistent whirring of foaming milk and the grrring of the grinder churned through her thoughts, although she'd tuned sounds out countless times before. Between whirs and grrrs, she kept running the same sentence through her head over and over, trying to focus on the words instead of Trip's impending entrance, and failing.

Nervous wasn't the right word, but she felt something along those lines.

In one of his letters, Trip said he'd always thought he had time. He'd assumed that down the road he'd meet someone who clicked. Then suddenly, there he was: down the road and alone. He'd written, "I guess I'll just have to hope that things work out with you."

She felt like that, too.

Down the road and alone, hoping things would work out with Trip.

He texted her. The "da-da-da-DA!" tones made her jolt. She wasn't used to text messages; she didn't understand why people didn't just call and talk.

Before Trip, only Sunny had texted her once, and she'd never read the message because she didn't know how to open it. But she'd recently gotten a new phone which popped messages right on the screen. Trip's message said, "Are you ready?"

Luna tried to write back but wasn't yet versed in quick return texts. She was fumbling over tiny touch-screen letters when Trip strolled in with a quirky, endearing smile on his face. Luna felt this weird pang of knowing, like they weren't strangers at all. She laughed and said, "I was trying to answer you, but couldn't quite work that out."

Trip wasn't particularly tall but carried himself high. He stepped to the counter and snagged a green tea. Then they relocated to a more secluded section, sinking into purple velvet armchairs and chatting about all those small-talk topics people use when they first meet. The weather, the movies, news of the day: preambles to any meaningful conversation. They talked about the pimple on her nose she'd warned him about in advance; he said he wouldn't have noticed. All this was kind of like wading at the edge of the water before plunging into the waves. And as though she were in the tide, she felt a tug. It wasn't sexual – well, it was partly, but this was more.

Trip was lean and well-toned, looking a lot younger than forty-nine. The one thing that revealed his age was his hair. What was left of it was curly grey, circling the lower outskirts of his head. If Luna were him, she'd ditch it. Bald was sexy. But it was his head…

He eyed her outfit. "Do you shop in thrift stores?" he asked.

She glanced down at her off –the–shoulder silky blouse, recently bought at retail. "Do I look like I shop in thrift stores?"

He shrugged. "I always shop in them." He tapped on his jeans. "Bought these there."

Her phone rang. Actually, Ozzy Osborne shrieked, "Allllll aboard! Hahahaha," the opening to *Crazy Train*, her ring tone. It was Sunny, calling to confirm that Luna hadn't been hacked to pieces by a maniac date.

"Alive!" Luna proclaimed.

"Cool! Call if you need me."

They hung up.

Then Luna told Trip she wanted to do what they'd talked about, via IMs. She wanted to go to the beach.

"Really?" he asked.

Really, she did.

Luna felt so secure that she got into Trip's car, a nondescript grey mid-sized sedan filled with paraphernalia for his alarm and computer businesses. He grabbed some stuff from the passenger seat and chucked it in the back.

The beach was five minutes away, if that. He parked by the boardwalk and they got out. From the other side the ocean called. As they walked, Trip asked if she was a Democrat or Republican. She knew he sometimes listened to Rush Limbaugh and therefore figured him a Republican, but answered truthfully that she leaned way more to the donkeys.

"Me too," he answered.

Then why did he listen to Rush Limbaugh?

He said, "I like to hear how the other half thinks."

They hit sand, passing through the beach entrance under the boardwalk and tramping through the mounds like clumsy camels. The sky glowed with sparkling stars. A new moon had yet to take shape.

Luna breathed fresh air in deep.

When they reached the hill piled high for the lifeguards with the chair on top, they dropped. Him first, on his back. Then her, on her stomach, on top of him. The cotton fabric of his polo shirt pressed through her sheer blouse.

Their energies were mingling. The current shifted, like when music switches tempo. It had spice now, zinging through it. An electro-magnetic tango.

The waves in front of them roared and rolled in and out, in and out. The air smelled like a beginning.

A little chilly, she pushed against him tighter. He felt so solid.

He said, sputtering, "I've got sand in my mouth… Now you'll never kiss me…"

He couldn't talk anymore because she kissed him. It was the perfect kiss, despite the grit, or maybe the grit enhanced it. It was the perfect fit, his tongue nestled in hers. Kissing him like she'd never kissed anyone, she wrapped her tongue around his in a long embrace.

Afterwards he said, "Boy, I hope you don't suck my nipples like that."

She laughed. "I won't."

His bristly whiskers brushed her cheek. She felt protected.

She kissed him again.

For some crazy reason they talked about old lovers. She told him about her sham marriage, and the men (some of them) that followed.

Trip talked about the endless supply of sex he'd had in the eighties, an overload which anaesthetized him. As a DJ at a local club, he'd had his pick of women.

He told her about one lover who'd been wearing glitter, how the bed was coated with it, the whole room covered in it, glimmering like Tinkerbell had exploded in there.

And he talked about the girl he'd loved three years ago - who'd suddenly fallen out of love with him and asked him to collect his things.

Maybe they'd shared all this to cleanse themselves, to make a fresh beginning like the air suggested. Or maybe it was a way to admit they were scared, without actually saying it.

Then they pushed their pasts aside and kissed some more.

The craggy sound of an idling motor interrupted them a while later. Loosening their embrace, they found themselves caught in the searing white beam of a searchlight, attached to a police jeep. Stunned and blinking, Luna and Trip were, at least, fully clothed. "Beach is closed," a shadowy female voice behind the light said. Only her elbow was showing, crooked from the jeep window. "You gotta go."

Evicted from their place in the sand, Luna and Trip lurched back to the exit, giddy and holding hands. Entangled, they stumbled even more, but to Luna the walk felt so smooth it was as if they were floating. Luna knew from Trip's emails that he'd always wanted a child. He'd told her in an IM about a woman who'd aborted his baby, confessing this to him only years later. Luna told him that down the road, she'd consider another baby. He liked that.

But, unromantic as it was, she said they'd have to 'spin the sperm' to ensure a girl.

He laughed, and said that would be fine.

In the car she asked, "You think we could find somewhere to park?"

"You wanna park? No one's asked me to park since high school."

She *did* want to park, so they headed to a lot by the bay next to the recreation center. She worried about it being too public. He said not to.

He moved his seat back and she climbed on his lap, facing him. He wore a small silver hoop that she found incredibly sexy.

"I like your earring," she said.

"Thank you!" he said, sounding quite pleased. "I got it three years ago. It was my niece's idea. She said, 'Unk, when you've had your heart broken, an earring's just the thing.'"

He showed Luna the woven bracelet knotted around his wrist. "This is from her. She met the Dalai Lama, and asked him to bless it for me." Luna ran her fingers over the colorful threads, and his surrounding skin. Maybe it was the power of suggestion, but she felt centered, like balance was tingling into her tips.

"I never take it off," Trip said.

He gave her that little, secretive smile again, lifting the corners of his mouth ever so covertly. He had glistening brown eyes with beautiful, flirty eyelashes. When he focused on her there was such magnetism between them, it really was like they already knew each other. They kissed again, and the energy level rose. He reached into her pants, touching the small of her back, and she climaxed.

He moved across her body, touching different parts and making her climax again and again. He asked her to take her pants off; she was nervous, but did it.

There was no denying him.

He didn't want anything in return. She asked, adding, "You know I'll do whatever you want."

He said, "Just enjoy yourself."

Sand sifted around them, moving from their clothes and bodies to the car. Luna's energy swirled and surged, relentless and euphoric to have found a mate. The window was open but still their bodies overheated. Trip said, "That's it! This shirt's coming off!" She helped him out of it, tugging it over his head and across his outstretched arms. Then he held her against him, against his chest. She nuzzled his neck. He smelled sweet and tangy, like butterscotch pudding.

He said, "You smell wonderful."

Trip was commanding, but gentle. He was masculine, not brutal.

Wrapped in Trip's bare arms, Luna said, "You're so tender."

"You're so soft," he said.

A little bit later Trip said quietly, "I can't tell if it's me you want, or just anyone."

She'd known it at the email, and now it was confirmed. Squeezing her fingers into his chest – it had just the right amount of hair and just the right amount of muscle – she said, "You're the man I've been waiting for."

THIRTY-NINE

LUNA WAS ON top of Trip in his front seat, kissing him to the tune of Alice in Chains' "Rooster" on the radio. Her jeans and underwear were off, and he was doing such beautiful things to her…

Her eyes were closed, her thoughts all wrapped up in the feeling Trip supplied. His woolly chest was comforting and strong.

A sharp light poked at her eyelids. She broke from the kiss and looked.

There was a police car creeping through the lot toward them, headlights in their faces.

"Oh my God," she said to Trip, freaking. She slid off him, squeaking against vinyl into the passenger seat. She snatched up her jeans from the floor, then dropped them again.

There was no way she'd ever shimmy back into them in time.

"It's okay," Trip said, and his voice was so sweet she actually relaxed a notch. She was still way up there on her ladder of terror, of course, but it was nice to be one rung down from the top. He pushed his t-shirt over her. She folded her legs on the seat, so that the shirt covered her whole lower half pretty well.

Trip said, "Just stay calm." He hit the radio off, just as the opening notes of "Born To Run" were playing.

It was the second time on this first date that they were being roused by a cop.

On the beach, they'd only been kissing.

This time they were doing something really wrong.

Dear Jesus, under Trip's shirt she was naked!

Her butt was stuck to the seat like a suction cup. She shifted to release it.

The cop pulled up to them sideways, his headlight beams bearing down on them like interrogation lamps in those old movies.

Where were you on the night of the eighth?

It wouldn't take much to crack a confession from Luna – even if she were innocent.

Leaving his engine idling, the cop got out, slammed his door and approached Trip's window with a flashlight. His tall, thick body blocked the bulk of the headlights now, but rays still poked in around his frame, illuminating Trip's dusty dashboard and the pile of parts and tools in his back seat.

Luna wanted to fade away, to melt into the floorboards.

Trip seemed stoic. He rolled down his window. "Evening, Officer."

The cop was young. His baby face probably looked fuller thanks to his crew cut. His eyes were big and round. Luna wanted to turn away – to look out at the dark ocean Trip's car was parked head-on against – but she thought it best to face him.

The cop said nothing back to Trip. He ran his light over Trip's bare chest, then down to Trip's jeans. Thank the lord Trip had his bottoms on!

Luna sucked in a breath and waited for the light to shine on her.

It didn't.

The cop said, "You folks need to be less obvious."

Trip said, "Yes, sir."

"You'd better be going," said the cop. He turned away and headed back to his car.

Luna and Trip sat still as the patrol car backed away, headlights growing dimmer until at last they were gone.

Trip chuckled mischievously. "See? That wasn't so bad."

Luna didn't have it in her to laugh at that moment. She was just trying to get her heart to stop jittering so she could be sure it wasn't going to burst through her chest.

It had been pretty bad.

But despite the heart-pounding interruption she felt happy.

So happy to be with Trip.

The next night they hung out in a vacant attic apartment Trip was working on, above a podiatrist's office. They couldn't go to Luna's house – the babysitter was there with the kids. They couldn't go to Trip's house, either. After his last relationship fell apart, Trip moved back in with his parents.

They sat cross-legged, comfortably mushed in a large sheet of egg-crate-style packing foam on the still-uncarpeted floor. They were surrounded by tools and fixtures yet to be installed. The room was tiny; its low ceiling was triangular. The faded wallpaper bore an ornate floral pattern. It felt like they were in a dollhouse, albeit one under construction.

They watched the show "House" while dining on Chinese take-out. The scent of garlic sauce filled the small space. Luna had tofu and broccoli; Trip had chicken and mixed vegetables. She used a Styrofoam plate and plastic fork; he ate his right out of the paper carton with chopsticks.

Finished, Trip stretched and moaned. He said, "My bones ache… I'm too old for all this hard labor. I'm falling apart."

Luna rubbed his neck and shoulders, and quoted a line from the opening credits of *The Six Million Dollar Man*: "We can rebuild him."

They talked a little, then they kissed a lot.

They sank into that foam and kissed and kissed and kissed. When they took a breather, Luna told him, "You're it for me, you know." She stroked his bristles. Eyes closed, Trip had the majestic peace of a lion at rest in the grass.

It was heaven in this attic, right in this clutter and foam.

A little while later, Trip made love to Luna.

It was exquisite, except Trip never opened his eyes.

The next evening Trip drove down to North Carolina to do a job. He worked all over the country –"Wherever they hire me."

Luna decided to go to the boardwalk. Nick had the kids.

She parked near the beach entrance she and Trip had used, and headed up the wooden ramp. It was warm—summer was holding on even in September, and she didn't need the sweatshirt she carried. The air smelled like salt and pizza.

Luna reached the top. There was nobody in sight. She walked over to a bench overlooking the water and sat.

"So what do you think, Jiminy?" Jiminy probably wouldn't answer, but she figured she'd give it a shot. It'd been a while since he'd piped in, and honestly, she missed his input. "This is a good one, right? A keeper?"

Her phone rang.

It was Trip, calling from some bleak interstate highway.

He was lonely on the road.

They talked about mundane things, like traffic and television. Then he mentioned some show he'd liked as a kid. Luna told him how much TV had meant to her when she was by herself at night, waiting for Loreena to come home. "I needed the voices… the distraction," she said.

"That sucks," said Trip. "I was never alone… but I do have one strange story about my childhood. Remember I told you we had a pet chicken?"

"Fred," said Luna.

"Right. Fred," Trip said. "One day I came home from school and Fred wasn't there. My mom loved to cook, and there was this aroma of soup filling the apartment. It made me so hungry that I couldn't wait for dinner. My mother gave me a bowl. So there I was slurping, and I asked her, 'Where's Fred?' and that's when Mom told me I was eating him."

"Oh my god!" said Luna. "That must've been devastating for you."

"It wasn't *really* my chicken," he said. "It was my brother's. He was the one who kicked up a fuss about it, when he came home from baseball practice."

Luna had no idea what to say. She didn't want to criticize Trip's mom, but damn, that was a cold thing to do to her kids. Unless they couldn't afford food. "Were you poor?"

"No. But if something had a use, my mother used it." He changed the subject. "Tell me about your ex-husband." What a transition: From a dead chicken to a deadbeat husband.

She told him a condensed version of her marriage.

Trip was disgusted by Nick's behavior. He especially didn't like him because "he had what I want, and he didn't appreciate it."

"You could have a family, too," Luna said. "I'll give you one."

Trip paused for a moment.

When he spoke again, his voice was quieter. "I can see you're in a period of transition."

After another pause he added, "Throughout my life women have come to me this way – on their way to somewhere else."

It wasn't true for her.

It wasn't!

Luna wanted to tell Trip this but somehow the words got stuck on their way out.

He said, "You scare me."

The boardwalk wood hummed under Luna's feet from passing bicyclists, and ahead, the ocean tumbled.

Trip said, "When you leave me, and you're with some other guy, at least I'll have spoiled you a little."

Luna stared at the empty lifeguard chair on a huge hill of sand. She and Trip had shared their first kiss at the bottom of that pile.

She said. "I'm not going to leave you. Why would I?"

But Trip went on like he hadn't heard her, and maybe he hadn't.

Over and over, the ocean rolled in and slid out under the moonlight.

"I don't know my purpose in life," Trip said, "but I think maybe part of it is to help women find their way to the next phase of their lives."

She didn't say anything then. She just looked at the waves.

"Have you seen the movie *City of Angels*? Trip asked.

"No," she answered. "Someone told me the end, and it's too sad. I can't watch that."

"It's not sad," he said. "You need to see it."

"Why?"

"You'll like it."

Luna wrote Trip an email when she got home.

She typed, "While I can't guarantee anything – who can? – I don't see this ending."

He wrote back, "Can't respond now."

And that's when everything changed.

When Trip came back, he was different. Distant. A great lover when he was there, but he wasn't there often. He always had to run to a job – always had to run somewhere far from her. He showed up late at night and crawled into her bed, but in the morning he was off like a starter's pistol had been fired.

"I gotta go to work," was his mantra.

His excuse.

His shield.

Just like that, the open, giving partner she'd thought she'd found had closed himself off.

During her next visit, Dr. Gold asked, "Have you ever heard of a self-fulfilling prophecy?"

Luna had, in *Oedipus Rex*.

Dr. Gold nodded. "But it's slightly different. Oedipus collided with his destiny trying to deny it. Trip is engineering his perceived destiny. He's doing everything he can to get you to do what he believes you're going to do anyway."

Luna decided to love Trip as much as she could, and then he'd see he was safe with her.

"You're out of your mind," Joe told her. "The guy's a scumbag. Simple as that. Any more discussion is just a waste of energy."

So Luna stopped talking to Joe about Trip.

It took a couple of weeks, but Luna located a copy of *City of Angels*.

It was about an angel named Seth who fell in love with a woman. He became human to be with her. Then she got hit by a truck and died.

She called Trip. "Why did you want me to watch that?"

"It was just a good movie, that's all."

There was more to it than that.

But the guy who would've told her the truth was gone.

FORTY

"I DON'T UNDERSTAND," Luna said to Sunny a few days later. "The beginning was so good."

Sunny said, "Beginnings are always good."

Then she amended, "Well, they're not always sooo good, but even when they're not, we pretend they are… You know how that 'hope for the best' shit goes."

Luna did know.

She could write a book about it.

Jiminy had said the same thing to Luna about beginnings, back when he was speaking to her. It seemed like forever since he'd chimed in. But what Luna had felt about Trip transcended beginnings.

It felt universal.

Grounded.

Right.

And yet, it had gone so wrong.

She was tired of thinking about Trip. Her brain hurt. So she changed the subject. "So what's new with you?"

"I met someone at IHOP," said Sunny.

"Really?"

"Yeah. I was out to lunch with the work crew. It was the waiter. He served me his number pierced on a toothpick in the middle of my Rooty Tooty Fresh and Fruity."

"That's… cute…"

"And he took my food off the check! Kachow!"

Free food was a sure way to Sunny's heart. Well, maybe not her heart. But it was good for at least a one-time visit to her vagina. "What's he like?"

Sunny paused. "He's twenty."

"Too young."

"He's got stamina. He says he's gonna rock my world."

Luna laughed. "A bit clichéd, but I admire his enthusiasm."

"I'd settle for a six pack of Bud and a foot massage," said Sunny. "But he's not old enough to buy beer."

"Well, have fun getting rocked."

"Unfortunately, I have to let him come to my place because he lives with his parents, and he doesn't make enough in tips to pay for a motel. But maybe he'll bring me one of those giant IHOP omelets with hash browns."

"A woman can dream..."

"I'll call you with an update," Sunny promised.

Luna hung in with Trip, accepting his late night visits, infrequent phone calls, general insensitivity...

And his sex.

God it was demeaning.

But it felt so good...

He called himself Thor in his erotic text messages, and in bed he *was* Thor.

Thundering into her.

Pure ecstasy, but joyless, too. Aunt Zelda said life was both heaven and hell, and here they were in one tough nutshell.

Luna and Trip were so spectacular together it was like fireworks bursting through their bodies. Yet when he looked at her, he was a terrified lamb caught in a trap.

She screamed in pleasure and cried in agony, and he never made a sound.

And she kept waiting for that guy from the beach to come back.

"You're gonna be waiting a long time," Sunny told her during their next conversation. It had been over a week since they'd spoken, due to Sunny's crazed work schedule (and hopefully also due to some world-rocking.) "Try: forever."

"How do you know?"

"Because Trip's an asshole like me. He doesn't want to be bothered with anything except what he wants."

"You're an asshole?"

"I am. But it bothers me to see him being an asshole to you."

"Thanks… I guess." But Luna wouldn't concede that Sunny was right about Trip.

She couldn't.

"So, did that young guy rock your world?"

"Oh, please. He couldn't rock a squirrel. And of course he wanted to stick around afterwards and watch *Shameless.*"

"Did you let him?"

"Hell no! If I wanted to watch dysfunction in action I'd go visit Sal's family."

"What did you do?"

"I threw him his pants and told him to get pedaling."

"Pedaling?"

"He rode his bike over. He claims he owns a car, but he wanted to drink when he got here."

"You could've picked him up."

"Goddamn good thing I didn't. Because after his shoddy performance, he'd have been walking home. And that fucker didn't even bring the omelet. He said he couldn't manage it on his handlebars. Loser!"

"Does he know you didn't like it?"

"No. He thinks he's stud of the year. He keeps calling and calling… wonder when he'll get sick of my voicemail."

"Why don't you just tell him you're not interested?"

"Because I'd rather stab myself in the eye than ever speak with him again."

"How about a text?"

"My way requires less effort," said Sunny. "The biggest problem is that I have to avoid IHOP now." She sighed. "Sayonara, Rooty Tooty Fresh and Fruity."

On Halloween, Trip called Luna at eleven p.m. She'd been under the impression he was working in Connecticut. Turned out he'd come home early that morning and constructed an elaborate haunted maze in his yard for the neighborhood trick-or-treaters.

"Why didn't you tell me?" she asked. "I would've brought my kids."

"I don't know. I didn't think of it."

There was silence on her end. On his, there was banging and scraping. He was taking down the maze, cell phone undoubtedly perched in the crook of his neck. He'd hang up soon, she knew, in a rush to finish his task. He never had time to talk to her.

"Okay, let me go finish. Bye." He was gone.

Luna held the phone against her chest and tried not to cry. This didn't seem right, no matter what kind of spin her mind tried to put on it to avoid a confrontation.

She called him back.

"Yeees?" he asked.

"I wish you'd called me earlier," she stammered out. "You're never around… it would've been nice to see you…"

He cut her off. "You know what's worse than calling late?"

She didn't say anything.

"Not calling at all, that's what," he told her.

Then she said what was really brewing inside—not because she was brave, but because she just couldn't hold it back. "I feel like I'm losing my self respect."

"Oh, calm down," said Trip. "There's always next year. I'll see you tomorrow night."

Click!

Trip showed up around midnight.

He gave her a puckerless kiss and tramped inside with a cardboard box.

"A gift for me?" she asked.

He laughed and pulled off the Marlboro ski cap he wore far too often, even though he didn't smoke. During his DJ years, he'd combed the club's parking lot for discarded cigarette packs so he could get free merchandise. He owned a Marlboro windbreaker and Marlboro luggage, too.

Then he took off his Jets jacket, which he'd gotten practically for free at Goodwill.

He wore a tattered sweatshirt and jeans so grungy even Tide couldn't save them.

"So what's in the box?" she asked.

"A costume," he said. "I found it in a dumpster outside a Halloween shop today. I don't know why they threw it away."

There was a noise from the stairs.

Dylan was attempting to sneak down, but the creaking wood had thwarted him. "I can't believe you're not sleeping!" Luna fumed. "What's the matter?"

"I wanted to see your boyfriend," Dylan said. "He's as hard to catch as Santa."

That was true. All these months, and Trip and the kids had never crossed paths. "Okay… Say hi to Trip."

Dylan looked at Trip, but said nothing.

Trip said, "Dude."

Dylan continued to eye Trip. "Mom, could you come in the laundry room? We need to talk."

Luna followed him. Dylan slammed the door to the tiny room, which smelled like detergent and fabric softener. There were more piles of laundry around then she cared to confront, especially at this late hour. But at least they were already clean and folded.

Luna's problem had always been actually putting the clothes away.

Dylan told her, "You need to break up with him right now."

"Why?"

"You didn't tell me he was homeless."

"He has a home—technically." Even though it was with his parents, and even though he lived more on the road than anywhere else.

"Look at him, Mom!" Dylan motioned toward the door like it was transparent.

"What about him?"

"He's got all those whiskers, and he's wearing those yucky clothes..."

"They're work clothes. He works a lot..."

"He's a mess!" Dylan broke in. "Your boyfriend's a hobo!"

The door opened and Trip poked his head in. "Finished talking about me yet?" he asked. "Come see my costume." He looked at Dylan. "You'll like it."

Luna and Dylan followed Trip into the kitchen, where Trip unfolded the nylon fabric costume, climbed into it and zipped himself in. "It looks like a beige blob," said Luna.

"Patience," Trip said. "I have no batteries, so I have to use an outlet."

He stuck the plug in the socket and began to inflate.

Luna thought maybe the tan costume was Scooby-Doo.

She thought the big round circles at the bottom were paws.

She asked Dylan, "What do you think he is?"

Dylan answered, "Stupid."

But as they watched the cylindrical outfit grow taunt and erect, Dylan hazarded a guess. "He looks like a giant wiener."

He was right.

Trip was a big dick.

"Oh my God," Dylan said, when his deduction was confirmed. He looked at Luna pointedly. "I'm going to bed."

With that, he stomped upstairs.

"May I ask why you invited my six-year-old son to watch you put on a penis costume—the first time you met him?" Luna asked Trip.

"I thought it would be funny."

Ben slept through the whole incident.

Good for him.

There was probably no point in introducing the two. It wasn't like either wanted to meet the other, and it was doubtful that Luna and Trip would ever have the sort of relationship where he'd have a role in her sons' lives.

Which might have been for the best.

A few days later, Luna decided to tackle the mess Nick had left in the back room. She really wanted to start getting things together, and it was best to do it when the kids were going to their dad's, so she didn't have to stop and cook them dinner.

She went in with a bunch of industrial-sized garbage bags and bent down to get to work. But something happened… she stalled. She just couldn't face dealing with all the things he'd left behind.

She sat for a while in the rubble, then finally left without picking up one thing.

Trip came over. She told him about how she'd frozen, trying to clean. He didn't know about the back room. She'd avoided discussing it, making believe that it didn't exist—until now, when she just couldn't pretend anymore.

He said, "Show me."

She led Trip to the room. They stood in the rubble.

"How did it get like this? Trip asked, kicking aside a copy of Bill O'Reilly's *Who's Looking Out for You?*

She told him.

Trip said quietly, "Don't you wish you could treat people like they've treated you?"

"No," she said. "No, I don't.

He surveyed the room again. "Well, I guess that's how we differ." They differed in many ways, but Luna was in no mood to start listing them. This room gave her a migraine.

Trip patted her hand. "I can't always be the man you want, but I can help you out here." He squeezed into her palm. "I have garbage bags in my truck. I'll clean this up for you and get it out of your hair." He ruffled her hair and smiled. "You go write."

So she did.

Luna was lost in her words when Trip came back. He knocked on the doorframe, and she jumped up.

"Sorry, I knocked so I wouldn't scare you," he said. "I found this in the office, buried in the rubble—and I figured it belonged to you." He held out a purple trinket box.

"Oh my God, I didn't know it was there." She got up and took it from Trip's extended hand. "My son Ben gave this to me. Thank you for noticing, and not throwing it out."

She opened the cover, and there was a little note from Ben inside. It said, "I lov u." She smiled. "He was so little when he wrote this."

"Cute," Trip said, in a deadpan voice. He pointed to a drop of glue on the cover. "The top was broken. I guess your ex stepped on it, or something. But I fixed it."

Trip gave her a toothy smile. This was what he loved: fixing things.

Luna kissed him. He didn't pucker back.

"I'm gonna go dump this garbage," he said. "I'll be back later."

And it was much later when he returned. Past dinner, past bedtime.

Even later, when Trip was asleep, Luna rolled over and touched his sturdy back. She felt protected behind it. He was the brick house, and she was the little pig hiding from the big bad wolf.

Except, sometimes he acted like he *was* the big bad wolf.

Could he protect her from himself?

Trip was out of town on Thanksgiving, visiting family. Luna could understand that, but he didn't even phone her. She typed him an email: "Are you interested in this relationship? People who care about each other talk on holidays."

He called.

"I'm sorry," he said. "The truth is, I've had this problem for years."

"What problem?"

"Whenever I get into a highly physical relationship like ours, my emotions go right out the window."

She was stunned. "Why didn't you warn me?"

"I thought it would be different with you. It started out so good…" his voice trailed off.

"So what now?" she asked.

"I'm trying… really…"

After they hung up, Luna thought about what Trip said. She had her minor in psychology and she remembered studying the symptoms he described.

She called him back. "You have the Madonna Complex."

"As in 'Like a Virgin'?"

"Kind of." She struggled to recall the reasons behind the complex. "Did you have an over-protective mother?"

"Nah. She didn't give a shit."

"Hmmm… I'll check into it more…"

She hung up and Googled the name. Turned out she'd only gotten it partially right. It was the Madonna-Whore Complex.

*Figures I leave out the whore… I **am** the whore*, she thought.

You've got to admit, it's funny, said Jiminy.

"Jiminy! Where have you been?"

I've been trying to let you find your own way. And here you are, lost again.

"I'm trying to figure out what's wrong with Trip."

How about figuring out what's wrong with this picture?

But Luna wasn't listening—she was reading. According to Wikipedia, a man with this complex separated women he could have a fulfilling sexual relationship with from women he could love.

It turned out, a "cold and distant mother" was a cause.

She called Trip back with this new information.

He said, "Wow. That stinks. Guess I'm screwed."

"No, you're not," said Luna. "Now that you know what your problem is, you can get help."

"Right." But he didn't sound convinced at all.

"This could work out for us."

"Sure." Then he said, "You wanna be the Madonna, don't you."

Not particularly. "I don't think I could be that immaculate," she confessed.

But Trip made no effort to seek therapy. "I have to work," he told her when she brought it up a couple of weeks later, during an *Elementary* commercial break.

There was no room for discussion.

The show was back on.

FORTY-ONE

THEN CAME CHRISTMAS.

Those gloves were a real ho, ho, ho.

True, he'd returned from his car with a steamy "real" gift: a Victoria's Secret satin and lace babydoll. That fogged her brain so much that she forgot all about her misgivings and hurt. It was all she could do to slip it on before she jumped him. But once Trip had delivered the goods and was snoring away, she realized the cold reality of the babydoll. It screamed "lust," not "love." Like Trip, it made her feel cheap in the aftermath.

When Luna woke up the next morning beside Trip, she kind of wanted to stab him with the scissors on her desk.

No, you don't, said Jiminy. *You'll miss your kids, and prison coffee sucks.*

"I hate him."

"Zzznmpfff… ," Trip snored.

Then wake him up and throw him out, said Jiminy.

"I can't."

Why not?

"I love him."

Therein lies the rub.

"What now?"

Tell him you love him.

"I told him last night." Right there, in the middle of making half-love, it'd come bursting from her mouth. She hadn't even known she was going to say it, until it was out. Exposed.

Trip had said nothing in return. Not even, "Thank you."

Tell him again.

"What's the point?"

Are you still questioning me, after all we've been through?

"Oh, fine."

Luna gazed at Trip's closed eyes. "I love you."

"Zzznmpfff… ," Trip snored.

"Happy now?" Luna asked Jiminy.

Well, it was more than he said last night.

"You think this is amusing, don't you?"

Maybe you think it's amusing… since I'm a part of you.

That was a bit much. "I need coffee."

Lucky you're not in prison.

"I guess I am." She glanced at Trip, who snored on. She pushed off her covers.

Remember what day this is?

How could she forget, after the night she'd had? "It's the day after Christmas."

What else?

She thought.

"Oh, fuck."

It was her father's birthday. And that meant it was a year since she'd seen him.

Then she shrugged. *Whatever.* She'd celebrate Lenny's birthday the way he'd celebrated all of her birthdays—without so much as a phone call.

"Why should I go see him, Jiminy? Last time I got nothing out of the visit, just like you predicted. What's the point?"

It's not what you're going to get out of him, it's what you need to face in yourself.

"That doesn't sound too appealing."

Jiminy's voice rang harsh in her head then, so loud that it stopped her cold: ***It's time to deal with your life, Luna…***

"I don't want to."

But Jiminy was gone. He'd made his point, leaving Luna to face what she had to do next.

"ZzzfffclmpACK!" Trip snored.

She couldn't agree with him more.

Blue Skies Extended Care Facility was a town away from Luna's—a two-minute drive once she crossed the Long Acre Bridge. But it might as well have been an ocean away.

She thought about her last visit, with Ben and Dylan. It had been confusing for the kids and upsetting for her. And what was going on in Lenny's stroked-out brain, anyway? He probably didn't even understand who they were.

That's what she told herself.

She was going to see him now, like Jiminy obviously wanted. But she wasn't armed with birthday wishes.

Today, Lenny Lampanelli would hear what he'd done to his only child.

Snow started falling just as Luna's minivan tires met the metal grid in the center of the bridge. Fat flakes splatting against her windshield, like kamikazes dropping from the sky and crash-landing. They were so big that she could see their individual patterns in the seconds before the wiper blades obliterated them. The air in the van smelled sweet, lilac-coated by the air freshener dangling from the radio knob. She'd turned the music off. It clashed too much with the din in her head. Beneath her, under the floor littered with hardened corn-muffin crumbs, the tires grooved their metallic murmur—a soundtrack for the flakes' demise.

Memories flurried through Luna's mind.

Lacey, spiky.

Unlike the snow, unbreakable.

Why can't you pick the things that last?

She remembered crossing the 59th Street Bridge with her parents. A rare appearance by Dad. They were in a little Fiat, driving down the long, winding exit ramp into Queens. The small backseat felt massive to her. She was tiny, shrunken into upholstery, watching the rhythmic flashing of the outside lampposts flickering reflections on her lap. Then she noticed something across the divider – a deflated red balloon. Only a flash, then they were past it. Her dad had said: "This kid, she doesn't miss a thing."

She wished she did miss things.

She wished she could shut down and rest.

She wished she couldn't recall the hurt… that she couldn't remember missing him.

Swoosh—more snowflakes met their maker. Was there a snowflake heaven?

All she'd ever wanted was in that moment with her parents.

The three of them, together.

The van's tires hummed on the bridge like a choir of monks.

She was crying. Damn it. She reached for one of the napkins wedged next to the seat belt buckle. If she couldn't wipe out her thoughts, at least she could cut off her tears. There was some small victory in that.

You have to let go, said Jiminy.

"Leave me alone. Unless you'd like me to drive off the side of this bridge." She couldn't take much more, between last night and now.

Let go, he repeated. *Let go or be dragged.*

"Dragged by the Fiat?"

Yes, said Jiminy. *Sort of. You'll get it eventually… Or it'll get you.*

Just what she needed. A vague, ominous warning. Coupled with that word she loved so much. "Eventually" sounded like something they'd say in hell. "Thanks a lot."

Anytime.

She was off the bridge now, passing McDonald's golden arches, the first landmark in Long Acre—a fast-food beacon through the snow. She didn't eat anything fried, but they did brew a mean cup of coffee. Much better than that fancy stuff in some other places that could burn a hole in your esophagus. A humongous Mack truck idled in their lot, delivering supplies. The side of the truck said: *Merge at taste and quality.*

She thought of Trip.

That motherfucker.

Where was his taste and quality?

Where was *hers*?

She'd wanted a daddy to take care of her back when she was a kid, and she wanted a man to take care of her now. Trip had presented himself as that man, and she'd clung to the relationship past all reason.

Now she felt like she was losing all reason.

She was around the corner of her father's street now. By Starbucks. Where she and Trip had met last August. Starbucks served that hole-in-your-esophagus coffee that felt like some first dates, but her meeting with Trip hadn't been gut-wrenching at all.

He'd texted her a little while ago about the basket full of treats she'd made for him: *U want 2 make me fat so no other women will look at me.*

She wrote back: *Yes, that's my plan. I love to sleep with fat guys.*

Trip didn't thank her for the basket.

Now, she had that burning-esophagus feeling. Who knew it you could get it four months later?

Her engine was off.

She was there.

Parked outside Blue Skies, where her dad sat parked inside.

This was his fault, all this groveling for love—and she was going to tell him so. Fuck him and his birthday. Was he ever there for hers?

Her hand grappled at the door handle, but she didn't open it. Instead, she wrapped her palms around her steering wheel, gripped, and prayed.

She said, " Please. God. Help me say the right thing."

Breathe in, breathe out. Rule number one.

She took a gulp of the water she kept in her van—rule number two—then climbed out. Door slam, lock click, footsteps crunching through the flakes settled on the street, the sidewalk, and the ramp leading inside.

All along the way, she tried to embrace rule number three. But it was a doozy.

She was all set to yell at Lenny when she walked into his room, to really let him have it, but he had this look on his face like a dog. This big, dopey grin. Like he was so thrilled to see her, like he'd thought he'd never see her again.

The TV above his head was playing *Wheel of Fortune*. The wheel was spinning. When it stopped, there was massive clapping. It had hit $5000.

He was staring at her all happy—all that was missing to make the canine analogy complete was the tongue hanging out of the side of his mouth—sunken pathetically into that engulfing hospital bed, in those same blue pajamas because Loreena had never brought him any other clothes. The pj's were faded and looking kind of worn. No doubt they'd endured many cycles of harsh detergent and bleach. These kinds of facilities focused on disinfecting, not fabric care. What did the nurses put him in when his pajamas were being washed? A hospital gown, Luna supposed.

It was his birthday, and here he was all alone with not even a roommate to share the emptiness, and he deserved it, and Luna hated him—god, she hated him, sometimes she wanted to kill him, she really did—but with that dippy dog-face on him, she clammed up. There was no more use or satisfaction in being mean to him than there would have been in doing it to a dog. He wouldn't even get it.

She stood there at his bedside, watching Vanna White in her heels and shimmering evening gown touch letters and show off shiny teeth so she wouldn't have to look at him. She said, "Aunt Zelda said to tell you 'happy birthday'," which was true. She'd phoned Zelda before leaving, to see if Zelda would be here, hoping her aunt's presence would defuse her—but her aunt had had a bad cold and couldn't make it.

"Gee, th-thanks," he said. Then he added, "H-how are you?"

It was jarring. He'd never done that before. Not in her whole life.

She answered, "I'm bad, Dad. I'm really bad. I'm in a messed-up relationship, and it's the latest one in a series, and...and it all started with you." Well, he'd asked.

She'd been holding the plastic railing of his bed, and suddenly the warmth of his hand was on hers. *Shit*, she was standing by his non-paralyzed side. She didn't like this touching at all.

Still, she watched the game show. Like it had to do with anything.

He said, "I'm s-sorry."

Lots of clapping from the crowd overhead. The puzzle was solved. But she didn't see the answer. It was hard to watch the show now; it was all blurry. Jesus. She was crying again. Such bullshit, crying twice in one day. *I need to get some sleep.* It was practically impossible to rest with all that snoring.

As for what her father had just said, she couldn't think about that. It was like the music she'd turned off in her van. Too much.

Luna's tears rolled down, down. She said nothing for a while, just cried as the wheel spun again—they were onto a new puzzle, the show must go on—and tried to swallow the lump in her throat. She wanted to pull her hand away, but she couldn't. She didn't know why.

"I-it'll be o-okay," he said.

What did he know about okay? He'd thrown his whole life away for a needle; he'd probably die in this stupid hospital bed. Pat Sajack's face would probably be the last one he saw. He'd thrown her away like nothing, for a fix…

What did he know?

"Y-you'll s-see," he said softly, patting at her hand. And she wanted to believe him, at the bottom of it all, but the man was more than half gone. He'd wanted to go to Mars!

And even if he did know what he was saying, how could he mean it?

It was way too hot in there. Sweat swept across her skin; under her coat and sweater she was drenched. She yanked her hand away, swatted at her eyes. His scent was there, on her hand. "I gotta go," she told him, still facing away.

And she did.

FORTY-TWO

SOMEHOW, LUNA MANAGED to muddle through the week and do the parenting thing. They went to the movies a lot. The kids were entertained and Luna could escape into the dark void, if only temporarily.

Then New Year's came.

Just like always, Luna and the kids were on board the barge.

It was even harder to avoid thinking of Trip than it had been with Alex, and she kept letting the champagne bubble up too high and run over. She wanted to be like those bubbles—to rise up and be free. But she still called Trip at midnight—he was visiting his sister in Delaware—because emancipated, Luna wasn't.

Yet again, all circuits were busy.

Did things ever change?

She finally got Trip's voice mail, but he didn't call back until the next day. "It's still New Year's," he told her. "But you're not making it happy with all this complaining."

Then, Valentine's Day.

"I can't take you out tomorrow," Trip told Luna on February 13. "My mom's getting lasik eye surgery, and I have to drive her."

He promised to make up for it on the weekend.

But he arrived so late on Friday night that the only place open was the diner, featuring a haggard old man at the register who was hunched so low Luna feared he might drop before the end of their meal, and an angry waitress who slammed their plates on the table.

Paradise was definitely lost.

Now her birthday was coming—in four days.

Luna and Sunny were in the parking lot shared by library system and a tabernacle church, leaning on Sunny's car. Sunny was on a smoking break.

Luna was not allowed inside Sunny's office.

No visitors could enter, not even to pee. That's because the crazies were always spotting the word "library" on the sign and trying to get in. Recently a woman wearing three knit scarves and a puffy ski jacket, magenta lipstick veering across her jaw, had rushed in behind an employee, raced to Sunny's desk and started grabbing. Christ in pajamas got stripped to his undies, and Sunny wrested her Angel Snot out of the woman's hands just before the precious fluids were released. "I like this branch. It got toys," the woman said as she was escorted outside.

"I wonder what Trip got me for my birthday," Luna said. She was staring at the empty church.

"I'm picturing something red with a Marlboro logo," said Sunny. "Is he taking you somewhere?"

"He's not gonna be here." Trip wasn't even on Long Island now—he was at a convention in Florida. Luna was picking him up at Kennedy Airport the following night, but he was flying out of town again the evening after.

"I guess you're stuck with us then," said Sunny. "I'll bring over a cake."

"Thanks."

"Don't forget to formally invite your mom, Dude."

"Right." Luna slumped a little. She kicked at a cigarette butt near her foot.

"What's wrong?"

"I'm afraid Trip's gonna give me a thoughtless gift. I don't think I can handle that."

A ruby Cadillac pulled into the lot.

It parked in the space next to Sunny's, even though the lot was at least two-thirds empty. A black woman in a chiffon dress matching her car and a huge round hat adorned with a tuft of feathers got out and headed for Sunny.

"Uh-oh," said Sunny.

The woman shook her fist. "We don't like smoking here!" she fumed.

"Who is 'we'?" Sunny asked.

"Well… I mean 'I,'" the woman amended.

"I'm sure you have authority over this lot," Sunny said. She blew a ring out.

The woman stamped her high-heeled foot down on the yellow line dividing the parking spaces. "*I* am the pastor's wife!"

"That explains the car. It's incredible what you can buy with those full collection plates."

The pastor's wife examined Sunny's sad Saturn, badly battered and missing its nose. "Our congregation *understands* that a sister needs her Cadillac." Her clump of feathers looked like they'd been snatched off a seagull. "So, are you gonna respect our lot?"

Sunny threw her cigarette on the pavement and crushed it with her sneaker. "We'll take that under advisement."

"We?" The pastor's wife eyed Luna like she was daring her to light up too.

"Oh, I mean 'I.'" Sunny took another cigarette out and ignited it.

The pastor's wife's eyes bulged. "Hmmmpf. I'm gonna have my husband order up some 'no smoking' signs for this area."

"Say goodbye to another few hundred in donations," Sunny said as the pastor's wife staggered off on her stilettos, feathers flapping.

"That was crazy," Luna said.

"Welcome to my life," Sunny said with a shrug. "But, speaking of crazy, back to you. I don't actually understand why you're still with Trip."

"I keep wondering what I can do…"

"Nothing. You can't fix people." Sunny inhaled the cigarette deeply. The pastor's wife had taken the second cigarette personally, but Sunny always chain-smoked during her break. She had to get enough tobacco in her system so she wouldn't go postal from the hours of deprivation.

"It was the chicken that made him like this..."

"Whatever, Dude." Sunny had heard the chicken soup story more than once. "You're not his shrink. Tell him to hop his sorry madonna-whorey ass on a transatlantic flight and tell it to Sigmund Freud's cremated remains, because no one else cares." She flicked the ashes from the tip of her cigarette. They fell to the pavement in a tiny grey heap.

"I care," said Luna.

"Oh, Chicky," said Sunny. "I know you do. And if it makes you feel any better, I'm a mess too."

"What's the matter?"

Sunny sighed. "Phil."

"What about him?"

"I miss him."

"Excuse me? You miss the man who came to bed with a bottle of gin?"

"Okay, it's not actually him I miss. It's his wallet."

"Are you serious?"

Sunny nodded. "He would've hooked me up. That useless fuck Sal cracked out again, so there went my back child-support up in smoke, and I'm about to be evicted." She puffed out a long trail of smoke. "I totally blew it with Phil."

"You didn't blow it," Luna said. "You saved yourself. How can you sacrifice your happiness for money?"

"Dude—no one would've died."

"He would've. You would've killed him eventually."

"Well... maybe."

Then Sunny spilled the real truth. She'd been e-mailing The Coconut, actively seeking reconciliation.

"How can you use The Coconut for money?" Luna said. "I'm disgusted."

"I am too—when other people do such things. It just doesn't seem so bad when it's me," said Sunny. She threw down her cigarette and stared at the rising white wisps. "I'm not a morally bankrupt person, usually."

"I know."

Dylan came home from school with a surprise for Luna. "Mommy, I got you a birthday present at the school book fair."

"That's great, sweetie. I can't wait to see it."

"I wanna give it to you now."

"It's not my birthday yet."

"I don't care." He reached into his backpack and dragged out a plump white stuffed chicken by its neck. "Isn't he cute? I spent two weeks' allowance on him."

"I love him," said Luna. She gave the chicken a hug, and then she hugged Dylan. "Thanks, baby."

"I didn't have enough money to buy you the book that came with him, but I think you're too old for it anyway. It was a counting book. You know how to count."

"Yes I do," she said. *I just don't know what I can count on.* "What should we name him?"

Dylan considered the chicken. "Fred."

FORTY-THREE

THE FOLLOWING NIGHT, Trip lay face down in a pillow, his usual pose in Luna's bed.

Luna was in her usual pre-sex spot, straddling Trip and giving him a massage. He hadn't pulled out any gift from his luggage; nor had he mentioned her birthday. They'd stopped for Chinese take-out on the way home from the airport, watched *Law & Order: Special Victims Unit* while they ate, and then gone upstairs.

Luna stared at the chicken, Fred, perched on top of her pillow, big orange feet facing forward and wide, worried eyes staring. She thought of Trip's poor, cooked Fred. Trip had insisted his brother was the one traumatized by eating Fred soup.

Luna could only imagine how that brother was now.

She could only imagine, because seven months after they'd met, Trip still hadn't introduced her to his family.

He hadn't met hers either, of course, because he was rarely around. It was probably better that he hadn't met Loreena, who was bound to be venomous, but she wanted Trip to meet Aunt Zelda.

Luna rubbed and rubbed and rubbed, while birthday candles burned in her brain.

Last year's birthday had held so much promise... she was free from Nick and on the road to recovery.

Now she was trapped in this half-relationship.

Trapped by her own self, because Trip clearly wasn't holding her in.

Where was the guy from the beach? Was he buried in the sand?

Trip finally turned over and took charge, doing those things to her that blew her mind, literally exploding all bad thoughts.

"I love you, Trip," she said. Those late-night words escaped from her lips every time she and Trip made half-love.

Trip remained silent. As always.

His eyes were closed, his lips out of reach.

All those other times she'd told herself, *It doesn't matter.*

Tonight, it did.

Trip worked his way around Luna's body like a blind, mute auto mechanic doing a tune-up.

Kiss me! Look at me! Luna screamed at Trip inside her head. *Say you love me, too!*

She ranted the whole time Trip made half-love to her, but the words never made it out. Part of her—one lucid little shard cowering in the corner of her mind—thought, *This is what it's like to go mad.*

Then it was over.

Luna was mentally hoarse and physically frustrated.

Trip was snoring.

Luna gathered Fred into her arms and squeezed. She stared at Trip's nearly bald head and wondered why she cared about him anyway.

To make herself not care, she tried picturing him in his Marlboro jacket.

It didn't work.

Outside, the patio light from downstairs illuminated the holes in the rotting deck wood like a glowing jack-o-lantern.

Next, she tried thinking of shitty things Trip had done to her.

How can I love this man? she questioned herself.

She lay there awhile, then decided to try and get the one thing she could from him: an orgasm.

If she could have sex again, maybe she could silence the voices and enjoy it.

She touched Trip in certain erogenous zones.

"Stop that!" he said harshly. "I need my sleep. I have to get up early.

If you're going to be like this, take me home!" He rolled over and gave an extra-loud snore.

Tell him to start walking, said Jiminy.

"You know I can't."

Let me ask you something, Luna: If you have a man in your bed and you're holding a chicken for comfort, what do you need the man for?

Luna had no answer.

She drifted into a fitful sleep, dreaming that she was a chicken and Trip's mother was chasing her with a hatchet, screaming, "Fair is fowl and fowl is fair!"

Waking up again before dawn, Luna wondered if she might have been Trip's chicken in a previous life. She was nine years younger than he was—the time sequence worked.

She glanced over at Trip, who was curled away from her, facing the wall.

Jiminy said, *Write him a note.*

She didn't want to, and yet she also did.

Oh, just do it, said Jiminy.

She sat at her desk and started up her laptop. Outside, the wind billowed in and out of the spaces between the glass slats in her deck doors. It used to whip through the room, until Luna had sealed a plastic covering around the frames. The temperature stayed warm now, but the plastic made an annoying swishing sound as it expanded and contracted. Trip had promised to fix the drafts so that she didn't need the plastic—but that was just something else he never got to.

Like telling her he loved her.

The wind pummeled the tree next to the dock. All of the tree's normally droopy leaves were raised, like they were giving her the finger en masse.

But at least the sun was on its way.

She started to type:

Dear Trip,

This isn't working for me.

Try as I may, you won't let me in. And more than that, you won't give me the affection I deserve.

I don't feel like you care.

I gave you so many chances, Trip. I wanted this to work, but I can't succeed alone. It takes two.

I'm sorry,

Luna

Finished, she printed it.

It was after nine when Trip awoke.

So much for getting up early.

He did whatever suited him at that moment and had no game plan past that.

The note was folded inside Luna's purse. She was going to give it to him when she dropped him off.

Part of Luna wanted to talk to him—to tell him how she felt instead of handing him the note—but he was rushing around zipping up his pants and gathering all his scattered things. She knew he wouldn't respond well to any attempts at conversation.

And there was also the fact that she was a chicken.

It had snowed in the hours between dawn and nine. Everything outside was white, as if it had all been sugar-coated.

The roads were slippery and Luna drove slowly. Trip was on the phone with one of his clients.

They inched along the normally twenty-minute route to Trip's parents' house. Trip was chatting it up with his client about plans for their project; Luna was a silent mix of resolution and squirm.

Half-way there, Trip finally got off his phone. They were passing a church sign that said: "Forgive your enemies. It messes with their minds."

Again there was an opportunity to speak with Trip.

So she did.

But not about their relationship.

Instead, she chose what might be the last moments they spent together to ask about "Homeland." They'd watched it once together, and she asked what had happened since.

"Haven't seen it," he said gruffly.

"Oh… you said you watched it all the time," she said.

"Nope… I gotta work, you know."

She did know that.

Then they were there.

In front of Trip's parents' house.

It looked like something that might've erupted from his cluttered mind. His parents' RV, his beat-up work truck with detached cap, and three cars—two of which were Trip's—were all in the driveway and on the lawn. The house—a ranch-style, probably built in the 50's, when the neighborhood was new—had a tired look. There was a security camera mounted above the garage and two signs on the door—one proclaiming "no solicitors," and the other alerting possible intruders to the camera. Thick curtains barricaded the front picture window.

It was not a warm and fuzzy house.

Trip got out and made a couple of trips to the door with his Marlboro luggage.

He lingered a bit then, checking out the bag with her boxing gear and pulling out her gloves. "These your gloves?" he asked, examining their worn red leather.

"Yeah," she said, wondering who else's gloves they could be.

She fingered the note. It was between two books wedged between the van's two front seats.

He opened the front door again, and gave her a peck on the lips.

She pulled out the note.

"What's this?" he asked, taking it from her extended hand.

"A note," she said, looking past him at all the junk on his lawn.

"A note for me?" His tone was half-cute, half-wistful. She wondered if he somehow knew.

"Yeah, a note for you," Luna said. She forced herself to look at him now.

Was it really the last time?

Oh God.

She wanted to snatch that note away and say 'never mind.'

But she couldn't stand living like this anymore.

"Okay," he said. Fingers around the doorframe, he paused. Then he said, "I'll call you later."

"Okay," she numbly agreed.

He slammed the door shut.

She drove away.

FORTY-FOUR

LUNA FELT ILL. She pulled into a shopping center and parked in front of Blimpie's. She turned her engine off and took deep breaths in and out, trying to follow rule number one.

She missed Trip so much. And it had only been a few minutes since she'd dropped him off.

The breathing wasn't working, so she took a sip from her water bottle.

That's when something really felt like it was coming up. *Click!* She unlocked her door and opened it. She leaned out over the pavement and stared down at the bright paint marking her parking space. Her stomach was churning, bile rose in her throat… She heaved right on that yellow line.

"What now, Jiminy? I feel like I'm dying… " It hurt so bad, like something had been ripped from her insides. *I'm gonna die without him.*

You sound like a teenager, Jiminy said. *Relax, you'll survive.*

She wiped a drop of vomit from her chin and leaned against the wheel. "How am I supposed to function?"

Keep going, said Jiminy. *The best way out is always through.*

"Why don't you go straight through to hell, Jiminy."

That's not nice, he scolded.

"Never said I was," she answered. She may not have said it, but she was actually nice, and she felt bad for what she'd said to Jiminy, and for what she'd written to Trip.

"I'm sorry, Jiminy." He didn't respond.

She looked in the window of Blimpie's – at the guy behind the counter. Any minute now people would start arriving for lunch. All his meats, cheeses and condiments were neatly laid out in front of him. He just had to wait.

She wanted to call Trip, to say, "Never mind the note" if he hadn't read it, or "April Fool's!" if he had—even though it wasn't April.

She called Sunny instead.

Sunny was stunned. "This is out of nowhere," she said. "You never said you were going to break up with Trip."

"I didn't know I was," Luna said. She told Sunny about holding the chicken and hearing Jiminy, who didn't take no for an answer.

Luna's voice was cracking, but she willed herself not to cry. She couldn't make a spectacle of herself in front of Blimpie's, especially with the lunch crowd coming.

Sunny said, "Well, Jiminy doesn't know everything. Maybe you're not done with Trip yet."

"So, what now?"

"How the hell should I know?" said Sunny. "I can't even make the right choices for myself. But come over for dinner and we'll discuss it. I'll order Chinese."

With something to look forward to, Luna coaxed herself into starting her engine and driving from the lot. Her stomach still twisted, but she didn't barf again.

She drove home and went to sleep.

Sunny's kids were at their grandmother's house and Luna's kids were at Nick's, which was a good thing, because Luna's morose mood gave the meal a very sad tone. "Cheer up, Chicky," Sunny said. "Give Trip a call if you feel like you have to."

"He wouldn't answer anyway," said Luna.

Sunny looked deeply at Luna. "Well, if you do decide to reach out to him, I want you to know that it's fine. You have to do things at your own speed, not Jiminy's."

"You're saying that I shouldn't have written the note?"

"I totally think you should've written the note… But I'm not sure *you* think you should've written it."

"Hmmmm…"

"Okay… so let's read our fortunes. You first." Sunny pushed one of the cellophane-wrapped cookies Luna's way.

Luna obediently opened it. "*When unsure, take the next small step*," she read. "Terrific."

Sunny read hers. "*Can I have the directions to your heart?*" She laughed. "Dude, that's like a cheesy pick-up line."

"It's not a pick-up line," said Luna. "It's a message from God."

"Whatever." Sunny shrugged. "By the way, I'm done flirting with Phil."

"That's good. What happened?"

"Nothing. I realized I don't want him back after all."

"Is this your final answer?"

"It is," said Sunny. "He answered my email, and even his reply was boring."

"Some things never change," said Luna.

Sunny continued, "It was the drinking that turned me. I forgot how bad it was until you reminded me about the gin at the side of my bed." She toyed with her fortune. "And you were right. I don't want to be that person… the person who uses someone."

"I didn't think you'd actually go through with it," said Luna.

"And anyway, I got a raise at both jobs, so I'm no longer in imminent danger of eviction."

"Congratulations."

Sunny made them both coffee. She put a box of Entenmann's chocolate chip cookies on the table. "Classy, aren't I?"

"You're a first-class friend," said Luna.

"Dude, that's another cheesy line." They both laughed. "Well, at least you're in better spirits now."

"I am."

"Good." Sunny finished the last of a cookie, swiped at the chocolatey remains and sighed. "God, look at the men I've chosen. A crackhead and a booze-hound. Do you think I'll ever meet someone who isn't completely substance-addicted?"

"Sure. You just need to change your aura."

"I'm too tired for aura-changing."

"Maybe we both need to do what my fortune said: Take the next small step."

"Any idea what step to take?"

"None."

They both laughed again.

Sitting in her cold, empty car in the municipal parking lot outside Sunny's after dinner, Luna had nothing to laugh at. As soon as she slammed her van door and sank into the dark interior, it all hit her again.

I'm alone.

Everyone's alone, said Jiminy.

"Some people have partners. *They're* not alone."

Everyone's alone, said Jiminy. *Anything else is a facade.*

"What are you, the grim reaper?" She was parked head-on to a humongous tree. Thick trunk stared through her windshield, rough bark straight in her face.

It's not a bad thing to be alone, Jiminy said. *Once you're comfortable with that, you can be unconditionally happy.*

Luna wasn't paying attention. She was thinking of Trip. She unzipped her purse and took out her phone. She entered her address book, scrolled to Trip's name and hit call.

She got his voice mail, of course.

His warm, inviting voice. So ironic now.

At the beep she said, "I'm sorry. I want to talk to you, to see how you are."

Even as she spoke the words, she felt how ridiculous they were.

But they were also true.

He didn't call her back.

The next day, Luna went for an adjustment.

Inside the examining room, lying on the table, Luna found herself staring at Dr. Gold's "Rules of the Office." The word "breathe" popped up at her.

"I'm having the hardest time doing the simplest things. Even breathing is an effort," she told him.

"You're going through a lot," he told her. "Relax."

That again.

"I still can't believe it's over with Trip." It was the third time she'd said that since she'd arrived.

"You were waiting for him to give you what you needed. That wasn't going to happen, Luna. You did the right thing, even though it hurts."

"I keep thinking of him…"

"You have to let go."

"I don't seem to be able to let go of anything… or anyone. I thought I was improving, but I feel so angry. At my dad, my mom, Nick, Trip…"

"Thank them."

"*Thank* them?"

Dr. Gold nodded with a totally Buddha face, except it wasn't round. "Be grateful."

"For what?"

"They challenged you in a way that allowed you to grow."

"So you expect me to walk up to these people and say, 'thank you for treating me bad'?"

"I don't expect anything, Luna. But I think it'll happen of its own accord. You won't have to say anything. When you're ready, you'll feel the gratitude sweeping through you.

"What will it feel like?"

"Like '*Ahhhhhh.*'"

"Sounds like one of those York Peppermint Patty commercials."

"It's better," he told her. "Way better."

At home, Luna kept trying to write. The end of *NWaN*, or anything at all.

Nothing came.

The day before her birthday, Luna had a workout with Joe.

"How's that book going?" he asked when they were taking a rest from their pad work. She knew he meant *NWaN*—they'd discussed it often.

"Pretty good… Okay, it's tough. I have no clue how it'll end. But I'm sure something productive will come out of all this."

"What are you calling it?" Joe asked.

"I was thinking maybe *She Loved Them All.*"

"Yeah, right. Try, *She Clubbed Them All.*"

The bell rang and she started pounding at the pads he held up again. "Are you saying I'm angry?" *Bam! Bam! Bam!*

He grinned in his psycho-killer way. "Yes, I am."

She stopped punching. "I miss Trip, Joe."

"I know, Kiddo," he said. "I know."

FORTY-FIVE

Trip is gone. I sent him away.

Luna woke up with this thought, just as she had the previous two mornings.

Trip and the lack of an ending for her book were all she thought about.

"Happy birthday, Mommy!" Luna opened her eyes. Dylan was holding a plate of pancakes. "We made you breakfast in bed!"

Ben entered her bedroom slowly, holding a steaming mug of coffee. "Happy birthday, Mom." He gave her a kiss. "Love you."

"You guys are the best," said Luna.

"And guess what?" asked Dylan.

"What?"

"When you're done eating, I'm gonna teach you to ride a bike." When Dylan had learned to ride, he'd wanted Luna to go riding with him. She'd had to admit that she didn't know how. He said, "You deserve to know the experience, too."

That was not thrilling news.

Every time Luna had ever gotten on a bike she'd fallen within seconds, and the plummet was a relief from those shaking, heart-racing moments. "I guess you can try," she said.

Gulp.

She sipped her coffee.

After breakfast, Luna and the kids headed to the school's grassy field. Ben came for moral support. They were wheeling his bike, which the kids had decided would be best for her, even though Luna had argued for Dylan's. Closer to the ground meant less of a fall.

The weather was warm for March. They were all wearing sweatshirts instead of coats, and Luna sported a purple hat.

Luna got on Ben's bike, with Dylan beside her. "Pedal, Mom," he instructed. So she did, even though she was scared.

She was moving, with Dylan holding her up.

"Go, Mom!' Ben cheered.

They went a short distance, which freaked Luna out even though Dylan was there. It was such a weird feeling, trying to negotiate gravity.

Then Dylan let go.

Plop! Down she went. "Ouch!"

Her thigh took the brunt of the impact. It throbbed. "Get up, Mommy," Dylan said. "We gotta keep going until you get it."

She didn't want to disappoint him, so she dragged herself up from the grass and got back on the bike.

They repeated the same scenario.

Plop! "Ouch!"

It was no use. She was too skittish. Even when she didn't fall, she halted at the first wobble. "I have to stop," she told the kids. "This is all too much."

"Oh, fine," said Dylan. "But this isn't over. I'm gonna have you riding before the summer."

"If you say so," Luna said.

They walked back to the house. Luna's whole body was throbbing now.

"So who's coming over for cake tonight?" Ben asked.

"Sunny and the kids, and Nonna," said Luna.

"What about grandpa in the wheelchair?" asked Dylan.

"How can he come? He can't drive," said Ben.

"Nonna could take him," said Dylan.

Luna was surprised at this mention of her father. "What made you bring him up?" she asked.

"Well, he *is* my grandpa," said Dylan.

There was something in Dylan's tone that struck Luna. Suddenly she felt bad, that she'd only brought the kids to visit Lenny once. "I thought you guys didn't enjoy seeing him."

"I don't mind," said Ben. "I liked the pizza we got after we left that place."

Luna pictured the last time she'd seen Lenny, lying in that bed, with only *The Wheel of Fortune* for companionship.

She'd spent her childhood waiting for him. But did that make it right to leave him in Blue Skies, waiting for her?

He'd apologized.

Then she'd run out of there.

It's time to finish that conversation.

Luna dropped the kids off with Sunny and headed across the Long Acre Bridge. Back across those humming monks, and past those golden arches. Millions and millions served… so many, they'd stopped counting.

This time, she played the radio super-loud to overpower her brain. She didn't want to think. If she did, she'd probably turn the van around.

Luna tried not to look at Starbucks when she turned the corner and parked in a head-on spot halfway down the block. She clicked the lock button on her van, slammed the door and crossed the street, still facing away from the place she'd met Trip.

She headed into Blue Skies, through the automatic doors. Up in the elevator to the sixth floor. Then, treading linoleum to her father's room, inhaling lemon disinfectant all the way.

His adjustable bed was empty.

The TV was silent.

Was she too late?

Wouldn't Loreena have told her if Lenny was dead?

A nurse ducked in the doorway. "Everyone's in the community room, baby," she said. "It's up the hall, past the elevators."

So Luna headed back down the hall, through the double doors into the huge room where all the sixth floor occupants were parked in their wheel chairs, facing a big flat-screen TV. They looked like the gang from *Awakenings*—pre-awakening.

An Oprah re-run was on. She was jumping around the stage all excited, playing *Deal or No Deal* with Howie Mandel.

Why, Luna didn't know.

Apparently some people got very thrilled playing *Deal or No Deal*, and Oprah was one of them.

The Blue Skies residents could've been watching static for all the enthusiasm they registered. They were negative on the recognition scale.

That disinfectant scent was in there, too.

Lenny was sitting in his wheelchair just inside the doors to the right. He actually looked good—his hair was cut and combed and he was clean-shaven. Also, he was wearing a button-down flannel shirt instead of his blue pajamas. Mom must've actually come through with some clothing.

But he looked petulant.

"Dad?" she asked.

He stared at her like he wasn't sure who she was.

"He just threw his glasses," an aide sitting with a frail female patient said. "He said he don't want them no more."

"You don't want your glasses, Dad?" Luna asked him.

"N… no."

She couldn't blame him. With his life, who would want to see clearly?

She picked up the plastic tortoise-shell frames, which were under the chair of the woman the aide was sitting with. One of the lenses was missing. "Were they like this already?"

"No, that one popped out when he threw them," the aide said.

"Ah," said Luna. She walked back and forth across the tiles until she found it. Unfortunately, he'd cracked the frame.

"The lens won't stay in, Dad," she informed her father.

He shrugged and waved the glasses away with his good arm.

Luna put them on the table. "Anyway, today's my birthday," she told him.

"H-happy b-birthday," he said.

Did he even get what he was saying, or was he just reciting lines? "Do you remember when I was here on your birthday?"

"Y-yes."

Well, there was a fifty-fifty chance of accuracy with that one. "Remember how you apologized to me?"

He nodded firmly. "Y-yes."

A nurse came up to them, interrupting. "Who's this?" she asked Luna's father.

"M-my s-sister," he said.

Terrific.

"How nice!" The nurse said. Luna didn't bother making the correction. "Have a good visit with your brother," she said as she headed away from them.

Exactly how old did she look to this woman? Luna wondered. It didn't matter though—she just wanted to leave.

On the TV, Oprah had lost and Howie had vanished. Oprah was speaking with some blonde woman. She said, "Tonight I'm gonna get out of bed to pee and I'm gonna think, 'I should've picked number eleven.'"

"Anyway, Dad," Luna continued. He squinted and listened. She took a deep breath and let it out. What she wanted to say was so simple, but it was hard to release the words.

It felt like she was going to choke on the disinfectant smell in there.

Finally, she managed to blurt it out: "I forgive you."

He blinked at her for a moment. Maybe he was processing what she said, or maybe he was just trying to get some kind of focus.

Then he said, "H-hey... th-thanks."

"You're welcome," she said.

On the big screen, Oprah broke into a great laugh.

Luna scanned the room again, searching for some sign of understanding. Only one woman had any expression on her face: her mouth was frozen open in a humongous wide 'O', like a permanent scream.

That sterile, cover-up smell was brutal. And even though she wasn't wearing a heavy winter coat this time, she was still sweating.

"H-how are the k-kids?"

Wow. Who knew he remembered them?

"They're good. Dylan asked about you today."

He smiled.

"I'll bring them to see you soon."

"O-Okay."

He was really beaming now. Could it be that they were having a nice moment together? Was that the gift clemency gave? "H-happy b-birthday," he said again.

"Thanks, Dad," she said. She meant it. "I'm glad I came." And she meant that, too.

Good job! Jiminy said as Luna headed out of the lobby. *Now you can focus on your mom.*

"My *mom*?" Oops. She'd spoken out loud to Jiminy in public. Several people stopped and stared. She moved a little faster and pushed through the door.

Luna had just climbed back into the driver's seat when her cell phone rang.

It was Nick.

She debated letting it go to voice mail, but then she answered. She was done avoiding things.

"Happy birthday," he said in his gravelly voice.

"Thanks."

"What are you doing?" That was Nick's standard telephone line, which Luna found terrible invasive. It was none of his business.

"Nothing." Like she was going to tell him.

"You going out with that guy tonight?"

Even though he surely knew "that guy's" name, Nick refused to say it, just as Loreena had never uttered "Nick" in all the years he was married to Luna. "We broke up," she said. Still she wouldn't look at Starbuck's.

"Oh. Sorry." But he didn't sound sorry at all.

"I gotta go. I'm driving," she told him. Not exactly true, but she wanted to be. She wanted to get the hell off that street.

"Oh." Again with the Oh. "Hey…"

"Yes?" For the love of God, she just wanted to leave, but she didn't have a Bluetooth.

"I just wanted to say, I'm sorry."

"For?"

"For everything I did to you. You didn't deserve it. I was an asshole."

Luna didn't say anything. She was so shocked that she accidentally looked at Starbucks. *Rats.*

"You there?" he asked.

"Yeah," she said. "I'm here."

"Anyway, I wanted to tell you that, and to thank you for being a really good mom."

"Uh… You're welcome."

There was a pause. Then he said, "I really did love you, you know."

She guessed he had, in his way. "Thanks," she said again. "We were good there for a while, weren't we?"

"We were."

"That's more than some people can say."

"It is."

Another pause. She took a deep breath and let it out. Then she said, "I forgive you." Who knew this would come up today, so soon after Lenny? Was forgiveness a domino effect?

"Thank you," he said, and he sounded relieved.

They exchanged goodbyes, and Luna started the car.

Then she turned it off again.

Now that she'd faced Starbucks, she might as well get a cup of caustic coffee. It might sharpen her up to focus on her mom.

Whatever *that* meant.

She gripped the handle, them paused. "I don't see how I can come to any terms with her, Jiminy. It would be like reasoning with an eggplant."

But Jiminy didn't reply.

FORTY-SIX

LUNA GOT HER coffee to go and drove home. She spent the rest of the afternoon outside on the water, sipping and writing.

At five o'clock, Sunny's in-need-of Midasizing ancient vehicle blasted up to the curb. Sunny, her kids, Ben and Dylan piled out. Dylan carried a bakery box.

Sunny lit a cigarette. "Happy birthday, Chicky." She took a drag. "This is all déjà vu and shit," she said. "Just like when we celebrated your release day, but our kids got taller."

"Just as long as everything that happened in-between doesn't happen again," Luna said. "I don't think I could take that."

"Amen and Christ windsurfing in a wetsuit," said Sunny.

They ordered their dinners. "I wish I could afford Chinese food all the time." Sunny said. "Just think of it: Meals brought to your door every day!"

"Wouldn't you get sick of it?"

"Nah. Do Chinese people get sick of Chinese food? They do not. You just gotta switch up the sauces."

"Ahhhh…"

It was after five, and therefore cocktail hour. Luna poured herself a glass of Riesling and handed Sunny a bottle of Bud from the fridge. The boys were upstairs playing X-Box, and Phoebe was using the computer in Luna's room. "I gotta tell you about my new boyfriend!" said Sunny.

"What? You didn't tell me you'd been dating."

"I wasn't. It's Layne's assistant soccer coach." Layne was on a team of Olympic hopefuls, training for the trials.

"What? Isn't he another really young one?" Luna had gone with the kids to a game once, to cheer Layne on. "What happened to your lesson that there's no substitute for experience?"

"That's not going to be an issue here."

"Why's that?"

"Because he has no idea we're involved."

"*What?*"

"It's simple." Sunny took a slug of her beer. "I'm having an imaginary relationship with JoshJohn."

"*JoshJohn?*"

Sunny shrugged. "His name is either Josh or John. I can't remember which, so I combined them."

That was the great thing about imaginary relationships, Sunny explained. Details like exact names ceased to matter. So did factors like getting to know each other and compatibility.

There was no need for any interaction, which suited Sunny just fine.

"We're gonna get married and be Mr. & Mrs. Assistant Coach!" said Sunny.

Sunny told Luna all she knew about JoshJohn, which was his soccer wardrobe. He wore the same outfit to each practice—a tan T-shirt and matching shorts. In cold weather he added a hat, gloves and sweatshirt, but the shorts remained.

He was bland, but he was consistent. Kind of like The Coconut, except she didn't have to talk to him.

Sunny decided it would be a blissful and fulfilling relationship, as long as he didn't know about it.

Sunny's lost it. Luna wasn't sure how to present this to her friend. She wanted to say, "Let's play a game called 'pretend you're not nuts!'" Instead she settled for the more diplomatic, "When was the last time you saw a doctor?"

"Never mind about that," Sunny said. ""JoshJohn and I are going to be very happy together."

"You might want to let him in on that," said Luna.

The doorbell rang. "It's not the Chinese man," Luna called up to the gaggle of youths who appeared at the top of the steps. "It's Nonna."

There was a group "Awwww." Then the four retreated back to their activities.

Luna answered the door. "What took you so long?" Loreena asked. "It's cold out here."

"I'm sorry," Luna said.

"Well, happy birthday." Loreena stepped inside and offered Luna her cheek. Luna gave Loreena's cold, vitaminy skin a peck. "Thanks for inviting me," Loreena said in a vague, flat way that could have been genuine or sarcastic. Luna decided to believe it was real.

Thank Sunny for reminding me, Luna thought. As if telepathic, Sunny gave Luna a nod.

"Did you eat without me?" Loreena asked suspiciously.

"Nope. The food's coming, and we ordered enough for you!" Luna and Sunny high-fived, proud that they'd remembered to include Loreena's meal.

"Do you know what I like?" Loreena sounded dubious.

"I told the woman it was for the lady who likes extra scallops and sauce on the side, like you always tell her when you order."

"Oh. Good!" Loreena was happy! Another high-five.

"Want some wine, Mom?"

"Do you have any green tea?"

Oh, crap. She never remembered to buy the tea. Luna was about to say 'no', when Sunny said, "Yes!" She opened her purse and took out a box of green tea. "I picked it up, just like you asked," she said, giving Luna another nod.

Loreena examined the box. "Lipton," she said with disdain. "I prefer Bigelow." She read the label. "I suppose it'll do."

"What's in it?" asked Luna.

"Green tea leaves," said Loreena.

Sunny circumvented the whole "How do I use the microwave?" conversation by taking on the task of preparing Loreena's tea.

Loreena sat at the table with Luna. Apropos of nothing, she said, "Didn't we have fun in Rome?"

They'd gone to Italy when Luna was a teen. The accommodations in each city were spare, since Loreena had found the places in a book called "Italy on $10 a Day." But nothing topped Rome, where they'd stayed (and eaten most of their meals) in an ancient, stone convent occupied by elderly nuns who'd taken a vow of silence.

Luna was about to say, "You gave me no religion, and then stuck me at a breakfast table with a bunch of scary, mute penguins bearing crosses," but the look on Loreena's face was so bright. Kind of like Lenny's on his birthday, when Luna had walked in.

That's when it hit Luna.

Loreena had done her best. She'd tried to take care of Luna. She just wasn't capable of it.

In Loreena's reality, they'd had an awesome European vacation. Somehow she'd missed or refused to see that Luna had been anorexic the whole time, eating nothing but vegetables in small portions for most of the trip. Even Luna had no idea why, on the plane home, she'd gobbled up the entire meal they served, including the roll and butter. After that, she'd started eating normally again, but Loreena did not seem to have noticed either the illness or the recovery. Like most things in Luna's life, she'd come through it alone, whether consciously or not.

As she flashed back on this, something shifted in her mind. She didn't feel so upset anymore.

The anger she'd harbored against her mother had split from the memory and vanished.

Just like that, it was gone.

I forgive you, she thought—not saying it aloud, because Loreena wasn't capable of grasping why she needed to be forgiven.

Instead, she smiled, and agreed with Loreena. "Yes. Mom. We did have fun in Rome." She gave Loreena a hug, and the vitamin smell didn't even bother her.

"I thought your boyfriend would be here," Loreena said. "I wanted to meet him."

"You wanted to meet Trip?"

"Of course."

"Why?"

"Why wouldn't I? He's practically part of the family."

"You never treated Nick as family—and he was!"

Loreena waved the comment off. "That was ages ago. And *anyone* would be better than *him*." She still wouldn't speak Nick's name. He was her Voldemort.

Luna and Sunny stared at each other. This was an unexpected conversation.

"I broke up with Trip, Mom."

"Oh? That's too bad. I'm sure you'll meet someone else soon." Loreena took a sip of tea. "You have so much to offer." She looked Luna right in the eyes. "I just want you to be happy."

The doorbell rang.

Footsteps of kids above them. It *had* to be dinner this time, they knew.

Luna rose to greet the Chinese delivery man. Sunny followed. She whispered to Luna, "I think your mom being normal is one of the seven signs. If Sal strolls in with dental implants and a fat check for years of child-support, we'll know it's all over."

When Sunny loses her sarcasm, that's when it's over, said Jiminy.

Luna laughed.

"What?" asked Sunny.

"I'll tell you later."

After dinner, everyone sang "Happy Birthday." Once again, Loreena's operatic voice rose above the rest, but this time Luna didn't mind. Loreena was just being herself. She didn't know how to tone it down.

The fiery candles were in front of her.

"Make a wish, Mommy!" Dylan urged.

What would she ask for?

Before she could form a request, something happened.

The last crusty bits of Luna's old resentments lifted from her stomach and her heart.

They rose though her throat.

She opened her mouth and they exited, extinguishing the candles before dissipating.

She was pure light inside, for just a moment, and everyone clapped, as if they knew.

Happy birthday, Luna, Jiminy said.

FORTY-SEVEN

THE NEXT DAY, Luna was on her way to a school visit and revising sentences of NWaN in her mind.

She'd let go of her anger against her dad, her mom and Nick. *That must be the end of the book!*

But it didn't feel right. Something was lacking, no matter how hard she tried to not see it.

Damn.

It was that old cliché about love again.

Did her story boil down to missing a man… and a missed period?

A week after Luna handed Trip the note, not only did she pine over him, but she also couldn't help wondering what had become of her period.

She never thought about "that time of the month" until she was suddenly bleeding, so the fact that she realized anything was wrong meant that her period was very, very late.

She'd only noticed because of the school visit. Getting ready to leave this morning, she'd checked out her nails and saw they were sporting the chipped purple remains of her last manicure. *Drat!* She poked her head inside the bathroom cabinet looking for polish remover and spotted a bag of sanitary napkins. *Hmmm. Haven't used those in a while…*

There was no polish remover, and no time to waste. She had to get on the road. But the lilac splotches on her nails no longer concerned Luna. Gripping the wheel tight she wondered: *Am I pregnant?*

She tried to distract herself by thinking about her book, but the only thing that led to was the certainty that she still hadn't found her end.

Altogether, it was a dreadful ride.

Fortunately, she went right into "presentation" mode when she spoke to the kids. The show must go on. And she really loved talking about writing, anyway. But the minute she got back in her van, it hit her again: *Am I pregnant?*

She couldn't stand the uncertainty, so when she saw a CVS she pulled into their lot.

After scanning the various pregnancy test boxes (why were there so many types?) she chose the simplest one. If a pink line appeared within three minutes… that meant she was knocked up.

She was still a long way from home. She needed to know now! She went next door to Trader Joe's, locked herself in the bathroom and peed on the stick.

Holding it gingerly between her thumb and forefinger, she checked for immediate results. No pink yet. She noted the time on her cell phone: 3:43.

Knock, knock, knock!

"Just a minute!" she called out to whoever was at the door. *Actually, just three minutes…*

She supposed she could take it with her, but if it got jangled around in her purse, would that tamper with the results? Plus, she didn't really want to put something she'd urinated on in her pocketbook, and she couldn't parade through the store holding it in the open.

3:44.

No pink yet.

Bang! Bang! Bang!

"Hang on!" she called out. *Yeesh.* This person didn't have any patience.

The door knob twisted.

Was he or she deaf?

"Almost done!" she yelled, extra loud.

3:45.

No pink yet.

The person was really going at that door, pounding away. Luna felt like she was under siege.

She stared at her cell phone until the five gave way to a six.

No pink line.

She wrapped the stick in a wad of toilet paper and chucked it in the trash. Then she opened the door and stepped out to face the urgent knocker. It was an old, gnarly, hunched man. "All yours," she told him, forcing a fake smile. He grunted and shuffled past her, slamming the bathroom door.

Luna headed down the cereal aisle toward the entrance, past all the people browsing bran flakes and granola.

She wasn't pregnant after all.

And even though it *was* a relief and *certainly* for the best, she also felt an overwhelming sadness, like she was grieving for something she'd never had.

Luna went home to try and write yet again. But Trip kept invading her thoughts. She mostly wasn't surprised he hadn't called her back, but part of her was. Her emotions were as complicated as her relationship with Trip.

She rolled her desk chair back and forth, back and forth. The wooden chair creaked just a little from the pressure; its wheels sank silently into the dense beige and white carpet.

Luna stared at the blank computer screen and considered Trip yet again.

Maybe he *was* like Seth from *City of Angels.*

A messenger.

Sent to teach her *what?*

She tried to distract herself by looking at the rippling inlet outside her window. The current was moving toward the right. After all these years, she'd recently noticed that the current changed directions. Didn't that disturb the fish? What about the ducks? Did they just go with the flow?

The current seemed so fast lately too, like it had picked up speed.

The water used to be so restful. Now it rushed, practically frantic to get wherever it was going.

Not to the ocean, at least not today—the Atlantic Ocean was to the left. It was a zigzaggy, bending path to the sea, but not that far if you had a boat and knew where you were going.

Luna didn't, but she hated the ocean anyway. She hated the way it had of being endless.

There were no ducks today, but her friend the egret plodded through the marsh grasses that stood sentry at the border between land and water.

Back and forth, back and forth he went, so slow that in each step he seemed to be awakening from a trance. Always searching for food, waiting for his next tiny meal to swim by and brush against his yellow, stickish legs; barely moving so as not to scare his prey. Every once in a while his head and long white neck would dart into the water and he'd snatch something with his beak.

You had to hand it to him—he had patience, spending his life practically on pause, all for a bite to eat.

She looked back at her screen, but it was no use. There was no writing to be done today.

She decided to try CraigsList again. If she found someone new, she could forget Trip.

Right?

She entered the site and placed a "woman looking for a man" ad: "A lot of love to give. Forty-year-old seeks emotionally available divorcee or widower for reciprocal long-term relationship."

The sleazy replies rolled in:

"I've got eight inches to reciprocate."

"I'm not only available emotionally, I'm available for your pleasure tonight."

"Let's start in bed and see where this goes." *It probably goes on this guy's hidden webcam*, Luna thought.

Within twenty minutes she'd gotten eighteen replies, all inappropriate and/or riddled with grammatical mistakes. *Ugh.* She was about to log off her e-mail when another response came in: "Hi. I just read your ad.

I'm 36, divorced and have a lot of love to give, too. Hope you'll write me back ☺ Perry"

Why not?

"Glad to hear from you, Perry," she wrote. "I was beginning to wonder if there were any nice guys left in the world." She felt a little pang when she hit the "send" button. She still felt loyal to Trip for some insane reason, but luckily there was no time to wallow. It was time to go work out with Joe.

Of course, Luna discussed everything with her boxing coach/guru.

Joe scoffed at Luna's suggestion that Trip was an angel. "That asshole ain't no angel. He's a pimp."

"A pimp?" Luna was hitting the heavy bag. Jab, Jab, right, right…

"Well, he's not really a pimp," Joe amended. "He's using a pimp's technique."

"What's that?"

"Every woman wants one thing desperately. A pimp finds out what that is and gives it to her. Then, he takes it away. She'll do anything to get it back."

Luna stumbled mid-twist. The heavy bag bopped her right in the face.

Joe was right.

Trip had given her what she wanted, then taken it away.

He'd given her love—in brief moments.

Luna balanced herself again, and did a combination. Jab, right, jab, right, left hook, right hook, left hook, right hook. The bell rang. "Rest," said Joe.

Between heavy breaths, Luna asked, "You think he did that on purpose?"

"Why does that even matter?" Joe shook his head. "You could spend your life analyzing pricks, but bottom line, they're pricks. What more do you need to know?"

"I guess." But Luna wasn't absolutely positive that Trip was a prick.

Joe laughed. "You still got it for him. He must've given it to you real good." The bell rang again. "On the upper cut bag. Go!"

Luna came home sweaty and exhausted.

She logged into her e-mail to see if Perry had written back.

He had: "Good news. There is at least one nice guy left, and I am him. Hope you'll allow me the opportunity to show you just how nice I am. I'm attaching my photo. Cheers!"

Perry's picture looked okay. Blond, Nordic-looking, nice eyes.

He was no Trip.

But wasn't that the point?

She wrote him back again, and sent her picture.

Minutes later, he responded again.

He asked her for a date on Friday night.

Am I ready for a date?

She didn't reply.

FORTY-EIGHT

LUNA DECIDED TO talk with Aunt Zelda, who had been pretty passionate towards the other sex in her day. In a recent interview she'd been asked, "What is your favorite sport?"

She'd replied, "Attracting men."

Zelda hadn't had much luck in the men department. Her first husband, a violinist, had been drafted into World War II and killed in combat within a month of their marriage.

Her second husband, also a violinist, died of alcoholism in a Las Vegas hotel room while touring with a road production of *Jesus Christ Superstar.*

Luna had only been six, but she remembered his violent temper. Sometimes when Luna had stayed with them, she'd woken up in the night because Uncle Toby was screaming at Aunt Zelda, and she could smell the gin on his breath from the top of the stairs.

Once little Luna had asked, "Why do you love Uncle Toby? He's so mean."

Aunt Zelda had replied, "Child, he plays the fiddle like a god."

Aunt Zelda was practicing her fiddle on the stage when Luna walked in.

"Dearheart!" she called. "I'm just finishing up."

Luna sat in a back row and watched Aunt Zelda play. Her fingers moved up and down the strings, while her bow plowed straight across with great gusto. It was a beautiful piece, even though Luna had no idea who had composed it. She'd never had a great interest in music no matter how hard Zelda tried to instill it, and unless it was something she'd heard many times, she was clueless about the composer.

"Chopin," Zelda said when she stopped, as if she'd heard Luna's thoughts.

She rose from her hard-backed chair and put her violin in its case. Then she strolled down the aisle to Luna and gave her a kiss. "How are you, kiddo?"

Aunt Zelda didn't remember Luna's birthday, because she didn't do birthdays. If Luna mentioned that it was her birthday, Zelda would write her a check, but she'd never buy a gift or pick up the phone. She just wasn't that way.

"I'm kind of sad," Luna answered. "I broke up with my boyfriend."

"If that made you sad, why'd you do it?"

Luna told Aunt Zelda the story of Trip. She'd never gone into it before, partly because it was complicated and Aunt Zelda always seemed so bogged down with enough stuff, and partly because she was afraid of what Aunt Zelda would say.

After hearing the beginning, Aunt Zelda said, "I think he's afraid. It's vulnerability."

But when Luna told her about how he'd show up in the middle of the night and display no emotions, Aunt Zelda said, "Fuck him! Out! He's a chiseler wearing at your soul!"

"I thought you said he was vulnerable."

Aunt Zelda shrugged, "He's a vulnerable chiseler." She took a swig of the red wine she always had at hand these days. "You know what I'd say to him, right?"

"I love you, darling, but the season is over."

"Right!"

"Well, the note I wrote him was a bit longer, but that was the gist of it."

"Good riddance!" She took Luna's hand and pressed it—a pretty hard squeeze for an old lady. (Zelda would describe herself as "one tough cookie.") Then Zelda said, "Although maybe he can't help his behavior. Each man is the sum total of all that's happened to him."

They were both silent for a moment. Luna considered what Aunt Zelda had said. Did it apply to her, too? Was she the product of all her experiences? Could she somehow add up to more than that? Could she use them to *become* more?

But all that was off topic, and it wasn't like Zelda had the answers, anyway. She'd just say something else deep and mysterious if Luna pursued that vein, and Luna already had Jiminy posing enough deep, mysterious things. So Luna said, "I miss Trip. A lot."

"Well, you can take him back, but you know what he's like and you have to accept that. Don't kid yourself into thinking you can change him."

"I know. And that's why I'm not going to call him."

"I think it's time for you to date someone else. Or a few someone elses." Aunt Zelda gave her a wink.

"Someone did ask me on a date...but, I don't know. It's so hard to find someone to like."

"It's fucking impossible to find someone to like!" Aunt Zelda declared, taking another big burgundy swig. "So you're saying that, in addition to loving him, you actually like this Trip, despite all that he's done?"

Luna nodded. "I'm sorry..."

"Never apologize, child!" Aunt Zelda thumped her hand on the table. "You are a loving person who I adore. Plus, you're pursuing your art, so you can't go wrong. I applaud you!"

"Thanks."

"But I would still go on that other date."

Luna laughed. "Okay."

When Luna got home, she wrote to Perry and agreed to go out on Friday night.

He got back to her within minutes, suggesting Ruby Tuesday's.

It was close to home and it had a salad bar, so she replied, "Sure."

So now she had a date. She could leave Trip behind.

Ding! She had a text — from Trip! Was he psychic?

Before she could tell herself not to read it, she read it: "I miss u."

Wow.

Easy there, Jiminy chided. *Remember what he's like.*

"But he misses me!"

That's all well and good. But that doesn't mean he can give you what you need. You have to recognize the difference.

She took a deep breath in and let it out. "You're right."

I really love it when you say that, Luna.

"And I really love you, Jiminy."

Luna didn't respond to Trip's text. Instead, she hunkered down on her writing.

He texted again, a few hours later. "I thought about the things you wrote in your letter."

Damn. She really wanted to answer him. "But thinking about them isn't the same as changing, right Jiminy?"

That's my girl!

A third text dinged, just as Luna was going to bed: "I want to try again."

She hit REPLY.

I thought we agreed you were a no! Jiminy piped in.

"I think he deserves an answer," she said. "I'd sure want one."

She typed: "No. Sorry, but you're out of chances."

Trip responded: "I can change."

"I don't think you can."

"Try me."

"Too late. I have a date on Friday night."

There was no reply for about fifteen minutes. She thought he'd given up. Then he wrote, "Let me coach you on dating."

"That's ridiculous."

"Why? I'm a guy. I can help."

Luna didn't think he could help her date, but he could help her out bed until the time was right to sleep with Perry—if ever. She wrote, "I don't want to date you or have your advice, but I wouldn't mind if you made half-love to me."

"Half-love?"

"That's what I called it when we had sex. Except now it's not going to be half-love anymore. Not it's just sex. Friends with benefits. Deal?"

He didn't answer for a while. Then finally he responded, "Deal."

They decided he would come over on Friday night.

Friday night arrived, and Trip was actually on time. He knocked on the back door, and Luna jolted from the noise. Honestly, she thought she still had at least an hour to write — judging by his previous track record.

A blast of cold hit her as she creaked open the door, raising hairs on her bare arms and goose bumps on the nape of her neck. Winter's last stand, holding out against spring.

Leaning on the edge of the doorway with his arms folded, Trip gave her the same quirky smile he'd shared in Starbucks the night they'd met. It was kind of sweet. His eyes gave out a sexy spark, but he also had a hesitant look—like a deer caught in the headlights, frozen in the dilemma of whether to run forward or go back.

She'd really hurt him.

And he'd hurt her.

They'd resolved nothing, except for the fact that they fucked well together.

For tonight, that was enough.

He sauntered in, and the wind blew the door closed behind him.

Luna clicked the lock, twisted the knob to double-check, and padded across the carpet behind Trip. Neither said a word.

They headed upstairs, Luna still following Trip. The stairs creaked. It seemed like they groaned with each step.

Trip groaned too as he kicked off his sneakers onto Luna's bedroom rug and stripped out of his thermal jacket, T-shirt, jeans and tube socks.

He looked at Luna hesitantly. "Do you suppose...Could I still get a massage? Just to unwind?"

Luna nodded. The truth was, she enjoyed massaging Trip. It was nice to relax him. She could do it as just friends. Professional masseuses did it all day long to people without any emotion or attachment.

"Thanks." He stretched across her bed, stomach and face down, sinking into her comforter.

Luna took off her oversized NYU T-shirt and Happy Bunny skull-and-crossbone pajama bottoms, dropping them on top of Trip's things. His clothes reminded her of how he'd never left anything with her—not even sweatpants. The times he'd brought them with him, he'd stowed them away safely in his backpack when he left in the morning.

Trip was nomadic, wandering with his toothbrush tucked in his backpack's side pocket, blue bristles peeking out like the face of a papoosed babe. That toothbrush was probably the closest thing to a baby he was going to get. He might've said he wanted a family that night they'd met, but his actions had done everything possible to avoid it.

Luna straddled Trip's back, smoothing her hands across his tired muscles.

When he rolled over and took her, it was in haste. It wasn't a good haste, springing from mutual urgency. This was an impersonal haste, in which everything seemed to be on fast-forward.

He cut right to the chase, entering her immediately. This might've turned out all right still, but it was quickly over.

He let out a grunt and fell backward off of her, plopping into the pile of throw pillows propped against her baseboard, his head landing right on top of poor Fred.

Next thing she knew, he was snoring.

Loudly.

Luna sighed.

Trip was a ragpicker, a hobo, just like Dylan had said.

Except Trip stored his rags internally, piled inside, insulating and muffling his heart.

He was lying the wrong way on the bed, his feet pressed against her butt, his head snuggled on Fred. Twiggy orange legs with webbed feet splayed out from under Trip's chin.

The wind outside beat at the two glass doors leading to the balcony, huffing and puffing only to be contained in plastic bubbles. Luna's sealant sheets had made it through the season without any tears. The wind shrieked; the plastic crinkled with every expansion and contraction. She'd gotten used to sound. The instructions had said to shrink the plastic taunt with a hair dryer, but Luna didn't own one.

A train horn shrilled. The tracks were across town, near where Nick lived, but the inlet carried noise, sometimes delivering warning blasts through the quiet as if the train actually approached her home.

Sometimes—like tonight—she could even hear the train's body rattling down the tracks.

The ragman slept, fitfully jerking every so often, whistling out his breaths.

If this was the way things were going to be between them, he could go fuck himself.

FORTY-NINE

At seven a.m., Trip groaned again and rose. It was weird how he made noise climbing in and out of bed, but he was stone silent during sex. "Gotta go to work," he said, putting on his clothes. She thought he was going to leave, but he reached out and grabbed her arm. "I'm sorry I let you down…last night, I mean. I was beat. I'll make it up to you Sunday night."

She looked him in the eyes. "Will you?"

She saw something so sincere in Trip's eyes that she thought maybe, just maybe, he actually cared about having let her down. Then the wind made the plastic wrap flap. Perfect timing for him to look away. "I'll take care of this for you, when I come back."

He let go of her wrist and gave her a peck on the cheek. "I am a handy man, if not a reliable one." He headed out the door, then peeked back in. "Have fun on your date tonight."

Luna vowed to think of her upcoming date with Perry, and not Trip.

She walked into the Ruby Tuesday's bar, and Perry waved.

He was pretty cute in person, and his picture had been an accurate representation of him. She should've been pleased, but she felt kind of ambivalent about the situation. They said hello and hugged in that awkward, first-date way.

"What would you like to drink?" Perry asked.

"Sangria would be nice," she said.

"Then sangria it is!"

Perry ordered a pitcher of sangria and a chicken wing platter for them both.

Luna opened her purse but Perry said, "Put your money away. It's no good here tonight."

The sangria helped. Luna loosened up and enjoyed herself. She and Perry were nibbling and drinking and laughing together.

Here are some of the things she learned about Perry:

STATS ON PERRY

Name: Perry Sorensen

Ethnic Background: Norwegian

Marital Status: Divorced. He'd almost died in a car accident a year and a half earlier. During the months he'd lain in a hospital bed, his wife had left him.

Children: None.

Body: Fit, but short. Luna was slightly taller than him.

Hair: Blond.

Occupation: Accountant.

Favorite Physical Activities: Brisk walking, occasional bowling.

Other likes: Watching football, baseball, basketball & pretty much any other sport you could observe.

Dislikes: Disagreement, diversity, extremes.

Religion: Lutheran.

Favorite Writers: Ayn Rand, Stephen Crane.

Favorite Dessert: Cheesecake.

Favorite expression: "What would life be like without arithmetic, but a scene of horrors?"

Luna felt that life *with* arithmetic was a scene of horrors. She'd been so disappointed that the play *Proof* was about math, and not the suspense thriller she'd imagined. Sitting in that audience, she'd wanted to murder someone.

Still, she figured she could deal with Perry's devotion to numbers.

She was devoted to words.

They could even each other out.

After dinner, they sat in Perry's grey Nissan Ultima.

He kissed her.

He did this sensational thing with his tongue, rubbing it in the rim of her upper lip. It must've been one of her erogenous zones, because it did the job immediately.

Perry was thrilled by her enthusiastic response, especially after so long a dry spell. He wanted to do more with her.

Luna knew she should wait to have sex with Perry. But he was so sweet, and it had been so long for him. Maybe this was meant to be. Maybe she was meant to find a replacement for Trip in bed quickly, and just be done with him. But right now she needed to pick up her kids from Sunny's.

They agreed to continue on Sunday, when the kids would be with Nick.

Before she went to bed, Luna texted Trip: "I don't need you on Sunday. My date went well."

He'd know what that meant.

Trip wrote back, "Don't you want me to at least fix the plastic?"

"No thanks."

"Suit yourself. But I doubt your new guy will be any use to you."

Did Trip mean in bed, or for fixing things?

She didn't write back to ask him.

FIFTY

LUNA SAT IN her kitchen with Perry eating Chinese food, toying with a shrimp and wondering how the hell she could get out of this without having sex with him.

The first sign that he was a boob had come when they ordered the food. "Let's get something to share!" he'd suggested, beaming. Luna stared, scarcely believing his words. Out of the whole diverse Chinese menu, why on earth did they have to eat the same thing? Was it supposed to demonstrate compatibility?

"I like bean curd and broccoli in garlic sauce with no corn starch or msg," she told him.

"How about General Tso's Chicken?" he asked, as though she hadn't spoken.

"Not so much," she replied in a tone she hoped would be cold enough for him to take a hint.

"Pepper steak?" he piped. Apparently he'd forgotten that she didn't eat red meat, or thought maybe she'd suddenly changed her diet.

She shook her head no, but she'd really felt like slumping on the table in despair.

Then she let him pick some shrimp thing, because it didn't mean that much to her and the debate was giving her a headache.

Perry wanted them to have the same meal, down to the soup. But here they could not agree.

Luna's sinuses were blocked up, and she looked forward to flushing them with hot and sour soup.

Perry was one of those guys who felt wonton soup was an integral part of a Chinese meal.

No way would Luna bite into any nasty wontons with their grey, mushy mystery meat. It looked like brain matter.

Perry was allergic to cloud ear fungus, one of the ingredients in hot and sour soup. Luna had never heard of cloud ear fungus, and wished she didn't know it was in her soup, but this nasty information wasn't enough to dissuade her from the thing guaranteed to unclog her head.

They agreed to disagree, reaching a soup detente—though Perry sighed deeply when Luna gave that part of the order to the Chinese restaurant.

Waiting for the delivery, they'd reached an awkward pause. *He's run out of things to say!* she realized. *Mental head slap!* Clearly she'd been fooled by "first date syndrome," during which anyone could come off intriguing just due to the sheer newness of them.

Then there was the sangria she'd been slugging…

Now, Perry started talking about his job again—just like he'd done at Ruby Tuesday's. It was like his pre-recorded tape had run out, and then rewound to begin again.

How could she have found accounting interesting?

She hated anything to do with numbers—they made her head spin.

She hated cold logic, which left no room for emotion and no room to breathe.

Most of all, she hated being held accountable.

In her determination to not need Trip—and in a sangria haze—Luna had somehow forgotten all this.

And now she had to listen to everything again!

As they sipped their different soups and ate the same main dish with white rice (she hadn't wanted to stir up any more controversy lobbying for brown) he launched into sports talk, which was apparently all he thought about when he wasn't thinking about work.

Why had that not appalled her the first time?

She wanted to jump ship, but didn't see how.

Damn!

The poor guy hadn't had sex in so long. No matter how annoying he was, Luna didn't have it in her to renege.

"Let's go upstairs," she suggested. If she couldn't get out of it, she could at least get it wrapped up.

They scraped back their chairs.

Luna tried to head for the stairs but Perry grabbed her hand. *Tell me he wants to hold hands climbing the stairs. I might barf,* she thought.

Perry pulled her close. "We need to talk," he said.

Uh-oh. "About?"

Hugging her tight to him he asked, "Have you heard of Crohn's Disease?"

"Um… I've heard the name…"

"It affects the intestines."

"Okay…" She didn't know what was coming, but it couldn't be good.

"I have a pouch," he said.

"Excuse me?"

"I have a… bag," he said. "I didn't know how to tell you, I got it while I was married, and so I've never had to come out and tell someone…"

Luna was not thrilled by the colostomy bag revelation, but she also felt sorry for Perry. A nearly fatal car accident *and* a colostomy bag! It seemed doubly unfair. She thought briefly about telling him it was bad form to spring it on someone suddenly like that, but decided not to. It wasn't like she had any alternative advice on breaking the news. That was a question for Dear Abby if she'd ever heard one.

"I'm sure it'll be fine," she told him.

Upstairs on the bed, Luna discovered that when it came to kissing, Perry was a one-trick pony.

He did that tongue thing on the upper gum of her mouth over and over.

It got old quick.

Plus, she was thinking about that pouch collecting his waste. She'd heard about colostomy bags. They'd sounded repulsive, but somehow she'd thought they were removable.

She'd thought wrong.

Luna made the mistake of leaving the light on, which she realized too late when she unbuckled Perry's belt and took off his pants.

For the love of God, why didn't they color the pouch, or at least make it opaque?

She felt a *real* possibility that she might vomit.

She looked away, but the bag was impossible to ignore. For one thing, it was huge, covering most of his stomach like a giant hot water bottle, except it wasn't filled with hot water.

For another, it made squishing sounds every time he moved.

She tried thinking of it like a wine sack—the kind she'd used to sneak booze into rock concerts as a teen, even though it made the alcohol taste like formaldehyde.

But this was no wine sack. No matter how much she wanted to believe, she simply could not get her brain to go along with it. Her brain wasn't stupid, even if her heart was. Her brain yelled "run!" but her stupid heart was way too polite, and unfortunately it called the shots.

And then there was the matter of his penis.

If you could call it that.

It appeared to be a nub.

Jesus H. Christ, she'd had no idea they came that small. What was the point?

On the plus side, a blowjob would be effortless.

If she could ignore the squishy colostomy bag just above.

He asked what her favorite position was and, truthfully in this case, she said, "It doesn't matter."

The only thing that would matter here was if he donned a strap-on.

He climbed on top of her and asked if he was in.

She didn't know.

She felt nothing, not the slightest pressure or movement or object inside her.

Fortunately, Luna could experience orgasm through touch, and so she closed her eyes and let her mind go to that place.

Unfortunately, Perry then thought he'd had something to do with her pleasure.

By the time Trip chimed in, she and Perry were done—Praise the Lord!—and lying in bed. She'd known Trip would text her—having been cancelled he had to barge in anyway—and she'd never been so grateful for the distraction that dinging tone provided.

Her cell phone was downstairs. In the dead silence that followed the so-called sex, she heard Ozzy shrieking. She practically leapt up to read it.

While Perry lay upstairs oblivious (she didn't know what he was thinking and she didn't care—she'd sacrificed enough), Luna and Trip texted back and forth.

He: How's ur date?

She: You were right.

He: About?

She: It wasn't good.

He: Wat wasn't?

She: Sex.

He: U HAD SEX?

She had, she replied. But it sucked.

Trip was stunned that she'd gone through with sex with someone else, but happy that it hadn't been good. He wanted details, to be assured that he really was a better lover. She related her experience briefly, omitting the part about the pouch because that was just too disgusting to admit.

You really needed to be attached to someone to accept a colostomy bag.

She told him about the gum-rimming thing and the nub and the general dullness that Perry was.

He offered to come over and do the job right.

Luna accepted. Although she'd been able to get off, there was no substitute for a good, hard fuck.

Perry left a short time later, saying he didn't want to go but he had to get up early, and, damn it all, she knew he was sincere.

She closed the door behind him and breathed a sigh of relief. *That was quite a lot to deal with*, said Jiminy.

"Talk about an understatement," said Luna. "You sure you didn't know about that pouch beforehand?"

I swear. I'm a guide, not a prophet.

"That would be funny if I wasn't so traumatized." She shuddered. "I can't believe I went through that."

There was a reason. Remember what you realized after you threw Nick out? There are no mistakes.

"Well, this sure felt like an accident." Luna went into the bathroom and brushed her hair. "Thank God I have Trip for the repairs."

Do you really think God has anything to do with that?

"I can't get into a theological inner discussion right now. Trip will be here any minute."

Are you sure you want to do this?

"Have actual sex?" She laughed. "Yeah, that's the one thing in all this I'm absolutely sure about. As Sunny would say, 'Christ in hiking gear on a Blue Ridge Mountain!'"

The doorbell rang.

She opened it, and Trip sauntered in. "Got anything to eat? I'm starved."

She fed him left over Chinese food. "Delicious!" he said. "But why'd you get white rice? You always get brown."

Of all that's happened, he mentions rice? She didn't feel like explaining, and it was none of his business. "They were out of brown," she said. He was scraping the last few grains onto his fork, making a grating sound. "Can we go upstairs now?"

"Sure we can, honeybunny." He dropped his fork to the plate and stood. "Let's go."

In bed, Luna found that her having had sex with another man prior to Trip made him circumvent all the pre-sex massaging. He was ready to go—eager to reclaim her and prove his superiority to Perry.

"Wow," Luna said when they finished. "That was superb."

"At least I can be your relief pitcher," Trip said. "If nothing else."

When Luna told Sunny all this the next day, Sunny said, "Good for you! You took lemons and made lemonade!"

"I'm surprised you have anything nice to say about this, considering how you feel about Trip."

"Desperate times deserve desperate measures," said Sunny. "At least that man's good for something."

Luna was forced to make the break-up call. Perry had gotten attached, and the only way to be free from his grip was to yank him off.

"I'm not ready for a relationship," she told him on the phone. It was sort of true – she wasn't ready for a relationship like the kind he was offering.

And she never would be.

He was stunned. "I thought everything was so awesome," he said.

"It was," she lied. "It's me, not you."

"Is there anything I can do to change your mind?"

A personality transplant, a penis-enhancement operation, and lose the gross pouch, she thought. "No," she said.

"You're sure?"

"I am."

"Then have a nice life, I guess," he said.

"You, too," she told him. She ended the call, breathed and felt relieved. But she also wondered if she could ever secure a successful relationship.

She worried not about the sex—she was bound to find good sex out there if she persisted—but the boring factor.

She liked "bad boys."

They were exciting.

But they were also bastards.

It was like a scene from the last James Bond movie she'd seen. James was in bed with a married woman. She'd asked him, "Why can't the good guys be like you?"

He answered very suavely, "Because then they would be bad."

Could a good guy be bad enough to keep her interested?

Luna shared these thoughts with Sunny at the diner the following day. She'd driven to Sunny's job to take her out to lunch.

Sunny responded, "This is all very disturbing."

"Speaking of disturbing, how's your imaginary relationship going?"

"As well as you can imagine."

"Seems like a dead-end situation."

"Yeah, but a dead end can be comforting. At least you always know where you are."

"Hmmm…"

"So what's your game plan?"

"I want to slow the sex down and just date," Luna said.

"If you think you can."

"You don't?"

"Let's put it this way, Luna. You'll never be a nun."

Luna shrugged. It was true. That was one habit she didn't want. "Yeah, but I need to get to know someone before I sleep with them."

"Sounds reasonable. What about Trip?"

"For now, he stays. I found the key to conjuring his 'A' game in bed."

"What's that?"

"Competition."

"That's an alpha male for you."

FIFTY-ONE

LUNA WAS SERIOUS about not starting her next relationship with sex. She'd never done this, but she'd heard that it worked. Dr. Gold had once told her, "The problem with having sex right away is that once you add that into the equation, everything else goes out the window."

Above all, she didn't want another Perry moment.

She met lots of guys on CraigsList, but weeded most of them out. Trip actually helped in the effort, coaching her on what to look for. "Make sure he's divorced or widowed. If he's never been married, that's a red flag."

Luna wished she'd known that before she'd gone out with Trip.

"He should be generous and willing to give you time most of all."

Ha! She thought. "So basically he should be everything you're not."

"Everything I was," he said. "I told you, I can change. You just won't give me the chance."

"That's right," she said. "Been there, done that."

A couple of weeks later Luna met another promising guy named Barry. He was a fifty-year-old contributor to a humor magazine. *A writer! Wow!*

When she told Trip how excited she was, he said, "Fifty? That's kind of old. He won't be able to keep up with you in bed."

Luna stared at him. "Do you know how old you are?"

He said, "I'm an exception. You'll see." Then he fucked her superbly.

Despite Trip's warning, Luna continued communicating with Barry. They wrote back and forth, sharing their backstories.

Here are some of the things Luna learned about Barry:

Name: Barry Black

Ethnic Background: Cornish.

Marital Status: Single, though he'd lived with a woman for over ten years.

Children: None.

Body: Hard to say from the picture. He told her he carried "a few extra pounds."

Hair: He had a bit of a bouffant, but Luna could look past that. It was his face that was off-putting, because Barry sort of resembled a llama.

Occupation: Humorist/satirist.

Favorite Physical Activities: Strolling to the theatre or a restaurant.

Other likes: Jokes such as: *A giraffe walks into a bar and says, "The high-balls are on me."*

Dislikes: Being left in the lurch. He ended every email with "Let me know…" even if he hadn't posed a question.

Religion: In the tradition of his ancestors, he called himself Celtic polytheistic, which he found amusing because it confused people.

Favorite Writers: Chuck Palahniuk, George Orwell, Gary Larson.

Favorite Dessert: Anything with wet walnuts.

Favorite Expression: "Welcome to Hell. Here's your accordion."

Soon they started talking on the phone. It was great, speaking with someone literary.

But for all of Luna's good intentions, the subject of sex slipped in fast.

Barry brought it up. "We need to talk."

Swell. "I'm listening,"she said, because it was clear that when someone said "we need to talk" there was never any room for discussion.

He told her he had this problem: He couldn't always "perform."

"Have you tried Viagra?" Luna asked, trying not to sound as tense as she felt.

He said he hadn't.

"Why don't you?"

Luna silently prayed that he'd take the not-so-subtle hint and get some.

She'd gone through too much in her life to deal with problems easily solved by medication.

Time for their big date!

Barry picked Luna up at six, arriving at her door bearing flowers and flan. Grinning widely, he looked even more like a llama. His teeth were quite broad.

"How sweet!" she exclaimed, giving him a hug and accepting the dozen white roses and the plastic container. She was more excited by the flan—the roses were going to be a lot of work.

He said, "Let's have the flan together, when we get back from dinner."

"Okay." She didn't really want to share, but she couldn't tell him that.

She showed him into the living room and excused herself to care for the roses. Trimming each stem on a slant under running water, filling the vase with the right temperature water – not too warm or too cold, searching for aspirin to drop into the water. All this to preserve things already on their way out – snipped from their roots in the name of affection. How ironic, killing something as a way to show you care.

The petals already had a brown hue to them.

Men apparently bought flowers without examining their condition.

She knew this because Sunny had frequently gotten wilted bouquets after Sal had fucked up. The Coconut also bestowed some iffy-looking bunches.

Nick had always given Luna extremely perky flowers in lavish displays, but he'd never picked them out.

No, he'd ordered them from a fancy florist, using Luna's credit cards.

Trip had never brought her flowers.

She finally got the roses settled in their vase. She put them on her nightstand upstairs and came back down.

"Ready?" he asked. There was that llama smile again.

"Yes." Up close, the llama thing was hard to ignore. But she was a trooper.

Once committed to something, she followed through.

And she'd committed to this evening with Barry.

She might find a way to be attracted to him, somehow. If only he would take her advice and some Viagra.

But Barry had not taken her advice.

"At this stage in my life, I just like to give pleasure," he told her as they climbed under the covers, having partaken in Japanese food and then flan. Outside, high winds beat at the house relentlessly. It sounded like the house—or at least the billowing plastic—was going to be ripped apart.

I guess we're at different stages of our lives, she thought. But she was too polite to say it. What was the point of saying anything, anyway? She'd already tried, and he hadn't listened.

So he gave her pleasure, and she enjoyed it, but there was no mutual energy exchange. She might as well have been alone.

She also didn't feel right unless she reciprocated.

Her mouth ached from her long attempt to bring Barry to completion—to no avail.

She was still trying when there was a loud banging against the house.

The wind *had* broken something.

The noise was a distraction. Bad in most situations, but in this case it was good. It gave her something rhythmic to focus on, like a meditation.

After forty minutes, fearing jaw dislocation, Luna finally gave up. She rose and wiped drool from her face. Then she looked at Barry and willed him to get out.

Suddenly she felt creeped out by the way he wrote "let me know" at the end of each e-mail, and it *really* bothered her that he resembled a llama.

She liked llamas, but not as dates.

"It's fine. I told you I like giving pleasure," he said. "But thanks for trying."

Leave, leave. She nodded numbly.

Finally, he got up. "I guess I'd better go. It's a long drive home."

"Ba-bye…"

"Unless you want me to stay…"

"That's okay."

The banging outside continued. "Want me to check that out for you?"

"No."

"Will you be able to sleep?"

"Yes."

"Okey dokey…"

Once she closed the door behind the still-talking Barry, she went to check on the noise. It was loudest in the bathroom. She opened the window and saw the problem: the gutter had been separated from the house.

"Shit." She didn't have any tools.

Her phone dinged from the bedroom, a text from Trip, who of course knew that she was seeing Barry tonight.

It said: *So?*

She wrote back: *He was attentive.*

Damned if she was going to tell him he'd been right about the age thing.

Trip wrote back: *Better than me?*

She didn't feel like soothing his ego at the moment—the banging was getting to her.

She wrote: *Oh just come fuck me, and bring something that slices metal.*

Trip was there in fifteen minutes and walked in silently.

He gave her a wounded look.

"You did this!" she exclaimed. "I would've been faithful forever." Still nothing from him.

"Oh, relax. We didn't have any chemistry." She wanted to make him feel better, but still didn't feel like revealing the entire truth. She didn't want to relive it.

He remained mute.

"For God's sake, I thought you'd be the last person I ever had sex with," Luna said.

He finally spoke. "I might be the last person you have good sex with." They stared at each other. Upstairs, the gutter banged.

She asked, "Did you bring the slicer?"

He handed her what looked like malformed, criminally insane pliers.

"They're called 'snips,' actually."

What a thing to care about. Metal-cutting semantics. "Whatever."

She took them and headed up the stairs.

"*You're* gonna handle this?" he called.

"I am," she replied. "I told you, I don't need your help for things, Trip."

"You know, it would be nice if you would at least take me up on the things I'm good at." He squinted his eyes at her. "And I'm good at fixing things.

"Go fix yourself a snack."

Determined to be independent and take care of this herself, Luna crawled out of the small bathroom window onto the ledge and clipped the jagged metal.

She tried not to think about being on a ledge. At least the wind had slowed.

It didn't take long to do the job. Trip's snips were effective.

She turned to climb back inside, but it was way more daunting than going out had been. The sink was so close… she didn't want to smash her head on its ceramic tiles.

"Trip!"

No answer.

"Trip!"

Nothing.

"TRIPPPPPPPP!"

He finally creaked up the stairs, appearing in the bathroom doorway with a two-thirds eaten banana split in hand. "You called?"

She looked at the bowl. "You ate my last banana?"

"I left you half." He ate a spoonful of split. "What's up?"

"I need your help. I can't get back in."

"Oh. Now you need my help? I should leave you there."

"But you won't."

"How do you know? If I'm such a bad guy."

She rolled her eyes and put her arms out. He didn't put his banana split down. "I might just go," he said.

"You wouldn't..."

"That's right, I wouldn't. But how about an apology?"

"For what?"

"For refusing my help."

She was tired on being on the edge. "Okay, I'm sorry I wouldn't let you help me."

"That's better." He put his sundae down, took hold of her and lifted her gently to the floor.

After their marathon session in bed, Luna and Trip were both breathless and sweaty.

"Would you open the window?" Trip asked her.

She cracked it, up to the safety lock. It wasn't much, maybe an inch.

"Do it more," he said. "Do it all the way."

"I can't," she said. "I'm afraid to leave it up all night."

"You don't have to be scared," he said. "I'm here."

Are you? She thought. *Are you here?*

But she didn't say it out loud.

He said, "I hope you know that I wouldn't let anything bad happen to you."

She wasn't sure she believed him. But God, she wanted to. "Sometimes you seem like an angel with your soothing words and those wings on your back, but other times I could swear you're the devil, Trip. Which is it?"

"Damned if I know."

She resisted the urge to turn over and face him. What would be the point? Instead, she counted petals on her roses. By the time she hit ten, Trip was snoring.

Pretty loud, said Jiminy. *Can you stand the noise?*

"Trip's snoring is the least of the problems."

What are the other problems?

She stared at the roses. "He doesn't bring me flowers."

Flowers die.

True. She'd thought that herself. But still…

"He doesn't bring me flan."

There's a Mexican restaurant down the block. You can get your own flan any time you want.

True. But it wasn't the same when she got it herself. Was it? "So you're saying there are no problems?"

I'm saying, decide what you want the most. You're not getting everything; this isn't a Julia Roberts movie. But for now, go to sleep.

So she did.

FIFTY-TWO

TWO DAYS LATER, the ringing of Luna's cell phone shocked her from sleep at 2:13 am. She knew without looking that it was Trip. Unless someone had died, no one else would call at this hour.

"Hi," she answered. She liked it when he called late, even though it wrecked her sleep. There was an added intimacy in the dark. With Trip, she had to take closeness where she could get it.

"Hey," he said. His voice was low and guarded. He sounded like maybe someone had died.

"What is it?" she asked, knowing he wasn't all right.

"I just left the emergency room. I was there all night," he said.

"Why?"

"I was having these stabbing pains. They still don't know what it was. They think maybe a kidney stone."

"How are you now?"

"Better… exhausted."

His car engine hummed in the background. Then he sucked in some air, so loud she could hear that too. "I thought I was going to die," he said.

Then he said, "I thought I was going to die there, alone."

"Oh, God."

"Yup."

"Come over."

"I can't have sex now."

"We don't have to have sex."

"But that's all I'm good for, remember?"

"I didn't say it exactly like that," she said. When had she turned into the bad guy? "We can cuddle. I care about you."

Silence. Then, "No thanks. But the caring part's good to know."

She said, "You just had a terrible experience. Don't you want someone to hold you?"

"Not on your terms."

He's a mess, Jiminy told Luna after Trip hung up.

"You think so?"

You obviously do. So why don't you get away from him?

"What's your deal anyway? Why are you fucking with my head? You're supposed to be helping me, and all you do is contradict yourself. You pushed me to write that note, and then two nights ago you seemed to want me to be with him. Remember all that talk about flowers and flan? And now you say he's a mess and I should be done with him...What do you want me to do?"

I'm merely reflecting the turmoil in your mind, Luna. It's you who can't decide, not me. This is all up to you.

Whoa. That was heavy.

Jiminy continued, *If you're not going to be done with him, at least stop this destructive dating path you're on. Deal with Trip and try to make it work.*

"That's hard."

What you're doing is harder. This isn't working for you, Luna.

"I know. I'll stop seeing other people, but I'll tell him I still am."

Jiminy said, *So much for honesty...*

"Where did honesty get me?"

That's also for you to decide, he answered. *But remember that Gandhi quote you love? If you're truly interested in being the change you wish to see in the world, I would imagine that honesty is a big part of that. Wasn't that what you wrote in your ad when you met Trip? If you want more honesty in the world, put it out there yourself. Be* ***that*** *change.*

"I am so sick of all this responsibility. Maybe I don't want to be the change any more. Maybe I don't believe there can be a change; the world's gone too far toward hell… Maybe I just give up."

Up to you. I'm basically just a sounding board. But I'll tell you this. Bottom line: Trip is utterly beside the point, Luna. He's just a means to an end.

She had to chew on that one alone.

Luna couldn't bear to think about her last conversation with Jiminy. She concentrated on finishing *NWaN*.

Except, she still couldn't.

Something was missing.

Every day she sat, staring at the computer screen, trying to figure out what that something was.

In the dark again with Trip a week later, Luna made up a story about Gabe, a twenty-nine-year-old male friend. "I'm thinking about hooking up with him," she lied.

He said, "Why? He's too young to know anything."

She said, "I had a younger boyfriend once. He was good in bed."

"A fluke."

"Whatever. I don't even care if Gabe is good. I just want to look at his body on top of me."

Trip's body went rigid. After a few moments he asked, "Don't I turn you on?"

Luna answered, "Of course you do." She hadn't meant to hurt him. Or had she?

Trip said, "Then why don't you open your eyes when you're with me?"

"I got tired of staring at your closed ones," she said, wondering what had made him open his at last.

But she asked a different question. "What are you worried about? You're the best lover, always."

He turned away from her, towards the flowers on the nightstand. They were looking kind of crispy. He said, "I'd rather be the only one."

Tell him the truth, Jiminy said.

And part of her wanted to…but she couldn't.

Or at least, she didn't.

I have the upper hand now, she told Jiminy.

Is that what's important here?

She didn't answer. She didn't actually have the answer. Part of her felt bad for Trip, and that was the part that wanted to tell him. *But* part of her felt good.

Part of her wanted to make him suffer, like she'd suffered.

I didn't peg you as an eye-for-an-eye type of girl.

Me, neither, she answered. *Shows you what we know.*

"You should throw those flowers out," Trip said. "They're dead."

FIFTY-THREE

LUNA INTERLOCKED HER hands behind her head, as Dr. Gold instructed. He stood behind her, his arms around her waist.

"Melt," he said.

She tried to relax.

"Melt more."

Again she tried, but she was still so stiff. "And more..."

He must've been satisfied this time because he pressed his arms tight against her middle like he was doing the Heimlich. Her back went *ccrrraaacckk*!

"Good," he said. "Lie on your back."

She complied.

"I'm mad at Trip," she told Dr. Gold. "I'm still angry that he changed from that guy on the beach."

Dr. Gold said, "He's a substitute for who you're really angry with—yourself."

Oh, damn.

He was right again.

She'd come to terms with her mom, her dad and even Nick.

But it was herself she found most daunting

She'd been doing the very thing she'd been appalled at her therapist Charlene for suggesting: she was going around the issue.

It was time to go through.

That night, Luna sat on her dock. The moon looked almost full. There was just the barest sliver missing. She stared into the water, at the ripples reflecting in the light.

The current was moving toward her at a pretty fast clip.

It was nippy out, as early spring nights often were – she tugged her knit cap further down on her ears and zipped her jacket to the max, until it touched her chin.

It was okay, though.

The air may have been chilly, but it was fresh, and that was all that mattered.

"So, Jiminy… we come to the real truth."

Of course, he didn't answer. She hadn't expected him to. She had to do all the hard stuff herself. That would've made her angry before, but not anymore.

It is what it is, she thought.

She took a deep breath and let it out. Then she closed her eyes and said the serenity prayer.

"I surrender," she said. "I'm ready to finish this now."

She saw it then.

In her mind, she saw the puddle.

And she fell into it, on her knees.

It felt so good, like when she was at Walden Pond.

"I forgive myself," she said.

Then she opened her eyes.

In the water below, the float swayed and creaked on the tide, bumping against the two tall beams it was attached to on either side.

The ramp bopped with it, rolling on its wheels slightly.

Luna felt a pop reverberating through her, just as the water carried sounds.

In her head it was like being on an airplane, when the pressure shifted and the ear canals were finally clear again.

In her body it was a crackling, like at Dr. Gold's.

Then came a cool sensation, a rush of relief from head to toe. Now she could breathe with absolute clarity.

She noticed two ducks then, swimming with the current, side by side. Gracefully, they headed under the dock and then out the other side.

She was at the other side, too.

She'd gone through.

She was free.

And she knew she had the ending of her novel.

Luna sat for a long time on the dock, just basking in being.

Sunny called.

"Dude, I'm on a break," she said. "I had to call and tell you what happened to me."

"Did you fall in a puddle?"

"Yuck! No," Sunny said, making a sucking sound. "I'm smoking an electronic cigarette, incidentally."

"Good for you! That's a start."

"We'll see. Anyway, we all got Taco Bell for dinner, and guess what?"

"Did you get a funny saying on a sauce packet?" Luna had actually framed her favorite packet and hung it in her kitchen: *You had me at taco.*

"No, but you're on the right track. It involves the sauce." She made another sucking sound, then continued. "When I squirted out the sauce into my napkin, it came out in a heart shape."

"Awww," said Luna.

"This is a sign that I'm on the right track," Sunny said. "I broke up with JoshJohn."

"Thank God! Did he take it badly?"

"Ha, ha. Anyway, I'm going to try dating again," said Sunny. "But this time I'm determined to filter out substance abusers, dullards and guys who don't know I'm dating them."

"Excellent!" said Luna.

"What I really want is a little voice that talks to me, like Jiminy," said Sunny.

"Well, Jiminy said all you have to do is be open to it."

Sunny said, "I want a female, so I can call it 'Jemama.'"

"Only you would have criteria for your inner conscience," said Luna. She looked up at the moon again. It suddenly seemed full.

"Oh, I almost forgot. I had a thought about you and Trip," Sunny said.

"Did it involve a sanitarium?'

"No." Sunny made a sucking noise again.

Luna stared at the moon. *How did it fill in like that?* "So?"

"This popped into my head," said Sunny. "It's an odd theory."

"Of course it is," said Luna. "Shoot."

"Have you considered that maybe this whole thing has been about two people afraid to have a relationship?"

"Huh." Luna still focused on that radiant moon. It looked so low and close, like she could just drive a few miles and grab onto it. "You know, you could be right."

She called Trip.

"Hey, I can't talk for long. I'm still working," he said.

"I just wanted to tell you something quick," she said.

"Shoot."

"I don't want any other lover but you," she said.

There was a pause. Then he asked, "But am I the only lover you have?"

"Yes."

"Good to know."

FIFTY-FOUR

THE NEXT MORNING was Easter.

Luna woke up to Dylan's sharp voice: "Wake up, Mommy! We have to see if the Easter bunny came!"

"Okey-dokey," Luna mumbled, forcing herself to rise. She was in Dylan's bed at Nick's, having stayed up until two a.m. making the kids' baskets. "I'm sure the bunny brought you something really special, baby."

Ben greeted them in the hall, rubbing his eyes. "Happy Easter, Mom." He hugged her.

Nick emerged from his room a few moments later, as a result of Dylan rushing in and shaking him awake.

Everyone headed into the living room to behold the baskets, which were humongous and packed.

"Look, the bunny got me Peeps!" Dylan exclaimed, ripping into the yellow package and snarfing a marshmallow chick with one hand while still rifling the basket with the other.

Dylan also got a kick out of seeing the carrot snacks he'd left for the bunny gnawed down to their green stems, with some orange spittle added for effect.

Ben was as tall as Luna now, and he'd grown past the bunny illusion. That was the difference five years made. He still appreciated a basket stuffed with goodies. He just knew who'd really stayed up late making it.

The kids feasted on a breakfast of chocolate bunnies' heads, with sugary sides of jellybeans and Cadbury Cream Eggs. Then everyone sat around the coffee table to play the games the "bunny" had also put in the baskets. Luna, Dylan and Nick played Operation, while Nick simultaneously played Connect Four with Ben.

Luna was surprised at how deftly she removed the patient's "spare rib."

Dylan came out on top after Nick purposely flubbed his attempt to retrieve the "funny bone," winking at Luna as the patient's bulbous red nose flashed and the game vibrated violently. Dylan then got it for double the money, because he held the "specialist" card.

"Ha!" Dylan said, brandishing the funny bone he clutched in the tweezers. "I win!"

"You do," Luna and Nick said in unison.

Nick was more competitive with his older son. Chips dropped and clinked rapidly, and they wound up tying in "games won": four to four; all in the time it took for one round of Operation.

He may have sucked as a husband, but Nick had grown into a good dad. She wondered if he'd had his own awakening, but not enough to ask. As long as the kids were being cared for, that was all that mattered.

After the games, Luna and Dylan left to go to her house. He was determined to teach her how to ride a bike today.

Today, she felt like she could do it.

"Look, Mommy, a snail!" Dylan said, pointing to the walkway as they headed toward the car.

Dylan loved all creatures.

"Hello, snail," she said.

"His name is Marvin," Dylan proclaimed.

"Okay. 'Bye, Marvin," she called, as they climbed in the van.

Luna got on the bike and pedaled, with Dylan gripping the rear and running. She wasn't scared this time. *If I fall, I'll just get up,* she thought. *No big deal.*

Still, she wanted Dylan to hold on until she said so. She rode across the field, getting ready. "Ok, let go!" she called out.

There was no answer.

Dylan wasn't there. He'd already released her!

She felt a slight tinge of panic, but then she laughed.

She laughed and laughed, like a madwoman. She was riding her bike solo, the wind in her hair, and even though she was still shaky, she oozed freedom.

She rode on for a little while, trying to get comfortable enough to maneuver and steer toward where she wanted to go.

Finally she managed to head back to Dylan. "Yea, Mommy!" He cheered.

"Why'd you let go before I said so?" Luna asked.

"Oh, Mommy. You're a big girl," he said. "It was time you went out on your own."

Luna stared at her wise son. "You're right, baby." She got off the bike—not very smoothly but not with a thunk to the ground, either—and embraced Dylan. "Thanks."

When they got back to Nick's, they found Marvin the snail squashed and eviscerated. "I should've moved him, Mommy," Dylan cried. "I could've saved him."

"Sweetie, you can't rescue everyone and everything in the world," Luna told him. "The most valiant thing you can do is to save yourself."

Dylan considered this. "Okay, Mommy. But can we have a funeral for Marvin?"

"Sure. Let's see if your dad has a box to bury him in."

"Nah, we can flush him. It'll be like a burial at sea."

"Whatever you say, baby."

At home again, alone, Luna drank coffee outside in weather fit for a Disney movie.

Birds chirped, squirrels bounded through the grass. Spring was here.

Above the water, the egret soared with his mate, white wings wide.

Beneath them, a long line of ducks floated along the current.

It was all very zippity-doo-dah, and while Luna had never subscribed to the resurrection in the literal sense, she felt reborn.

Life was beautiful. She was beautiful.

Every breath was beautiful.

She was so happy to be with herself, alone.

Jiminy was right, she thought.

Well, thank you, he said. *It's nice to be appreciated.*

Trip came over with Easter turkey dinners in take-out tins from the diner.

And an Easter basket wrapped in purple cellophane!

"Some bunny brought you a present," he said, handing the gift over. He gave her a kiss.

""That's so sweet," she said. Then she saw the centerpiece inside. Surrounded by all kinds of chocolates and candies was T*he Catcher in the Rye.*

"It's a first edition," Trip told her.

"*What*?" This was an unbelievably generous gift, both on the money *and* on the thought scale. "Holy smoke! I can't believe you got this for me."

"I had to make up for those gloves," he said. "And I owed you a birthday present, too."

"You didn't find this in a dumpster, did you?"

"No." He laughed. "I guess I had that coming. And truthfully, if I had found it in a dumpster, I would've still given it to you. I don't think where you find something has anything to do with how you can treasure it."

That was a deep thought. She always knew Trip was capable of depth, and it was nice to see him flexing those muscles. "What made you think of Salinger?"

"I wanted to give you something you love. And you told me how much you love this book."

"I really do." She put her basket down and embraced Trip.

In bed later, Trip looked her in the eyes. He said, "I love you, Luna."

Going to sleep, they lay side by side.

Trip reached out and held Luna's hand.

Luna woke up a while later. She'd rolled over in her sleep, and Trip was curled against her back, arm around her.

This was a relationship, she realized. Everything else had been drama.

It wasn't perfect, but *this* was calm.

She was calm.

Being in a relationship was like falling into water. Sink or swim.

And a relationship was like water. No matter how hard you tried, there was only so much of it you could hold in your palms, and even that was bound to seep through cracks, eventually.

The only thing to do was splash around in it while you could, or get out.

Trip's body pressed warm on hers.

And she was happy.

Congratulations, Luna, said Jiminy. *Our work is done.*

"You're leaving me?"

You don't need me anymore.

She started to protest, but he was right.

I'm proud of you, Luna.

"Wait! What about Trip?"

What about him?

"Is… Is he the partner I'm meant to be with?"

I told you, it was never about Trip. It was about why you were with him. Your book is finished. What comes next is up to you.

What a profound little fucker he was. She was going to miss him.

There was nothing more to say, except… "Goodbye, Jiminy."

Goodbye, Luna.

Trip sighed in his sleep. Amazingly, he wasn't snoring.

Enjoy this excerpt from

MELT

Book One of the Rough Romance Trilogy

Selene Castrovilla

Winner of six awards

Praise for MELT

"Dorothy and Joey's plight is both an inner and an outer struggle, a reckoning with a cold world, and a psychological drama about the stakes of truth-telling that ends with a gratifying act of mercy… A fresh, emotionally complex bildungsroman of young American love that looks long and hard at violence, and at what can overcome it."

—Kirkus Reviews

"Melt is evocative, emotional, vivid, and powerful. Beautiful, painful, and ultimately healing, Melt is a gripping read that will make you feel and care about the characters."

— Cheryl Rainfield, award-winning author of SCARS and STAINED

"It was so well-written. If I were to meet Selene right now, I'd clap in front of her for she has written something painfully real and beautiful."

—The Quirky Reader

"MELT was one of the most powerful, stunning books I've read all year... Castrovilla sets MELT against a WIZARD of OZ backdrop and the L. Frank Baum passages offer a unique insight into the plot of MELT.

The plot was incredibly real, raw, and painful. Castrovilla takes on many different subjects, such as abuse, addiction, and first love. Despite the heavy subject matter, this novel reads extremely quickly and is amazingly well-written.

If you are a fan of realistic, contemporary fiction, this novel should be a MUST READ."

—Lady Reader's Bookstuff

"Melt... reminded me of why I love to read. My heart was literally pounding... I couldn't put it down."

—Eve's Fan Garden

"This is such a captivating read from the start. I got so involved with the characters that I was afraid to leave them, afraid that I might miss out on something big if I stop reading."

—The Cursed Empire

"I get the writing style of "Melt" isn't for everyone. It's written as verse, poetic-like. But the book is so deep, but yet such an easy read. I'll never forget it. NEVER. And I'll forever recommend it as a must-read. The fact that she could introduce these deep characters in such a structure and make me feel like I know them is mind blowing. I have nothing but praise to the author… she created a powerful book that will forever haunt the reader. Poignant and entirely realistic, MELT is a book that should NEVER be missed."

—Her Book Thoughts!

"All I could think was 'God help them'.
And I couldn't stop reading."

—Sheri's Reviews, Goodreads

"Different. Intense. Perfect. This story was
all of these, and so much more."

—Bibilophilia, Goodreads

No Place Like Home

"'What shall we do?' asked the Tin Woodman.
'If we leave her here she will die,' said the Lion."
—From *The Wonderful Wizard of OZ* by L. Frank Baum

Mom stopped crying a
long
time ago.
Now
she don't even
whimper
when he does it. He comes
home
in his steel blue shirt shiny black shoes shiny tie clip shining
badge
he blows in and the screen door
slams
behind him like it's pissed off
he's
back.

He comes in shuts the front door clicks the lock closed
he wipes his shoes on the mat
back and forth
back
and
forth he pads across the shit-brown carpet without a sound
his eyes are empty his eyes are
dark his eyes are
wrought
lead like his
Glock.
          I catch a whiff of his favorite mouthwash
Jack
Daniel's
he used to smell of Listerine and Jack but he don't bother trying
to
cover
up
these days.
Without a look he goes past me and Jimmy and Warren. Warren's
got his textbooks spread out across the couch but he ain't studying
not
no more. Grim music drifts from our video game low
chilling
sounds like any second the reaper's gonna
strike. Me and Jimmy we're playing *Halo* on Xbox, least we were
'til
he
came

back. It's like we're paused
we're all on
pause whenever
Pop
comes
home.
We ain't putting down the controls 'cause if we look at him if we
act like we're paying attention to what he's doing then he
might
come
after
us
next.
The freakish *Halo* music plays on and
on and
on. He heads through the arch to the kitchen his shoes
stamping on the green
linoleum he goes right over to
her
at the stove cooking his goddamn mashed potatoes stirring
stirring
stirring she don't move she don't run she just stirs
stirs
stirs
he says
nothing
to her to the
girl he married to the
mother

of his kids he comes behind her at the stove
his shoes squeak he
grabs
her
the spoon plops in the potatoes no not even a plop not a sound it
sinks soundless
like
her.
He holds her against him blue sleeve on white apron
squeezing
squeezing
squeezing into her ribs like he's doing the Heimlich
his tie clip presses in her back
he sticks his semi-automatic piece of crap weapon in her mouth
clanks
it against her teeth shoves
it
down
her
throat clicks
off the safety and she don't
make a sound
she
just
stands there and takes it. Not a peep not a flinch not a blink of
panic
nothing she just takes it she
melts
for him

melts like the butter she stirred in his mashed potatoes made from
scratch
peeled one by one
eyes carved out
she
melts she just disappears
she's
gone.
Like every husband in the world kisses his wife like this.
Like she
deserves
it like she did something that'd
make
it
okay
for the man who
swore
to
love and cherish her
to do
this
in front of
me.

Hey, I saw the video.
There wasn't nothing in those vows 'bout guns or fists neither
for that matter. Do you Caitlyn Ruby Shields promise to take
a pounding anytime Joseph Thomas Riley damn well feels like
laying one on? No, I don't think Father Gallagher mentioned that.
God I

hate
that name I
hate that I'm
named
after
him. My pop I mean. Not Father Gallagher.

Mom in her satin white dress with the lacy veil and the
puffed
sleeves the long
train
dragging
behind her the big-ass bouquet of white roses she
cradled
in her arms
poor
Mom she looked so happy no one told her 'bout the guns. And
him
he's standing there by Father Gallagher in his black tux black
bow-tie
that
prick
he's always
so neat
looking
so smug
hair slicked
back I could've killed him even then if
only
I was born.

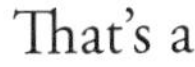

That's a
lie
I can't even
kill
him
now.
I just sit here
pretending
to
play
Halo while my mom gets a Glock rammed down her throat I can't even save my mom from this piece of shit who goes out to serve
and
protect
all day
some
joke.

She stopped crying like five years ago.

She stopped crying when I was twelve.

Me I never cried much not in front of him he warned me not to.
He told us me and my brothers not to let one tear drop on the carpet or we'd get it too. He don't hit us much he just
says
he might.
Me and Jimmy we're pussies I guess Warren's nine what could he do but me and Jimmy we sit there
day
after

day fingers touching stupid useless buttons day after
day night after
night he hits her hits
her hits
her and we watch.
Week after
week month
after month we
watch.
She gets slammed
into walls so hard pictures fall she gets shoved
so rough his finger marks are in her arm she gets thrown
to the floor and kicked
kicked
kicked
and we hold our controls and we hold our breaths and watch we
watch
we watch.

Warren cries in bed. I check on him before I go to sleep,
stick my head in his door. The blankets are pulled up over him
he's just a
lump
underneath. There's no noise but the covers shake he's under there
holding it
all
in
I know 'cause I did that too.
He's only nine.
He'll learn to cut that shit

soon
enough.
	Me and Jimmy we don't cry.
	And she don't cry neither.
	So
what's the
problem maybe this is
normal maybe this is
life maybe everybody on Long Island does this behind the doors
they close and lock when they come
home.
	This's all I know and
maybe
this's right but it
don't feel right I wanna help her
but
I
don't.
	I watch Mom suck steel and then we all eat. We sit at the
table slide our chairs in
we pick up our forks
like
nothing.
Pass the potatoes.

PART ONE

MUNCHKINLAND

"She was awakened by a shock, so sudden and severe that if Dorothy had not been lying on the soft bed she might have been hurt. As it was, the jar made her catch her breath and wonder what had happened; and Toto put his cold little nose into her face and whined dismally. Dorothy sat up and noticed that the house was not moving; nor was it dark, for the bright sunshine came in at the window, flooding the little room. She sprang from her bed and with Toto at her heels ran and opened the door."

—From *The Wonderful Wizard of Oz* by L. Frank Baum

ONE

Dorothy

He looks like a sculpture by Michelangelo. Like his body was intricately carved, chip by chip until it was perfect.

He's beautiful.

When I saw his muscles—even half covered by his Metallica T-shirt they couldn't be denied—when I saw his arms, I knew they could keep me safe. Funny, I never thought I needed protection, but there it was, that thought, and just like that everything changed.

He was sitting with a bunch of guys in Dunkin' Donuts when Amy and I walked in. Dunkin' Donuts is apparently the mecca of teen society in Highland Park. Not that there's much to choose from in this one-square-mile town. There's a pizza place, a Chinese restaurant, a laundry ... well, you get the picture. Manhattan, it's not. Anyway, the cool crowd gathers in Munchkinland.

Personally, I find the bright fuchsia and orange colors a tad aggressive on the eyes, but what the hey. When in Rome .... And it looks like I'm going to be in Rome for a while.

So Amy—the one friend I've made thus far in my two

days here—she headed right past all those guys, just ignored them and headed for the counter. I meant to follow, but those biceps … they held me back.

Imagine if they were holding me.

The rest of the guys, they were yammering away, making crude jokes and cracking themselves up. He sat slightly apart, leaning his wrought iron chair back against the oh-so-pink wall.

My eyes scanned higher, rising over his thick, strong neck to his finely chiseled jaw, lips, cheeks, nose.

He's a work of art.

To his eyes then, to his smoky-grey eyes that stared back at me. He had the look of an animal caught in a trap. It was like he was caged inside that beautiful body, like he was asking me to carve deeper and set his soul free.

"What are you doing, Dorothy?"

I guess I didn't answer fast enough because Amy grabbed at my arm, pulled me closer to the counter. "Those guys, they're jerks. We don't talk to them."

"I wasn't actually talking to …."

"Listen, they're losers. Get your donut and come in the back room, that's where everyone is."

I turned and looked at him. He was still watching me, tracking me with those eyes ….

"Are you insane?" Amy yanked me around again. "That's Joey Riley. He's the biggest loser of them all."

"He doesn't look like a loser."

"Hel-*lo*, do you think losers come with big 'loser' signs attached? No, they can come in some exceptional packaging. But when you unwrap them and you peel away all that plastic coating stuff and rip off the safety tags, then guess what, it's too late to return them."

"Could you be more specific?" I asked.

"How about Joey Riley beats people up for fun, sends them to the hospital. How about Joey Riley drinks and smokes weed. How about Joey Riley's been arrested, sent to jai—Oh, crap, he's coming over .... Hey, Joey! What's up?" Amy's lips widened into a faux smile. I was beginning to not like my only friend. Maybe it was time to make another.

I turned around, faced him.

Faced those muscles, faced those eyes. If Amy was correct about him fighting he must've been awfully good, because he didn't have a visible mark. I tried to think of him as bad; I tried to shut him down in my head, but who was I kidding? He didn't answer Amy, he didn't even glance at her. He was all about me, and it was reciprocal.

"Hi, Doll," he said in a voice low and husky.

"Doll?" I echoed. "Are we in some sort of 1940s gangster movie?"

"What? No, I ... I didn't mean anything by ...." His face tensed, reddened.

"It's okay," I jumped in. "Doll should be the worst name I'm ever called."

His jaw loosened, and he smiled just a little, around the edges. "Haven't seen you around before," he said.

"I just moved here, from New York."

He nodded, his long brown hair brushing ever so slightly against his shoulders. Lucky hair. "That's cool. I'm Joey."

He hesitated, then offered me his hand. It was calloused,

kind of bent and bumpy-looking. His knuckles were uneven, bruised. I guessed he did punch people.

I hesitated, then took it.

A warm energy moved through me when we touched. It was all I could do not to melt into his arms, and I'm not the melting type.

I swallowed deeply. "I'm Dorothy."

Joey

She looks like a
doll
like one of them
porcelain
dolls something so
fragile and
precious
you should put
high
on
a
shelf to keep
safe and never
never
touch.

Mom had a bunch of them three shelves full 'til Pop had enough
he said he couldn't stand them all
staring
while he was sleeping.

And he didn't want
me
and
Jimmy near no girly shit neither he said
no sons
of his
were gonna
wind
up
fags. So Mom had to
pack
them up she
wrapped
them in that
bubble stuff she
taped
the boxes
real
good
so no dust would get in and she
left
them in Grandma's
basement.
I still remember them I remember their
faces all
smooth and delicate their
eyes so
wide so innocent like
nothing bad's

ever
happened
to them. Pure that's it they were
so
pure.
    She's like that.
    Hey
Doll,
I said that's what I
called her
without even thinking.
I almost didn't go over there she was with frigging Amy Farber her
crowd
don't
see
me
even when they see me. But she had those big blue eyes like my
mom's dolls so I went.
    She said something 'bout
the
movies
I didn't know
what
she was talking about. I thought
she was pissed but
then
she smiled
and
it

was
okay.
    Her hair's like those dolls' too.
Long and glossy.
And wavy.
It's wavy
like you could just
unfurl
your fingers in it and set course.
    You could just drift far
far away.
    There was all this noise in there. There was people
yakking on line ordering
donuts and shit
there was registers ringing there was tip
cups clinking
there was background music some kind of top forty whining b.s.
but when we started talking there was
only
our voices.
    She's new
here
she's from New
York, she said. You could tell she had class she was wearing a top
that actually fit her it
covered her not like these girls who let their stomachs hang out all
over the place like that's
supposed to be attractive.
I must be

crazy even
talking to her, I thought. She's probably used to all these
rich
fancy
dudes but the way she kept
looking
at me
I thought, Well maybe ....
          There was all these eyes
watching.
There was Jimmy and the guys at the table
there was
frigging
Amy
there was the people buying
donuts and shit there was the people
ringing
shit
up.
But when we looked at each other there was
only us.
          So I introduced myself I didn't wanna
stick
out
my hand
partly 'cause it's a
disaster all twisted
up from fights and I thought
for

sure
it would spook her but also ‘cause she looked like a
doll
like one of Mom’s
dolls
and you
shouldn’t
ever
touch
them
they might break.
          But I did it.
I
forced
myself
‘cause that’s what you’re supposed to do
especially
when someone’s from a place all classy and
polished
like New
York that’s what they do there and anyway
I
can’t
lie
I really did wanna do it, I wanted to
touch
her.
          And she took it.
          She

took
it.
          I thought she
wasn't
gonna but she slipped her
soft
soft
fingers round my
rough
scabby
hand.
          She
touched me she
touched me she touched
me
and something warm
crackled
through my body.
It didn't start in me it didn't start in her it started right between
our hands like two sticks rubbing
like some kind of
friction
we caused together.
          For sure I thought she'd
drop
my hand like a
hot
potato
and run right outta Dunkin' Donuts but

she didn't.
    She said
her name was
Dorothy
and I thought,
Where's
Toto? But thank god I kept my trap shut that time 'cause how
many chances
do
you
get
really before you're chalked up for the
jerk
you
are?
    We were still holding hands looking at each other I was
just glad I wasn't
drooling
or something I'm such a
doofus and then
fucking
Amy
cleared her throat
A-hem
and Dorothy
let
go.
    You coming or what, Amy asked her and she said
yes

she
was.
She said
nice
to meet
me and all that crap.
        I figured,
That's
that.
        She went to the counter and ordered a croissant and a
mocha latte for crying
out
loud. What made me think
someone
like
that
would like
someone
like
me?
Someone who'd pick a
croissant
over a bagel or a donut.
Someone willing to pay
three
times
the
price to have
foamy

milk
on her coffee.
She could have anything
she could have
anyone.
So
why
the
hell
would she ever want
me?

I started heading to the guys. I stared straight at the
psychedelically
pink
wall tried not to catch their eyes 'cause defeat's hard enough
without having to
look your friends
in
the
face.
The smell of
brewing
lattes
was making me dizzy.
The white ceiling lights beamed
down
on my head
bright
bright

bright.
The noises in that place were
way
too
loud.
My Nikes
slipped across
pale smoke tile
I could barely lift my feet.
It was all I could do not to
shut my lids and
melt
right
into
the
gray.
        But then I heard
my
name.
        She called
my name
she called my name she
called
my
name.
        She called me
back over.
        So I
went.